THE WAY BACK TO YOU

michelle andreani & mindi scott

The WAY BACK TO YOU

 KATHERINE TEGEN BOOKS
An Imprint of HarperCollins Publishers

Katherine Tegen Books is an imprint of HarperCollins Publishers.

The Way Back to You
Copyright © 2016 by Michelle Andreani and Mindi Scott
All rights reserved. Printed in the United States of America.
No part of this book may be used or reproduced in any manner whatsoever without written
permission except in the case of brief quotations embodied in critical articles and reviews.
For information address HarperCollins Children's Books, a division of
HarperCollins Publishers, 195 Broadway, New York, NY 10007.
www.epicreads.com

Library of Congress Control Number: 2015952419
ISBN 978-0-06-238630-4

Typography by Kate J. Engbring
16 17 18 19 20   PC/RRDH   10 9 8 7 6 5 4 3 2 1
❖
First Edition

For my grandparents, with every beat of my heart
—M.A.

For my mom, who has loved me the longest
—M.S.

OREGON

Dear Recipient:

It was suggested to me that I take time to grieve before reaching out to each of you. However, if I were in your position, I'd be curious about the sixteen-year-old girl whose organs I received. And since I was her mother, I'm absolutely bursting to tell you about her.

If there's one thing to say about Ashlyn, it's that she was a person who cared deeply. This was especially apparent in her love of animals. When she was a little girl, she would groom her grandparents' horses, and try to pet every dog and cat she came across. She talked about growing up to be a vet, a zoologist, or an animal-rights activist. The beauty of being young is that you can change your mind a hundred times and life is still before you with all the options. We'll never know what she'd have decided when the time came, but after volunteering at local animal shelters for the past couple of years, she seemed most excited about the idea of one day running her own nonprofit animal rescue center.

Ashlyn was athletic and a member of her school's cheer squad. She was busy, busy, busy with practices, performing at games, competing statewide, and summer cheer camps. Community outreach is also a big part of being on the team, so between cheer obligations and her own ambitions, she was always on her way out the door to go help someone in some way or other.

What else can I tell you? Aside from me, Ashlyn had her dad, her younger brother, her best friend, her boyfriend, and countless friends and extended family members. She was a good student. Outgoing, talkative, opinionated. Bossy, even, depending on whom you might ask. She liked it best when things were going her way. (Don't most of us, though?) She was also sensitive and loyal to the extreme. She laughed a lot. She made me laugh a lot. She was my first baby, and I have always been so proud of her. I still am.

When Ashlyn got her driver's permit last year, she made the choice to register as an organ donor. It was her wish that if she lost her life, she might save others. Our family is deeply bereaved, but it brings us solace that our girl was able to help you in your need.

If you'd be comfortable with it, I'd love to get acquainted with you and hear how you're progressing with your transplant. Either way, please know that I'm thankful for you, and I wish you a speedy recovery and a joyful, meaningful life.

All my best,
Paige (and Enrique and Tyler, too)

Cloudy

I t's not that I never think about Ashlyn. I do.

Especially on days like this.

This is what it used to be like on pep rally day: Ashlyn and I would meet at my locker, we'd complain about having to wear our cheerleading uniforms in class, declare whose Bend High blue-and-yellow hair bow looked perkier, gobble down some granola bars, and walk to the gym, together.

This is what it's like now: I'm sitting on the gym floor, alone, attempting to blow life into a yellow balloon. We're using them in the relay race later, so once I'm done, I toss it into an emptied trash can along with the others. The rest of the varsity squad is scattered around—hanging signs, draping streamers, and painting faces.

Face-painting used to be mine and Ashlyn's. Then junior year—this year—started, and I told Coach Voss I was bored of staring into people's pores while brushing bear paws on their cheeks, and that my talents could be used elsewhere. Now those talents include transferring carbon dioxide from my mouth and into a balloon, all without passing out.

From my spot on the sidelines, I've been watching the rest of the school file in. Most students are dressed to fit the rally's theme: *Bounce the Blackhawks into the Past!*, a nod to our boys' basketball team making the play-offs. Every class was assigned a different decade—freshmen are the 1920s; sophomores are the 1950s; juniors are the 1960s; and the seniors, the highly coveted 1980s.

As yet another Madonna climbs the bleachers, Lita and Izzy march over to me, Zoë in between them. As the team manager, Zoë's not required to dress in theme, but she did anyway. And leave it to my little sister to come as Dorothy Parker, a 1920s-era writer hardly anyone here would recognize.

When they reach me, Lita sweeps her deep brown bangs off her forehead. "Zoë says I can't use the word 'douchebag' at a pep rally."

Zoë huffs and adjusts her hat—her *cloche*; that's what she called it this morning, not that I asked. "It's *crass*," she says, glancing down at me. "It sucks all the enthusiasm out of the room!"

There's probably a rule for this. *Thou shalt defend thy sister, even if she's an interloper.*

Cheer was never Zoë's thing. It's always only been mine. But when our previous team manager moved away, Zoë swooped in to snatch the job, and she did it all without a word to me first. Suddenly, she's so eager to coordinate our fund-raisers and bus rides, and it's crossing a line I didn't know existed. She's trespassing. And if she can break a rule, so can I.

"We must have skipped that lesson at cheer camp," I snipe.

"Really." Izzy slumps beneath the *Lava Bear Country* banner on the wall at her back. "Is there a list of things we're not supposed to say?"

I tie off the last balloon and cradle it to my chest. "Erectile dysfunction."

Lita taps her chin. "Moist?"

"Nibble," Izzy adds. "Secrete."

My eyes flash on Zoë, and a grin lights up her face.

"Chlamydia!" She yells it as the marching band transitions to a Prince song, and I cringe at the volume of her voice.

But that doesn't matter anymore because "1999" is our cue.

Nervous buzzing swarms my stomach as I stand up to join Lita, Izzy, and the girls at center court. There's an energy springing around the place; it crackles on my skin. The last time we performed in front of a crowd was a week ago at Nationals, and I'm antsy to do it again.

The delicate scent of lavender wafts over to me. I whirl around to ask Ashlyn where she's been and—

See a girl in a poodle skirt, her auburn ponytail swinging as she walks away.

Not Ashlyn.

"What's up?" Zoë was messing with her hat again, so she missed it. But I must look how I feel—bloodless, weightless, boneless—because her eyebrows are up in a question.

"Nothing," I say, keeping my voice practiced and careful. I smooth down my white, pleated uniform skirt so she won't catch my fingers trembling. I remind myself to breathe—it's all about breathing.

Shit.

What was that?

It's been almost six months since my best friend died, and I've never fumbled like that. Not in public, anyway. I've been holding it together just fine, and I'm sure as hell not losing it now—not in front of the whole school and, like, four different James Deans.

The stuffy gym air isn't doing anything to cool down my cheeks. "I need to get some water. I'll be right back."

Before Zoë can say anything, I elbow past a group of junior hippies. My sneakers squeak against the waxy court as I hustle to the girls' locker room. I focus on that. The squeakier, the better, the faster I go, until everything is a smudgy blur of neon and sequins and synthetic hair.

"Cloudy!"

I stop short at my name; the locker room is so close. When I turn, there's Matty Ocie, that ever-present quirk to his lips. He gives me a small smile—small for Matty, anyway. My return smile's wattage is a flicker in comparison.

Things with Matty and me are complicated. As in, he might be my ex-boyfriend and he might have seen me naked, but we're still able to look each other in the eye. Which is lucky because his are a nice, M&M-y brown, and meeting his gaze is keeping me upright at the moment.

My heartbeat steadies enough to take in the rest of him. His slim, dark blue suit is iridescent under the lights, something I failed to notice earlier in Spanish. "Wow."

"I know," he says, smiling bigger.

"Who are you supposed to be?"

He sighs like he's gotten the question a lot today and gestures at his hair. "I'm JFK! Check out the majestic side part."

He spins to show off the entire ensemble, and I spot someone else standing behind him. A year of practice has made trying to ignore Kyle second nature, but this might be the only time it's actually worked.

A familiar carbonated frothiness courses through me, then fizzles flat. I never let it last long enough to enjoy it.

"Hi," I say to Kyle.

"Hey," he says back.

"Nice work, guys." Matty claps a few times. "Those were real words, and you were *nearly* looking at each other."

Next to Matty, Kyle is completely underdressed for the rally in plain jeans and a sweatshirt—he's not even wearing blue or yellow.

"Did you leave your pep in your locker?" I ask him. The stupid joke clogs up my throat. There was a time it wouldn't have, but that was before Kyle started dating Ashlyn. Before I dated—and broke up with—Matty. Kyle and I are a study in Before and After. And if things with Matty and me are complicated, then my relationship with Kyle is something along the lines of splitting the atom.

"I've got to find Coach," Kyle mutters, then shuffles off.

Matty watches him leave with an expression that's full of things only I understand. Months of concern and anxiety and unease, all for his cousin.

"How is he?" I ask Matty.

Kyle and I might not be friends, but Ashlyn wouldn't want her boyfriend turning into some tragic epilogue. He kind of fell apart when she died, but he's been doing better. That's what Matty says, and he wouldn't lie about that.

"Probably nervous," Matty says, shrugging. "Slawson's making him announce baseball tryouts today. But the question is"—he clamps a hand on my shoulder—"what's your pep emergency? You were hauling ass pretty quick."

Of everyone, I could tell Matty about my Ashlyn slipup. That remembering practically knocked me over, and if I ever let myself go there, I might not get up. This was a tiny lapse, though. It won't happen again. And anyway, he has enough to worry about.

"I'm fine," I tell him. Auto-reply: on. "Just getting a pen and paper so I won't forget I can't say 'Chlamydia.'"

SOPHIE PAXTON'S VOICE trembles so much during "The Star-Spangled Banner," I need a Dramamine. But we both power through it. Then the basketball team storms out, ripping and running through a paper banner that takes six cheerleaders to hold up. Once at a football game, we used only two, and it was a grass-stained disaster for everyone involved.

As the boys assemble on the giant bear paw painted on center court, four of the cheerleaders, including me, hike up into the bleachers to lead the class yell contest, while the rest do it from the floor. I always get stuck with the sophomores because they're the least enthused, and I'm the least tolerant of that too-cool-for-school bullshit. Unsurprisingly, the seniors win.

Afterward, I join the squad on the free-throw lane as the general announcements start. Coach Voss is lingering at the end of the line, and three people ahead of her, I see Matty—but no Kyle. My pulse beats in my ears as I check the junior section for him, then every other section, the exit doors, and the shadowy corners of the gym. He's not anywhere. But that's not possible; he wouldn't skip out on a responsibility like this. Aside from Slawson giving him all kinds of crap for it, Kyle would never let his team down.

At half-court, the student council president hands off the microphone to Matty. The first words out of his mouth are about baseball tryouts.

"No way," I mumble. Kyle bailed.

Beside me, Zoë presses close, her arm against mine. "Would you ever date Matty again?" she whispers, completely oblivious. "Because I think he'd date you again, if you wanted to."

"I don't want to," I tell her, even if it's none of her business. She may have inserted herself into cheer, but that doesn't mean every other scrap of my life is fair game.

Matty spouts off details I'm not paying attention to. Then he turns to hand the mic to the girl behind him before sauntering calmly back to his seat.

And Zoë is still going: "See, I'd believe that if you guys hadn't already been together twice. Third time's the charm, right?"

"No third time. No charm." My teeth clench around the words.

Besides, what happened between Matty and me after Ashlyn

died doesn't really count as dating. But there are some details I don't need to share with my little sister.

I tune back in when Coach Voss clears her throat and it ricochets around the gym. Her mouth is a tense, flat line on her fairly line-free face, and with her feet slightly apart, she commands attention like this is cheer practice.

"As you might know," she's saying, "the varsity cheerleaders just came back from Nationals, where they placed third in the country." She stands back and waits for applause. Which comes—eventually. Damn sophomores. "It wasn't an easy victory. We lost a bright spot on our squad the very first week of the school year."

Like that, the room goes static, I go static, and part of me is relieved that Kyle isn't here for this.

"Ashlyn Montiel was an integral member of our team, and we miss her commitment and positivity every day. But," she says, her voice switching from sweet to steel, "these girls fought and worked and earned their success. And because of that . . . I'm honored to announce that Bend High Varsity Cheer will be featured in the nationally syndicated *Cheer Insider* magazine."

A shriek bomb explodes around me, and I must go momentarily deaf because I'm stunned, right there in the middle of it. This can't be true—*Cheer Insider* can't care that we exist. But then Zoë is hopping beside me, shaking my shoulders, and her grin is so big, I find myself grinning back. Believing it. And whatever energy the team has saved up for the rest of the day comes off of us in waves. Beyond our ecstatic huddle, no one else in the gym seems to understand what's going on, but their indifference doesn't touch us. This is it. This is real. This is fucking incredible.

Voss isn't done. She's still smiling as she adds, "And, because of her tireless dedication this year, they've chosen to spotlight our own"—her eyes lock on me, and my stomach drops as she extends a hand in my direction—"Claudia Marlowe."

That's when it happens again. I stand there as my teammates crowd around me in an eager rush of congratulations and hugs, and all I can do is remind myself to breathe.

It's all about breathing.

Kyle

In movies, they make it look so easy. Someone has a crisis, so they wander into a random church where they find peace staring at statues, or are comforted by the vague yet inspirational words of a priest, nun, or stranger. Or, if those first two things don't happen, the character leaves all discouraged but soon discovers the answer they were seeking awaits them right outside.

I'll be glad if any of this happens for me today, but my hopes aren't high. Right now, I'm pulling up to Random Church Number Four after having found the doors at Random Churches One, Two, and Three locked. Unlike those others, there's one car in this lot, which means I might have a shot at getting inside.

After steering into a space near the entrance, I slam my SUV into park, cut the engine, and hop out. The pavement and the church throw echoes back and forth with every step I take.

I climb the short staircase—two at a time. At the top, the foyer is dark behind glass double doors, but there's a set of keys dangling from the lock. I pull the handle and the door swings outward. Aiming a fist bump toward the sky (hallelujah?), I rush in.

Coming here was a last-ditch move and I hate that I'm this desperate. It's just that 1) today one of the assistant baseball coaches made me sit through an epic "your absenteeism drags us all down" lecture and 2) this should've been my one-year anniversary with my dead girlfriend, Ashlyn.

As it turns out, 1 + 2 = me kind of losing it again.

Kind of *a lot* losing it, actually.

I tread farther into the darkness. Then, making a guess about where to go next, I pull the handle of one of the wooden carved doors ahead. It leads to a large, dim room with raised ceilings where row after row after row of cushioned benches face a wood podium and a two-story-high stained glass window.

I'm in now. I make my way to a row near the middle of the room and sit.

Why here? I don't know. This place is 100 percent empty, but the idea of going to the front somehow seems as dickheaded as grabbing the last of the chips and salsa when everyone else is starving and waiting for their enchiladas, too. It'd be like I'm trying to hoard all the enlightenment for myself.

Because I was born to a "not a Christian but still deeply, *deeply* spiritual" mother and an "agnostic with hope" father, this is only my second time inside a church. (The first was almost six months ago for Ashlyn's memorial.) If my parents had been different, maybe *I'd* be different, but I don't think so. I just don't connect with anything religious or mystical. Before, it never bothered me that I didn't inherit my mother's ability to believe in an afterlife or my dad's ability to hope for one. Since Ashlyn's death, it's been bothering me a lot.

In this church, there's no organ music playing or lit candles or statues. The heat doesn't seem to be turned on. It's also dingy, with pea-green fuzzy seats and yellowish beige carpeting.

I sit perfectly still, perfectly quiet. There's rustling up front. Church mice, maybe? (Are those a thing in real life, or just in kids' books?) It's probably good that I'm back here, after all.

Digging into the pocket of my hoodie, I grab my phone and earbuds so I can cover up the potential-rodent sounds. I consider making this experience more authentic by putting on some gospel channel, but decide instead to leave it on my usual music (which isn't emo, no matter what my cousin Matty thinks). I turn it up and wait for answers to end my crisis. I'm more than ready to become the Back to Normal Kyle everyone wants me to be.

I wait.

I stare ahead.

I focus on the light-colored cross on the dark-wood podium.

I get lost in the stained glass's kaleidoscope-type circle design.

I glance left, right, down, up.

I wait some more.

At the last church I was in, the minister spoke Words of Encouragement to the hundreds of people who showed up for Ashlyn's memorial. Later in the service, Matty read aloud friends' and family members' memories he'd collected. I was surprised when Claudia (Ashlyn's best friend, who mostly answers to "Cloudy") didn't go up front with him, and even more surprised when I realized afterward that none of the stories had been from her.

The cheer coach's note was all about the inspiring drive, perfectionism, and positive outlook Ashlyn brought to the squad. My aunt Robin's was about eight-year-old Ashlyn showing up at their house next door after having "run away" with only a suitcase of stuffed animals. Ashlyn's mother had Matty share the letter she was sending to Ashlyn's organ recipients. There were happy stories, thoughtful stories, silly stories. So many, I couldn't recall all of them now even if I wanted to.

The audience chuckled while Matty read what I'd written about Ashlyn's laugh and how it had taken me completely off guard at first. They could relate because no one ever expected such a strange sound to come out of such a cute girl.

When she really got going, she sometimes sounded like a farm animal, and I teased her once, asking if she'd been a donkey in her past life. (Not that I believe in the past-lives thing, obviously. Even though I kind of want to.) My stomach twists up now at how douchey that was for me to say, but Ashlyn wasn't even bothered. She just pushed me all playful and laughed her unique, endearing, and contagious laugh.

The laugh no one will hear again. Not in the flesh, at least.

I pause my music. And even though I know it's going to be a mistake, I check my phone for the last video I got of her.

There was a time when it would have taken a lot of searching to find something from half a year ago, but since there hasn't been a single moment I've wanted to record since she died, I'm able to go straight to it and press play. A wiggly shot sweeps toward the darkening sky and settles on two girls in the stadium parking lot with their arms around each other. The sides of their faces are smushed together and Ashlyn's glossy black ponytail is flipped over both their heads, covering most of Cloudy's reddish-blond hair.

On that Friday night, they'd already changed out of their uniforms after having cheered for the first football game of the year, and were waiting with me for Matty to come out of the locker room. School had started that week, and it was one of those rare occasions when Cloudy and I were in the same place at the same time and I wasn't getting the feeling she wished we weren't.

In my earbuds, my disembodied voice says, "Okay, ready? One. Two. Three."

The seconds tick by and the girls' smiles on my screen get bigger, fade a little, and then get big again. Ashlyn's eyes look extra bright, bright green. (She once said her eyes were the color of a 7Up can, while Cloudy's were dark blue like a Pepsi can.) On the screen, Ashlyn raises her eyebrows and Cloudy scrunches her nose and they both giggle. While still holding a stiff grin, Ashlyn asks, "Did you take the picture, Kyle?"

Me: "I don't think so. You didn't see my flash, right?"

Cloudy whispers something to her (I'll never know what, but I assume it had to do with "flashing"), and they both burst out laughing.

Me again: "Oh, wait. I accidentally set it on video mode."

The view gets all wavy again and the only sound is the girls as they laugh and laugh and laugh. It's all accidental by this point since I was changing the settings, but the camera goes back to them and follows as they slide their backs down my Xterra and land on the cement, where they laugh some more.

Then the clip ends. My eyes tear up at the blurred, frozen image of Ashlyn and Cloudy sprawled on the ground, looking both silly and pretty at the same time.

People say stuff about how Ashlyn's in a better place and gazing down from heaven, but I can't stand to think of her as some stalker in the sky who has nothing better to do than use her telescopic, 7Up can–green eyes to watch me all day while I shower and eat and go to school and do homework and (sometimes) hit the weight room and play video games and sleep.

I can't stand to think of her watching me now.

Secretly, I do want to have hope that reincarnation is real and she's a baby. Or a donkey, cat, raccoon, seagull, zebra, tropical fish. Or something else. Anything. I don't care *what* she is; I just wish some part of her could be living somewhere on this planet. Because if she isn't, what's the point of any of this?

My chest tightens and my jaw does its thing to try to prevent me from crying. Most of the time these days, it works, but I hate the soreness afterward, like someone wadded my face up in their fist like a candy wrapper. I pull my earbuds out, drop my phone on the seat beside me, and cover both hands over my eyes.

It was two days after that first football game when Ashlyn went for a bike ride with her parents and her little brother. She lost control going downhill and took the landing so hard, her helmet was knocked loose and she hit her head. At first, the doctors thought there was a chance she'd come out of her coma—that she'd be okay. But after only a few days, they determined she was brain dead.

If Ashlyn hadn't been in that accident, I don't know what today would have been like. It was important to her that we do something special for our "monthiversaries" (which meant we always did—except for the time last June when I forgot), so obviously, she would have wanted our one-year anniversary to be a much bigger deal. A twelve-times-bigger deal, probably.

The entire past month has been filled with gut-punching reminders about how my relationship with Ashlyn first began last year. And each week there's been something to trigger more "what if?" thoughts: *If Ashlyn were here, what would she have given me on my birthday? What would we have done on Valentine's Day? What would she have picked out for me to wear to Winter Formal?*

And on and on and on.

The rustling up front kicks in again and someone whispers, "Did you hear something?"

Wiping my eyes, I lift my gaze in time for a girl's head to pop up from the front row. My vision has adjusted to the dim lighting and I recognize her as Danielle, one of the cheerleaders. I also recognize she's wearing nothing on top except a black bra.

She sits up a bit higher, squinting at me, and then disappears again. "Oh my gosh! *Kyle's* here!"

Another head appears. This one belongs to my cousin Matty, who isn't wearing a shirt, either. "Kyle?" he asks.

I raise my hand in greeting, even as the rest of me threatens to collapse in sudden exhaustion. Matty waves back and a goofy grin spreads across his face.

"What is he *doing*?" Danielle loud-whispers.

Matty ducks out of view. "Not sure."

The conversation continues, but they're speaking too quietly for me to make out words.

I'm not sure what my next move should be. What *is* the proper etiquette when you wander into a random church in search of enlightenment and your cousin and his ex-girlfriend's teammate happen to be hooking up ten rows in front of you?

Just as I've made the decision to leave, Danielle beats me to it. She rushes down the aisle (with her shirt and coat on now), staring very fixedly at something that isn't my face.

Up front, there's a loud *zip!* Matty gets up, ambling toward me with his Lava Bears baseball T-shirt on inside out. (He plays both football and baseball, but he's better at baseball.) His smile is bigger than any he's directed my way since I got overwhelmed and left before the pep rally yesterday.

"So, Kyle." He plops down beside me. "What are you doing here?"

"Looking for peace and quiet. Which, obviously, is not the same as what you're doing." I sweep my hand to encompass the room. "Who knew this would be where it all happens?"

"I know, right?" Matty says. "Pastor's daughters. Watch out when they're driving you home and say they need to stop at church to pick something up real quick."

"Thanks for the tip." The odds of me having to get a ride are minuscule compared with his; Uncle Matthew and Aunt

Robin's favorite method of punishment is taking Matty's car away. Whether he gets a bad grade, misses curfew, gets caught stealing a beer from the fridge, or says "shit" in front of them, it's a guarantee his car will then spend a week or more in "purgatory," as he calls it. (It's also a guarantee that the rest of us will be suffering the consequences along with him, since we'll have to drive him everywhere.) "I thought you were getting your car back today."

"No. Sunday."

"It's impossible to keep track. So, am I the last to know about"—I gesture in the direction Danielle headed—"all this?"

"This just happened. I mean, *just* happened. So you're the first." He picks up my phone and I brace myself. Is he going to notice the Ashlyn video and figure out what's going on with me? Instead, he hands it over, still smiling. "Take my picture. Then when I start to wonder if this was a dream, I'll have a way to remember."

Exactly what I want, to be part of my cousin's kinky memories. I drop the phone back into my pocket. "Or, we can forget I was here."

"That works, too." He sinks back against the bench's stiff cushioning. "But seriously. Now that you've found me, what were you needing?"

"Nothing. I mean, I wasn't looking for you. Or for anyone. I'm just . . . here. For the quiet, like I said."

Matty studies me for a long moment, wearing his Kyle-you're-freaking-me-out face. Pep-rally-skipping aside, I do what I can to avoid causing him to make this face, so it's especially frustrating that, of all the places in the world either of us could be right now, we both ended up in Random Church Number Four.

"I should leave." I stand and step around his legs to get to the aisle.

"And I should find Danielle."

Matty goes back up front for the rest of his clothes while I head for the carved doors.

When I step into the lobby, Danielle is waiting at the entrance. "I figured out how you got in." She jangles a set of keys and aims a shy smile at me. "Is everything . . . okay with you now?"

I put on a smile for her. Like Matty, she seems to think I came here for him. "I'm fine. And I'm sorry for startling you. Just so you know, I had no idea you guys were in there. In movies, it seems like people go into churches whenever they feel like it."

"It isn't like that here. My dad keeps set office hours."

"Which don't happen to be Thursday afternoons?"

She giggles. "Definitely not."

I push the door to leave, and cold air hits my face like I've opened a freezer.

Danielle follows me out. "Oh, no. The Dirty-Pawed Avenger strikes again!"

At first, I can't figure out what she's pointing at, but then I spot a brown, smudgy trail across the hood of my vehicle, leading to a black cat that almost blends into the paint job. "Whose cat is that?" I ask.

"She's a stray. Always on the hunt for a warm engine. When

she first turned up here, she was such a tiny thing. Every Sunday she goes from car to car. It's kind of funny."

The temperature outside has been in the twenties and thirties for weeks; no wonder the poor cat is curled up so tightly.

Matty barrels out to join Danielle and me, and the vibe gets weird as they smirk at each other in embarrassed, secretive ways. I guess it's all good for Matty, though. He's been telling me for months he likes Cloudy "*only* as a friend," but I didn't believe it until now.

"Well, it seems I have no choice except to become the villain who sends this stray cat back to the mean streets of Bend, Oregon." I give Danielle and Matty a quick nod and start down the stairs. "See you guys at school."

"Kyle, wait!" Matty calls out. "You want to do something tonight?"

I turn. "Nah. Maybe tomorrow."

"Well, *obviously* tomorrow."

I lift the corners of my mouth into the approximation of a pleasant expression to hide my irritation. "Right."

Official baseball tryouts aren't happening until after we get back from midwinter break, but Matty decided everyone who played varsity last year (aside from the guys who graduated, obviously) should hang out Friday night for some preseason bonding or whatever. I told him this morning I'd go (after he guilt-tripped me for leaving him to make the announcement yesterday), but the truth is, the closer it gets to the start of the season, the less I want anything to do with the team.

Without waiting for Matty to say more, I skip down the stairs. Before I even reach the bottom, my false smile dies and depression slams into me all over again. I came here for answers, for a sign, for *something*. But there were no statues, no nuns, no priests, and no helpful strangers. All I got out of this was Matty on my case again and muddy little paw prints all over my vehicle.

"Sorry, Dirty-Pawed Avenger." I'm at my driver's-side door now. "It's time to find another heater."

It turns out the cat is actually a kitten. She keeps lying there with her eyes squeezed shut, so I step forward and give her a light poke in the side. "I mean it. I'm going home now."

She curves herself into an even tighter ball. Her stomach rises and falls as she breathes. What was Danielle talking about, saying she was tiny back whenever she first came around? She's still super little now.

Aside from a carnival-won goldfish, Dad and I have never had a pet, and Matty's cat, Hercules, is the only one I've spent much time with. He likes to show his "affection" by hooking his claws into my legs and biting my wrists, so I haven't always been his biggest fan.

I rub the kitten between her ears. Her glossy black fur is softer than it looks. She responds by butting her head against my hand, flicking her tail, and opening her eyes.

Her eyes, which happen to be green. Bright, bright green. The color of a 7Up can, to be exact. My heart stops for a second.

She blinks at me and I blink right back.

I don't know what this means, if it means anything. I really, really don't. But I can't help hoping maybe, just maybe, I've found the answer I was seeking after all.

Cloudy

We finally pull into a parking spot.

"Thank God," I groan, reaching forward to click off the radio. The sounds of overlapping guitars and the la-la-la-ing singer cut off abruptly, the speakers now mercifully silent. I shudder all over like the power button was covered in raw meatloaf. "No more music by sad boys."

Zoë, in the passenger seat, crosses her arms over her chest. "You said I could choose."

"My mistake." I put my Honda in park and turn off the engine.

"Anyway, they're not *sad*. They're—"

"Crybabies."

"Passionate," she says, decisively and dreamy-eyed.

"Oh, gag." I snap off my seat belt and twist to grab my puffy coat from the backseat. Slipping it on, I say, "Just so you know, on the way home we're listening to someone who wears glitter."

Zoë's eyes scrunch up behind her glasses. "Glitter? Really?"

"Glitter"—I count it off on one finger, then more—"with a

fondness for drum machines. And clapping."

"I'd rather crawl home." She grins and slides out of the car.

As soon as I open my own door, icy February air ribbons in. It has to be the coldest day of the year so far. The sun is about to set, and the sky is a mix of purples and pinks against the pine trees that border the Target parking lot—possibly the only parking lot in Bend without a mountain view.

We make our way toward the big red bull's-eye, Zoë bobbing beside me in her green Converse sneakers and orange knit cap. The lot is mostly empty for a Friday evening; everyone's probably skipped out for midwinter break vacations already.

Zoë and I are not so lucky, however. We're homebound while Mom and Dad are away on a cruise to Mexico. They haven't taken a trip by themselves since Zoë was born and now they're going for it. Which is all very nice until you get to the part where they ditch their dependents for ten days. I'd be on board with fending for myself if it wasn't the reason why Ashlyn's parents asked Zoë and me over tonight. Accepting their invitation felt more like a sentencing. I dread being back in that house, but I couldn't refuse. Although there's always the chance I'll break an ankle and have to cancel before dinnertime.

"Candy first," I announce once we're inside. The Montiels aren't expecting us for another hour, so I'll fill up every minute of it with distraction.

Usually, the cosmetics section is always the first stop in Target, a tradition that began when Ashlyn and I both got our driver's licenses and could be here on a whim. Makeup, then magazines, then kitchen appliances, where we'd screw around with the coffeemakers. That's the way we worked through this place, no matter what—except for some quieter nights, when Ashlyn would dare me to do full twisting layouts in the patio furniture department. She'd always ask me in the same way, her eyes lighting with a challenge, as if she didn't already know I'd take the dare.

The makeup section never comes first anymore, if I go there at all.

Zoë stands by while I grab the essentials: a bag of sour gummy worms for my personal stash and some Dum Dums for the gift basket I'm making for tomorrow's cheer event. Zoë eschews empty calories and preservatives, and is obviously of alien stock, so she ignores the candy.

Then she follows me to the home decor department, where I pick a stalk of fake daffodils that I'll cut up and drop into the basket for extra flair. If it were warmer, I'd pluck real ones from our garden, but these will do. Afterward, Zoë leads me to the DVD section. She is the last human being under thirty who still visits it, and five bucks says she leaves with something black and white and boring all over.

I'm elbow-deep in the comedies when Zoë comes up behind me and shoves a DVD case under my nose. I'm surprised it was made this century; on the other hand, it looks like it has enough slash and gore to trigger a fit.

"Come on, Zoë." I raise an eyebrow. "A scary movie?"

Bunching her lips to one side, she says, "So what?"

I peer over her shoulder at the other racks. "No new

docudrama snoozefest out this week?"

"I'm allowed to like different things, you know."

She passes the case over, and I take it, reluctant. I barely read the story synopsis on the back cover, focusing instead on the snapshots of attractive, desperate-looking actors, their eyes and mouths open wide. A creepy, bloody movie is so un-Zoë—oh, but there's the magic word: subtitled.

"It's a foreign film."

"Korean," she clarifies.

"How did you even hear about it?"

"This boy Owen told me. It's one of his favorites."

My fingers freeze. A month ago, Zoë came home from school jabbering nonstop. Owen had recommended a thriller about a guy who'd had a brain transplant; afterward he started having visions of his donor's life, and isn't that just so metaphysical. Zoë speculated, out loud, to me, about whether it could actually happen, but I shut her down. It wasn't real, and it wasn't worth wondering.

"Sounds like This Boy Owen needs a rom-com weekend," I say, tossing the DVD back at her.

She blinks at me. "He has exceptionally eclectic taste."

I force an interested smile, steering the topic elsewhere. "So what's up with you and This Boy Owen?"

Zoë's cheeks redden and her eyes go round. She's fallen for it. "We have some of the same classes. That's it."

"If he's trying to woo you with the slaughter of innocents, I feel like I should know more about him. Like, okay: How many decapitated dolls does he keep in his locker?"

She rolls her eyes, but she's smiling. "Enjoying well-made horror films does not make someone a psychopath, Cloudy."

"*De*-fensive." I waggle my eyebrows.

"It's not like that," she says, a little breathless, so it's obvious that it's *exactly* like that. "He has a girlfriend, anyway."

I watch her for a moment more, a familiar slump in her shoulders. *He has a girlfriend, anyway* must be the Marlowe sister motto. "Well. Plenty of other single doll decapitators out there for you, I promise."

And if anyone knows that feeling something for a guy who's into someone else is a black hole, so willing to suck you in and twist you up, it's me. Better to cut the heartstrings now while they're not so tangled.

I HEAD TOWARD the toy section so I can pick up more things for the gift basket. The squad is raffling them off at tomorrow's fund-raiser for the public library. On my way across the store, my phone buzzes in my bag.

Cheer Insider is obsessed with you! Slight exaggeration, but let's talk, please?

A text from my friend Jade, with a screenshot of *Cheer Insider* announcing our interview—including my solo profile—on their Twitter. Super.

Jade lived in town and cheered with us until two years ago, when her family moved to California. We keep in touch and meet up every summer at cheer camp—ideally, we'd also meet up at Nationals every year, but the Bend squad didn't get past Regionals last season, and Santa Monica's didn't get there this time.

I tap out a quick reply to her last message—HUGE exaggeration. Talk later?

I might miss her more than ever these days, but I'm not as eager to discuss the interview as she is.

I've just pressed send when I see him.

Kyle.

Even with his back to me, I can tell.

I really hate that I can tell.

And I hate the emotional lightning storm that immediately charges up in my body. *Zap!* Excitement. *Zing!* Dread. *Sizzle!* Full-body tingles. *Singe!* All-consuming guilt.

He's standing in front of a display at the end of an aisle, his hands in his pockets, the hood of his black coat coming up to meet the straight line of his short blond hair.

I can't help it: I flash back to him at the hospital, and there's a heaviness in my limbs. It was the day after the accident, and Ashlyn was still in a coma. All I wanted was to be there when she woke up. But my car had stalled on the ride over, and I was beyond stressed because it was time wasted, less time for me to be with her. Kyle was already there, though, near the waiting room. His stance was exactly the same as it is now, with his hands in his pockets, except then he was staring at a vending machine. He stood there longer than the hospital's snack selection was worthy of: old, crappy chips versus older, crappier candy bars. So part of me wondered if he was even hungry. There were a lot of blank stares all around then. I ended up blowing past Kyle and heading for the ICU. I doubt he even noticed.

I'm about to do the same now—pass behind him and go

straight for what I'm really here for—but I stop when I see what has him so preoccupied. An entire wall full of bright, plushy cushions shaped like animals. Why the hell is Kyle shopping for a Pillow Pet?

At the pep rally, Matty was certain that Kyle wasn't backsliding. That he's okay. But a seventeen-year-old guy with no younger siblings, shopping in the stuffed animal department, seems definitively *not* okay. So the same part of me that needed to ask Matty about him two days ago needs to get closer—just to make sure he's not about to rip the heads off those pillows and wear them as hats.

He picks up a koala in one hand and a panda in the other. He's deliberating.

Holy shit.

"Kyle." His name slips out before I can wrangle it back.

He startles, straightening up as he whips around to face me. I'm instantly aware of my messy hair and salt-caked snow boots. "Cloudy. Hey." His fingers tighten on the koala, his voice a low, thundery rumble. "What's going on?"

Crack! Heat.

"Here with my sister. How about you?" I peek at the shelf behind him. "Redecorating?"

"Um," he says, following my glance. "Not exactly. Just looking, I guess."

Then his eyebrows do the Thing. The Thing where they kind of slope up in a slant, like he's contemplating something too big, and it makes me want to smooth them flat. The Thing has done bad things to my insides since he walked into my biology class sophomore year.

I used to wonder if being attracted to Kyle felt like a weather event to Ashlyn, too. Or maybe it was more serene for her, because her feelings weren't constantly battling. The first time she told me about him, her eyes were as lit up as sparklers.

"Kyle. Ocie."

She'd steered me into an alcove under the stairs. Her grin was so giddy and nervous, I giggled before I knew what was going on. At the time, Kyle felt like my little secret, although he was hardly a secret at all. "The guy who stole my bio notes all last semester?"

Ashlyn had put her palms to her cheeks, endearingly shy. "I like him," she whispered. "A lot. I think I like him a lot."

My smile was so big and stiff; I must have looked like a wax figure. "Since when?"

"Seven thirty-three. This morning."

"Ashlyn, *what*? He's been here for months—"

"I know! I mean, I've seen him around Matty's house before and I've always thought he was cute. But he walked me inside the main entrance and held the door open for me, and all of a sudden I have cartoon hearts in my eyes. *For Kyle*."

I pressed my spine into the wall. "Does he like you, too?"

"Maybe?"

A tornado rioted through me. I could have told her the truth, and she would have dropped it. But then what? That weirdness would be a constant wedge between us. And in that moment, I believed that giving Kyle up could be simple, but I'd never forgive myself for ruining this for Ashlyn. I wouldn't carve that line into our friendship. What I didn't anticipate was that keeping the secret could be just as damaging. And that I wouldn't get over Kyle the way I wanted to. "What are you going to do?"

"Invite him to Winter Formal. They're announcing it at the assembly later, and I could ask him right away." She bounced up on her toes, and her expression was so hopeful it made my stomach hurt. "You're a bold, self-sufficient woman. Tell me: Should I just do it?"

It was as if poisonous gas had leaked from the heating system. I knew Kyle would say yes—he'd be a total cretin not to. Ashlyn was a star. She was warm, and fierce, and the prettiest person I'd ever seen. She was happiest when she was making other people happy. So I told her yes. Ask him.

"Ashlyn loved pandas," I blurt out now, motioning to the pillow in Kyle's right hand. I brace myself to melt from embarrassment. As if he doesn't know that Ashlyn loved pandas. As if he didn't adopt the symbolic kind for her on one of their monthiversaries, only to have her agonize over what to name it (Pandy Warhol). As if that's not the reason he picked up that pillow in the first place.

"I remember," he mumbles, putting both pillows back on the shelf.

"I'm sure." It comes out snappy and I peek over my own shoulder, reflexively checking for the exits.

We stand opposite each other, shifting and silent. A woman pushing a shopping cart filled with paper towel rolls sashays between us. It's like she can't tell we're even in the middle of a conversation. I guess we aren't, really.

"Hey, do you want to . . ." I trail off, gesturing behind me. "I need to buy something for a gift basket. You could help. If you're not busy."

And maybe if we're walking, and he's not looking at me, I won't be such a disaster.

Kyle's mouth opens a bit, and he hesitates before letting out a strangled "Okay." Then he scoops up the shopping basket at his feet and follows my lead until we get to the action figure aisle. We're completely uneasy around each other, and it sucks, but it's all my doing, anyway.

Talking to him used to come easy, *too easy*, for me. I was actually impatient for first-period bio and dissecting virtual animals—after all the animal-rights speeches from Ashlyn, I refused to slice into the real ones. It meant sharing a computer with him, one focal point for a few minutes. But outside of class, there was always Matty, and his other friends, and eventually, Ashlyn. After she asked him to Formal, they started getting closer, and I purposely forgot how to talk to Kyle.

So shopping with him will be new.

"What are you looking for?" he asks. We're alone, and it seems darker in here, not as starkly bright and exposed as the center aisles.

"Basically anything that'll make a six-year-old's day."

He laughs softly and it sounds right, like something I've heard before, and maybe if he sounds like familiar Kyle, he really is okay. "Is this a cheer thing?"

"What else?" I say, wandering farther away. "It's for the library—we're raffling off some gift baskets to raise money for the youth literacy program. And from past experience, kids like you better when you throw presents at them. They're like bridge trolls that way." I pull a dinosaur—that also launches tiny rockets—off the wall. "Or the really bad kings in the Bible."

What.

I hope Kyle's had an embolism and missed all of that.

Nope. He's looking back at me. "I'll take your word for it," he says.

Fueled by desperation, I hone in on these crayon-slash-robot toys from a cartoon—everything's a hybrid these days; can a crayon not *just* be a crayon anymore? The green robot is hooked on the top-shelf rung, and I put the toe of my boot on the lower shelf to hoist myself up. Before I can, Kyle's behind me, his chest brushing my shoulder as he snatches the package for me. He's such a frigging oak tree, he doesn't even need to stretch much to get it.

Once he does, he steps away quickly. I hold my breath so I don't inhale the minty Kyle smell that clings to him. It happened all the time in bio—we'd be sitting at our table, bent over our lab workbooks, and he'd move in a way that set off these mini wintergreen explosions. Ashlyn once told me he used this tea tree mint shampoo, and she always mooned over how his kisses tasted like all the Junior Mints he ate. I filed the info away with the other things I shouldn't remember about Kyle.

"I could've gotten it," I say instead of thanking him.

He looks at me. "I know." Then he hesitates before handing over the robot. "It didn't seem worth breaking an arm for."

We turn away from each other at the same time, facing

opposite shelves. I can't believe he's still helping me look for a dumb toy after I was such an ass.

I slip over to a pole stacked high with stuffed Yodas. "So are you stuck here over break?"

Kyle is deeply engrossed in a display of rubber balls. He sticks his hand in and palms a red one. Then he holds it up, and I shake my head, declining. "Yeah," he says, tossing the ball back with the others. "You too?"

"Yep." I stroke one Yoda on the head, tug another one's ear. "My mom and dad deserted us for Mexico this morning."

"They left you two alone for the whole week?"

"Total abandonment. They're taking a cruise, so they'll only be able to contact us once they reach port."

"That's not so bad."

"My mom told me I'm not allowed to use the stove."

"Ah." A small smile lingers on his lips, and this warm-honey feeling spreads in my belly. I want to kick him in the shins for it. "It's cool your parents get to be away, though. I wish I could've gone somewhere, just to . . . get out of here."

I hug a toy Yoda to my chest as I meet Kyle in the middle of the row. I don't want to know if he said that because he's depressed, or because he's as restless as all of us are. "Tell me about it."

After a few more beats of silence, he bends to pick up his shopping basket again. "I should probably get going," he says, before I have to say it myself, and my shoulders sag. Being around Kyle is exhausting, but so is examining how I destroy our every interaction once he's gone.

We're back in the glaring fluorescents of the middle aisle, and I take a few steps backward, away from him. Kyle switches the basket to his other arm and everything in it shifts, so I peek in this time. It's filled with cans of cat food and tiny, fuzzy cat toys.

"You've got a cat?" I ask.

Suddenly, he finds the cat toys as interesting as I do. "It's kind of complicated." Then he raises his head and says, "I'll see you around, Cloudy."

"Yeah. Thanks for your help, Kyle." I spin on my heel to head back into the aisle—I'm not sure the crayon robot or Yoda will make the cut, and I need to keep searching.

But I can't get my mind off the cat supplies. During the few times I was in Kyle's house, I never noticed a cat, and Ashlyn never mentioned anything about him having one. Though it's possible he's gotten one since she died. People adopt pets when they're grieving. It's totally and acceptably normal. The opposite of a downward spiral.

Right.

What else could it be?

All the recycled air in this plane hangar of a store is messing with me.

But I look back anyway, and pretend not to see Kyle go straight to the panda pillow when I do.

Kyle

Dad's car is already in the garage when I get home from Target. Which means he's back from his office and the gym already. Which means I might have a problem here.

Parking my vehicle next to his, I leave the panda Pillow Pet and a bag filled with canned cat food on the passenger seat. (Yesterday, I picked up a litter box and dry kibble. Later, I read it's better to feed cats both wet and dry food.) A couple of lights are on already when I head inside through the laundry room, but my dad isn't in the kitchen or on the couch.

"Dad?" I call out.

A nonresponse is what I'm hoping for, and the faint sloshing of water through the pipes overhead clinches it: he's in the shower. I hurry back out to grab the stuff, race upstairs with it, and close myself into my room.

All day, I imagined coming home to a kitten-shaped hole in my door like a Road Runner cartoon and no other sign of my secret roommate, so it's a relief to spot the scrawny black kitten curled up in my walk-in closet exactly where I left her this morning.

"Hey." I set down the bag and kneel beside her. "How's it going?"

She opens her eyes. "Mrrowwww."

Her voice is low and scratchy. It doesn't match up. She sounds like a two-pack-a-day smoker of fifty years instead of a tiny new kitten.

"Would you say you had a good day or bad day?"

This time, she yawns in response.

"My feelings, too."

My closet is for sure a warmer and more comfortable place than wherever she was sleeping before. That's part of why I felt I had to bring her home; Ashlyn would have wanted me to. She was passionate about rescue shelters and adoption.

But another reason is because I'm hoping this stray animal somehow *is* Ashlyn.

Which is why I still haven't admitted to anyone that I did this. Not Matty. Not my dad. Not Cloudy—even after she flat-out asked why I was buying cat food twenty minutes ago.

Cloudy Marlowe is the one person I could have shared my thoughts with that this kitten might be (but probably isn't) Ashlyn. Because, of anyone, Cloudy would understand completely why I'd want it to be true. The fact that she went out of her way to talk to me the day after I brought this kitten home is a major coincidence.

Almost a year ago, Cloudy broke up with my cousin. At the time, I thought it was my fault, but it turned out to be a huge misunderstanding all around. Unfortunately, I made the mistake of trying to talk to her about it afterward. She went off on me for butting in and said, basically, she'd tolerate my presence moving forward for Ashlyn's sake, but that was *it*. Even after Ashlyn died, even after Cloudy and Matty temporarily got back together, Cloudy didn't go out of her way to have any real conversations with me. Not until today.

The kitten stretches herself to be as long as possible while I unfold the panda Pillow Pet. This was an idea I got from Matty. He has a puppy-shaped one for his cat to sleep on, which is his big statement about what a badass he thinks Hercules is. ("Dude, he sleeps on top of a *dog*!")

I pat the pillow a few times to entice her to sit. She isn't interested, though. Instead, she tiptoes over to her food and water dishes (which happen to be as far from her litter box as possible), in the exact spot where my shoes were until I chucked them all under the bed last night.

The always-embarrassing clip from the song Matty set on my phone as his personal ring and text tone starts playing ("I don't want anybody else / When I think about you, I touch myself"), and I check his text: Everyone's here but YOU. Am I going to have to drag you from that house? Haha!

I send back: Haha

Of course, it isn't an answer to his question and it isn't going to get me out of anything.

Now that I've seen the cat is okay, I should take off. I was supposed to meet everyone fifteen minutes ago at the bowling alley for pizza, pool, and darts. (But no bowling. Go figure.) I still have my coat and shoes on. Keys and phone are in my pocket. I'm set. I just need to walk out of this room, drive back to town, and do the thing I said I'd do.

I stand up, leaving the closet door open so the kitten can wander around my room if she wants to. "I'll be back later."

But as I'm reaching for the doorknob, I imagine the conversations I'll be forced to have with the guys about girls they're hooking up with, midwinter break plans, the upcoming baseball season, and whatever else. Then I glance back at my bed and picture myself sprawling across it listening to music.

Even though I should feel like a jerk for this, I breathe easier as I toss my coat on the chair, kick my shoes off, and get started on making my second vision a reality.

HELPING ANIMALS WAS probably Ashlyn's favorite thing. I'd known from the beginning, but it really hit home when she showed up at my door last January with a sewing machine and a bag of fabric.

"What's this for?" I asked as I helped her lug it inside.

"Koala mittens," she told me. "There's an animal hospital in Australia taking care of koala bears that got severe burns on their paws in brush fires. They're asking people to sew these little cotton coverings to slide over the wound dressings. You want to help?"

"Okay."

We settled in next to each other at my kitchen table, and she handed me the pattern: basically a five-by-six-inch rectangle, but it was curved across the top like a cartoon gravestone. I traced and cut out red plaid while she threaded her machine.

Being around Ashlyn at that time was exciting and weird.

She'd invited me to Winter Formal, and we'd started holding hands at school and kissing good-bye, but she wasn't officially my girlfriend. We still barely knew each other. (She and Matty had lived next door to each other for years, but my summer visits had somehow always matched up with the times she was away at camp or on family vacations.)

"How'd your cat hunt go this morning?" I asked Ashlyn.

Since she volunteered a few days a month for the Bend Spay and Neuter Project, it was a guaranteed icebreaker topic.

"Really good! Except I found out one of the females from last weekend had already been spayed. They noticed the scars right before surgery. If she'd been ear tipped, we'd have known without having to bring her in. Oh, well."

I wasn't sure what to say, so I simply nodded. Before I'd started hanging out with her, I had no clue there was a system in place for trapping (*humanely*, she always emphasized) feral cats, taking them in for spaying/neutering and vaccinations, and setting them loose again. I also had no clue that veterinarians cut the tip of one ear so people could spot these feral cats easily.

I slid both pieces of one soon-to-be mitten to Ashlyn, which she lined up and pinned together. "I wanted to tell you," she said, "the reason I'm late is because I picked up the sweetest little Pomeranian on my way. She was prancing down Greenwood, so I pulled over, coaxed her into my car with treats, and drove to the address on her tag. Her name was Charisma and she was out of her mind with joy when her owners opened the door."

Chuckling, I shook my head.

"What's funny? Her name? I think it's perfect."

"Oh, no. I wasn't making fun of it. I'm just comparing our days. You helped homeless cats, retrieved a lost Pomeranian, and now you're sewing for injured koalas. Guess what I did? Went snowboarding and ate three quarters of a pizza. I mean, really. What could you possibly see in someone this lazy?"

After the words were out, I wished Matty had been there to cut me off midsentence and drag me from the room. Sometimes, he was all I had to save me from my pathetic self. It had been on my mind a lot, though: *Why does Ashlyn like me?* We didn't have much in common and there were cooler guys she could have picked. I couldn't help wondering whether she somehow saw me as another stray who needed her help.

She smiled. "There's nothing wrong with snowboarding. And you're not lazy. You're constantly working out and training for baseball season. That takes up a lot of time."

"Me playing ball isn't changing anyone's world, though."

"Not true. It's changing mine."

"In what way?"

"In the way that"—she leaned over, almost whispering—"I can't wait to see how good your butt looks in a uniform."

"What?"

She burst out with that wild laugh of hers, and then clamped her hand over her mouth. "I didn't mean to blurt that out. I'm allowed to be shallow, though, right?"

"Sure." Suddenly feeling so much better about us, I scooted my chair closer to hers. "So what are you saying exactly? I'm just a piece of meat to you?"

"Kyle Ryan, I'm a vegetarian." She leaned in and kissed my cheek. "You're more like a seitan and pineapple shish kebab to me."

I'M ON MY back with my arm slung over my face as symbols of light migrate through grayness behind my eyelids. The overhead light is causing this distracting effect, but I haven't turned it off because I'm not sure I want to commit to being *in* bed instead of just *on* it at six o'clock on a Friday night.

Dad and I already got our conversation through my door over with before I cranked up the music. Matty stopped texting me probably an hour ago, so I'm not expecting it when my door bangs open and Matty calls out, "Time to join the living!"

My heart leaps and I move my arm for a better view of the closet. The kitten isn't visible at the moment. I remain silent while trying to recover my calm, hoping she won't make an appearance before I can get rid of Matty.

"All right. Tyrell's waiting in the driveway." He claps his hands together. "Let's go, K.O.!"

(*K* and *O* are my first and last initials. They've also been used as my baseball nickname since I was a kid. It's *K.O.* as in "Knock Out," as in "Knock it Out of the park.")

I don't move to get up. Even with Matty here to coerce me, I'm not feeling it. I breathe deeply and exhale slowly, trying to get lost in the music again.

"St. Peter's Cathedral" by Death Cab for Cutie has been on repeat the entire time I've been lying here, and Ben Gibbard is once again singing, *"When our hearts stop ticking, this is the end.*

And there's nothing past this."

"Hang on." Matty leans his head close to the speaker on my nightstand. "What did you just say?"

Ben responds in the song, like Matty had known he would. *"There's nothing past this."*

"Can you repeat that?" Matty cups his hand around his ear.
"There's nothing past this."

"Still not getting it. One more time?"
"There's nothing past this."

"So what you're saying is"—Matty stands straight and belts out the next line—*"there's nothing paaaaaast thiiiiis."*

The phrase keeps repeating through my speakers. It's soothing, which is why I haven't been able to stop listening to it. Some days (like every day this week), it's the only thing that makes me feel (sort of) okay.

"I know you're all about the atheist anthems these days," Matty says, "but this shit's going to make you kill yourself. And if you kill yourself, I'm going to have to kill myself. Then your dad will. And my dad. My mom will be so pissed, she'll kill herself so she can come kick all our asses in the afterlife."

"There is no afterlife," I mumble.

I'm pretty sure he doesn't hear me, which is fine because I can't change his mind. I don't even want to. There have been so many times since losing Ashlyn when I've wished I could believe in something big the way Matty does. The way the vast majority of the population does. Having that certainty seems so much easier.

Matty strides to my desk and turns the music off. At this

moment, it's the worst thing he could have done to me. In a cheerful tone, he says, "I'm telling you. You've got to stop with this music. Because only *you* can prevent the Ocie suicides."

Does he honestly think he's being funny?

"Fuck off, Matty."

"Hell, yeah." He climbs on the bed and bounces by my feet. "That's the spirit. Cussing is a good sign. A *great* sign. Give me some more. How about an 'asshole'? Or a 'cocksucker'? Let's hear it! You *do* have something to live for."

Pushing myself up onto my elbows, I shout, "Enough with the suicide jokes, you fucking asshole cocksucker!"

The movement at the end of my mattress halts. He asked for it, but by his wounded expression, it wasn't what he'd expected. "You're right. I shouldn't have said that. I was just—"

"Just get *out* already!"

His mouth moves a few times, making no sound, until he's finally able to burst out with, "I've been texting you for, like, an hour! You couldn't be bothered to tell me you were bailing on me again?"

"*You* couldn't be bothered to take a hint?"

He glares at me. "No! Not with how much you've been freaking me out lately. You keep disappearing. I'm always covering for you and I don't know why. It clearly isn't helping. The season hasn't even started and you're already stressing the coaches out."

"I don't care," I lie.

"Well, you should." Matty's voice is getting fiercer by the second. "You're the best player on our team. If your head isn't in it right now, how do you expect—"

"I don't care about *any* of this crap."

Another lie. It isn't as if I suddenly hate baseball. I just can't handle the pressure of everyone counting on me when I can't count on myself.

Matty jumps to his feet. "Since when did it become 'this crap'?"

"Since . . . I don't know! But I've decided not to play this year." Matty is staring down at me with his mouth open wide, but it's a relief, finally having said the words aloud. "I'm done," I add.

"Are you *kidding* me with this? I mean, what are you even saying? It's like you're speaking in tongues."

"Whatever that means."

Just then, my dad pokes his head in. "Hey, what's going on?"

I shoot Matty a warning look. Based on his reaction, I don't want to have this discussion with both of them at the same time. "It's nothing, Dad."

"Right." Matty stares straight back at me. "*Nothing* other than the fact that Kyle is quitting baseball."

So much for him "always covering" for me.

"What?" Dad's expression matches Matty's from a few seconds ago.

I've put off making this decision forever. Still, I'm surprised they're this surprised. Baseball is a spring sport, but training is a year-round expectation. During the past several months, I've skipped almost as many sessions as I've attended. The coach wasn't getting on my case yesterday for being *too* committed.

Dad makes his way into the room. He moves my jacket to

sit on my chair, while Matty remains standing at the foot of my bed.

"Kyle, what's going on?" Dad asks.

"I'm not quitting anything. I'm just not trying out for the team this year."

Matty says, "You started playing T-ball when you were, what? Four years old?"

"So?"

"So, not trying out after thirteen years—after making fricken MVP as a fricken sophomore last year? That's exactly what I call quitting. Don't you want to play in college?"

I shrug. "Maybe not."

"What are you going to do, then? Stare at your ceiling and listen to this god-awful music? Because that's a useful way to spend your life."

"Matt," Dad cuts in, "you should let Kyle and me talk, okay?"

"Good luck with that," Matty says, scowling.

In a flash, he's out of the room, his shoes pounding down the stairs.

Ten seconds later, the front door slams and Dad lets out a loud breath. "That was a first."

He's right. It isn't like Matty to get pissed off and aggressive toward me (or anyone). Of course, I don't blow up at him, either. We're both *off* right now—all because I'm not Back to Normal Kyle.

"I don't know where this not-playing-baseball thing is coming from," Dad says, "but Matt did make a good point. You need something to focus on. Something other than . . . what happened. We've all been waiting it out, thinking baseball season would be the thing to get you on track. You used to be busy all the time. You always had somewhere to go, something to do, people to spend time with."

I hate Back to Normal Kyle for being so out of reach.

It's true; I was never alone last school year. I hung out with Matty, along with different combinations of his friends. Being his cousin meant I was instantly more popular after I moved to Bend two summers ago than I was for the entire fifteen years that I lived in Arizona. Then Ashlyn and I got together and, aside from her out-of-town cheer camps in July and August, being with her was a huge part of my daily routine, too. When she died a few days after school started, I stayed home for the next two weeks. I full-on sobbed at least once a day for three months. I didn't want to be around people who didn't get it, people who were telling me they'd "see" her again someday when I was sure I wouldn't. And that meant I didn't want to be around anyone.

Everyone thinks I changed because I can't get over Ashlyn. But I know that even if she were to come back somehow, I'll never be who I was before. I can't unexperience the shock of having her ripped from my life.

Dad goes on. "If you don't want to play anymore, I won't force you. This is a big deal and it deserves serious consideration, though. It can't be a hasty decision you made because you're pissed at Matt."

"It isn't about him. It isn't about anyone."

But really, it *is* about him. It's about everyone.

"All right. If it turns out this is what you really want, you need a plan for what you're going to do instead."

Dad's a dentist (he shares a practice with Matty's dad, his fraternal twin brother), and he's very big on plans. Pretty much the only unplanned things he ever did in his life were getting my mother pregnant and, later, divorcing her.

"Staring at the ceiling can't be my plan?" I ask.

"Probably not," he says with a small smile. "I've been thinking. How do you feel about talking to a counselor now?"

I sit up taller against my pillow. "Dad, not this again. No matter what Matty says, I'm not suicidal. Okay? I'm *not*."

"I didn't say you were. But I know you've been having a hard time, which is understandable. Now you're saying you don't want to be involved in the thing you've always loved most. And since you haven't been talking to anyone about it—"

"We're talking now, aren't we?"

"—maybe a professional can help you in ways I can't." He stares at the floor. "Sometimes it's good to sit down with someone who doesn't know you, who can give an outside perspective."

Since Ashlyn's death, I've been thinking a lot more about my mother (who for sure is in the category of Someone Who Doesn't Know Me), and wondering if she'd be better than Dad at helping me get through this. During conversations like this one, it's hard to imagine she'd be worse.

"Your aunt Robin recommended a therapist," Dad says. "We can try to get you in while you're off from school. I think it will be good for you."

"No. Look, I'll leave the house, okay? I'm going snowboarding tomorrow. I'll find something to do every single day of the week, if that's what it's going to take to make you happy."

"This isn't about making *me* happy. You know that, right?" I don't answer, so Dad speaks in a rush. "I'll call on Monday for an appointment. And I'll even go with you if you want. Unless it will be easier if I don't go?"

I shrug.

"Think it over. Now, there's a *Terminator* marathon on TV. You want to come down and watch with me?"

What choice do I have? Only a therapist-needing person would say no to watching *Terminator* movies so he can spend more time alone in his room listening to "god-awful music."

"Sure," I tell him.

Dad gets up first, and as soon as he does, a furry black face peeks out of my closet. I sit frozen, hoping he'll walk out without noticing her.

Naturally, the next words out of his mouth are "Kyle, are you aware that there's a cat in your room?"

Cloudy

The plastic lei is still in Ashlyn's room.

After months away, that's the first thing I notice when I peer in from the doorway. I've decided that limiting where I go in the Montiels' house is my best option. Not that even keeping still is safe. In this hallway, Ashlyn and I would use pillowcases instead of potato sacks and bounce around from one end to the other. Or there was the night we convinced ourselves a ghost lived in Ashlyn's vanity mirror, so we slept right over in that corner.

Best option or not, the memory booby traps are all over this place.

I did visit twice after the funeral. It was mostly Mrs. Montiel and me sifting through Ashlyn's stuff. We never threw any of it out, or even moved any of it, but both times she asked if I wanted to take something, a relic from Ashlyn's life to keep for myself. So far I've only taken the cheer camp shirt from our first summer there together. But that was to please Mrs. Montiel. I'm not sure she's ready to part with any of it yet.

I'm not sure I'm ready to have any of it.

The Montiels didn't invite me over after that. They needed space to grieve, is what my parents told me, and I understood, even if their choice of words was completely misguided. Grief doesn't seem to need much space at all; it's more like it tightens and squeezes until there's no more of you left. But whatever their reason, I never offered to stop by, either. If I wasn't around, it was easier to avoid the picture of Ashlyn and me on her nightstand and the grape Kool-Aid stain I left by her closet. And now looking in on Ashlyn's unlived-in room is like wearing my own old clothes. Not completely uncomfortable but still fundamentally . . . *off.*

I guess Mrs. Montiel finally put away the stacks of laundry and threw out the trash, but the things that matter—the mail from various animal welfare groups, the *Almond Blossom* mug that doubles as a pen holder, the *Cheer Insider* magazines that I'm ignoring—they're all still here. Everything is still here, pretty much the way she left it before going on that last bike ride with her family. Almost exactly the same as I remember it.

Including the radioactively orange lei hanging from her bedside lamp. Ashlyn almost had a meltdown when I walked into her kitchen with it last May.

"A luau kit," she said, peering into the Party Town shopping bags. She was sitting at the island surrounded by pre-fruit-punch orange and apple slices, part of the prep for Kyle's surprise. My job was decorations detail, and I'd clearly screwed up. Epically. "This is what you got for today?"

"You don't like it?" I reached inside the bag for a tiny pink drink umbrella and stuck it behind my ear. "It's festive. See?"

A warm breeze blew in through the patio doors, and she lifted her black hair off her shoulders. "But we're not having a luau."

"It's your party." I grinned. "You can luau if you want to."

"It's *Kyle's* party." Her voice was getting squeaky—proof she was about to reach panic-button mode. "We're celebrating him getting MVP! Not . . . Hawaii."

I hopped onto one of the stools surrounding the island. Everything had been about Kyle then—and everything that fell into Kyle's trajectory had to be flawless. "News flash: Kyle has no idea he's even having a party. And"—I leaned across the countertop to take back a bag—"I'm pretty sure he doesn't care if I wear this kick-ass grass skirt or not."

She gave me a stabby look.

"What?" I said. "You think he'll want to wear it?"

"Cloudy," she warned.

"I'm not judging, Ashlyn. I just would've gotten another if I'd known."

With a groan, she started pulling stuff out of the bags: more paper umbrellas, some cardboard hula girls, a sign that read Get Low and Limbo! Her eyes flashed. "They didn't have anything regular? Like with boy stuff or . . . primary colors?" Ashlyn moved a plate of apple wedges between us. As I bit into one, I could feel her watching me, although her stare had gone softer, more butter knife than machete. "This is because you hate Kyle, isn't it?"

I choked on my apple. "No, but that is why I poisoned the cake."

"You could give him a chance."

My mouth fell open. "Like you gave Aidan a chance?"

"Aidan was a snob." The twist in her lips was almost a smile. She had hardly tolerated my first boyfriend, and she wasn't shy about it.

I shook my head, smirking. "You are such a hypocrite."

"And you are such a brat." She propped her elbows on the countertop, sitting up straighter. "You and Kyle are the most important people to me in the whole world, and you can barely be in the same room."

It felt like my insides were getting bigger and bigger, like they were trying to be my outsides. Whenever she talked like that, it made my feelings for Kyle seem a thousand times worse. And any righteous resentment, those dangerous I-knew-him-first thoughts, crumbled into this dusty guilt that coated everything.

I was never supposed to fall for him. But I screwed up.

In freshman year, I had Aidan: a senior with great hair, whose only comment about what would happen with us after he graduated was "let's play it by ear." By the time he was set to start college in the fall, he had apparently played it and, by ear, decided to dump me. Somehow, I hadn't seen it coming. So I did what anyone does when they're lost: I Googled. Most of the articles about breakups offered the same slice of wisdom: it takes half the time your relationship lasted to get over your ex. Get involved with anyone before that and you were doomed. And so, the day Aidan drove to Oregon State, my five-month guy embargo began.

Ashlyn said it was ridiculous. According to her, I should've been dating *more* to get him out of my system. But she'd never liked Aidan, and at the time, her advice seemed like a slight to my hairline-fractured heart, as if Aidan's and my ten-month relationship wasn't worth the time it would take to recover from it.

My Boy Ban felt like an extended summer vacation. Like I had all this free time and nothing—no *one*—to answer to. I started running every morning and finally finished reading *Jane Eyre*. I did the bravest thing I could imagine: I went to the movies *alone*. And that's when I discovered the mural, in an alley behind the Tin Pan Theater. It was taller than I am, and the words "All good things are wild and free"—a Thoreau quote— filled the entire canvas. The letters were painted as if they'd been formed out of wildflowers and tree bark and leaves—a few were coated in actual, velvety moss.

I was stunned. It was nothing like the van Gogh painting Ashlyn was so smitten with. *Almond Blossom* is pretty and soothing and classic. But no matter how often I'd seen it in her room, it never sent jolts through my system like the "Wild and Free" mural. The words seemed crafted just for me in that instant, and the whole piece was energetic and *alive* and looked as if it might explode off the brick wall.

On the way home, I noticed all kinds of flowers and plant life growing around town. I couldn't believe it had taken seeing them on a canvas to appreciate the real things.

I also kept up the Boy Ban. Even though Kyle and I were assigned as lab partners, and I discovered there was a family of bumblebees living in my chest that zipped around only when he smiled at me, I never said anything. Not to Ashlyn, because liking someone else so soon would be admitting she was right about Aidan—and certainly not to Kyle. I really did believe in waiting it out. And then, with one month left in the Ban, Ashlyn had pulled me aside in that alcove and told me about Kyle.

Like I said, I screwed up.

"Well," I told Ashlyn, "I got the luau stuff because I thought it was fun. Not because I hate Kyle—I don't hate Kyle."

She sighed, wistful. "My life would be a lot simpler if you'd get back with Matty. Can't you do that for me?"

I laughed. "For you, anything."

"Things were the best when you were together. We were neighbors-in-law!"

Ashlyn was always gunning for Matty and me to couple up. It was this fantasy she had—that the four of us would fit in this perfect way, a puzzle made from only her favorite pieces. The most ludicrous thing about it was, for a while, she was getting her wish. The same day she asked Kyle to Winter Formal, Matty asked me. I didn't have a reason not to, so I said yes. And then Matty and I just tumbled into each other. We weren't Ashlyn and Kyle, who were taking steady and measured steps into a relationship. We were apart, and as swiftly as flipping a page, we were together.

Until WinterFest happened and I screwed up again.

Three months later and Ashlyn still didn't know about that. All she did know was that I ended it with Matty the week following WinterFest because "I wasn't ready for a relationship"—which was sort of true; I *had* broken the Boy Ban early—and that things were weird between Kyle and me because he was staying loyal to his cousin, which was also sort of true. Keeping that many truths from her was agony, but it was the least I deserved.

"I just want everyone to be happy,"Ashlyn said as she considered the Party Town loot.

"In that case"—I dropped off the stool, my flip-flops slapping the tiled floor—"I'll go return this stuff."

"You will?"

"Yes," I whined, joking, like it was the hardest thing in the world, like the bags each weighed fifty pounds and I would have to carry them back in my teeth. "For you, anything. Remember?"

But I kept the orange lei for myself and wore it until, after a raging sugar high from too much punch, Ashlyn made Kyle wear it. Supposedly, he had it on for the rest of the night, but I only stuck around long enough to catch Ashlyn placing it around his neck as he smiled bashfully.

I KNOW THE Montiels invited us both, but it feels like Zoë has attached herself to me barnacle style. She's everywhere I am lately, impossible to shake off. It's also hard to resist telling her she's preparing the salad all wrong. Once Ashlyn became a vegetarian, she was especially invested in dinner salads. And she never cut the tomatoes like *that*.

"So where's Mr. Montiel?" Zoë asks, wiping tomato goo from the cutting board.

Ashlyn's mom dries her hands on a dish towel, then hands

Zoë more vegetables to massacre. "Out at the market with Tyler, buying charcoal for the grill," she says.

I smile a little from my spot against the doorjamb. Tyler, who's only eight, must be thrilled. He loves cold-night cook-outs. Mr. Montiel is always doing stuff like this in the winter, grilling outside, even opening the pool. "You can't stop doing things you love just because the outside world is telling you different," he'd say.

It's nice that hasn't changed when everything else has.

"Thanks for having us over tonight," I say, finally stepping into the kitchen.

"It's our pleasure," Mrs. Montiel says. "And you're more than welcome here any time, especially while your parents are away."

Ashlyn didn't look much like her mom, except for the grassy green eyes. That's how my mom's been rating Mrs. Montiel's progress over the past few months; her eyes. Dark circles? Bad day. Bloodshot? Worse day. But now they're the tiniest bit rimmed in red, which I'm hoping means at least a slightly-better-than-bad day.

I clutch the cuffs of my sweatshirt. "That's really gener-ous, but you wouldn't believe how busy we are this week. We'll hardly have time to eat at home."

Zoë glances at me, puzzled. It's not completely false—there's cheer practice and homework and probably something in our house that needs a thorough cleaning. Lots of things to stop me from coming back here next week.

Mrs. Montiel slings the towel over the sink. "Have your mom and dad checked in with you yet?"

"Right when they landed in LA," I say. "The ship is leaving tomorrow, so we won't hear from them until they reach Cabo on Sunday."

Although the connection is excruciatingly slow, not to mention expensive, my parents still considered calling us from the cruise ship. Then my dad read a horror story about some guy racking up a thousand-dollar phone bill because he'd called outside of the proper zones. The debate ended there. "Good to know what our safety's worth to you," I'd said to him. "Your safety is priceless until we're in international waters," he'd said back. So Mom and Dad will only be in contact once they make port in Mexico and find free wifi.

Mrs. Montiel grabs a bowl of rinsed-off raw chicken. She stares into it, then smiles weakly at me. "I never thought I'd miss seeing all of Ashlyn's tofu in the fridge."

I smile back. I think. I'm too numb and nauseated to know for sure.

She places the bowl on the counter. "Would you mind sitting with me?" she says to us, walking over to their butcher-block table. Her back is straight but her shoulders seem loose, so her body language is one big mixed message. "I was going to wait until we were having dinner, but this feels like a good time."

My heart pounds hard, just once, like the last emphatic beat of a song. "What's going on?"

Without a word, Zoë obediently takes a seat opposite Mrs. Montiel. I follow, a little slower, so frozen I'm convinced my knees will splinter when I sit, but they don't.

Once I hit the padded cushion, Mrs. Montiel flattens her

palms against the wooden tabletop. "You know that some of Ashlyn's organs were donated when she passed. And that we— Mr. Montiel, Tyler, and I—wrote a letter so that we could contact her recipients."

Beside me, Zoë nods.

Matty read the letter at Ashlyn's funeral. Afterward, everyone talked about how lovely it was, and how brave the Montiels were, reaching out to the recipients like that. I'd mostly tried not to think of it.

"Well, we haven't told this to many people"—suddenly, Mrs. Montiel's smile is a glow, like its own light source—"but out of the seven, three of them wrote back."

"Three!" My sister leans forward, entranced. "Who are they? Are they all young? Are they all girls?"

"Zoë," I hiss. "Don't be nosy."

"Oh, no, it's fine." Mrs. Montiel tilts her head at Zoë. "Sonia was the first to write back. And then there was Ethan, who's only ten years old. And Freddie, who's . . . considerably older than that."

She starts listing facts about each of them: Ethan likes animals and has part of Ashlyn's liver. Freddie is planning a vacation to Australia and New Zealand. I shove my fingers under my thighs so I won't plug my ears shut.

"How often do you write to each other?" Zoë asks.

"Whenever we can." Mrs. Montiel's face is bright, as if she just got back from getting a facial or something. "After our initial letters, we had to communicate through the transplant center. But now that some time has passed, we're not required to do that anymore. So we decided that we'd like to contact each other separately."

"That's amazing," I say, because it's what you say when you're ready for a conversation to be over.

"I don't get it." Zoë furrows her brow. "What's the difference?"

"Basically," Mrs. Montiel starts, "we're able to share more with each other now. Our notes had to be filtered through the donor organization. They're very strict about people disclosing private information, so we couldn't say where we live or anything too personal. But we all felt ready to take the next step. So recently we started emailing. Maybe we'll even talk on the phone one day."

Zoë hops in her chair. "Seriously? That's very cool! Right, Cloudy?"

"Yeah, very cool," I add, then clear my achy throat.

"What do you guys talk about?" Zoë pokes at her glasses. "Anything juicy?"

"No deep-down secrets yet," Mrs. Montiel laughs. "But Ethan's mom told me he's acting in a play. It's the first time he's felt healthy enough to participate in an extracurricular activity."

My skin goes rigid, like it's made of tiny pieces of metal that have all suddenly snapped together.

"And I did get one extremely exciting piece of news about Sonia today."

Instantly, without wanting to, I recall the Sonia trivia she dispensed a minute ago: twenty-eight-year-old receptionist, with a dog, and Ashlyn's heart.

There's glee in Mrs. Montiel's voice. "She sent us a wedding invitation."

Zoë gasps. "She's getting married?"

"Her fiancé proposed after the transplant. Isn't that wonderful?"

"It's so romantic! Will you go?"

"Unfortunately, no. It was too short notice," she says, her tone gentle. "But it was kind of her to invite us. Don't you think so, Cloudy?"

My fingers curl around the edge of the stool. Somewhere in my mind, I'm aware it *is* really kind. But I can't breathe enough air to say what I'm thinking out loud, so I just smile and nod.

Bing-bing-bing!

"Shoot," Mrs. Montiel says, bending back to look at the oven. "I forgot I was preheating that and I haven't even gotten the biscuit recipe from the printer."

"I'll grab it," I say, darting up.

As I rush from the room, Zoë's and Mrs. Montiel's spirited chatter bites at my feet.

I knew about the recipients. I figured that they were out there, somewhere in the world, walking around. They weren't supposed to have names and interests and futures.

Flicking the light on in the Montiels' office, I cross the room to the family computer, the printer right next to it. They both sit on the desk that faces a picture window overlooking the backyard. If I press my face to the glass, I'll be able to see Matty's basketball hoop in the Ocies' driveway next door on the right.

But it's so dark outside, all that's visible in the glass is my reflection.

The biscuit recipe is waiting in the printer tray. When I reach over to grab it, I knock the mouse aside with my wrist, jolting the computer from sleep mode. The monitor blinks back on, revealing Mrs. Montiel's inbox. Revealing Sonia's email.

It's not even that long. A few short paragraphs that transformed Mrs. Montiel, if not completely, then just enough. Contacting the recipients is filling in some part of her, maybe in a way nothing else can.

Kyle flits through my mind. There was no hiding the little bit of lost in his expression earlier today. I didn't do much for him after Ashlyn died, but what if I can give him some kind of evidence now that not everything sucks? Not for everyone, anyway, and that counts for something. If it's helping Ashlyn's mom, it might help him.

I twist to check the doorway, listening closely for the sound of someone nearby.

The subject line of Sonia's email says: YOU'RE INVITED! And I don't know why, exactly, but I speed-read through her wedding plans, the Las Vegas hotel her fiancé, Paco, picked out, absorbing more details I don't want in my head. And I feel guilty for only a moment before clicking print.

THE THING IS, you don't just pull up to a guy's house, present him with stolen documents, and expect him to perk up. Not guys like Kyle, anyway. He might be horrified that I printed out emails from these three organ recipients without the Montiels' permission. And he might not care that Sonia is getting married or that Ethan is in a community theater play this weekend. All of that could mean nothing to him, because all that matters is his girlfriend isn't here. What if it makes him worse?

"Oh my God," my sister grumbles from the hallway. She waves her phone around as she stomps into my room. "We left the Montiels' an hour ago, and this thing's been ringing non-stop since. It's like it's having a seizure."

I take the Dum Dums from the Target bag, then rip open their plastic packaging. Crisis or not, gift basket production stops for no one. "Don't make fun of seizures," I tell her flatly.

"Why are fund-raisers always so chaotic? My instructions in that email were incredibly clear."

"You're the one who wanted to manage twenty-two cheerleaders." I sprinkle the candy around the basket, then carefully arrange the faux daffodils around the pencils with pom-pom toppers.

"I still do." The mattress creaks as Zoë flops on my bed. She's up on her knees, checking out my lineup of small cacti on the windowsill. "But I wasn't prepared for how needy you all are," she laughs.

I roll my eyes, but my own phone buzzes before I can say anything.

It's a text from Matty. I reread it about four billion times.

Kyle didn't show at the bowling alley tonight. I had to go find him. He was home. In bed.

Quickly, I type out a message back. Is he ok?

He's Kyle.

Are YOU ok?

Pissed off.

Damn.

It's one thing to skip a pep rally—weird in itself for Kyle—but he is completely devoted to the guys on the team. He wouldn't miss a night out with them. Matty being mad at him is even more bizarre. I've seen Matty angry a handful of times, and while it was usually Xbox-related, it was never Kyle-related.

Wanna talk?

Still out with everyone. Just wanted to tell you, figured you'd get it.

I do, I write back immediately.

Okay. No more deliberation necessary.

Shooting up from the floor, I go straight to my sweatshirt. After printing out the emails, I stashed them in the front pouch pocket.

"What's up?" Zoë is on her stomach, assessing me. "You look . . . anxious."

I realize I've been clutching the printouts and chewing my lip. "Do you mind if I leave for a few minutes?"

"You're going out? For what?"

"Not anything fun." I shove my arms into the shirt, then pull it over my head. "I need to drop something off."

"Where?"

I roll the papers into a tube. "First," I warn, pointing it at her, "you cannot say a word about this to anyone."

She straightens up. "Whoa."

"Second, if you do say a word about this, I will duct tape you to a chair and leave you at a local children's beauty pageant."

"*All right.*"

I drop down beside her and unroll the papers, smoothing them on my lap. "I printed these out earlier at Ashlyn's. They're from the organ recipients."

Zoë looks up at me, her eyes big, and takes the pages. "You're not allowed to do that."

"That's why you can't say anything. But I thought—I think Kyle's having a hard time lately. Maybe these will make him feel better. They might prove that something not-terrible came out of this or something."

She doesn't comment, just starts reading each email, "They all live kind of close to each other. I wonder if they've met."

"What?"

"Well, Ethan's family must live near Sacramento if his play is at the Sacramento Children's Theater." She shuffles through the other papers, her eyes running across them. "This guy, Freddie, mentioned his new house in Palm Springs. And I don't know where Sonia's from, but she said they're *driving down* to Las Vegas, so it can't be that far."

Zoë reaches for her phone and opens the map app. "Oh, wait. Palm Springs is farther south than I thought," she says, thumbing down California. When she zooms in to the cluster of cities near LA, my eyes catch on Santa Monica, nestled right on the coast.

"That's where Jade lives," I say, waving a finger at the map as Zoë scrolls to the east.

"See?" She zooms out enough to show Nevada and part of

Oregon. "They still form this wonky triangle. So it's possible that they've met. Or will meet." She presses her lips together. "I mean, I'd want to, if I were them. It's like they all have a little bit of the same person inside them."

My heart beats faster and faster, trying to tell me something.

I'm up again, pacing my room, hoping the motion will help shake the pieces into place. Of course Zoë's right; the recipients do have a little bit of Ashlyn in them—that's the whole point of showing the emails to Kyle. But what I didn't consider was how close they are to each other. Which is not so far from us.

I grab her phone. There are 437 miles between Bend and Sacramento, a seven-hour drive.

"We can go," I say to Zoë. "We can go and find them."

She stills, then swings her legs around into a sitting position. "You don't have their addresses. And even if you find out, isn't that illegal?"

I scratch the back of my head. "They won't know who we are. We probably won't even talk to them. But we can go to Ethan's play tomorrow, and there's Sonia's wedding. We'll blend in if we're sitting with everyone else." Then, because I know it'll clinch it for her, I say, "Remember that movie Owen told you about?"

Zoë's eyes sparkle. "Maybe they're all like Ashlyn now!"

I smile a little because it sort of seems possible—not that it *is* possible, that the recipients are suddenly like Ashlyn. But a few hours ago, they barely existed, and now they're points on a map.

The lightness in my chest turns tight. "Forget it. You can't be alone while Kyle and I leave town for an entire week."

Her face freeze-frames for a moment, then thaws out, but only slightly. "Alone?"

"Mom and Dad are gone. You'd be stranded here on your own."

Zoë's flustered; it's how she gets when she's working to make a point. "I know how to take care of myself, Cloudy," she tells me, rushing the words out.

"How? By walking a mile back and forth to the market?"

"Someone needs to water your plants."

Our closest family lives in Redmond, but it's not like I can tell them I'm crossing state lines without supervision and without my sister. Zoë would need assistance of the non-blood-related kind.

Matty comes to mind first. I'm sure he'd keep an eye on Zoë, but I don't want to unload any more on him when he's had his share lately. Other friends and acquaintances like Lita and Izzy pop into my head, but they're dismissed just as quickly. The only person I'd put my faith in is Ashlyn and, needless to say, this would not be an issue if she were available to babysit.

I cannot believe I'm doing this. "You sure you'll be okay if I go?"

"Of course," Zoë says. Her eyes are the same deep brown as Mom's, introspective but sharp. "This is a you-and-Kyle thing. And I can't wait to hear about Sonia's wedding."

"Let's not get too excited. None of this will matter if Kyle says no."

Plucking my phone from the carpet, I key up Kyle's contact info. We exchanged numbers when we were lab partners, in case of a biology emergency, but texted only a handful of times. As I press the call button, I don't even hope for his voice mail.

He answers; his voice is gruff.

"Kyle. Hi."

"Is everything okay?"

"Yeah." I slide onto my desk chair. "Everything okay with you?"

"I guess."

Complete awkward silence, just like in Target, but this time I can hear him breathing. "I was wondering if you were busy tomorrow."

"Um . . ."

"There's this play I *really* want to see"—I grimace at Zoë, who is nodding supportively—I should've come up with a better pitch than this—"but it's not exactly local, and there's no way my car can make it. And since you said you wanted to get out of here for a bit, I thought you could do me a favor. By driving. And I'll pay for gas and stuff, obviously."

Oh God. Drowning is probably less painful.

My mouth goes completely dry as I wait for Kyle's questions: Why should I? What play? Where is it? Why would I go anywhere with you? How long will we be gone? Why would I do you a favor? *Why why why?*

Because I owe you this much, I tell him, but not out loud.

I brace myself as he takes another breath. And then he says, "I'm in."

Kyle

Ever since the bizarre phone call I got last night, the same four words have been running on repeat through my brain:

What

Am

I

Doing?

It's ten hours later, and I still don't have an answer. Not one that makes sense.

Fresh snow fell overnight and it's still below freezing outside, and yet when I turn down Cloudy's street, she's waiting on the sidewalk. She asked me to pick her up at "eight thirtyish," and it's 8:34 a.m. You can't get any more "ish" of eight thirty, so she must be impatient to get on the road. Either that, or she hoped keeping me off her porch would also make me forget she yelled at me last time I was here: "Get over yourself! Not everything is your problem to fix!"

As if I'll ever forget *that*.

Bundled up in her sky-blue coat, Cloudy is holding a large

gift basket. She has a duffel bag slung over one shoulder and a bulky pink cloud-print pillow tucked under her other arm. I park by the curb, and as I rush to meet her, the words "Sorry I'm late" come out of my mouth—even though I'm not. (Late, that is. The sorry part remains to be seen.)

I carefully take the basket from her. Most often, when we make eye contact, she frowns and glances elsewhere in a hurry, but this time, her expression is filled with so much I'm-happy-to-see-you, I'm the one who has to look away as I fumble the basket and almost drop it onto the snow.

"You're not late," she says, tucking back a few rusty blond strands that already came loose from her bun. "I did promise to drop off that tool of bribery at Lita Tamsin's this morning so she can add the finishing touches before tonight's fund-raiser. But I've padded in extra time, and we'll get to Sacramento before the play at six o'clock no matter what."

"Okay, sounds good."

Truly, I have no idea why Cloudy wants to see a play all the way in Sacramento or why, out of the blue, she's decided I'm the person who should go with her, but I'm not going to question it right now. Leaving this frigid weather behind for a day and (much more importantly) showing my dad exactly what it looks like when I get out of the house is too good to pass up. A break from Matty would be considered a bonus, too, but he won't be bugging me until later anyway. Every Saturday morning by this time, he's heading up to Mount Bachelor to snowboard all day. I haven't heard from him since he left my house last night, so he obviously got a ride from someone else.

I open the back door and set Cloudy's gift basket on the seat. But when I turn to take the rest of her stuff, she's already made her way to the rear of the vehicle and is lifting the hatch.

"Oh!" she says.

I join her. Side by side, we stare down at my kitten, who's lying on top of the panda pillow and is surrounded by a disposable litter box, fuzzy toys, and bowls of water and food that I'm hoping won't spill. The kitten gives an inquisitive, growly, "Mrroww?"

"This must be the 'complicated' cat you were talking about yesterday," Cloudy says.

"Yeah. But things are pretty much noncomplicated now that my dad knows about her." He seemed glad, too, like me bringing home a stray animal was an encouraging sign. (Not that I told him what I'd been doing before I found her or exactly what it was that prompted me to bring her home.) "I found her in a parking lot the other day. Her name's Arm."

Cloudy jerks her head up. "Arm? As in, A-R-M?"

My face gets hot under her gaze. I settled on the weird name last night, not thinking about how Cloudy would recognize right off that "Arm" is Ashlyn's initials spelled out. "It's short for"—I consider for a second—"Armadillo."

She lifts her eyebrows and I can't tell whether she believes me. "And . . . *Armadillo* is coming with us?"

"That was my plan." My heart beats faster. Is she spotting the similarities between Ashlyn and this black-haired, green-eyed kitten? "I hope you aren't allergic."

Cloudy watches Arm for a few seconds more and then gives

a small shake of her head. "I'm not allergic. And this will be an adventure. Just think," she says, in a teasing voice, "millions of boring humans go on road trips *without* cats. Total losers. All of them."

We both laugh a little. I don't want this to be awkward, but it is.

I close the hatch and motion to Cloudy that we should set her stuff on the backseat. "Is it still called a 'road trip' if it's only for one day?" I nod toward her duffel bag. "And what's all this you're bringing? A pillow and a week's worth of outfits?"

"It might be hot down there." A hint of panic rises in her voice. "And we don't know what we'll want to wear. You packed clothes, too, right? Like we talked about last night?"

"Yup." I have my coat on and am wearing last year's baseball hoodie over a long-sleeved shirt and jeans. I also brought along shorts and a T-shirt to change into. From this not-so-new invention called "the Weather Channel app," I found out Sacramento is supposed to get up to the low seventies. It's more than forty degrees warmer than here, and it'll be comfortable—definitely not the Phoenix-during-July type of misery that, for some weird reason, she seems to have planned for.

After we've loaded her things in and taken our seats, Cloudy says, "Once we drop the basket off with Lita, we can grab breakfast to eat on the road, if you want."

"Sure." I reach behind my seat for the bag of snacks I bought on my way here. "I got a few things for later, too. Still your favorite?" I ask, holding out a package of sour gummy worms.

She gives me a look like . . . I don't know. Like she's amazed

I would remember. The truth is, while she was always chowing down on sour gummy worms next to me in bio sophomore year (even on the day when I had to dissect a real worm by myself because she felt so bad for it), I kind of had a crush on her. She had some college boyfriend at the start of the year, and after it ended Matty was biding his time, so I knew I didn't stand a chance. But I do still remember what it was like when getting to talk to her was a cool part of my day.

"Still my favorite." Cloudy accepts the candy from me. "What about you? Still addicted to Junior Mints?"

In answer, I show her the white-and-green king-sized box I bought this morning and ripped into first thing.

We smile at each other and it's nice. Maybe everything else has changed since back when Cloudy and I used to be friends, but I'm glad there's this one tiny thing we each know about the other that's still true.

AT CROW'S FEET Commons, there's always an herby-skunky pot scent that hangs in the air—even at nine in the morning when no one's outside sneaking a joint. I kind of hold my breath against it while Cloudy and I make our way across the slushy sidewalk with food and coffees.

Beside me, Cloudy groans. "Don't you hate that bullshit slogan?"

I assume she's talking about something for WinterFest. It's everywhere right now. With the onslaught of posters and flyers and cashiers all over town trying to sell discounted admission buttons, the reminders about Bend's winter festival extravaganza next weekend are inescapable. I'm surprised Cloudy would want to chat about it with *me*, but maybe this is a good thing. Maybe we can have a casual WinterFest conversation and the whole mess that happened there last year will officially be behind us.

I scan the huge banner flapping overhead. "There's a slogan?"

"Not up there. In front of us."

This time, I follow her glare to a sticker on the back window of a parked sedan: "My Life Is Better than Your Vacation ~Bend, Oregon."

Now I sigh, too. Partly because I'd braced myself for nothing, but mostly because the sticker *is* bullshit.

I mean, I get the meaning behind it. Central Oregon is a vacation area for people from all over the state and beyond. The ski season here lasts six months a year, and it's sunny most of the time (even on cold days). In warmer weather, there are tons of spots for hiking, biking, kayaking, fishing, golfing, rock climbing, caving, and just about every other outdoor activity imaginable. Being surrounded by mountains, rivers, lakes, and waterfalls in our regular lives and not *only* while on vacation is cool, but I don't get why some of the residents are so smug about it.

"Sedona is a tourist town, too. Probably more than here," I say to Cloudy. "But the vibe in Arizona is like, 'Please visit, enjoy yourself, spend lots of money, and come back again.' In Bend it's more like, 'This is rad, and if you don't live here, then get the hell out.'"

"Because freezing our asses off for the majority of the year is *so* brag-worthy. For the record, I am determined to always have a better vacation than that person's life."

I chuckle. "Exotic Sacramento, here we come."

"Yes!" She touches her cup to mine and the gentle collision of our lids makes a *clunk* sound.

As we approach my vehicle, "I Touch Myself," starts up on my phone. I stop to read Matty's text: Hey, maybe this would be a good thing to check out? FindYourTruth.com

I click the link and a site appears offering "powerful seminars to help you FIND YOUR TRUTH." The words *depression* and *grief* pop out at me. I close the browser and tuck my phone away in a hurry.

Cloudy recognized the ringtone; Matty's mission in life is to download that song onto the phone of every Earth inhabitant, so it might be on hers, too. She's watching me, maybe expecting that I'm about to tell her what he wanted. Instead, I peek in at Arm, still asleep on her Pillow Pet. "You think she's going to be okay back here all day?"

Before Cloudy can answer, a loud voice interrupts with: "Well, if it isn't Miss Teen Royal Galaxy Cheerleader herself! We meet again."

We both turn as Jacob Tamsin slams the door of his red Chevy truck—the same red truck I was parked behind while Cloudy left the basket with Jacob's sister, Lita.

Dressed for snowboarding, Jacob strolls over in the slouching, cocky way he has. Unsurprisingly, he keeps his eyes on Cloudy and ignores me. By Jacob's perspective, he "had" to play second base last season because I "stole" the shortstop position from him. By my perspective, he's a dick. Acknowledging each other is something we avoid equally.

"'Miss Teen Royal Galaxy Cheerleader'?" Cloudy scrunches her nose. "That's so . . . snooty-sounding."

"Because you are. You're Bend High's most princessy princess."

"That means so much to me coming from our douchiest douche."

Jacob smirks. It's the only version of a smile that halfway works on him. As Ashlyn pointed out, Jacob's yearbook picture last year was disturbing: it was as if he was mimicking what he thinks smiling looks like from having seen other people do it. "A douche is something girls put up their hoo-hahs, right? So I should take it as a compliment?"

"You really shouldn't." Cloudy smiles extra sweetly. "They're considered unnecessary and harmful to women. Just like you. Now what do you want?"

"To get some grub before me and Quincy head up to the mountain." He stares into my backseat. "But since I saw you here, I thought I'd congratulate you on your big-deal magazine interview. Lita won't stop blabbing about it. It's great that hopping around in short skirts is finally getting you girls the recognition you deserve."

Cloudy ditches her fake smile in an instant.

I have no clue what magazine interview he's talking about, but Cloudy's likely to explode at any second. She owns a T-shirt that reads, "Not a Sport? Meet Me at the Mat" to shut down anyone who says cheerleaders aren't real athletes.

"Did you learn nothing last weekend?" Cloudy asks him.

"Because if half a bottle of maple syrup didn't do it"—she holds her drink up high and takes a step toward him—"this time I'm happy to pour an entire latte in your hair."

"Always so violent," Jacob mutters.

Matty told me about Cloudy's revenge when Jacob sexually harassed one of the other cheerleaders at last week's pancake breakfast fund-raiser. Cloudy can always hold her own against him (against anyone, really), but she shouldn't have to. "Just back off, Tamsin," I say. "Cloudy, are you ready to go?"

"Definitely."

I open the passenger's-side door and she leans in to set her drink in a cup holder.

"Hey, what up, K.O.," Jacob says, as if he's just noticed me. "Glad you have it in you to finally crawl out of your cave, since you couldn't be bothered last night to do it for your team."

And with that, he ambles off.

THE MUSIC'S PLAYING on random and the heat's on high. I've been driving, not long. (Fifteen minutes.) I've been speaking, not much. (Three sentences.) I've been eating, nonstop. (Breakfast sandwich first, then Junior Mints.)

With every passing mile marker, the snow on the side of the highway is getting thicker and thicker, and I'm becoming more and more pissed at my cousin. Obviously, Matty went back to the bowling alley with Tyrell last night and complained to everyone about me.

In the passenger seat, Cloudy's been quiet while spooning up her oatmeal with berries, but as she turns the music all the way down, I sense our nonconversing time is about to come to an end. Silently, I beg: *Don't speak, don't speak, don't speak.*

"I'm so hungry, I could eat an antler!" she announces.

"Um, okay? I brought beef jerky and—"

"You haven't heard of Eat the Alphabet? It's a road-trip game Zoë and I have played for years. We take turns. Letter by letter. I did *A*. Antler. Now you could say, 'I'm so hungry, I could eat an antler and a battery.' Or whatever you want that starts with *B*. Then I'll be like, 'I'm so hungry, I could eat an antler, a battery, and a chrysanthemum.' We have to memorize and say the words in order until we get to *Z*."

"Okay." I don't especially want to play a game or talk or do anything other than drive while music plays, but I need to snap out of my bad mood. "I'm so hungry, I could eat an antler, a battery, a chrysanthemum, and a . . . douchey ball player."

Cloudy laughs. "God. Jacob is the *worst*. I don't know how Lita can stand sharing DNA with him."

"Yeah."

It comes out exactly how I didn't want it to: sulky.

"What's wrong? You're not letting him get to you, are you?"

"No," I say. "I don't care about Jacob. It just sucks that Matty was complaining about me to him."

"He didn't. Matty would never do that."

Cloudy doesn't even know what happened, but she sure is quick to defend him.

"I know he did. I was supposed to meet the guys at the bowling alley last night. I wasn't up for it, so Matty busted into my room, yelling about how I'm always freaking him out and letting him down. And now today, Jacob's talking about me not leaving my cave. Gee, I wonder where he heard that from."

"I think Matty told him the truth. You decided to stay home. And Jacob came up with the rest on his own. Because Matty wouldn't have complained about you or tried to make you sound—"

"Depressed?" The seminar link he texted pops into my head. "Miserable? Pathetic? I think he might."

She lets out a loud breath. "Kyle, no. He just . . . he worries about you."

I side-eye her. She's biting her bottom lip and staring at her lap.

That's when it hits me: she knows. Cloudy knows exactly what Matty said about me because she heard it. From Matty. And suddenly her out-of-the-blue invitation to California isn't so out of the blue.

Anger pulses through me. "This trip today. It was his idea, wasn't it? He filled you in about our argument last night. He asked you to get me out of the house and cheer me up or whatever."

"This has nothing to do with him," she says, shaking her head. "Unless *you* told him, he doesn't know anything about it."

"Look. I'm not stupid. Before yesterday, you hadn't really talked to me since, when? A few days after WinterFest? That's, like, fifty-one weeks. Why do you suddenly want to hang out with me now?"

"Like I told you"—her voice gets sharper with every word— "my car wouldn't make it. And you said at Target you wanted to get away, so I figured it was win-win."

I don't respond. I can't. I'd let myself believe she asked me to do this because she actually wanted to. What an *idiot*.

After several seconds of silence, Cloudy says, "Fine. Believe whatever you want, but I'm not lying."

"Right. Because you never lie."

She turns, glaring at me. "And what is *that* supposed to mean?"

"Come on. The whole thing at last year's WinterFest. You lied to Matty. You lied to Ashlyn."

"So did you."

"You're right. And what did I get out of it? You stayed friends with both of them, and treated me like what happened was my fault." Words are bursting out of me now. Words I never thought I'd be saying to her. "But the fact is, *you* kissed *me* and—"

"I would have kissed *anyone* that night!"

"I know!" My heart is hammering now. "It was a complete accident. It had nothing to do with me. You've said it all before. And I *get* it. So why—"

"Kyle, stop. Please. I don't want to talk about this."

"Haven't we not talked about it for long enough? We kept it a secret because it meant nothing, right? And it wouldn't have done Ashlyn and Matty any good to know. But then you stopped speaking to me. Why? And what's changed all of a sudden? If you needed a ride to California, why not ask one of your actual friends? Like, you know, *Matty*."

Instead of answering my question, she reaches over, cranks up the music, crosses her arms over her chest, and turns to face the window.

Clamping my mouth shut, I stay focused straight ahead as we pass a sign for La Pine.

I could turn the car around. I *should* turn around. But Dad wants me out of the house, I'm definitely not ready to deal with Matty, and I need to experience some warm California weather now more than ever. So I keep driving south even as these four words repeat in my brain:

This

Is

A

Mistake.

NORTHERN
CALIFORNIA

Dear Paige,

My name is Ethan. I am ten years old. My mom said I can write to you and she will write to you.

I was sick so I got a new liver. I am getting better. It was part of Ashlyns liver that I got. She sounds nice and I like animals to. I like dogs and I like wolfs the best. I also like drawing and comics.

I want to say thank you to you and your family for my new liver and I hope you will not be sad.

From Ethan

Cloudy

We'd wanted to get drunk, and WinterFest was as good a time as any.

It's always in February; the first outdoor festival after a long, frigid few months, and the whole town comes out for it. There's this eagerness to everyone, like we're ready to burst, and I felt it, too, especially last year. After wallowing over the cheer team not qualifying for Nationals—which had been a couple of weeks earlier—not to mention everything else, I needed to have fun and forget for a while. So when Lita and Izzy proposed the idea, I went with it. Enthusiastically.

We'd camped beside the amphitheater, waiting for the bands to start playing. There was already a huge crowd on the main lawn, and farther behind us, booths were set up with fire pits, local shop owners selling food, and people showing off their boarding skills on the snow imported from Mount Bachelor. The moon was a shiny silver and the wind was whipping off the Deschutes River. The alcohol was helping with the cold, though. That was the one and only part of the plan: to sneak it in, mixed with juice, in our travel thermoses—and not get so hammered that we got caught.

Izzy mentioned Ashlyn once, to see if she was joining us, and I quickly waved it off. Ashlyn was somewhere at WinterFest with Kyle, I'd told her. They'd casually dated up until Formal, and a few days after, Kyle had asked Ashlyn to be his girlfriend. So Ashlyn was occupied that night. Ashlyn didn't need to forget.

My eyes went heavy and pinched, like I would cry right there. I didn't want to be that person, someone who wished her best friend away, whose muscles clenched at the thought of her best friend's happiness. It felt like a turning point, a place I could never come back from. So I took another gulp to get the bitter taste out of my mouth, and hoped I wouldn't remember feeling that way the next morning. But then I got hungry—and annoyed that my teammate Danielle had shown up and been a total sober downer.

It was while I was waiting in line for homemade pretzels that I lazily glanced to my right and saw Kyle. He was only a few feet from me, around the corner of a large canvas tent and out of the crowd, staring down at his phone. His other hand was in his pocket, and it was probably warm. I thought if I held it, I'd be able to touch the tiny scar on his knuckle, and he could—

My brain yelled at me to ignore him.

Except the rum had snipped any connection between my body and my brain—and the truth was, I really, really wanted to talk to him. We hadn't done much of that since our teacher switched up our class's lab partner assignments at the beginning of January. Standing there, it felt right to go to him, like I had the power to be okay near him. So I scurried over, swerving around a small group until I stood opposite him in the shadow of the tent.

"HEY!"

Kyle started at the noise. "Cloudy," he said sharply. "Where did you come from?"

"I've been waiting in the loooooooongest—" I gasped. "Oh, shit, I got out of my line."

He barked a laugh. "I guess so."

I sighed, jerking a thumb over my shoulder. "I was standing in the pretzel line and then I saw you and . . . now I'm not standing in the pretzel line."

He was watching me, his eyes narrowed. "Have you been drinking?" he whispered.

Cupping my hands around my mouth, I said in a perfect— at least I'd thought so—impersonation of our biology teacher, "A-plus for observation, Mr. Ocie."

He held up his phone, smiling. "That explains why you never answered your boyfriend's texts."

"Oops." By then, Matty and I had been together for over a month. And it's not like he was a consolation. Matty was fun and hot and actually into me.

I spotted a row of folding chairs lined up against the tent and hopped on top of one, the seat shaking under my feet. "I left my phone with Lita."

"Well, he's been attempting to tell you he's running late. And Ashlyn's in this never-ending bathroom line," he said, glancing

90

down at his phone again. "We're supposed to meet up near the ice sculptures. If she gets out before spring."

We're, I'd thought. Ten days as a couple, and he and Ashlyn were already, officially, a We. My stomach curdled, but the sensation passed quickly, and I was back to being fine. Why didn't people drink rum all the time?

"Yeah, this place," I said. "More like LineFest, right?"

I paused, absorbing my joke, then giggled. A lot. So much my face hurt, even though it didn't register as pain. It made me bobble on the chair, and the toe of my boot slipped off the seat.

Kyle swooped in as I fell, his hands ready to spot me. He was the one looking up at me then, and it was borderline obnoxious that he was almost cuter from this angle. No, it *was* obnoxious, and I was abruptly enraged. This was *his* fault. If he'd only just liked me back. How difficult was it? To like me? It's all hormones and firing neurons, so what the hell were wrong with his? Life would have been so much simpler, and not even all that different. This is how I imagined it: the Earth would continue to spin on its axis, and I wouldn't be lying to my best friend, or dating someone I didn't totally want to, or feeling guilty for noticing Kyle's stupid, cute face.

Maybe I was drunker than I thought.

I pressed my heels into the metal seat to re-steady myself and studied his eyes. They were a deeper blue—not the in-between-blue-and-green color they normally were—as if they were reflecting off the night sky.

"You sure it's safe to stay up there?" he said, surveying the chair.

I let my head drop; it weighed a thousand pounds. "Kyle, please. I stand on other people's hands and get launched twenty feet into the air on a weekly basis. This is . . . *pie*."

"Not that you're bragging."

"No, I was definitely bragging."

"In that case, I think you mean it's 'cake.' Not 'pie.' Unless you were going for 'easy as pie.'"

I groaned. "Keep that up and your new lab partner will, for sure, stab you with a scalpel."

"Sam was pretty enthusiastic with that crayfish last week." He gave me a pointed look. "He believes dissecting on a computer isn't as educational as the real thing."

"Said every future serial killer ever."

"Or maybe future surgeon."

I scoffed, my head rearing back. "Like I believe anyone in our class could be a surgeon."

Crossing his arms over his chest, Kyle said, "So your theory is everyone in first-period bio will turn out to be a serial killer—including me."

"I'm sorry you had to find out this way."

"But *excluding* you, since you do the virtual dissection thing. That's pretty convenient."

"I don't make the rules, Kyle!" I said, flinging my arms out wide, and when I did, my entire foot slid out from beneath me. This time, I reached out for Kyle's shoulders just as he placed his hands on my waist.

"You okay?" he breathed, spooked.

I dug my nails into his coat. I didn't want him to go—and

what scared me most was that I dreaded Ashlyn ever showing up. "Uh-huh."

My teeth stung from the cold, which meant I hadn't stopped grinning the whole time, but Kyle was smiling, too. At me. He was so close; suddenly eye level when only a few seconds ago, I could see the top of his head.

That rightness wrapped me up again like a warm blanket, and I felt myself tipping forward, to him, a houseplant arcing toward a sunny window. And I kissed him, breathing in his Junior Mint-y exhale. I kissed him until I realized he wasn't kissing me back. He was pulling away, his eyes panicked, checking if anyone had spotted what I'd done.

My arms dropped; my lungs shriveled up. "Don't tell anyone" was all I said.

Then I bolted. Jumped right off the chair before he could give an apology or a rejection. I didn't want to hear it. I didn't want either of us to even acknowledge how I'd massively wrecked this. So I'd avoided him and Ashlyn after that—and the only reason I hadn't completely avoided Matty was so I could dump him.

Six days after I kissed him, Kyle rang my doorbell. He'd come over to talk about how worried Ashlyn was about me, and what was worse, he wanted to know if I was *okay* after what happened at WinterFest. I couldn't let him believe that the kiss had meant anything, not when it could be erased if we ignored it.

We. Kyle and I were a We—and this was why. Because We had a secret.

So while we froze solid on my front porch, I told him to stay out of my business, that as far as I was concerned, the kiss never happened, and he was taking it all way too personally, anyway. He didn't have to play peacemaker because there was nothing for him to come and fix. Everything was fine. And I was determined to keep it that way. I'd be a better friend; the kind Ashlyn deserved. Matty would get over the breakup soon enough, and Kyle would forget what happened.

Except Kyle clearly hasn't forgotten. And now here we are.

Five hours in the somber-mobile.

Five hours of Kyle's "Mood Disorders for Beginners" playlist. Except for one song that he purposely skips every time; one that opens with these earnest, twinkly piano chords. How he finds it any more unbearable than the rest is a mystery, but it's not like I'm asking.

Five hours of basically no talking, aside from the occasional necessary "I need the bathroom" or "I have to stretch my legs before they shrivel."

Five hours of those words bouncing around in my head, wondering how long they've been in his.

Because you never lie.

He thinks I'm a liar, and he said it out loud, so now it feels like a truth.

I was ready to deny it and instead the first thing that came out of my mouth was another lie. That's what shut me up, smothered the outrage crackling through me. He was right. And something about being in his car, with its freakishly comfortable seats and dumb tree-shaped air freshener, made fighting with him impossible. I have lied. I *am* lying, whenever I don't tell him why we're actually on our way to Sacramento.

But I'm hoping it won't be the kind of lie that breaks every-thing apart.

The car slows and I check Kyle's phone, where the GPS app is tracking our progress. We're a couple-ish hours from Sacra-mento now—my time is running out. But if I'd come clean when he asked, just twenty minutes outside of Bend, he could have turned us right around. Then I'd go back to my house for the week and he'd go back to his. With the kitten.

Arm.

Like I'm falling for that Armadillo bullshit. There's no ques-tion Kyle named her after Ashlyn. If anything, it proves that he needs to see the recipients for himself. The cat is an enormous sign. We've passed smaller billboards on I-5.

I risk a glance at Kyle. His anger—or whatever that was earlier—quickly simmered into that quiet, contemplative thing he does so well. As if he's running on this hamster wheel inside his own mind. And I'm partially responsible for it. If I hadn't defended Matty, Kyle wouldn't have gotten so worked up. He wouldn't now believe we pity him or swap stories behind his back. Or that we're ganging up on him.

I slump lower in my seat.

How am I already losing control of this?

"You look the same from this side, you know." It comes out louder than I want it to. Maybe I've forgotten how to use my vocal cords.

Kyle blinks twice at the windshield. "What?"

I clear my throat. "When we were lab partners, I always sat on your left side. I'm not used to seeing you from this angle."

"Oh." He places a palm over the heating vents. "Did you think I wouldn't?"

"Anything's possible."

My heart bumps around my rib cage even as relief settles my nerves. He's answering back, which hopefully means he hasn't spent the entire ride counting the ways he hates me. But the silence between us returns in full force, and these few seconds might be worse than the entire five hours that came before them. I'm trying. Can't he tell I'm trying?

Something hot prickles on my skin, the same aggravation from when he lashed out this morning. So I untie my bun, and coil it back up, and breathe through it. Giving him attitude now will only make things worse.

"Look, isn't it too long a trip for us not to talk at all?"

Kyle pauses, then reaches over to turn down the music. "I'm not *not* talking to you. I'm just . . . driving. When I drive, I think."

"About kicking me from a moving car?"

He smiles, but not enough to put me at ease. "Nothing that vicious."

"Great."

"I'm kidding." His fingers curl around the steering wheel tightly before loosening up. "Cloudy, I didn't mean all that before. I—"

"No, don't. It's fine." I tap my armrest. "Let's drop it."

"I can't drop it," he says quickly, and it isn't resentment—it sounds like part of an apology. "I'm not sure I function that way."

I nod once, afraid of encouraging him to keep going. But he does.

"I was pissed about Matty—and Jacob is *such* an *ass*. But I couldn't blow up at them, and you were sitting right there, so I blew up at you. I'm sorry; it wasn't fair. And bringing up that stuff from last year wasn't fair either." He sighs again. "That's all I wanted to say."

I look out the passenger window as we zip by signs for towns I don't recognize. Every second means we're a littler farther away from Bend, and the thought makes something in my chest contract. I can't tell if it's a good feeling or not.

"Keeping WinterFest a secret, I did it for her," I say quietly, my gaze stuck on the California plates of the cars that pass us. "And for Matty, and even for you, I guess. But I didn't mean to hurt anyone."

It's not enough, but it's all I have right now. Maybe we'll go the rest of the way not talking, until I unload the whole story on him, and who knows what'll happen then.

"Hey."

When I turn my head to him, Kyle says, "You're the same from this side, too." And he's smiling like that's a good thing.

WE GET THERE earlier than expected, right around five-thirty. Even more time to come clean.

"Sacramento Children's Theater?" Kyle asks, though the awning on the building pretty much clears up any confusion.

"I told you we were coming for a play." I dig through my bag, looking for the email from Ethan's mom. The last couple of hours in the car have been practically pleasant—despite the playlist—and I'm finally ready to tell Kyle. Not that I have a choice anymore.

Kyle swings the car into a long driveway that leads behind the theater. He pulls into a spot under a tree. "Is it for extra credit or something?"

Snorting, I say, "You think a teacher would give me extra credit for watching some kids in *Snow White and the Seven Dwarfs*? In another state?"

Kyle shrugs stiffly, and I'm nervous his patience is running on low. Perhaps making him drive for seven hours, then mocking him, wasn't the greatest warm-up.

I swivel in my seat to face him. "I need to tell you something, but if you yell at me again, your phone's eating sidewalk."

He chuckles, embarrassed. "I'm not going to yell at you."

I fold my hands in my lap so I won't fiddle with them. "Do you know anything about what happened after Ashlyn died? About her organs being donated?"

Everything about him goes still. So still his cells have probably stopped dividing. "I guess." He's staring at a candy wrapper in the center console. "I remember her parents mentioning it at the memorial service."

"Apparently, they've been in contact with a few of the recipients. Including Ethan, the boy who got Ashlyn's liver—well, some of it. I was over at the Montiels' yesterday and I read an email from his mom saying he's in this play." I hold up the crinkled paper. "And I printed it out. Without telling anyone."

His eyes meet mine. "Can you do that?"

Why is that everyone's first reaction?

I lift my chin. "No, I can't do that, but I did. And I couldn't ignore this, not when we're on break from school and Ethan's so close." Kyle's undoubtedly about to disagree with my "so close" comment, so I jump in first. "I thought it would be cool to see him. And I thought you might think so, too."

His eyebrows slant up in that way they do. "This is the email?" he asks, nodding at my hand. When I tell him it is, he reaches for it.

Suddenly, there's too little air in here, so I open my door and wait outside. According to the dashboard, it's sixty-four degrees out, but it feels warmer—anything feels warmer than Bend in February.

The back door of the theater is in clear view. Ethan's probably already inside getting ready for his performance. I don't know what he looks like. His mom may have sent the Montiels photos, but I couldn't risk getting caught to search for them last night. Does he look different than he did before getting part of Ashlyn?

I fight every impulse to spy on Kyle. He deserves his privacy, but the longer he takes, the more likely he is to peel out and strand me here.

Finally, after an endless few minutes, Kyle's door slams shut. He comes closer, but stops before reaching my side of the car. He's not veiny or panting or anything, but he seems . . . shattered. Not completely, but something about him has definitely cracked. His face is flushed and his gaze is far away, as if he's about to cry or already has. Regret and empathy see-saw inside me. I've had only one day more of knowing about the recipients, but I've been able to box up thoughts of them. Organizing them in a way I can deal with. Kyle's different.

How else did I expect him to react?

"This is for real," he says, squinting.

I nod. "Are you all right?"

His mouth is open, like he's rearranging the words in his mouth. "Yeah. I am. And this kid with Ashlyn's—Ethan. He's here?" Kyle gives his head a slight shake and gestures behind me. "In there?"

"You read that he's playing Sneezy, right? And the play completely sucks—we did it in second grade—but his mom sounds pretty optimistic about it."

His cap is off, and his blond hair picks up whatever light the early evening sun has left. I notice the email, all folded up, clenched between his fingers. "So this whole trip is about Ethan."

"Partly," I say, wishing I could see his eyes. "There are others nearby. But I wasn't going to tell you that until later."

"That's why you brought a duffel bag. You packed for longer than a day."

I bite my lip. "I packed for the *possibility* of longer than a day."

"And this is why you asked me to take you, not your friends. Because—"

"Don't be stupid; you know why I asked you." I have to say it before he babbles out the truth—that he's falling into a rut again. That Matty's right: Kyle's sadness is so obvious, and that's why I'm going this far to help him. "It wouldn't mean the same thing to someone else. Plus, my car really couldn't have made it."

Kyle lifts his arms, placing his hands on his head, and when his eyes do meet mine, his expression changes, opens. "We basically drove seven hours to spy on a ten-year-old."

"Don't you want to see what he's like?"

He sighs deeply, staring at the theater. "The play really sucks?"

"YOU'LL GET KICKED out," I tell him.

"No, I won't." Kyle is trailing behind me on the path to the entrance. He's walking *so slowly*, and gripping my duffel bag in one hand.

"Then arrested for animal cruelty, probably."

"I'm not leaving her alone in a car for two hours, so what I'm doing is the opposite of cruel."

I tried convincing him that Arm would be fine in the car—the temperature's comfortable enough and we could've cracked a window for extra airflow. He pretended to humor me, then asked to borrow my duffel. And it's not that I mind him using it for a cat carrier; I just didn't count on temporarily storing my bras and underwear under his backseat.

I wait for them to catch up, watching as Kyle holds the bag gingerly. "If you keep walking like that, someone's going to think you have a bomb."

He makes a visible effort to loosen up, and I laugh. "An overprotective dad," I say to Arm as I squat down. She's sniffing at the mesh around the sides. "Good luck getting any dates, kitty cat."

When we get inside, parents and siblings and friends are grinning in every corner of the small, rectangular foyer. So maybe I was wrong about the play sucking so much. Or, what's more likely, these people don't care. Any of these women could be Ethan's mom—I imagine she's the one grinning the biggest.

The guy at the box office window offers us a student discount—no word on any smuggled-cat deals. "I've got this," Kyle says, all gallantly, pulling out a ten-dollar bill. I'm set to tease him, but after he hands me my ticket, his hand gently brushes my back, and my lips snap shut.

Inside the auditorium, a girl about our age waits to exchange our tickets for programs. When she moves, I smell her cotton-candy perfume. It's only then that her eyes graze over me, then Kyle, and for the first time it occurs to me that people might think we're a couple. It makes me feel like I've swallowed tissue paper.

I walk away first, forcing Kyle to navigate his and Arm's way down the center aisle alone. Then I drop down onto a seat in our assigned row and flip open the program.

Kyle eases in beside me and carefully slides Arm's duffel underneath his chair. We're sitting close, closer than in the Xterra. I press the program to my face and hope the cotton-candy-perfume molecules are somehow more powerful than whatever Junior Mint-y freshness comes from Kyle.

"What part were you in the play?" Kyle says, shifting his legs around the little space they have. "When you were in second grade?"

"A hummingbird."

"For real?" Kyle laughs.

"There was this huge tree onstage; it was in the background, behind the dwarfs' cottage, for almost the entire play. I was the only forest animal who wasn't scared to sit in it, so they made me an owl. I negotiated them to hummingbird."

"Why a hummingbird?"

"They eat half their weight in sugar every day." I shrug. "And they're the cutest, obviously."

"Obviously," he repeats quietly, with a small smile.

It scares me how aware of him I am, even when I'm not trying to be.

"Ashlyn got a speaking part, though. It was only her first year in Bend, so it was a big deal. Kiera Mahoney was *pissed*."

Kyle turns his head, his smile getting broader. "Who did Ashlyn play?"

"Young Snow White. She kind of let it go to her head, to be honest." I smirk so he knows I'm kidding. "I told her she got the part because she had black hair."

Then I pretend to pick at my nail polish, and Kyle pretends not to fuss over Arm, until the lights go down and the show starts.

There is *a lot* of Snow White singing about being perfect. And the actress playing the Evil Queen is putting on this pseudo-British accent that I guess is supposed to make her sound royal but instead makes her sound as if her tongue is swollen.

But none of that matters when the dwarfs finally come onstage. Beside me, Kyle stiffens, and without realizing it, I've scooted to the front of my seat. Sneezy—Ethan—is in a deep green, belted tunic with a matching pointy hat, and his nose is streaked with rosy makeup that makes him look more red-nosed reindeer than allergy-ridden dwarf. He is small compared with the other kids. Is it because he was so sick? Will he get bigger now that he's not fighting to stay alive? Ethan cuts across the stage with the others, and Zoë's theory flickers through my mind. Whether I like it or not, I'm waiting for a little sign of Ashlyn; I want one. In the way Ethan walks or stands or taps his shoes. And I want it for Kyle, too.

Maybe we did come here to watch Ethan, but we really came to see Ashlyn.

Snow White hands Ethan an oversized prop flower. His nose twitches and he lets out a big, squeaky sneeze that the audience laughs at, even Kyle. My fingers are digging into the seat, and my body fills with a panicky heat as Ethan starts to walk offstage. I don't want him to leave before I glimpse something. Why couldn't he play a bird and be onstage the whole time?

But before he disappears behind the curtain, he stops short. No one else notices because Snow White is singing another sap-tacular song at center stage, but my eyes are only on the kid in the corner. He turns his head slightly, probably to where his family is sitting, and he unleashes a toothy grin. It relaxes me, as if someone cut the string that tied me tightly. Because maybe Ashlyn never smiled exactly like that, but I know she gave that grin to Ethan.

And when Kyle turns to me, I know he saw it, too.

THE THEATER'S BACK door opens, letting some of the noise from inside slip out before it clangs shut. I tilt sideways around the front of the car. Kyle is halfway inside the trunk, fretting over Arm, and we share a nervous look.

"Are you going to talk to him?" Kyle asks.

"And say what?" I sort-of whisper. I don't want anyone to overhear. "'Hey, you know your liver? The part that's not yours? It's our friend's! Wanna chat?'"

Kyle presses the hatchback closed. "It's just a little weird that we came all this way to not even say anything to him."

I can't exactly argue with this. But as nice as it would be to talk to Ethan, there's no way we can without it being suspicious. I do another front walkover—I've got residual energy like crazy—and Kyle hoists himself up on the front hood.

"The Montiels'll get into major trouble if Ethan's parents think they're giving out information," I tell him.

"And you'll get into trouble for being nosy?"

I shoot him a half smile. "You're technically my accomplice, so I wouldn't get all judgy."

Kyle holds his hands up in surrender. No arguing with *that*, either.

Sighing, I say, "Wasn't Ethan so good in the play? He sneezed like a professional!"

"Totally believable sneezing," Kyle murmurs.

"Yeah, he was great." I rub my hands on my pants, sore after pressing against the concrete. "Do you think he's like Ashlyn at all?"

"Ethan?" His eyebrows come together. "You mean, because of the . . ."

I tell him about Zoë and that movie. I don't say that after seeing Ethan, I'm starting to hope that it's true. "It's not the same, of course. I know he's not possessed. But maybe he's got something. A little bit of Ashlyn."

Kyle stares across the small lot at the brick wall bordering it, and I'm sure he thinks I've gone bonkers. Then he says, "Like he brushes his hair five times a day now?"

Startled, I look up at him. "Yeah," I say, grinning. "And listens to Whitney Houston every single morning."

He laughs. "And can never remember his own phone number."

"And hates the color coral because it can't decide if it's pink or orange."

"And has to sit right in the center seat at the movies—or else."

I groan, knowing just what he's talking about. "And mainlines iced coffee."

His eyes go round, and he sucks in a breath like he can't get the words out fast enough. "What was with the iced coffee? And then she'd eat the ice, too. Who does that?"

We're both smiling, facing opposite directions, and I'm warm all over despite the temperature having dropped. If things had been different—if *I'd* been different—it could've been this way, us cracking jokes about Ashlyn's silly quirks when she was alive. God, she would've loved it.

Suddenly there's giggling coming from the theater. Maybe we were too preoccupied roasting Ashlyn to hear the door open, but someone's coming—someone young and decidedly Ethan-shaped.

"It's him," I whisper as Kyle slides off the car and steps up beside me.

We're standing side by side, like some human wall of idiocy, especially if Kyle's doing what I'm doing—beaming nervously at Ethan and his family as they pass us. His mom and his dad, and maybe his big brother, they're all circled around Ethan, who is grinning that same grin I saw onstage.

I take in as much of him as I can and try to match him up with Ashlyn. Like placing a traced picture over the original. But there's not enough time and I don't know enough about him, except that he's so, so happy and so . . . *here.*

"Look, he's got freckles."

Something about Kyle's observation sends me over the edge. I trap a laugh in my throat so it doesn't spill over, but I'm shaking from the effort. Kyle eyes me, and his smile is the second best thing about tonight, which is saying a lot.

I turn to the first best thing. His family passes by without noticing us, but Ethan must sense our attention. He waves. At us. And he does it the way little kids do it, moving his hand furiously for those three seconds. I trap the memory of it in my mind while holding up my own hand to wave back.

I CARRY THE bags and drink tray outside to Kyle, whose long legs are dangling from the back of the Xterra. He was doing a dead-on Kyle-driving-from-Bend-to-Sacramento impression on the way here, totally silent, while I could barely shut up—even though all I did was point out the different fast food places along the street and why we couldn't eat there: "They don't have healthier options," "Ashlyn said they buy from a supplier that's inhumane to animals," "I heard someone found a tumor on their chicken sandwich once."

That didn't help Kyle's mood, whatever his mood even is. Being so near Ethan put a stopper on his easy laughter in the theater parking lot.

When I reach the back bumper, I drop his grease-spotted Taco Bell bag into his lap, then hop in the trunk beside him. Arm's snuggled up in a fleece blanket, but her eyes are open and her teeny nose perks up, probably scenting Kyle's crunchy tacos. He tears into one, finishing most of it in one bite.

Him chomping on his food is the sound of progress being crushed, because we are back on mute.

I jiggle my feet, then cross my legs into a yoga pose. Talking isn't supposed to take this much work or thought. I picture every silent second that's stretching out ahead of us. They're piling up and over to bury us in a mountain of boredom, and the only way out is to reach with my hand and—

"Are you taking the SATs in the spring?"

School. I might as well have asked Kyle to explain his cell phone plan.

It's a safe topic, sure, but who cares? He'll say yes or no and I'll say "Cool." Then I'll shove the rest of this salad into my face and let boredom take us down quietly.

Kyle wipes his fingers on a napkin. "Probably, yeah."

So I say, "Cool."

I'm stabbing a huge plastic forkful of lettuce, shredded cheese, and grilled chicken when Kyle does the unexpected. "Have you been thinking about college at all?"

A follow-up question. About school. Surely, in some universe, two planets have just collided.

"Sort of." If this is his version of an outstretched hand, I'm grabbing it. "The front-runners so far are USC and the University of Washington."

Arm is now up and moving, tottering around the trunk, and Kyle and I both smile as she hoists herself up on my ankle and sniffs at the rim of my salad bowl.

"Why those two?" He leans back against the car, crunching more of his food. "I mean, why not somewhere in Oregon, or . . . I don't know, West Virginia."

Something twists in my throat, and I take a sip of iced tea to drown it. "Both schools have a nonprofit-management degree," I murmur.

He presses his lips together. "For Ashlyn."

"Yep."

She was going to run an animal shelter, and I was going to . . . figure it out. My career prospects were hazy and uncertain, but I'd solve that at whatever school I attended with Ashlyn. And we were going to try for cheer scholarships—*try* because, although we were both capable of getting one, so were lots of others. The odds could've gone either way. Maybe mine are better now that *Cheer Insider* has noticed me.

That was the plan, and Ashlyn excelled at those. She always had forward momentum, some kind of goal, and she'd blueprint her way to it. I'd been envious of that, even when I told myself that I was someone who took things as they happened, without a safety net. But I was kidding myself—of course I had a safety net. If I slipped up, I had Ashlyn—who'd be ready with a hug, a *Freaks and Geeks* marathon, and both chocolate-covered pretzels and sour gummy worms. Now the idea of winging it, alone, is paralyzing.

"What about you?" I say to Kyle. "What does your future hold?"

He squirms, pulling at the hem of his sweatshirt. "When I was little, I figured I'd be a dentist."

"Like your dad and your uncle."

"The Family Footsteps," he says, his lips curving up. "Back then I thought dentistry was what all Ocie men were destined for. But now I'm not so sure about it."

I squint across the narrow lot, over the shrub borders, to 25th Street. "You'd be defying your destiny, then."

"That makes me sound like a Greek tragedy."

"I was picturing more . . . Buffy the Vampire Slayer."

He smiles again, crumpling his food wrappers into a ball. "So I guess I don't have a plan."

"Probably for the best."

Plans hardly ever behave like they're supposed to.

"Speaking of plans," Kyle says, "where does the squad think you are right now instead of the library fund-raiser?"

"Oh." I blow out a breath. "About an hour ago, I came down with a very gross, very contagious stomach virus. That's what Zoë's telling them."

"You are freakishly good at this," he says, and I'm not sure it's a compliment, but my cheeks burn anyway.

Arm is back to snuggling in her blanket, and I lift a finger to stroke the top of her head. She's so soft and tiny. "Is she going to develop parking-lot PTSD?"

Kyle raises his eyebrows. "What do you mean?"

I shrug one shoulder. "Aside from a whirlwind tour of my duffel bag, it's like all she's seen is parking lots so far. Not where you should spend your first days."

"Isn't she probably a couple of months old? She's seen more than parking lots."

My turn to raise my eyebrows. "Where did you say you found her?"

He shoves the food-wrapper ball into the empty paper bag. "A parking lot."

I laugh. "Would she be opposed to Palm Springs?"

"Palm Springs?"

"There's another recipient there. I thought we'd swing by, and maybe Vegas, too." I peer at Kyle. "If Arm's okay with it."

He frowns down at his taco remnants, and I know he's not going to say no. "I'll need to stop off for supplies—clothes and a toothbrush, at least."

"Not a problem." He'll also need something to wear for Sonia's wedding, but I can mention that later. The ceremony's at a fancy hotel on the Strip, so hoodies and jeans won't help us blend in with the other guests. It's why I packed one of my nicer skirts and a blouse from home.

Kyle checks his watch. "And I guess we should find a hotel for the night. It's too late to drive down there now."

"Good idea," I say, even though renting a room with Kyle has never ever been in the realm of possible for me.

Okay, not *never ever*. Last night, while I was throwing things into my duffel bag, it did occur to me that we'd have to sleep somewhere—many somewheres, together—if Kyle wanted to keep going. But I'd shouldered the concern out of my brain to make room for more pressing ones, like Mom and Dad being forced to come home early because of a viral outbreak on their cruise ship, and discovering I was gone.

I leave Kyle tapping at his phone—searching for the cheapest room with two beds in Sacramento, I assume—to go dump our paper bags in the trash. Then I fish my own phone out of my pocket. It's been off since before the play, mostly to conserve the battery, but also because you can't ignore people if you don't know they're calling.

As soon as the home screen blinks up, my phone sputters and beeps and dings like it can't wait to tell me something. A lot of somethings. All the texts and voice mails I've received in the past few hours, who they're from, and how many. Many.

So, so, so, so many.

My eyes lock on one in particular.

It's from Zoë.

I've made a huge mistake.

Kyle

I 'm turning into the Good-Night Motel parking lot when
Cloudy's phone goes off for what has to be the twentieth
time in seven minutes. In the darkness, the small screen in her
hand illuminates her frowning face.

"Something has to be done about this," she says.

From what Cloudy explained during the drive from Taco
Bell, Zoë never got a chance to tell the other cheerleaders about
Cloudy's imaginary sudden illness. Lita Tamsin heard from
Jacob that there was a pink pillow on my backseat this morning and Cloudy and I were "looking very cozy." So Lita rattled
off a bunch of questions about us, which got Zoë so flustered
she ended up admitting we'd driven to California together. She
tried to fix it by adding that we were visiting Cloudy's friend
Jade, but the Jade cover story was pretty much beside the point.

Cloudy's teammates latched on to the fact that she had left
town unexpectedly *and* with me. As a result, a flood of texts,
call notifications, and emails poured in as soon as she turned
her phone back on. Luckily for me, I didn't get the same treatment.

"What do you think *can* be done about this?" I ask Cloudy as I pull into a spot near the main office.

"One: I can have you run over my phone a few times. Or two: I can suck it up and call Lita." She tilts her head as if she's in deep thought. "But do I care more about keeping my phone intact or my sanity?"

"Talking to Lita is going to help?"

"She's my best shot at making sure the version of the story I *want* to have spread actually *gets* spread."

Since so many people know we're gone, Matty probably does, too. Which means other members of our family could be finding out at any time. "I have to tell my dad where I am. I can call him now if you want to call Lita?"

"If I *want* to call her? You're funny."

But she taps on her screen, and then holds the phone to her ear.

It's impossible to have a conversation while sitting beside someone having their own, so I open the door to make my call outside. I'm fine without a coat since it's still warm. As I climb out, Lita's voice comes through loud and clear. "*Finally* you call me back! Kyle's with you, right? So let's do this in secret code. Blink twice if he abducted you. Wait! That's not going to work. *Cough* twice—"

I close the door. Despite being related to Jacob, Lita is mostly harmless (I think), but her talking about me like I'm a psycho isn't exactly my favorite thing. It must not be Cloudy's, either, because she points a finger gun to her temple and jerks back like she's shot herself.

She's slumped over like she's miserable, but I can't help

smiling. I'm on a road trip with a kitten (asleep in the back on her Pillow Pet) and visiting a city with palm trees. Cloudy and I are talking about visiting two more of the people who have Ashlyn's organs, and I can't believe any of this is happening.

Under the glow of parking lot lights, I make my way to sit on a rickety bench with two slats missing. I have a good view of the wide avenue from here, with headlights streaking past every few seconds. I dial my dad and ready myself for the coming reality check. I left home before he was up this morning, knowing he'd assume I was with Matty. At the time, I was looking forward to the shock in his voice when I told him I'd taken off for California. But that was back when I thought it wouldn't matter, back when I thought I'd be driving home tonight.

Dad answers, skipping past hello and going straight to: "I was about to call you! I can't find your cat."

I hesitate. "She's with me."

"At the mountain?"

Here goes nothing. "No, I drove the cat and Cloudy Marlowe. To . . . Sacramento."

"You did *what*?"

"Remember you said you wanted me to get out of the house?" I say in a rush. "So I—"

"Drove to California without telling me?"

My dad yelling at me is rare. "I'm sorry. I should have talked to you first."

"Damn right, you should have." He replaces his mad voice with his weary voice. "Is this because of the counseling appointment?"

"Not entirely." I explain how Cloudy called last night and asked for a ride to the play, and that I'd told her yes because I wanted to get away. "When we arrived, she showed me an email. It was from the mother of one of Ashlyn's organ recipients." I take a deep breath and let it out. "This woman has been writing to the Montiels about her ten-year-old kid, and . . ."

I trail off, because even though the email from Ethan's mom was super upbeat, it was difficult to read her words: *It's still hard to believe that six months ago, doctors were saying my son had mere days left in this world. Now, he has his whole life ahead of him.*

After I finished reading, I'd sat gripping the steering wheel and pressing my forehead hard against it as I fought to keep from crying. Then I made myself read the email again and again until the pain dulled enough to allow me to get out of the car.

"You all right?" Dad asks.

"Yeah. It's just. This kid. Ethan. He was really sick. I mean, he was *dying*, Dad. He got Ashlyn's liver just in time. And tonight, Cloudy and I saw him. He was in that play."

"Oh, wow."

"No one knew we were coming, so we didn't talk to him and his family or anything. We just watched the performance."

"And how was it for you?" he asks. "Seeing him?"

Cloudy's energy through dinner (along with what ended up being my second conversation in two days about how I don't have any kind of Life Plan) kept me distracted, so I wasn't dwelling on the fact that, as a result of something that sucks more than anything, the lives of these people in Sacramento are now better. "It wasn't upsetting or anything. It was cool, actually. But it was weird, too, because the reason why he's even alive now is because—I mean, I'm not bitter. Even if he hadn't been given her liver, Ashlyn couldn't have been saved. So I'm glad for him. I just . . . I don't know."

"That's understandable," Dad says quietly.

Is it? "Cloudy told me there are two other organ recipients who've written to Ashlyn's parents. They're in Palm Springs and Vegas. We don't have school this week, so we're talking about traveling to see them, too. What do you think?"

"If it's something you want to do, if it's going to help you, you should know I'm all for it. Why isn't Matt with you, though?"

I stare at silhouettes of power-line towers hovering behind the streetlights. They're like tall, angry robots. "We need a break from each other."

"I doubt he feels the same. You know how much he's always admired his big cousin."

"He's the big cousin. I'm four months younger."

"Really?"

"Really. His birthday's October and mine's February."

"Oh. Well, I don't know why he admires you, then."

I laugh.

"Where are you going to stay?" Dad asks.

"I'd like to detour to Sedona for a few days, once we're done in California. If we have time." I haven't been back to the town where I grew up since we moved almost two years ago. I haven't been great at keeping in contact, either, so my old friends might not care about seeing me. "For tonight, though, we're getting a motel."

"You be careful, Kyle. You got that?"

"I will."

"And by 'careful' I mean, be *safe*."

Suddenly, this conversation took a turn I wasn't expecting. I groan. "I know what you mean and—"

"And by 'safe' I mean, use protection."

"Dad, stop!" I'm almost yelling, but at the same time trying not to laugh. "It isn't like that, okay?"

"Maybe not. But you said the words 'getting a motel' to your father. Not to mention that Sedona happens to be the most romantic place in the country. I visited there a little less than eighteen years ago, met a pretty girl, and now I have a son. A son who might be going to Sedona with a pretty girl. See what I'm getting at?"

The girl Dad met in Sedona (and who he moved away from Oregon and his family to be with, after he found out he'd gotten her pregnant) was my mom, obviously. But on the rare occasion when we talk about her, she's just "Shannon." I figure that a mother who was gone more than she was around, and who left without a real good-bye when I was ten, doesn't get to be called "Mom."

Dad gave me this same "be careful" speech repeatedly when I was with Ashlyn, and there's only one thing that will shut him up. "I'll be safe," I say. "I promise." Across the parking lot, my passenger door opens, and Cloudy steps out. Lita's done with her for now. Or vice versa. "Dad, Cloudy's on her way over, so we should either get off the phone or you should stop talking about the sex that I'm not going to have with her."

He laughs. "I'll let you go. But I want you to call me every day. And let me know if you need anything. And you should check in with your cousin. And be careful. And *safe*. And—"

"*Bye*, Dad."

"Love you, Kyle."

"You too."

Cloudy approaches as I'm dropping my phone into my pocket. "How'd it go?"

"He was pissed that I left without telling him, but he came around to the idea of me being gone for the rest of the week. He's pretty easygoing most of the time. What about Lita?"

"*Not* easygoing." She flashes a grin. "But she won't be a bigger problem than usual. I take it this was the cheapest motel you could find?"

"Pretty much." I gesture at the neon Welcome sign on the street, which advertises Vacancy/Color/Cable/Fridges/Suites/L.H.K./Pets O.K. "But more importantly, Arm is allowed here. What do you think 'L.H.K.' means?"

"Love, hugs, and kisses?"

"You think it's *that* kind of a motel?

She giggles.

We follow the sidewalk to the front office, and as Cloudy pushes the door open, jingle bells on the handle announce our arrival. A customer is already at the counter, facing a clerk who's behind a sliding window.

We hang back several feet, breathing in flowery room spray over microwave popcorn and scorched coffee. I glance at the brochure stand that's almost as tall as I am (6'1"), and displays more glossy pages of places to see and things to do than we could get to in a month. Golf courses, the Sacramento Zoo, Fairytale Town, the California State Capitol, the Governor's Mansion, Old Sacramento, state parks. And then the museums: art, history, Native American culture, the railroad, automobiles. I never knew there was so much going on in Sacramento.

When I was a kid and Shannon still lived with Dad and me, she once complained that she'd grown up in "the armpit of California." As I got older, I wondered if she'd meant that it smelled bad, was sweaty and hot, or something else. I checked online to figure out which city she'd been talking about. Sacramento, Fresno, and Bakersfield came up in my searches as the armpittiest. After reading that, I'd assumed they wouldn't be good places to visit.

The man in front of us finally finishes at the counter, and Cloudy and I step forward.

The clerk's massive black mustache covers his mouth, but when he speaks, his bottom lip appears. "How can I help?"

"Hi," Cloudy says. "We'd like a nonsmoking room, please. With two beds."

"Sure thing." The mustache lifts on both sides. "Just need a driver's license and credit card for the reservation."

"I'll get this," Cloudy tells me as she reaches into her messenger bag and pulls out a small stack of plastic cards. She slides off the hair band holding them together and hands the clerk the two on top. His lip disappears again as he holds up the license in his left hand and types using only his right index finger.

Cloudy's so in charge here—like she rents motel rooms in

other states all the time. The strangeness of the situation hits me yet again. I've never stayed in a place like this (Dad's kind of picky), and I've never slept in the same room with a girl. (Ashlyn and I only "slept together" in the nonsleeping way. And she was always worried my dad would come home early, so taking a nap together or anything afterward wasn't an option.) But this is real. I'm actually doing this, and it's kind of a rush.

The slow typing tapers off as the clerk squints at Cloudy's license. "Sorry, kids. The person who reserves the room has to be eighteen or older."

Cloudy turns to me with her eyebrows lifted in surprise.

"Neither of you is eighteen?" He holds the plastic out for Cloudy to take. "Then I can't rent you a room. I'm sorry."

"Hang on," I say. "Can I have my dad call to give permission? He's fine with this. I just talked to him."

"Permission isn't the problem. We need a person eighteen or over to sign for the room and stay in the room. If he can't do that . . ." He shrugs.

"We're traveling from Oregon," Cloudy says. "Alone. And we have nowhere to sleep. Can't you make an exception? If his dad promises to be liable if we overflow the toilet or—"

"Sorry," he says again. "We need the contract signed in person. A minor's signature isn't binding, and I'm not taking the risk. Been burned too many times."

Cloudy's shoulders sag as she tucks her things back into her bag and steps away. "What should we do?"

No matter what, I'm not going home now. I ask the clerk, "Do you have any suggestions?"

He keeps his eyes on his computer. "Try a youth hostel. Or some campground might let seventeen-year-olds rent a spot."

"Okay, thanks," I say.

Cloudy and I head back outside. "Stupid age discrimination," she grumbles as we walk back to the car under the parking lot lights. "Do you want to try a hostel?"

"Are you serious? Haven't you seen that movie?"

"*Hostel*? Yeah. So?"

"So, I happen to like my Achilles tendons the way they are, if that's okay with you." I give an exaggerated shudder. "And my eyeballs. Say it with me, Cloudy. No hostels. Not ever."

She laughs. "Do you make all your decisions based on what happens to fictional characters?"

"Not necessarily. But the thing is, in movies, fictional characters our age never have to show ID. This is uncharted territory."

"Real life loses this round."

"It really does. It's kind of late, but we can buy a tent and find a campsite."

"Wait. You want to *camp*?"

Now it's my turn to laugh while she gapes at me, horrified. "You've lived in Bend your whole life. Don't tell me you're afraid of camping."

"I'm afraid of needing an osteopath before I'm legal. But sure, let's sleep on the ground. It's not like we were cramped up all day. Or better yet, why not sleep in the car?"

I stare at the Xterra for a long moment.

"Oh, no," she says.

Cloudy

Y ou'd be surprised how much action a twenty-four-hour Home Depot gets after midnight.

A lot, it turns out, and enough to keep the Xterra—and the three squatters inside of it—unnoticed by security. For now.

Shifting as quietly as possible, I scrunch my body into a tighter ball and shiver under my coat. Earlier, when he saw me messing with the passenger seat's adjustment handle, Kyle offered to stay up front while I took the cargo area. I turned him down, though. He'd just be origamied up where I am now, worse because he's so tall, and I owe him a goodish night's rest after driving all day. He also proposed that we share the back of the Xterra—with the backseat folded down, it's big enough for the both of us. I brushed that off, too, and told him I kick when I dream, a cheerleader side effect. It's a lie, but honestly, the image of Arm settled in safely between us, like our newborn or something, was too much.

It's weird enough being in the same cramped space as Kyle, but thinking that he and I have a cat baby is proof I'm close to the edge.

I look out the sunroof—it's steamed up like the other

windows—and listen to Kyle breathe, in and out, evenly. The idea of sharing a hotel room with him seemed like a nightmare, but this is torture. Actually, being tortured with Kyle might be preferable to trying to sleep in this car with him. At least then I wouldn't be wondering how it would feel to be next to him, to watch his chest rise and fall.

I crane my neck to check the time on the dash—four thirty a.m.—instead of powering up my cell again. I've had enough phone trauma for tonight.

Lita was practically foaming at the mouth when I spoke to her. And by the end of our conversation, I'd managed to convince her that:

No, Kyle did not kidnap me.

No, Kyle and I were *definitely not* eloping.

Yes, this was all last minute, spur of the moment, unplanned, etc.

Yep, Zoë will tell Coach that I won't be at practice this week. Coach won't be thrilled, but she won't punish me for it, either. She'll give me the Responsibility Lecture when I get back and her eyes will go soft in that way they have since Ashlyn died. Adults never let it go. They hold on to things like a brand, with them all the time. I see it in the way teachers treat me, even months later. As if I'm wearing a Dead Girl's #1 Best Friend T-shirt. Not that it's a bad thing, people handling you more carefully because you've had a shit time of it. But it doesn't make moving on any easier when someone's pinning you in one place.

And finally, of course I would tell Jade that Lita said hi.

I wasn't serious about that last one, obviously. Since the

drama threat level has been downgraded, Jade won't ever know Zoë threw her name into this.

My blood is still humming with residual aggravation. Yesterday was supposed to be easy. I didn't have to worry about my parents since they were somewhere in the middle of the Pacific, and my pretend illness would've kept me off the radar at home for at least a couple more days. Except less than twelve hours into the trip, Zoë crumbled. From now on, the less I tell her, the better.

It's impossible to get comfortable, so I sit up to check over the backseat. The light from the lampposts ringing the lot is enough to show Kyle passed out like a pro, his head on the panda Pillow Pet. Arm is pressed to his bicep. After how he reacted to the email from Ethan's mom, I'm relieved he's taking this so well.

But there's been an undercurrent rippling through me. Ever since he agreed to see the other recipients. Dread or bitterness or something else that stretches my skin taut. I'd thought seeing Ethan was like having Ashlyn nearby. Now I realize it wasn't— not at all. She isn't nearby. The only parts of her that are still alive on this planet are inside of Ethan and the other recipients. They're here because she isn't; they're with their friends and families, and she's not. I'll never be with her again.

I inhale deeply, slowly breathe out.

I punch my cloud-print pillow, fluffing it up.

It's the worst at night. When there aren't daytime things to distract me, my thoughts always drift to Ashlyn. They creep in to catch me, drowsy and unguarded, but I chase them away before they gain any real ground.

Arm's supersonic ears must sense me moving around because she picks up her head.

"Hey, kitty," I whisper, carefully reaching over the seat to pet her with my pointer finger. "Some slumber party, right?"

She yawns and stands, her tiny body vibrating as she arches into a stretch. Without hesitating, she leaps onto Kyle's chest and curls up. He jerks awake immediately, then blinks down at Arm and up at the roof, before bending his head to catch me. The near darkness and quiet make it painfully intimate when he gives me a groggy smile. It's a moment before it registers I should smile, but Kyle has already fallen back to sleep. The whole sky could fall on the Xterra and I'd be okay with that.

Then my body temperature goes up a few degrees, and I consider smothering myself with my pillow.

UNLIKE ETHAN, FREDDIE Blackwell isn't debuting at any local playhouses. But his email did mention the street where his new house is, so after a few minutes of Google stalking, it wasn't too hard to find him. Now all we have to sort out is what to do when we get there.

At least we have time to work on a plan.

"Palm Springs is, like, seven hours from here. We could be there by dinnertime," Kyle tells me, tearing at the corner of a sugar packet for his coffee.

Maybe it's the sunlight coming in through the diner window, but Kyle looks *awake.* He's zinging with a new energy this morning, excited to get the day started, despite the rumpled chic of wearing the clothes he slept in. We were both able to clean up in the Home Depot bathroom, but the store was unfortunately lacking in a menswear department. So our first stop on the way to Palm Springs will be a seriously needed shopping mall.

It's seven thirty and we're at a diner that smells like coffee and bacon, and looks exactly like the diners everywhere else—chrome and vinyl, a long counter, and everything covered with a thin layer of maple syrup. It's kind of nice. Cozy, even. Like this is any other Sunday morning and we're having any other Sunday breakfast.

Except there's nothing really any-other about being here alone with Kyle and a cat in a duffel bag, sitting at a table that overlooks the Sacramento River.

From the corner of my eye, I spot our waitress, Wendy, strolling back to our table. She's probably around fifty years old, with her curly, dark hair tied back. Her bright red lipstick made me like her right away. "Ready to order?"

After Kyle asks for the eggs Benedict and bacon, and I settle on an egg-white omelet, Wendy takes our menus and examines us. "You know, we usually don't see anyone under retirement age here this early." She gestures to her left, where a large group of older men are seated at the counter, bent over newspapers.

"We haven't been to bed yet," I say. Kyle's eyes narrow on me. He doesn't want Wendy lingering because she might notice Arm, but I can't help myself. "We're celebrating."

Wendy braces a hand on the booth, near my ear. "Oh, yeah?" She smiles, curious. "Celebrating what?"

I rest on my forearms, scooting forward, and point at Kyle. "My brother got into Harvard. Early decision."

Which is so clearly not true. Aside from Kyle not having a "plan," neither of us can even apply to college for months.

"Harvard!" she says to him, all giddy. Kyle, on the other hand, tosses her a queasy-looking smile while shifting to block the duffel beside him. He shoots me a discreet glare that could propel his knife across the table.

"Yale, too, but"—I wave my hand—"everyone knows that place barely counts."

Wendy laughs. And while Kyle scratches his head, the distress in his expression shifts to challenge.

"My *sister's* being modest," he says to Wendy. "Sitting right there? Miss Teen Royal Galaxy Cheerleader."

What a dick.

I choke, unable to stop the grin that breaks across my face. When I notice Wendy eyeing me, a cheerleader with a title, I nod. "My Herkie is *out of this world.*"

Wendy tilts her head. "I'm not sure what any of that means, but I better get those orders in. Don't want to keep my most talented customers waiting," she says with a knock on the tabletop.

"It's a cheer stunt," I call to her back, then shrug at Kyle. "My Liberties are even better."

"You're out of control," he says on an exhale.

"Come on, Wendy bought it." I take a sip of coffee, flattening my grin. "She might give us extra home fries now."

"Only in your mind could I get into Harvard."

"No kidding. 'Miss Teen Royal Galaxy Cheerleader'? No Ivy Leaguer would ever quote Jacob Tamsin."

Kyle absently scratches at the light stubble across his jaw.

"What was that all about, anyway? He said something about you winning a cheer award?"

"It's not an award. It's just an interview in this cheer magazine."

"*Just* an interview?" he laughs. "You're aware they don't give those out to everyone, right?"

"They might as well. It's stupid."

He dips his head. "Is it the same magazine Ashlyn's article was in? The one she wrote about you two?"

"Um, yeah," I say, tracing the scalloped edge of my paper place mat. "I think so."

I know so. Last year, *Cheer Insider* put out a call for stories about cheering with your best friend, and Ashlyn had been all over it. She'd submitted a short essay about how we'd been competing and cheering together since we were kids—with nothing but glowing things about me, she promised. It was a hideous coincidence that they published it the same month she died. When I saw the issue on Ashlyn's desk, most likely placed there by her mom after it came in the mail, I tucked it into a drawer without ever flipping it open.

"She was going to display it," Kyle says, smiling again. "She had the frame all picked out."

I shake my head. "She must be so pissed she never got to use it."

Kyle pauses at that, then says, "Her mom stopped by my house one day to give me a copy. I was really glad to read it . . . you know, after. Weren't you?"

The coffee and cream have congealed in my stomach. "Totally."

"I read it more times than I could count at first. The way she wrote it was like listening to her talk. Like she was reading it out loud. I could even hear the weird way she pronounced 'family.' Faaamily," he says, drawing out the *A*s like a sheep would. "Where did she get that from?"

Thank God Wendy shows up with the food.

It gives me a moment to avoid saying anything else. There's this openness about Kyle that makes you want to talk. Except when I open my mouth around him, what usually comes out is pointless, or babbling, or abrasive.

Right now I want to say a lot. About how I haven't read Ashlyn's essay. How reading about *us*, in that way, in her own words, would be getting my hopes up; because spending too much time in the past would make the reality of her being gone unbearable. And I'd tell him that I can't face doing my own interview for the same reasons. How I'm not sure I fit with the other girls anymore, and how sometimes it feels majorly fucked up to be dancing and clapping to the same four songs as if Ashlyn isn't dead.

But no one needs to know all that.

Instead, I say, "Anyway, the magazine thing: not a big deal."

"Really? It sounds like one. It makes *you* sound like one, and from what I remember, you kind of are." Suddenly very focused on cutting his bacon into perfect tiny squares, the corner of his mouth quirks up. "Not that it's Harvard or anything."

I smile a little, too, watching him drop the small pieces of meat into the duffel bag for Arm. And I let his praise sink in, a buzzing that charges me up more than my coffee.

MY PHONE VIBRATES as soon as Wendy drops the check off.

I press my forehead into the table and groan. "I bet you gas money that's Zoë."

Kyle pitches forward to glance at the screen. "'Did you know parts of Sacramento are underground?'" he recites, deadpan. "'They had to raise the streets after a flood in the 1800s.' Exclamation point."

I laugh. "My sister loves her fun facts."

She's been texting them to me every hour, and I'm hoping my parents will be too obsessed with their part of our phone bill to realize I was texting back from a different state.

Did you know the Sacramento Zoo opened in 1927?

Guess what, Sacramento is one of the most haunted cities in the country.

Sacramento's the Camellia Capital of the World!

It's really my own fault for leaving her alone with too much time on her hands.

We're counting out our cash when my phone starts up *again*, shaking and trilling, all attention-seeking—an actual phone call this time.

My fingernails dig into the vinyl seat. I'm not sure anymore that unexpected phone calls ever happen for good reasons.

Maybe it's Zoë and it's something urgent. Something *else* urgent.

Could she have spoken to my parents—and caved like she did with Lita?

Could Mom, who always knows who the killer is—and tells you—before the movie's halfway done, have coaxed the truth out of her? Maybe Mom's the one calling. To vocally murder me.

"Do you mind checking?" I ask Kyle, the words rushing out as the ringing goes on and on.

He reaches for it calmly. I guess he *can* be calm. He doesn't have to cover his ass for so many people, what with him only having one parent, who apparently doesn't care where he goes.

God, he is so lucky.

"Jade?" he says.

I huff out a relieved breath. It's not Mom. Mom still believes I'm in Bend, and it's just Jade calling.

Jade, who I'm supposedly visiting right now.

The call finally goes to voice mail and, after a few seconds, a blip announcing a new message cuts through the diner.

"Oh, no," I mumble.

Kyle furrows his brow. "Isn't she—?"

"Our cover story," I say before he can finish the thought.

I stab at the evil, taunting icon, and play Jade's message on speaker as Kyle and I curve over the table.

"Hey, Cloudy. I'd like to congratulate you on this invisibility thing. Your sister called in some bizarre attempt at damage control, and she told me that everyone thinks you're in my house right now. With Ashlyn's boyfriend? So that's cool, but I figure since Zoë's not spilling any more details, you better poof yourself into reality. CALL ME BACK."

Kyle remains quiet as I bite down hard on my thumbnail

and stare out the window. Two little kids streak by, towing a golden retriever along with them. "I am going to destroy my sister."

"It sounds like she was trying to help."

Rubbing my eyes, I say, "What should we do?"

"What do you want to do?"

Could things get much worse for us if I ignore Jade? If I don't call her back, she might tell her parents, or my parents, or someone on the squad, and this trip will be over. She might never speak to me again.

I focus on everything Jade's ever mentioned about her house, like how it's near the ocean, and there's a big bird-of-paradise plant out front, and that it definitely has a shower.

Taking a deep breath, I sit up straight. "I think we should go to the beach."

SOUTHERN
CALIFORNIA

Dear Paige,

It has been a month since I received the gift of your daughter's organ donation. Please accept my deepest sympathies for your loss.

My name is Freddie and I am in my midfifties and married. Before my lung transplant, I was unable to do the things I've always loved, such as running, golfing, and traveling. Even the most basic of tasks had become an exhausting chore. Getting dressed and walking to the mailbox were too taxing on my body.

I thought there were no words for what this transplant has given me, but there is. One word: life. Life and all it encompasses. I can now do the things that I was incapable of before. My wife and I just relocated to a different state and bought a new house, a dream of ours for years. In the spring, we will celebrate our thirtieth wedding anniversary with an extended trip to Australia and New Zealand. The itinerary includes hiking, sailing, snorkeling, and perhaps even surfing lessons.

Without the transplant, none of this would have been possible for me. Every breath I take is a testament to Ashlyn's generosity, and she and your family will always be close in our hearts.

I look forward to hearing from you again.

Most sincerely,
Freddie

Kyle

"Ready?" I ask, removing my key from the ignition.

Cloudy gestures at her lap, where Arm is sleeping. "How can I be ready for anything when all this cuteness is happening?"

She pulls down the visor, which illuminates the inside of the vehicle. With no urgency whatsoever, she digs inside her bag. I bounce my legs and drum my fingers on the steering wheel.

Jade lives in Santa Monica, but asked us to meet her fifteen miles inland at an all-ages club to see her girlfriend's band. I'm never in a huge hurry to get to something like this, but I was dealing with Arm's litter box while Cloudy made a run for the bathroom at our last I-5 rest area visit. I thought I'd be fine not stopping again during these last few hours. Let's just say I was mistaken.

"I really am dying to shower," Cloudy says, dabbing her lips with a pinkish-colored makeup crayon.

Mostly, I'm dying to pee, but I don't want to announce it. "Thirty-six hours and counting."

Cloudy puts her lipstick thing away and removes her seat

belt. I spring to action, gently taking Arm from Cloudy's lap. I set her on the Pillow Pet in the backseat, careful not to wake her.

The fact that Arm is so laid-back makes me think she can't possibly be Ashlyn, who was this high-energy control freak, always sweeping up the rest of us in her plans. Then again, maybe Arm's calmer than every other kitten in the history of kittens because she already knows Cloudy and me?

Over my shoulder, there are no approaching headlights, so I pull open my door and step onto the street. Cloudy still hasn't made a move to get out. She has, however, removed her hair tie and is combing her fingers through her long hair.

"I hope it's okay that I'm not dressed for going out," she says. "LA clubs are picky about that in movies. Jade would have mentioned if there was a dress code, right?"

I'm in jeans and one of the new shirts I bought at the mall in Stockton this morning (I also got dress clothes to wear to the wedding later this week), and Cloudy has on a T-shirt, a loose skirt, and sandals. "I think you'll be fine. But the thing is, could you maybe hurry up? I need to go. Like, really. Like, *now*."

Her expression turns distant for a second, like she can't understand why I, of all people, would be talking like this. Then her eyes widen. "Oh! You mean the bathroom? Why didn't you say so?"

In an instant, she's climbing out with her bag over her shoulder. We slam our doors in unison and I jog to join her on the sidewalk.

The GPS showed us approximately where the club is, but we had to park a couple of blocks away. As we're speed walking under palm trees and streetlights, we pass tiny single-story homes filling the space between large two-story apartment buildings. Cloudy pulls out her phone after we turn the corner onto North Gower Street. "So Jade's text says that AMPLYFi doesn't have a sign out front, but the entrance is a green door in the alley behind Astro Burger."

Quickening my pace, I chant in my head: *Get to the green door. Get to the green door.*

Cloudy runs to catch up, giggling. "Who'd have guessed that my first time in Hollywood, I'd be by the *real* Melrose Avenue standing across the street from the *real* Paramount Studios, hurrying straight into a dark alley?"

At the green door, a guy in a black shirt with the thickest arms I've ever seen in real life blocks the way. "I have to wait until this song ends to let you in," he says. "Noise ordinance laws."

I give Cloudy my most pained expression.

"Maybe you can run and use the bathroom at Astro Burger?" she suggests.

"It'll be quicker to wait," the bouncer says. "The band tonight is this all-chick Beatles tribute band. Luckily for you, they finished the long one, 'Hey Jude,' two songs ago. They're partway into 'Can't Buy Me Love,' so you've got maybe a minute and half, tops."

"Okay," I say.

I try not to squirm, and finally, after the longest ninety seconds of my life have passed, he pulls the door open, revealing a long, rectangular room below, about the size of a three-car garage. With several dozen people clapping for the band and facing the stage with their backs to us, the club is at about full capacity. Cloudy follows as I race down the staircase to the cement floor. Once I've handed a woman with purple-streaked blond hair the money for admission, I get directions to the restroom, which happens to be about six feet directly behind me. I hurry off without another word.

When I come out again, feeling much better about life, I take a quick look around for Cloudy. The way this place is arranged is like being in someone's very large, very cool, very crowded living room. It's partially lit up with lava lamps, paper lanterns, and spotlights pointed at the stage. There are also weird pictures and framed gold records on the walls, mismatched tables and chairs, and a red velvet couch. Nothing goes together, but somehow, in this room, it all works.

Cloudy is studying a painting. She really had no reason to worry about her clothes; some girls are in flashy dresses and heels, but she looks just as good.

The music and singing are loud, so she raises her voice when I approach. "Pick one!"

She holds up two kazoos, printed with the words: She Loves You.

I take the yellow one and my voice becomes buzzy and Donald Duck–like as I lean close and speak through it by Cloudy's ear. "Now the question is, who is 'she' and what exactly does she love about 'you'?"

Cloudy uses her own purple kazoo to answer. "It's the name of Jade's girlfriend's band." She switches back to yelling. "The girl at the door told me 'She Loves You' is from a Beatles song."

We turn toward the band, and I stand as tall as possible so I can see over everyone. The four girls onstage are our age, wearing matching white blouses, black ties, black skirts, and black vests. One of them repeats "all right" over and over, and the song ends to applause and kazoos. Once the noise dies down, they go straight into the next song, with two of the girls singing "Help!" into the microphone they're sharing.

I don't listen to a lot of oldies, but I do vaguely recognize these songs. "You texted Jade?"

"Yes." Cloudy pulls out her phone for a quick glance. "No response yet."

"Should we look for her?"

Cloudy nods. As she weaves around people to get nearer the stage, I stay close, keeping my hand lightly on her shoulder so we don't get separated. I spot Jade at the front just as she's turning her head in our direction.

Jade moved from Bend to California the summer between freshman and sophomore year, which was the same summer I moved to Bend from Arizona. We missed each other by a few weeks, but I've heard a lot about her and recognize her from Ashlyn's camp pictures taken last summer.

"There she is," I tell Cloudy.

Beneath my hand, her shoulder goes stiff.

Jade's dark brown skin and thick, wavy black hair look the same now as in her photos, but it turns out she doesn't grin non-stop in real life. In fact, the slight lift of her mouth reverses as recognition sets in. Jade's eyes brighten with tears and she rushes to fold Cloudy into a long hug.

While it's happening, Cloudy stands very straight, with one

arm hanging limp and the other curved up to rest on the back of Jade's lacy top. Jade finally lets go and dabs at her eyes. "I wasn't expecting that to happen!" she calls out over the music. "I'm so happy you're here!"

"Me too!" Cloudy says. "Kyle, this is Jade."

Cloudy's trying to act normal, but it's all over her face that she feels uncomfortable.

Jade and I smile and shout, "Hi!"

Then Jade hooks her arm through Cloudy's. "You want to stay for the rest of the set or head outside where it's easier to talk?"

Cloudy casually pulls free, gesturing at the stage. "This is our one chance! We can't miss Theresa's band."

"Prudence, actually."

"What?"

"Theresa's stage name is 'Dear Prudence'!"

"Let me guess," Cloudy says. "From a Beatles song?"

"Exactly!" Without further discussion, Jades flashes another smile, and then eases back into the space where she was standing before. A few people make room so Cloudy and I can crowd in behind her. (Which is nice—especially considering that most of them are shorter than I am.)

"Hey, everyone!" the lead singer says into her microphone. "We have a few more. If you grabbed a kazoo, this next song is when we need your help the most. Whenever we 'dood'n doo-doo,' you know what to do!"

The girls sway with their instruments and launch into "Here Comes the Sun."

Today was a good day, but maybe meeting up with Jade was

a mistake. Cloudy and I had fun sneaking Arm into the mall in the duffel, taking turns driving, and making jokes about each other's playlists. But encountering Jade has made Cloudy tense, which makes me tense.

As the song picks up speed about two minutes in, Cloudy elbows my ribs. She's smiling and singing along—something about feeling ice slowly melting. At the next chorus, I'm quick to "Dood'n doo-doo" into my kazoo. She laughs, and when she sings "It's all right!" I hope it's safe to believe her.

SHE LOVES YOU is about to wrap up and Jade's girlfriend is speaking to the audience once more: "Thank you, AMPLYFi, for letting us play your amazing stage! And thanks to all of you for coming! Now, I'm going to let you in on a little secret: Sexy Sadie"—she points at the drummer—"Eleanor Rigby, Lucy in the Sky with Diamonds"—she nods at the two sharing the front of the stage with her—"and myself are pretty fond of a band you might have heard of. They're called the Beatles?"

The crowd whistles and kazoos in response.

"Now, these girls and I also happen to adore a song the Beatles recorded, which is *not* an original of theirs. So the other day I said to myself, 'Dear Prudence'—because that's what I always call myself—'Dear Prudence, what could possibly be more meta than a kick-ass Beatles cover band doing a kick-ass cover of the Beatles doing a kick-ass cover?' I couldn't think of *anything*. So, for our last song, I want every one of you to 'Twist and Shout' with us!"

This time when the music starts, the energy onstage and throughout the room ramps up even higher as everyone jumps around and swings their arms.

Spinning to face Cloudy, Jade yells, "Let's twist! Come on. You too, Kyle. It's easy!" She motions at her jeans and demonstrates bending her knees a bit, while also turning her waist rapidly as if she's working an invisible Hula-Hoop.

Lifting her eyebrows, Cloudy looks at me like *Should we humor her?*

I shrug like *I'll do it if you will.*

Then I just go for it, and Cloudy joins in, which earns us both grins from Jade.

At first it's awkward and I can't help laughing at myself, but soon I find a rhythm. Cloudy and I are getting bumped on all sides, so we move in closer. We aren't exactly dancing *together*, but we *almost* are, and my stomach flip-flops with this realization. My heart beats way faster than it should and everything in my periphery goes blurry and all I can focus on is how Cloudy's T-shirt and skirt move as she moves, how she's smiling up at me, how her blue eyes are locked on mine, how beautiful her face is, and—

"We love you!" Theresa/Prudence shouts.

The song, the twisting, and the eye contact between Cloudy and me all come to an abrupt end, leaving me wondering, *What was* that?

The chandeliers overhead switch on as She Loves You exits the stage to applause.

"I'll ride home with you guys," Jade announces, "since you're staying at my house and all. But I want to introduce you to Theresa after she's done packing up."

"Don't you mean 'Prudence'?" Cloudy teases.

Jade gives a dismissive wave. "Eh. Show's over. She's Theresa again. Want to get milkshakes while we wait?"

I nod, but Cloudy narrows her eyes. "Wait. You said last summer you're lactose intolerant."

Jade laughs. "Hey, I'll say whatever it takes to keep Ashlyn from forcing her disgusting yogurt-kale-avocado smoothies on me."

The present-tense slipup is jarring—like Ashlyn can run a blender any old time. All three of us go silent.

"I'm sorry," Jade says.

"It's fine." Cloudy shrugs. "She also added kiwi and banana to those drinks and they were delicious. But, yes, a milkshake sounds good." She heads through the crowd, back up the stairs, and into the dark alleyway with Jade and me behind her.

Cloudy's on edge again and my stomach clenches. Her sandals slap, slap, slap ahead of us, while Jade's heels click, click, click on the concrete next to me.

Jade says, "I can't believe I'm finally in the presence of the famous Kyle Ryan Ocie."

Ashlyn started calling me "Kyle Ryan" when we were first getting together, and I called her "Ashlyn Rose." We didn't have actual nicknames for each other—just first and middle names. Last names, too, when we were being especially sappy. ("I adore you, Kyle Ryan Ocie." "And I adore *you*, Ashlyn Rose Montiel.")

"I'm really not famous," I tell Jade.

"Sure you are. We've never met, yet I'm able to first-middle-last name you. That should tell you something."

"I'm able to first and last name you, Jade Decker. Maybe you're famous."

With a smile, Jade shakes her head. "Um, no. First and last name? Not the same at all."

Cloudy reaches the door first, and Jade and I follow her into Astro Burger. From the outside, the place is generic, but inside, it has a 1950s theme with tiny jukeboxes at each table.

"I want to enjoy the nonfreezingness of LA as much as possible," Cloudy says, standing in line. "You two go grab one of those outside tables. I'll buy the shakes, which also means I get to surprise you."

Jade and I do as we're told, and settle in across from each other at a round table with an umbrella on the lit-up patio. "Tell me the truth," she says. "How's Cloudy been doing since . . . you know. Everything that happened with Ashlyn?"

It's weird—someone asking a question like that about Cloudy. A million times weirder still that *I'm* the person being asked. For the first time, someone's assuming I'm not the one who's most wrecked over Ashlyn's death. "She's all right, I think."

Jade lifts her eyebrows. "Really? Because the Cloudy Marlowe I've known since elementary school has always been the girl who walks into a room and owns it. Right now, it's like she doesn't want to be seen. I had to catch her in a lie to get her to visit me today. I had to beg her to start dancing at the club. Before, she was always up for anything at any time."

Annoyance stabs at me. Especially since, okay, maybe Cloudy had to be coaxed to dance, but she was already singing and having fun with me before that. According to Jade, if Cloudy isn't generating maximum energy every moment, there's something wrong with her? "We've been on the road for two days and had to sleep in my car last night. She's tired."

"It's more than that. One glance confirmed it for me." Jade purses her lips. "What's the big mystery, anyway? Why are you two in California?"

Cloudy knows I told my dad about the organ recipients, but we agreed not to let anyone else in on the secret. "It gets so cold in Bend. We're on midwinter break, so we figured, why not go somewhere warm?"

Jade nods, but I can tell she isn't satisfied. "You hang out with Cloudy all the time?"

Ashlyn used to call me from camp, complaining about Jade being pushy. At the time, I'd chalked it up to jealousy over her having to share Cloudy, but now I get it. I wait several seconds before answering Jade's question. "Do you mean in the past day and a half, or in general? I can write you our hanging-out schedule, if it helps."

Jade lets out a short laugh. "You feel like you're being interrogated?"

"Aren't I?"

She eases back against her chair, as if she no longer intends to pounce. "It's hard for me to be there for Cloudy the way I want to be. She's eight hundred miles away. After losing Ashlyn, it makes sense that the two of you would gravitate toward each other. More than anyone, you can understand what the other is feeling and help each other get through it, right?"

Now it's my turn to nod. Not because I'm trying to lie or rewrite history, but because there actually was one specific day when it was true—a day I try never to think about.

While Ashlyn was in the ICU, Cloudy and I went every day. The hospital had strict rules about how many visitors could go in at a time and for how long. We took our turns whenever we could get them without complaint.

One morning, the Montiels were gathered in Ashlyn's room, waiting to hear test results. Cloudy and I had skipped school for this. We hadn't talked about it. We didn't do it together. But we both showed up. We sat alone in the waiting room, elbow to elbow, no empty seats between us. She had a magazine open on her lap, but wasn't turning pages. I'd never prayed in my life, but I did then, inside my head, for half an hour: *I don't believe anyone's reading my mind, but if I'm wrong, you should help Ashlyn, okay? Please. Because she deserves to get better. She should have a full recovery.*

I went over what she'd told me she wanted to do in the future: *She's never left the US, but she hopes to visit every continent in the world. She's saving up to volunteer for a month in Costa Rica at a rescue center for endangered animals. She wants saving animals to be her career. Her life, basically . . .*

I listed off things Ashlyn had done that proved she was a good person: *She visits nursing homes and takes up collections for clothing and toy drives with her team during the holidays. She served food to the homeless one Thanksgiving. She smiles at random people in the hallway at school. If someone spills something, she'll help clean it up. . . .*

In my thoughts, I repeated and rephrased everything so my argument became even more convincing. Ashlyn would get better, I'd decided. It wouldn't make any kind of sense for her not to. There were animals that needed her. People who needed her. Her team, her friends, her family. And me. *I* needed for her to be okay.

But then Ashlyn's mom came stumbling out of the ICU. From her expression, I could tell right away she'd forgotten we were out there, the doctor's news hadn't been positive, and she was trying to get space from what she'd been told.

My mind went all over the place. Ashlyn's recovery was going to take a long time? She'd never fully recover? No more cheer? Or walking? Or . . . *what?*

Cloudy asked the questions I was unable to speak aloud: "What's wrong? What did they say?"

Mrs. Montiel let out a shaky breath, dropped into a seat across from Cloudy and me, and told us Ashlyn wasn't coming out of her coma. Not ever. Tears ran down her face as she explained that machines were keeping Ashlyn's body alive, but her brain was dead.

Dead.

Ashlyn was dead.

My bones turned to liquid and I slid onto the floor.

Cloudy's magazine landed next to me with a *whump!* She leaned forward, took my liquid hand in her solid one, and said, "Kyle."

Just that. Just my name.

DEAD.

I couldn't breathe, but my bones slowly solidified and I was able to slide myself over to kneel in front of Cloudy. I sobbed onto her knees. She wrapped her arms around me and her tears fell into my hair. I knew, in that moment, that we were in this together.

JADE JOLTS ME out of it. "Cloudy's hands are full."

She jumps up and pulls the glass door open. I blink hard a couple of times to make sure I'm going to be okay.

Cloudy sets down a tray with three Astro Burger cups and slides onto the chair next to mine. "This place blends strange ingredients into vanilla ice cream. But not avocado, so here's banana for Jade," she says, pushing it across the table. "And sadly, Kyle, no chocolate mint. I got you pineapple, but if you hate it, we can trade. Mine's apple cinnamon, which I was told tastes like apple pie minus the crust." As we unwrap straws to stab into our shakes, Cloudy says, "Tomorrow's Monday and you have school. What do you recommend Kyle and I do all day?"

Jade talks about the Santa Monica Pier, Third Street Promenade, and Venice Beach Boardwalk, but I kind of zone out.

After I'd gotten up from the hospital waiting room floor, Cloudy convinced me to go see Ashlyn for the last time. I didn't say good-bye because I knew Ashlyn couldn't hear me, but I did sit beside her. I studied her face. I wanted to memorize her tan skin, her thick lashes, her shiny black hair spread over the white pillow, but I couldn't stay focused. It was as if I was somehow outside my body, watching myself watch her through a haze of tears. I held her hand, and it felt like the warmest hand in the world. At that moment, I was the colder of the two of us, shaking all over and nauseated, knowing her warmth was artificial and temporary. Afterward, Cloudy drove me to Matty's and all I could think as I lay on the couch and cried until I passed out was that I had sat in a room alone with Ashlyn, but since she wasn't really there anymore, what had actually happened?

I still can't answer that question, but I do know this: the worst day of my life was also the worst day of Cloudy's. I was completely useless to her, but she helped me get through it.

Jade pulls out her phone to tell Theresa where to meet us, and I watch Cloudy in profile. She catches me looking and smiles, nodding toward my shake. "How's the pineapple? Any good?"

"It's perfect," I tell her.

Cloudy

"Y ou've got to come out here."

I look up from the kitchen table—and the long list of "Things to See" Jade's parents left for us: Hollywood, Beverly Hills, the Griffith Observatory, the Getty. It's almost like they don't want us alone in their house all day.

Even though I've known the Deckers since I was ten, they wanted to talk to Kyle and me before we settled in last night. But "want" may be the wrong word. I don't think they desired our company at eleven thirty p.m. so much as needed to be sure I'm not suddenly a cultist on the run—or that when Kyle mentioned bringing in Arm, he wasn't talking about, you know, an *arm*. Afterward, I took the guest room, claiming I didn't want to disrupt Jade's regular school-night routine by bunking with her. Mr. and Mrs. Decker ate that up.

Not Jade, though.

From the moment she zeroed in on me at AMPLYFi, she was . . . studying me. It was in the way her eyes scrunched up at the corners whenever she looked my way. And if anyone could spot a difference in me, it would be Jade. I suspect that friendship plus distance has a way of magnifying the things that should stay hidden. When you change so gradually, the people you're with every day don't have a chance to notice.

So all I have to do is avoid the kind of time she wants to spend together. Last night, a separate room and a locked door seemed like a decent start.

Now Kyle's standing in the doorway, fresh from a shower, in his brand-new clothes.

"I thought you were checking on the car," I say.

"I was. Then I saw it."

I follow Kyle out into the foyer, then pat my back pocket for the extra house key Jade left before going to school. Arm is still curled up on the couch—hopefully the Deckers don't mind her crashing here while we're out. I'm not sure Rodeo Drive is as welcoming as half-empty diners in Sacramento.

We're out the door, onto the porch, then down the stairs. The sun and the wind have an agreement going here—just when the breeze gets too chilly, the sun picks up the slack. Kyle jogs into the street, right across to Ocean Park Boulevard's thin, grassy median. The Deckers live in a small bungalow on a street that points straight to the ocean—the same direction Kyle's gesturing now.

"Holy. Shit."

Kyle shakes his head, incredulous. "It was too dark when we got here last night. I didn't notice it."

"Jade said it was close, but . . . *it's so close*." Well, not really. The Pacific is barely an inch-wide stripe across the horizon, but I can see it clearly. It's as if I can hold up my thumb and smudge the inky blue of the ocean into the sky. "Let's go."

"To the beach?"

"Yeah, I want to go in the water."

He glances at me, dubious. "Cloudy, it's February."

"Kyle," I mimic, "it's frigging Southern California. It's not like they shut down the ocean."

There's an amused twist to his lips. "I think sometimes they do, actually. Something about rain runoff."

"Oh. My. God," I whine. "Come on."

I set off, Kyle chuckling behind me. Neither of us knows where we're going, but straight ahead should be as good a direction as any.

We walk for fifteen minutes along a path that lies parallel to the beach and should be front and center in a postcard. The perfectly spaced date palms reach way up into a vibrantly blue sky. Santa Monica might border on annoyingly perfect, but I'm already too in love to care.

Once we cross over onto the beach, I kick off my shoes and roll the cuffs of my jeans. We shuffle through a long stretch of cool sand, and Kyle stops where it starts to dampen. I go on, right to the shoreline, ignoring the chill that creeps up into my bare feet. So maybe I was a little overzealous earlier, but after being a brat about the whole thing, some part of me is going into the goddamn Pacific.

"How is it?"

I don't bother turning around as I give Kyle the finger. "It's freezing," I admit. "Satisfied?"

"Nah. Just curious."

"You can come feel it for yourself."

"It's freezing enough right here," he says, "but thanks."

A small wave swells up, foamy around my ankles, and I have to grit my teeth so I don't shriek. It gets easier to adjust every time, so much so that it becomes close to comfortable. Or my feet have gone numb.

Eventually, Kyle comes up beside me, his sneakers dangling from his fingertips. "Are we really here, looking at this?" he says.

I cluck my tongue. "Sedona desert boys. So impressed with water."

"And Bend girls?" He elbows me. "You prefer your water at a glacial temperature?"

Bend might have every other body of water—rivers, lakes, streams, waterfalls—but we're totally lacking in saltwater. "This one summer, my parents took us to Lincoln City. It was the first time I'd ever been to the ocean, and I ran straight in because I thought it was a lake."

"Not so much?"

"Most lakes don't have waves that'll knock a five-year-old on her butt."

"True," he laughs. "But if you do end up at USC, you could get some practice in."

"What do you mean?"

He gives me a sideways glance. "USC's only a few miles from here. I looked it up. You'd be able to come here every day, if you wanted."

I could. Every single day. Without Ashlyn.

I've never imagined myself anywhere without her—certainly not college. Before, our course was so set. And now, it's all up to me. There are hundreds of places I could end up, schools or programs or neither of those things because I don't know where I'm going. The thought seizes me, ping-ponging around my brain until I'm light-headed.

I anchor myself here with this: Ashlyn and I will never go to USC like she intended. We'll never be on this beach together. Yet in her own way, she still managed to get me here.

Kyle and I stand, shoulder to shoulder, at the edge of Santa Monica. Up and down the beach there are others, all determined tourists probably, doing the same—staring ahead, watching the water, hypnotized by the vastness of it. It's so big out there, so much more mysterious and promising than what's at our feet.

Behind me, a kid squeals, and I imagine her bolting across the sand, her mom or dad or someone who loves her chasing closely behind. The people riding bikes on the same walkway Kyle and I were on earlier. Beach apartments and small cafés and a few blocks inland, a high school where one of my oldest friends might have already figured me out. And everyone here, looking the opposite way. We're all staring out to the ocean like the answers are in front of us when, really, the whole world is at our backs. Waiting for us, hoping we'll turn around and take notice.

But I'll let it wait. I won't worry about the rest of the world, or USC, or Jade. I just pick out a spot on the horizon as my feet sink deeper into the sand.

KYLE AND I are having fun. Possibly. It might be fun. Fun or it's that we're showered and not wearing our parkas and the salty air is going to our heads. Either way, Kyle hasn't frowned in an hour, so I'm checking that off in the having-a-blast column. And I'm feeling it, too—a lightness, in the way the beachy wind flirts with the curly ends of my hair and how the sun warms but never burns.

We end up doubling back, away from the Pacific, up to wide Ocean Avenue—we want to see the Santa Monica Pier from where it begins. I'm disappointed we're a couple of months too early to catch the jacarandas in bloom. The spindly trees fan out with trumpet-shaped purple flowers, like in a Dr. Seuss book. We definitely don't grow those in Bend.

The big blue Yacht Harbor, Sport Fishing, Boating, Cafés sign curves above the street. I dig my phone from my pocket and tap into the camera.

"I can take it," Kyle says. "If you want to get in there."

My eyes move to him and the sign, the cars zooming by on the street behind him, the palm trees canopying above us. And I'm so . . . present. Grounded on this sidewalk, with Kyle, on a trip that Ashlyn is leading us on. It makes me say, "We should get one together."

His forehead wrinkles. "Um, okay. Good idea."

He doesn't sound so sure, but I hand over my phone anyway—he *is* the tall one. As he raises his arm to aim it, I inch closer until my sleeve just barely brushes his chest. We stretch and duck around, trying to find the best pose; when we do, my shoulder is digging into Kyle's torso; his fingertips are pressed to my back. I keep entirely still.

"Ready?" he asks.

"Ready."

Once he snaps the photo, time catches up with itself.

He gives back my phone, where Zoë's Fact of the Hour is waiting: **The Ferris wheel at the end of the Pier is solar-powered!** She spoke to my parents yesterday, and managed to cover for me without self-destructing, but it's my turn next. There's no chance they're letting today go by without hearing my voice.

Kyle and I move under the archway and down the big ramp. My phone is still in my hand when we reach the old-fashioned blue-and-beige building at the bottom. That's how we both hear the familiar words—*"I don't want anybody else"*—sing from its speakers.

"Not again," I murmur, my head falling back. I saw his missed call before bed last night, and judging from the time, Matty tried me when we were still at AMPLYFi. Probably right when Kyle and I were kazooing to the Beatles.

"Again? He already called you?" Kyle is staring at my phone like Matty might mist out of it like a genie from a lamp. Is he still upset, or does he wish Matty would call him instead?

"I was going to tell you—" No, there's no time to get into it, so I pick up.

"Matty, hey." I look at Kyle as I say it. He gestures vaguely over his shoulder, which I assume is his way of saying he'll meet up with me later. After. "Hey," I repeat once he's gone, "I meant to call you back, but—"

"But you're in California with Kyle?"

So we're all caught up, then.

"You've heard."

"Yeah." His voice is gritty—Matty is *pissed*. You'd think for

someone that doesn't happen to often, he'd be worse at it, but he's not much of a half-asser. "Let's see who I've heard it from. Jacob," he starts like he's ticking the names off on his fingers. "Tyrell, everyone else on the baseball team, *my uncle.*"

My stomach curdles with each name, one more person waiting for us when we go home. "What did they tell you?"

"Kyle's dad says you're visiting Ashlyn's organ recipients. And you took a cat with you?"

"Arm," I say.

"*. . . Arm?*"

"She's the cat." Settling between two of the old building's domed windows, I whisper, "Matty, you didn't tell anyone about the recipients, did you? Because this could get us into a lot of trouble."

"Why?"

"We don't exactly have permission." I shift my weight from one foot to the other, back and forth. "So please, *please*, you have to keep it a secret."

"What the hell, Cloudy?" He sighs out, long and loud, and I instantly regret asking him for a favor. "Not only did you take off without telling anyone, you took off *with Kyle* without telling *me.*"

I'm trying to keep my voice down but it's hard to hear it over my own heartbeat. "We didn't plan it. And since when do I need your approval to go anywhere?"

He mumbles something away from the phone. Then more intently: "Maybe I'd like a heads-up when my ex skips town with my cousin."

I wait until a woman pushes a stroller out of earshot. "Don't be an asshole," I grind out through my teeth. "I asked him to come and he agreed. That's all."

"Kyle wouldn't get out of bed on Friday night and the next day he's road-tripping with you? You aren't even friends."

My thumb is poised to end the call. "If you're so puzzled, maybe you should be having this conversation with Kyle instead of bitching at me. Oh, right! You're not talking to Kyle."

He sighs another time, right into the receiver, right into my ear, and it's so familiar. How many times have I felt his breath in my ear? On my neck, down my stomach, wherever else he put his lips, which was lots of places. I never loved Matty, not like that, but he was a better boyfriend than I deserved. And maybe things were awkward after I broke it off, but when Ashlyn died, he was there again—my friend, and more than that, it turned out. If he thought our hookups would lead to more, he never said so.

There's a muffled noise on his end; I picture him rubbing his forehead like he used to in geometry. "Look, I promise I won't say anything, okay? But Kyle's dad told me about the kid in Sacramento."

I spill a little more of our secret. "Ethan."

"How'd that go?"

"He's really happy. And we're hoping we might actually talk to this other guy, Freddie. He's in Palm Springs."

Matty hesitates. "Why didn't you tell me any of this? We texted the night before you left."

I inhale air that's dense with the scent of funnel cake. I hadn't considered asking Matty along. Is that what this is about? Sure, he's worried about Kyle, but does he believe we purposely left him behind?

"You were fighting. It seemed like you both could use the space."

Matty's laugh is flat. "I figured he'd tell you about our fight."

"Kyle didn't know what was going on until we were in Sacramento, so don't be mad at him. Not for being here, anyway."

Again he's quiet. Then: "It's good he's with you. You've been really strong through this."

That's what people tell me. I'm *strong*. "Yeah."

"And seeing these people could be good for him. Right? Closure or something?"

"That's the idea."

He chuckles, and tension snakes out of my shoulders. "Only you would come up with that idea. What did you tell your parents?"

"They're away," I say, "and *will never know about this*."

"Your sister, too?"

"Oh." I pause, praying my phone will spontaneously drain itself. "She knows. She's . . . not away."

"Zoë's home?!" He puffs out a breath. "Do you need me to check on her?"

She may be a total pest, but I can't refuse this. "Would you? She might want a ride to the grocery store or library—wait, is your car out of purgatory yet?"

Knowing Matty, he's already done something to get it taken away again.

"Nope," he says, his lips popping on the *P*. "And I'd rather not talk about it. But it's cool, I can ask Danielle to drive me."

Hold on.

"Danielle?"

He coughs once. "We've been hanging out lately."

"Danielle from my cheer squad?"

"We're sort of together," he tells me, carefully. Matty being nervous is almost as unusual as him being pissed. "It just kind of happened last week. Is that weird for you?"

"You've had other girlfriends since we dated."

"Yeah, but we've never talked about it. Not after . . . everything, you know?"

He means last fall.

A few weeks after Ashlyn died, the school held a candlelight vigil for her in the Bend High parking lot. Afterward, there was a party at some senior's house—a better way to honor Ashlyn, everyone said, except hardly anyone mentioned her. But Matty did; he sat on top of a picnic table in the backyard and told stories about growing up next door to Ashlyn, like the time they went trick-or-treating and she dressed up as a jellyfish, and when they were twelve and snuck beer from a cooler at their Fourth of July block party. He talked about Ashlyn to anyone who'd listen, until the sky was dark and the porch railing was lined with empty plastic cups. When he was finished, I kissed him and led him from the party into the basement.

That was the first time. When I was with Matty, I was thinking of only one thing, not a million. Not if it hurt when Ashlyn flipped over her bike, or if she'd gone unconscious immediately. Not if the doctors could've done more for her, or if I should've asked her to come with me while I got my hair cut, so she wouldn't have gone on that bike ride in the first place. For a month, whenever Matty and I could steal some time away from school and football and cheer, I was okay. Then he ended things. He felt like he was losing himself more and more every time; like somehow it made him feel more alone. I pretended that I didn't understand what he meant—I did, though. Losing myself was the whole point. But in the end, I didn't want to risk losing him, too. I didn't have many people left.

"No, it's not weird," I say to him, my voice steady. And I don't get that churning-stomach, frozen-veins sensation when I picture them together, so I know it's the truth. "You and I are friends, Matty."

"We are."

"She makes you happy, I hope?"

"Well, she does this thing where—"

"No!" I shout. "Matthew Ocie Junior, do not say another word. We are not *those* kind of friends."

He's cackling, and I can picture him, wherever he is, with his hand on his stomach. "We're not? Really? I think we might be."

"Never. And we never, ever, ever will be."

"I can live with that," he says, smiling bigger than ever—you can just tell.

THE BUILDING I'VE been leaning against ends up also housing an old carousel and its gift shop. I find Kyle there, near a tall stand of refrigerator magnets. The one he's focused on is colorful metal, shaped like the big Ferris wheel outside. When he puts his finger to it, it actually spins.

"Like the real thing," I say.

He straightens up, his eyes avoiding the phone in my hand. "Let's see for ourselves."

We walk the length of the pier, our feet thumping against the faded wooden slats, past bike racks, a full-on trapeze setup, and an arcade.

"So Matty was furious," I tell Kyle, even though he didn't ask. "I guess I deserve it. I did chloroform you, dump you in the back of your car, and drive you and your cat to Sacramento."

"Then we're even," he laughs. "Since Lita's convinced *I* abducted *you*."

I slap his arm. "Eavesdropper."

Kyle takes a few more steps, his hands in his pockets. "What else did he say?"

"Your dad told him about the recipients." Kyle's eyes go big and round, afraid he's blown the whole thing, and I wave it away. "Don't worry. Matty won't rat us out."

"He must think I'm really losing it now."

I grin. "He sounds pretty into it, honestly."

We stop outside the entrance to Pacific Park, a small amusement park right on the pier. There's a roller coaster that loops around a good chunk of the grounds, including other rides and a bunch of carnival-type games. In back, the enormous Pacific Wheel stands tall, glinting under the clear sky.

Once we buy our tickets, we head straight for it. The wheel has a spiral design in the center that's lit up in neon, and the cars that dangle around it alternate colors: red and yellow and red and yellow.

Kyle and I end up in a yellow one. We slip onto the bench seats opposite each other, a thick metal pole between us—my guess is for grabbing on to. The cars have no windows, just seat backs that reach our shoulders, an umbrella-like cover on top of us, and open air in between. Shortly after we're locked in, the ride starts, and the car swings as we move slowly up, up, up, until we're coming down, down, down again.

"What happened with Matty that was so bad?" I ask. "You guys never fight."

Kyle clears his throat, shifting on the hard seat. "I'm not trying out for baseball this year."

My mouth goes dry. That is so not what I expected—mostly because I wasn't expecting an answer at all. "Repeat that."

He shrugs. "I'm not trying out for the team this year and Matty . . . disagrees with my choice."

No wonder Matty flipped; he loves playing with Kyle. Not to mention that Kyle missing an entire season isn't quite an indication that he's moving on.

My first instinct is to question him until he tries to rappel down the side of the Ferris wheel. But badgering him didn't work out so well for Matty. "Last time I checked, you're only supposed to quit the stuff you suck at."

He weaves his fingers together. "It's not about being good or bad at it," he says. "I need a break."

Over Kyle's shoulders, the ocean sparkles in the sunshine. I shield my eyes and look into his. "From baseball?"

"From having all those people depend on me. I could use

a few months off from that. And from Matty. Or his expectations, I guess." He laughs, but it's halfhearted. "You know how intense he gets when he's really excited about something."

I nod because I understand, but it's like I've swallowed a knot. There's more to Kyle's life than baseball, but it's one of the things that made him happiest. I could see it on his face whenever Ashlyn dragged me to a game. We'd sit up in the bleachers on the third base side and talk about anything but baseball, eyes on Kyle the whole time. It was hard to ignore him out there. He was the only one on the team who wore his uniform socks pulled up to his knees, like an old-time player. His personal hat tip to tradition. And he was all grace and confidence on the field. He never made a flashy play to get attention; he treated each boring, routine ground ball with respect. Every so often, he'd crouch down and run his fingers through the infield dirt, as if he needed to keep the contact.

For Kyle and baseball, it was true love. So maybe this will be only a short break for him, but what if it's not? What if he gives up and regrets it?

Something tells me that what Kyle really needs now is a distraction. "Confession time," I say, slapping my palms on my thighs. "My last Ferris wheel experience was not my finest moment."

He folds his arms over his chest. "Really?"

"It was at this end-of-the-school-year carnival in fifth grade. Nicholas Morgan promised to take me on the Ferris wheel, *just the two of us*. Huge stuff." Kyle's mouth twitches in a smile. Encouraged, I go on. "But by the time I made it there, he was already getting on with Raquel Harrison. Raquel Harrison! Who started a rumor that I never washed my gym shorts."

He leans back, bracing a foot on the pole. "That is the worst Ferris wheel story I've ever heard. You weren't even on a Ferris wheel."

"That," I tell him, "is the entire point. I should have been. Entire lives could have changed if I'd only been there sooner and gotten the chance."

Our car comes to a stop as it reaches the pinnacle of the ride. We both slide over, peering all the way down at the boardwalk.

"Maybe this is it, then," he says, closing his eyes to the wind. "This is your second chance."

A spiky, charged *buzz* goes through me at the sight of him.

Maybe it's my first chance. One I didn't get five years ago so I could have it here, on the sunniest day I've ever seen, hovering above a postcard city.

The Ferris wheel churns again, jolting us forward.

What am I doing?

This isn't some cutesy first date. I'm not here sightseeing with Kyle. We're not even supposed to be in Santa Monica. This is a stopover on a trip that matters more than tourist attractions and silly stories. It matters more than anything.

Our car dips lower, dropping back down to the pier, scattering whatever electricity thrum there was left.

JADE POUNCES AS soon as her front gate clicks shut. "So how does Kyle look naked?"

It's like the time a sheet of snow fell off our garage and onto my hatless head: stupefying and obnoxious and a little painful. Not that I wasn't expecting Jade to get straight to the point as soon as we were alone, but Kyle naked is a little too . . . pointy.

My lungs ache, even though we're just starting our run. I haven't taken a decent breath since Jade suggested it. She asked Kyle along, too, but he doesn't have any of his exercise clothes to run in. Neither do I, really, except for my sneakers—and Jade kindly offered to lend me shorts and a T-shirt. We were all in the kitchen, setting up for dinner, and I'd been edgy from a phone call with my mom that included telling her I was making quesadillas for Zoë. So when Jade brought up the run, I couldn't come up with an excuse fast enough. Not that she would've taken an excuse, anyway.

"Don't tell me you two do it with your clothes on," she says now, watching my face. "What a waste."

"Would you stop?" I hiss, glancing over my shoulder. When we left, Kyle was with Jade's father in the backyard, checking out the new hammocks. With any luck he's still there, an entire house-sized distance between him and this conversation.

Jade snickers, but her pace quickens to a light jog and I follow. "Okay, you're looking at me like *I'm* absurd when you're the one on a road trip you're obviously lying about. And I'm not supposed to believe this is an interstate sex romp?"

"No, you're not, you hornball." I stretch out an arm, briefly hiding my face as it reddens. Matty had insinuated something similar—not that he actually believed it. But everyone back home . . . they might. "And we wouldn't have to leave Bend to have sex."

She purses her lips. "You would for it to count as a romp."

"There's no romping!"

"If you say so," she snorts, her eyes sparking, "Then what's up? You'd really come all the way to California and not tell me?"

My exhale is shaky. This is the warm-up to whatever else she has in store for me. "We were six hours away. That's not exactly in the neighborhood."

"I know there's a story here. Zoë was way too much of a jittery mess on the phone."

I wipe sweat from my forehead. "Do you remember when Mr. Ordell used to say, 'If I can hear you talking, you're not running hard enough'?"

Jade grins. She must be picturing our middle school gym teacher, complete with track pants, polo shirt, and top-notch farmer's tan. "I think it was more like, 'If I can hear you talking, or see any shred of joy on your face, you're not running hard enough.' But this isn't gym class. I want to talk!"

I fix my eyes straight ahead. There's a full moon, and the palm trees and condos along Barnard Way are burnished orange by streetlights. Kyle and I walked this same street only a few hours ago—the ocean is *right there*. Although it's too dark to see it beyond the boardwalk, I can smell its briny scent, more powerful here than up near Jade's house.

I breathe out a sigh. "Okay, then. How does Theresa look naked?"

She laughs and reaches over to poke me sharply in the forehead. "I missed you, idiot."

I take the opportunity to spring ahead, my feet pressing

down hard into the cement. I can't get away from Jade, or her questions, but running away right now tastes a little bit like freedom.

When I'm running—or tumbling, or practicing cheers, or exercising—my mind goes clear. Distracting myself constantly is exhausting, but when I'm active, I'm centered. I can let everything go.

We continue on to Ocean Avenue, then Santa Monica Boulevard, before turning into the Third Street Promenade. White fairy lights hang from the trees, glittering in the dark. It makes the place feel enchanted, like so much more than a few blocks of retail shops and restaurants.

Once we're back on the street, there's less to gawk at and fewer people to maneuver around. My legs blaze from ankle to thigh, and my arms throb—stretching before the run didn't prepare my muscles at all, not with how tight they've been. But I want to get back to Jade's quickly, so I push myself to run faster. She glances at me every so often with her eyebrows pulled together. She's cataloging everything I do, and the sooner we're with Kyle, and Arm, and even her parents, the better.

We pass a mural on Main Street—it's an entire wall painted red, with the words "you are beautiful" scrawled across it in a neat white script. My mind pulls up the Thoreau mural back home, and a twinge darts up my chest. It makes me stumble and when Jade notices, her pace slows to a walk.

I keep jogging, not willing to slow down, but my skin goes cold and clammy. "Come on, Jade," I huff. "A little farther."

Her forehead wrinkles when she looks at me. "Aren't we ever

going to talk about her?"

Stupefying. Obnoxious. Painful.

I finally fall into step with her, panting. "What?"

"Ashlyn."

My veins contract or expand or whatever they need to do so they won't burst. Blood thunders in my ears as I steer myself around a woman walking her beagle. "What about Ashlyn?"

She pulls at the waist of her red shorts—"Vikings Cheer" is stitched onto the right leg. "How have you been? For real?"

I've answered that so often, it doesn't register anymore. But this is Jade, not a random classmate or one of my mom's friends who I've run into at the supermarket.

"It's hard," I tell her, my gaze on the squat and square blue building across the street. "Not having her around, I mean. But I'm doing okay."

"Are you? Because it doesn't seem like it." I turn to her, and she holds up her hand. "She was your best friend. You're more than entitled to not be okay."

My shirt is heavy with sweat and rough against my skin. I just want it *off.* "Then what's your point?"

Her voice is gentle when she says, "You're different."

I stop under a low, leafy tree. All I wanted was to avoid this conversation, but now that it's happening, I'm aggravated Jade started it in front of a car wash. "How would you know if I'm different? We barely ever see each other."

Jade rubs a hand down her face, weary. "I am so sorry that I couldn't make it to her funeral. My mom was still looking for work back then and we didn't have . . . I'm not trying to make this about me. What I'm saying is, even though we live far apart, I'm always going to be around for you. And I want you to know that you can talk to me."

It hurts to smile, but I do. "I do know that, you sap."

Her expression softens. "*That.* That's what you do whenever I bring up Ashlyn. It's like shutters come down over your eyes, or someone turned off your switch. You check out and change the subject."

Nausea roils deep in my belly, a pit that gets bigger and bigger. "You're imagining things."

"You can't bottle everything up, Cloudy," she says. "If you do, you'll never move on."

I swallow hard. The school counselor, my parents, they all said the same thing. If I didn't talk about Ashlyn's death, how it made me feel, I'd never get past it. But here's the thing about talking: every conversation ends the same way, with Ashlyn still dead and me missing her so much that it's overwhelming, excruciating, and relentless. And when you talk enough about something, you give it a shape. You make it real.

Why doesn't anyone get that?

Jade puts her hands behind her back. "Don't get me wrong, Cloudy, I understand needing to get out of Bend. But this trip is kind of . . . *unlike* you."

I roll my lips together. "Meaning?"

"You're lying to your parents, your friends, skipping practice—you've never left the squad behind like that. Your sister's home alone. And all for a spur-of-the-moment road trip with Ashlyn's boyfriend? That's not you."

My skin is tight enough to split open. So what if I left things back in Bend? It's not as if I'm doing this for myself. This trip is about Kyle getting through something big—and I'm not sorry for it. Not when I'm finally helping him. How can I look out for Zoë, for the squad, and for Kyle at the same time? How many people can I be there for at once?

"You haven't given me a straight answer since you got here," Jade pushes. "What's going on?"

Warning bells and shrieking alarms and blaring sirens sound in my head, but I say it, anyway. "You really want to know what this trip's about?"

She shrugs at me like *of course. Of course I do.*

So I tell her.

I tell her everything. Kyle's rut, and the emails, and Ethan, and Palm Springs, and the Vegas wedding.

Her mouth opens the slightest bit as she absorbs it all, and before she can answer, I add, "I'm going to finish our run."

Then, with my heart beating double-time and halfway up my throat, I turn away. And this time, I *am* running away from her, and her questions, but there's nothing freeing about it.

Kyle

It's nine fifteen in the morning, and Cloudy and I have already been *go, go, go!* for over three hours. My amped-up mood as I breathe in dry Palm Springs air in a strip mall parking lot reminds me of how I used to feel around Ashlyn or Matty (or especially Ashlyn *and* Matty): motivated, energized, ready for anything.

"I wish you'd have stolen more emails," I tell Cloudy, waving around Freddie Blackwell's printed words. "He's so formal. I can't get a handle on his personality. Unless this *is* his personality."

I'm sitting at the back of my vehicle beneath the open hatch with my legs dangling above the cement. Three feet to my left, Cloudy is using the cargo area as her craft table. She's standing as she arranges mugs, artificial daisies, chocolate bars, biscotti, and a variety of coffees, teas, and hot cocoas in a basket. Once she's done, we're going to deliver it to Freddie, Ashlyn's lung recipient. We're going to try, at least.

"There weren't other emails to steal," Cloudy says. "Before, the Montiels communicated with the recipients only by letters through the transplant organization. And there was no way I was going to take official United States mail from their house."

"Oh, fine."

At this point, I'm talking just to talk. I've become *so distracted* by this girl. Officially, it started during "Twist and Shout" in LA the night before last, and has only gotten more intense since. I like it, though.

I like that we're able to converse again. I like getting to spend our days together. I like that she looks at me as if I'm her friend. I like . . . her. More than I should. This bland email from Freddie is the only thing keeping me from staring nonstop at her face while she concentrates on taping each item where she wants it in the configuration.

An elderly couple strolls past us. Like everyone I've seen out and about in Palm Springs, they're wearing sweaters and long pants, while I'm in shorts. It's hard for me to believe they all find it cold here.

"What else do you know about this guy?" I ask. "What are we getting ourselves into?"

"I haven't read the actual letters. But Freddie's a former golf instructor, I think?"

"It says here he has a new job lined up for when he gets back from his trip, so maybe it won't be 'former' for long. I wonder where he and his wife are headed."

"Australia and New Zealand. That's what Mrs. Montiel told me." Cloudy holds out the basket, so I take it from her. "I think it would be cool to travel there someday."

"Me too," I say. "If you could go anywhere in the world, where would you pick?"

She hops up, holding the sides of her skirt against her thighs as she takes a seat beside me. "South America and especially Machu Picchu in Peru."

"I've never heard of that."

"It was a lost city to the outside world until, like, a hundred years ago, and the engineering was supposedly very advanced. People still don't know what it was used for, so it's this great mystery."

"So that's the one thing you want to see more than anything else, then?" I ask.

"Um." Cloudy motions for me to lift the basket, and then I kind of maneuver it around while she wraps it in crinkly, plasticky stuff. "No, that would be the tulip fields in Holland."

I laugh. "Holland? That is nowhere near South America!"

"I know. I'd say that Machu Picchu is my ideal *destination*. But you asked for one *thing*. And that would be beautiful, colorful tulips surrounding me in all directions. What about you?"

"For my one thing? I guess just something ancient? I'm into checking out places people built hundreds of years ago. Like, there's this cliff dwelling near Sedona called Montezuma Castle. It's from the twelfth century. People aren't allowed inside anymore, but you can look up at it from the ground. I used to imagine living there. That was before I understood the meaning of 'national monument.'"

"Will we have time to go there today?" she asks.

"Yup. It'll be on our way."

Excitement and nervousness swirl through me. At this moment, I'm closer to Arizona than I've been in almost two years, and as long as everything goes according to our new plan, I'll be there with Cloudy before the day is over.

At the pier yesterday, Cloudy told me she wanted to stay with Jade's family for at least a couple of nights. Today was supposed to be the day we explored Los Angeles. But after she came back from her run with Jade last night, she'd changed her mind. Matty's parents let him book their time-share in Las Vegas for us for Thursday and Friday nights, and since this is Tuesday, Cloudy said we should try to find Freddie this morning, and then head to Sedona afterward. This way, I'll get to spend time with some of my own friends during our trip, too.

I'm very on board with this plan. I want to show Cloudy my old town, which is different from anywhere in the world (or so people say). I want to catch up with my friends—especially Will, who we're going to stay with. I want to discover if me spending time in the place I lived before I lost Ashlyn will help me find a way to become someone who resembles Back to Normal Kyle. It's an ambitious goal for a two-day visit, but I'm hopeful.

Cloudy takes the basket and her hand brushes mine. It shouldn't be a big deal, but when our skin touches, all this heat radiates through me. It's so strange to be feeling anything about another girl—and stranger still that the girl would turn out to be Ashlyn's best friend, who seemed to hate me until this trip. With the convoluted history of Cloudy and me, I know I should tamp it down, knock it off, *get over it*.

I don't want to, though.

She slides the wrapped basket behind us and then pulls out a spool of ribbon and tiny scissors from the shopping bag beside her. "You still didn't answer your own question. What's the *one* ancient thing that's going to make your life complete?"

I consider. "Probably the Egyptian pyramids. I've seen them in pictures and movies all my life, but to be there in person? That would be amazing. They're five thousand years old. Did the people who created them have any idea they'd last so long? I mean, what were their lives even like then?"

"From what I've heard, not so different from now. They had indoor bathrooms, played board games, and, you know, occasionally shaved off their eyebrows to keep away evil spirits. Or is that what they wore black eyeliner for?"

I chuckle. "I'm not sure. But do you remember Crystal Curby shaving her eyebrows last year? She told Matty it was a sign of mourning because her cat died. I checked online and that was a real thing in ancient Egypt."

"Whenever someone died, they'd shave off their eyebrows?"

"*Only* when their cats died."

"Ohhh. Because they worshipped them." Cloudy glances up from the intricate bow she's tying and nods toward Arm, sleeping in the backseat. "Kind of like how you are with a certain bundle of fur?"

"She *is* the coolest cat to come around in several millennia."

I wonder if Cloudy believes in reincarnation. A couple of days ago, she said Ashlyn must be pissed about not getting to use the frame she'd picked out for her magazine article. That doesn't sound like any kind of heaven I've heard of before, but it's probably what she was meaning?

She trims the ribbon and attaches it to the basket. "All done."

We both climb down and view her handiwork from a couple of feet away. "If I'd tried to make a gift basket," I say, "it would literally be a basket with a pile of gifts in it. You're insanely skilled at this."

"I'm all right. Lita's the team's designated bow maker. She does these pretty loops and uses a needle and thread to make them stay perfect. Mine is atrocious in comparison."

"Well, I think yours looks awesome. So there."

Cloudy smiles at her sandals. "What do you think? Are we ready for Freddie now?"

"We're ready."

AFTER I'VE MADE a couple of turns from the parking lot to get us headed the right direction on East Vista Chino, two things happen at once: Cloudy reads from her phone that my next turn will be in 1.3 miles and "What Sarah Said" by Death Cab for Cutie starts playing on my stereo.

This song. This is the song I've been avoiding for months because it's too honest, too real, too painful. The opening piano notes alone have made me cry more times than I like to think about. But I haven't deleted it from my playlist for one reason: this song means more to me than any other.

"What Sarah Said" describes what's it like when someone you love is in the ICU. The lyrics nail every detail. The nonsensical thought that maybe slowing your own breathing could help them somehow. The smells, the sounds, the vitals monitors, the waiting room, the magazines, the vending machines, the nervous pacing. The complete helplessness of knowing there's nothing you can do, that you have no choice except to wait for whatever's going to happen.

I move my finger to the button that will skip the song like I've done hundreds of times before. Then I hesitate. Maybe it's because I'm sitting next to this cool girl who's come up with a scheme to help us both move on. Maybe it's because the kitten crawling in the backseat gives me irrational hope. But mostly, it's because even though I don't want to listen to this, part of me is curious to discover whether I can. I want to know if I'm physically capable, after all these many weeks, of hearing these words set to this music and not losing it.

So I let it play.

The first sixteen seconds is piano only, then the drums and cymbals kick in, and at forty-two seconds, the vocals.

The piano is relentless. That's how it's always felt to me. My hands squeeze the steering wheel tighter with every verse. Each description in the song conjures up a real memory from my own time visiting Ashlyn in the ICU and it makes my eyes sting and my chest ache. This song might have been written for the sole purpose of killing me, but I'm not letting it.

I'm not breaking down.

At the three-minute, ten-second mark, Ben Gibbard sings about what Sarah said ("Love is watching someone die"), and I know I've made it. I let out a loud, relieved breath like I've sat up again after body-weight bench pressing.

And that's when, with three minutes still remaining, the music stops.

I turn my head toward Cloudy, who's holding my phone and

staring at me wide-eyed like I heaved the weights right onto her. Her voice is accusing. "You didn't skip it."

It hadn't occurred to me she'd been paying attention the other times. "It was an endurance test. And I passed. It's the first time I've not skipped 'What Sarah Said' since, like, November. Have you listened to it before?"

She shakes her head and sets my phone down to focus on her own again. "North Palm Canyon Drive. That's us. Stay in this lane and go left at the light."

"A couple of weeks after Ashlyn died," I tell her, "it randomly came on the radio, and I felt like the singer was stealing thoughts straight from my brain. I listened to it over and over again until one day, I couldn't anymore." I wait at the traffic signal for a few seconds, and then make the turn. "I was kind of starting to hate myself because I hadn't wanted to stay until the very end with her. I didn't want to watch her die."

"Kyle, we didn't have the choice to stay. Mrs. Montiel said only the surgical team was allowed in the room when they turned off life support. Because of how organ donation works."

"I know. But deep down, I was relieved. This song made me wish I'd been strong enough to have gotten upset about not being given the option, you know?"

"Turn right on North Via Las Palmas." Cloudy removes her sunglasses from the top of her head and puts them on properly. "Then it will be another right onto South Via Las Palmas."

Her tone is clipped. I can't tell if she's upset about this discussion or simply trying to keep us from getting lost. I'd like to talk it through, though. Of anyone, I know she's the person who can understand.

"While listening to that song again," I say, "there's one thing I just now realized. I used to think I'd never get the image of her in the hospital out of my head. I thought I'd always be haunted by it. But it's mostly gone now. If I try really, really hard, I can sort of picture the scrapes on her face and hands, the bandages, all the tubes and cords, but my brain has rewritten the memory. All I see is her, looking the way she'd always looked before."

Cloudy sighs so softly it's barely louder than breathing, and my stomach tightens. I'm pushing this too far. The last thing I want is for her to think I'm being a jerk. "I'm glad I can survive that song again." I speak in a rush. "That's all I was trying to say."

It takes a few seconds for Cloudy to put on a small smile. "Song conquering is a very good thing."

At that, I shut up and let her continue guiding me toward our destination.

THE DIRECTIONS LOOP us back to the main drag once, but it isn't long before we've figured out where things went wrong and I'm pulling us into a circular driveway. Freddie's house is an A-frame with an attached flat-roofed garage jutting forward from the far side. Behind the property, the palm trees are overpowered by mountains, which are now so much bigger than when we were three miles away.

"Here we are!" Cloudy sings. "Are we really ready for this?"

"Yup. And I'll let you do all the talking so I don't screw it up."

"I don't see a car, so let's hope it's in the garage. It's already seventy degrees. If we have to wait for him to come home, this might be one miserable, sweaty stakeout. Plus, the chocolate won't survive."

I put down the windows all the way so Arm won't get too hot while she waits. "You don't think she'll jump out and run away to live in the mountains, do you?"

"No way. She *lurves* you. She'd never leave without you."

"If you're wrong, I'll be shaving my eyebrows off."

"We both will be."

Cloudy retrieves the gift basket and together, we head up the walkway past the flower beds. Due to the house's design, we're standing completely under shade almost ten feet before we reach the front door. A big red-and-white sign demands our attention as we get close: NO SOLICITING. No Charities. No Food or Menus. No Home Estimates. No Petitions. No Politics. No Religion. No Salespeople.

"That covers just about everyone," I say.

"But not gift-basket bringers. So we're in luck."

Cloudy rings the bell. After about thirty seconds, the door flies open, revealing a guy maybe around Cloudy's height (5'5") and my dad's age (51). It isn't like we woke him up or anything (he's dressed in slacks and a collared shirt like he's on his way to hit golf balls), so I can't begin to guess why his face is scrunched up like he's just downed a shot of vinegar.

Cloudy puts on her best cheer smile as she moves her sunglasses back to the top of her head. "Good morning!"

The man's voice is stern as he nods toward his warning sign. "Before we go any further, did you read this?"

I clear my throat. "We did."

His eyes bore through mine. "And do you understand that I will slam this door *in a heartbeat* if you're here for any of what's listed?"

"We're here to deliver a prize," Cloudy says, holding out the basket with a smile.

The man peers at it from his side of the threshold, but doesn't take it. "A prize for what?"

"It was a raffle drawing," she says. "The winner is Freddie Blackwell. Is that you?"

"Yes. My wife must have entered me, but I don't drink coffee." He calls over his shoulder, *"Bettie!"*

Now we have an answer as to whether this particular recipient has inherited Ashlyn's iced-coffee habit. I'm not sure what else we'll learn, but I'm not spotting anything about him right off that's Ashlyn-like—except his size. Which makes sense, I guess. Only someone with a small body could get enough oxygen using lungs that had belonged to another small person.

I try to catch Cloudy's eye, but she's staring straight ahead. Her cheer smile has vanished.

When Freddie turns to us again, he has the decency to soften his expression and his voice. "I'm sorry. What organization did you kids say you're with again?"

"We're not," I tell him.

"Then who sent you to deliver this?"

"Oh," Cloudy says. "I think . . . the card's in the car."

She thrusts the basket at me and rushes off in search of an imaginary card, leaving me alone with Freddie. I consider dropping the basket at his feet and getting the hell off his property without another word, but then he's joined at the door by a platinum-haired woman who's even shorter than he is.

She smiles up at me. "What's this?"

"Apparently, you put in my name to win coffee," Freddie explains.

Bettie reaches for the basket, so I let her take it.

"I put in *your* name?" She examines their "prize" through the plastic. "That doesn't sound like something I'd do. Not for delicious coffee and chocolates. I'd want to make sure they went to someone who appreciates them. Like myself, for instance. Look at this chocolate caramel bar. Yum!"

Freddie shrugs. "The girl he has with him said it was specifically for Freddie."

"Oh, you know what?" I say. "This was one of the runner-up gifts. The raffle was done through a hospital. I'm, um, not sure which one, but maybe only patients could win? The grand prize was a trip to anywhere in the world."

For a millisecond, Bettie's eyes go glassy, like she's trying to puzzle out whether a teenager hand-delivering a basket in Southern California could possibly be aware of the other prizes some unknown Oregon hospital had up for grabs nearly six months ago. But then she smiles. "Oh, yes. Freddie was in the hospital last year. I think I remember signing up for something in the cafeteria. I spent a lot of time there to keep from pacing holes in the waiting room floor during his surgery. We're actually headed Down Under to Australia and New Zealand in March for our pearl anniversary. That's thirty years! We'd sure have loved to win the trip for free, but thank you for bringing this by."

"No problem. And congratulations on . . . everything."

Freddie looks past me. "Your girlfriend doesn't have to round up the card. Or do you think she's taking her time because she doesn't like me?"

"That wouldn't surprise me in the least." Bettie laughs. "He's such an ogre when people drop by. We moved here from Portland, Oregon. He survived all the rain and living on an oxygen tank for years, but he still hasn't recovered from dealing with the door-to-door salesmen."

"Relentless little pricks." Freddie nods toward his sign. "They don't care what you post or what you say to them. They call it 'freedom of speech' and felt very free to pound on my door all day until I could manage to drag myself over to answer it."

Bettie grins at me. "He forgets that in this town, we're among the young people. Especially Freddie, now that he's had a double lung transplant. He's turning fifty-six next month, but his donor was only sixteen. So he has sixteen-year-old lungs."

I can't help it—my gaze goes straight to Freddie's chest. He referred to Cloudy as my girlfriend a minute ago and I didn't bother correcting him; we're never going to see him again. But it's incredible that he's breathing *right now* through the lungs of the only girlfriend I've ever had.

"Sounds like the surgery was a success, then?" I ask. "I mean, no more oxygen tank. That's got to feel good."

"No more oxygen tank," Bettie says. "No more constant fear that my husband and I won't get to grow old together. The transplant changed everything for us. *Everything.* We never could have taken our Australia trip otherwise." She rests her head on Freddie's shoulder as he wraps one arm around her. "And he's doing so well he's going to run a marathon in two weeks."

"Woman," he says with a laugh, "I keep telling you the race is only three miles. I'd still fall down dead in a real marathon."

"Okay, mister. But for a man who could hardly walk from the couch to the kitchen six months ago, I think three miles *should* be called a marathon."

Bettie bumps her hip on his thigh, and as Freddie holds her tighter, something in their hallway captures my attention: a painting of tangled tree branches covered in beige blossoms over a greenish-blue background.

Almond Blossom. That's what it's called. I know because it's the same artwork as Ashlyn's phone case. The same artwork as the thick bracelet I gave her for our third monthiversary because she loved it so much.

"That's a cool picture," I blurt out as my heart rate slams into overdrive. "In your hallway."

"Oh, thanks!" Betty says. "The color scheme is perfect for this house. A van Gogh on canvas maybe isn't the most unique choice, but we love it. If only we could have afforded the original! Can you imagine? We'd be living somewhere a *bit* more exotic than Palm Springs, California, if that were the case."

We all chuckle, and then there's a silence long enough for me to decide the Blackwells' conversation with any other delivery kid would be coming to an end now. Plus, I need to check on Cloudy. "Well, good luck with the race. And, um, have a great rest of your day."

"Likewise," Freddie says.

Bettie lifts the basket in my direction—like it's a glass of champagne and she's toasting.

I rush back to the Xterra, where Cloudy's waiting in the driver's seat with her sunglasses on her face again. It probably worked out that she didn't come back to their door, since she might have unknowingly contradicted my grand-prize story. Still, it would have been better if she'd gotten to meet Bettie, seen Ashlyn's favorite picture hanging in their house, and heard for herself the few details they shared about Freddie's sixteen-year-old lungs.

Wait. Sixteen?

My breath catches as I pull the door open. Bettie said sixteen, but she was wrong.

When I turned seventeen a couple of weeks ago, I had the sucky realization that Ashlyn was born 138 days before I was, but since she died at sixteen, I'm going to be older than her for the rest of my life. It hadn't occurred to me until now that her lungs (and the rest of her transplanted parts) actually *are* seventeen now.

It isn't a huge consolation. But still, how cool is that?

DETOUR:
ARIZONA

Cloudy

"We saw the burros."

I tear my eyes away from the pages I'm reading and there she is: a tiny girl, maybe five or six, right at my elbow. She squints up at me and I scan the grounds for whoever might belong to her. We're at a rest area on the way to Montezuma Castle; it's a smallish plaza with a well-kept brick building, surrounded by concrete, gravel, and prickly looking trees. It's also the last rest stop for miles, so it's not like the girl could be on her own. And yet, here she is, alone.

"You what?" I ask her.

Moving a bronze curl off her forehead, she says, "They didn't let us feed them, though."

"They?"

"The ghosts."

As we hold each other's stare, I carefully readjust the duffel—with Arm inside of it—on my shoulder. "You'll have to fill in the blanks, kid."

She lets out this pathetic whine that's bordering on cute, then jabs her finger at the display beside us. *"There."*

The words "On Your Way" are up top, with photographs and descriptions of roadside attractions below it. That much I already know—I saw it ten minutes ago, when I first propped myself against this brick wall.

After taking off from Freddie's porch this morning, all I wanted was to find my iPod. Even though my hands were shaking too hard to be useful, I kept sifting through the Xterra's cargo space for it. Two reasons: 1) No chance in hell was I listening to Death Cab all the way to Sedona, the words "love is watching someone die" poking at me. Because no, we weren't with Ashlyn when she was taken off life support, but I remember what she looked like. Like she was some kind of science experiment, not my best friend. Maybe Kyle's been able to overwrite his memories, but Ashlyn in that bed is still the image embossed in mine. And now that Kyle's had some kind of breakthrough, how many times will he let that Sarah song play through? Not happening.

And 2), if I didn't keep myself busy, focused on that one absurdly minor task, it was very likely I'd short circuit, right on the most solicitor-free street in America. Because I'd spotted it almost immediately. *Almond Blossom*. Ashlyn's painting. When my eyes locked on it, the oxygen had left my body. It was a punch in the stomach, or that breathless feeling when there's unexpected plane turbulence.

In the middle of the search, my phone buzzed in my pocket.

So how did it go with Freddie??

Zoë's text made me feel monitored. Caught.

I'd nearly fallen apart in front of the Blackwells, and I didn't need Zoë pressing me for the details.

So I turned my phone to silent and tossed it onto the dashboard to be forgotten.

"See?"

Blinking, I yank my thoughts back to the rest stop, to the young girl chattering away. I follow her pointed finger up to the corner of the sign labeled *Oatman, AZ: A Living Ghost Town*. Well, that explains the "ghosts" telling her not to do things. I hope. There's a short write-up below the heading that describes Oatman's history as a gold-mining town, and with that, a photo of some donkeys in the middle of a dusty road.

"Those guys, you mean?" I ask her, tapping the donkeys. Burros.

She grins, balancing on her toes. "They were everywhere," she says, her small arms stretching out around her, "and they smelled kinda bad, but I got real close anyway, and one tried to kiss my dad!"

"Wow."

"I know." She bends her head all the way back to goggle at me. "What's your name?"

"Cloudy," I tell her, then peruse the area again, this time for her dad. Unless there was some tragic burro-kissing incident, it sounds like she's with him. If not literally at this very moment. "What's yours?"

"Rosey. Are you going to the burros?"

"Maybe. If we have time."

"You should make time," she says, very seriously, so I can't help but smile.

"I'll ask my friend if he's into it. Deal?"

Her nose scrunches up. "Where's your friend?"

I squat down beside her, arranging the duffel on the ground between us and flattening the emails across my lap, then gesture over at Kyle. He's away from the paved-over center of the rest stop, pacing in the dirt beside two shrubs. "See that boy?" I ask Rosey, and she nods. "He's my friend."

Kyle must sense the attention because he glances over at us, eyebrows furrowed and his cell pressed to his ear. Rosey and I wave. It seems to confuse him more.

"So where's your dad?" I try to say this to her casually, and not like a stranger with candy.

Nevertheless, Rosey ignores me as she pirouettes, ending with some flair. "Are you a fairy? You have a name like a fairy."

"Rosey!" We both turn our heads. A woman is stalking over, her face a mix of worry and exasperation. "I told you to wait inside the bathroom for me." Rosey's mom, I'm assuming. "You can't run off. It's very dangerous," she adds, giving me the once-over.

I stand up—crouching never sells your innocence. "She was just telling me about the burros."

"Cloudy said she's going, too. We made a deal!" As she squeals the last word, she launches herself into the woman's arms.

Kyle walks up as Rosey and her mom start off toward the parking lot. He's still gripping his phone, and motions at their backs with it. "What was that about?"

Arching a brow, I say, "Oh, you're the only one who can pick up strays?"

He laughs, then reaches inside the duffel to stroke Arm on the head. "Will wants us to meet him before sunset, so it'll have to be a quick stop at Montezuma Castle."

"He's not building a moat to keep you away, huh?" Kyle was trying to hide it earlier, but he was apprehensive about asking Will if we could stay at his house. It all worked out exactly as I'd thought—without a problem—which is why it feels so good to mess with him.

"It's already past two in the afternoon. He'd never have the time," he says, sliding the bag off my shoulder. As we head for the Xterra, our shoes kick up dust. "What's Arm doing with you?" he asks. "I thought we decided it was cool enough for her in the car."

"Are you joking? I couldn't leave her by herself." I sweep my arm out, taking in the numerous signs dotting the area that warn against having your pets loose—Poisonous Snakes and Insects in Area. Danger! Death Trap! "Face it, Kyle. Your home-land wants to murder your cat."

Kyle points the remote to unlock the doors. "I hate to break this to you, but she was probably safer in the car than outside."

"Maybe if she actually *was* an armadillo instead of just named after them," I scoff, opening my door and climbing up inside. "She'd be completely defenseless in here."

Kyle's smile is distracted as he leans across to deposit Arm—now liberated from the duffel—in my lap, then quietly slides into the driver's seat. It's such a difference from how hopped up he was when we left Palm Springs. His mood was so upbeat, he could have floated to Arizona. He didn't even complain when

I synced up some old Marina and the Diamonds without asking, or notice that my fingers were wrapped around the steering wheel so tightly, I had to massage them every few miles. Instead he went on and on about Freddie and Bettie, how grateful they are for the transplant, and how Kyle realized that Ashlyn's lungs will grow older even though she won't, but isn't that amazing? That had me lowering my window, desperate for fresh air, despite the whipping wind.

And Ashlyn's painting—that really got Kyle going. I nodded and made the appropriate mm-hmming noises, adding in the occasional exclamation point, while Kyle gushed about how impossible it was. That they liked the same painting as Ashlyn. But the idea of it was more like antifreeze in my arteries. *Almond Blossom*, perfectly placed in the Blackwells' hallway, was a taunt. I thought of the people who'll pass by that wall. Would they even notice it hanging there? Or would it only be background scenery?

Ever since she'd seen a print of it in a museum gift shop, Ashlyn had loved that painting. She'd say it was welcoming and exquisite. Everyone who knew her knew that. It was practically her coat of arms. She flashed the bracelet Kyle gave her whenever she could, and I would tease her for being a show-off. But she'll never get to show it off like the Blackwells have, in a brand-new house, or apartment, or dorm room. No one will see her phone case again, not until the Montiels take it from her desk and stuff it into some cardboard box to put away or donate—or worse, send to some landfill. Soon, enough time will pass that no one will randomly come across *Almond Blossom* and automatically think of Ashlyn. The unfairness of it wriggled through me until

I felt like I might scream from it.

But I'm happy for Kyle—I am. Visiting the recipients is doing exactly what I hoped it would. His grins come easier now, and his shoulders don't seem to carry as much weight. It's important he doesn't figure out what went wrong with me in Palm Springs. And at least one thing went right: within a couple of hours, we were able to put Jade and Freddie permanently behind us. In a few more, we'll be even farther away, in Sedona.

Arm nestles into the crook of my elbow and, while I'm not sure Kyle will need them, I pull up the directions on my phone. As I do, I notice he hasn't turned on the engine yet—his stare is fixed on the dashboard. I snatch an unused straw from the center console and javelin-throw it at his neck. "Did you forget how cars start?"

The tips of his ears are pink, and he runs a hand through his hair. "So . . . that whole 'armadillo' thing, with Arm. I sort of came up with it on the spot that morning."

I smile. "You don't say."

He glances at me sideways. "You knew the whole time?"

"A-R-M? It's pretty obvious. To me, anyway." I shrug, absently stroking Arm's back and belly. Her little paws knead through the thin fabric of my skirt. "But naming her after Ashlyn is sweet. She'd love it. You know how passionate she was about the furry and adorable."

Kyle swivels in his seat. "Do you ever think about what happened to Ashlyn? I mean, her . . . spirit or whatever."

I blow out a sharp breath. "Um, sure. Heaven. The normal route."

"I've never believed in heaven or anything like that. The

afterlife." He rubs at the skin right below his lower lip. "But ever since she died, I've sometimes wished I had it in me to believe in *something.*"

"Something like what?"

He nods almost imperceptibly toward the cat in my lap. I follow his gaze to Arm, who's turned on her back, her legs outstretched. So Kyle wants to believe in, what, animals? Animal rights? Or something more Arm-specific? Arm. Arm . . . A-R-M.

With a gasp, it hits me: "Reincarnation?"

His eyes search me frantically. "I'm not saying Arm *is* Ashlyn. . . . Not really." He props an elbow on the steering wheel, hiding his face with his hand. "Forget it. I sound delusional."

"Kyle, no." I jostle him, and he groans. "Come on, I'm listening."

"I just . . . When I saw her—Arm—in the parking lot, I got this feeling. Like there was something familiar about her."

My lips tug up at the sides. "The green eyes? The black fur?"

He lifts one shoulder, sheepish. "I don't know. But I thought if there was even the slightest chance that reincarnation is real and Ashlyn might be alive again . . . I couldn't leave her there, outside, all alone. I had to look out for her."

"You're doing a good job of it," I say, forcing my voice to keep from cracking.

"It's not like I'm in love with a cat or anything," he says. I burst out laughing, and I spy Kyle's mouth tilting in a lopsided grin. "I needed to be clear on that," he tells me.

"You're clear."

"And I didn't keep her so I could fixate on Ashlyn dying,

or as an excuse not to move on. It's about doing some good for Ashlyn now. I wanted to return the favor." He brings up his fingers, kneading them into his forehead. "Damn, I really do sound insane."

Shaking my head, I say, "Not any crazier than wondering if Ashlyn is possessing her organ recipients."

He sags against the seat. "You think?"

I narrow my eyes out the windshield, taking in the rest area once more. So far, Arizona is greener than I ever pictured. Not as burned-looking as the sandy and cracked-earth desert I was expecting. "I think that we can believe whatever it takes to get us through," I tell Kyle. "As long as she's okay. Somewhere she deserves to be."

"Yeah." He's still holding on to the steering wheel, his arms straight, and he exhales. "Exactly."

Then he turns the engine on. I'm not sure he wants to talk about Arm or Ashlyn anymore, so I lean back and tell him about Rosey and the burros.

THERE'S NOT MUCH I know about Kyle's life before he moved to Bend. Even when he first got there, he was never all that forthcoming about it. Ashlyn thought it might have to do with his mom—bad memories, maybe. If she ever asked him, she didn't tell me. And besides, with Matty around, Kyle eased in so seamlessly; it was practically like he'd belonged to Bend all along.

But when we stop at Montezuma Castle, he tells me it isn't technically a castle but an apartment-type complex carved into a limestone cliff, and that up until the 1950s, tourists would climb questionably safe ladders to peek inside. His smile stretches wider with every word. And as we pass over into Sedona, the change in Kyle is even more obvious. His shoulders are pressed into the seat, and only one of his hands holds on to the steering wheel. He's relaxed, loose. Like he knows the way.

And the way is unreal.

We're on a one-lane highway that's bordered on each side by clumpy, reddish dirt and vibrant green brush. But as much as I love the greenery, the rock formations—that's what Kyle called them—are my favorite. They're these natural structures that look like stony layer cakes: a layer of red rock, and brown, and orange, and beige. Some even have clusters of bushes and trees at the top and sides, like frosting. Others are shaped like ancient temples or alien architecture, something that's distinctly otherworldly. They're so different from the hills and mountains at home that I snap a few photos. I catch Kyle smiling to himself when I'm done.

After a while, sidewalks and commercial buildings start popping up on the side of the road. The shops are low, mostly one story tall, and they were clearly designed to blend in with the earthy color scheme of the city's landscape. The rock formations tower over everything, a constant backdrop.

"I cannot believe you grew up here," I say to Kyle, giddy as we pass the millionth storefront advertising some variation of the words *psychic*, *healing*, or *enlightenment*. "Be honest: were you birthed on a bed of quartz crystals?"

He laughs. "It's trippy, I know."

"Was your school on a commune? Did you learn how to read auras instead of, like, history?"

"Even Hogwarts teaches history, Cloudy," he says, a playful smirk on his lips. "This is mostly tourist bait. Not that it's all bullshit. Native Americans did believe Sedona was a sacred space; some of the locals have run with it."

I tilt closer to my window, gaping at our surroundings. "It's like a New Age theme park."

We turn it into a game—a point for every mystical establishment one of us spots. But we're laughing so much, we lose track before Kyle pulls off the highway and onto a more secluded drive. We stop for a quick bathroom break at the local McDonald's, and even that is charming, with a pink facade and the famous golden arches turned a pastel blue. Once we're on the road again, the shops and businesses fall away, and I go back to ogling the rocks.

"Wait until you see them at sunset," Kyle tells me. We're meeting Will at the parking lot that serves a few different hiking trails—including the Teacup Trail, which is how we plan to trek up a mountain called Sugarloaf Rock. It all sounds very Candy Land, but according to Kyle, it'll be worth it once we reach the top.

"Sunsets are an *event* here. You have to see one on your first night. And the higher you go, the better the view." He glances at me quickly, nodding down at my sandals. "Actually, you might want to put on pants and change your shoes. It'll get a little colder up there."

"*Colder?*" My voice breaks as it rises. Four days out of Oregon and I've already adapted to the warmth.

"It's the desert." And he says it so fondly, I don't even care that I woke up a few blocks from the Pacific Ocean this morning.

As he swings into the small lot, Kyle inspects the five cars lined up side by side, then eases the Xterra into the closest available spot. The area is ringed with trees, so the space is mostly shade.

He shuts off the engine. "Looks like Will isn't here yet."

"Are you nervous?"

Kyle pauses, tapping the wheel. "No," he says, and he sounds surprised but firm.

Through my window, I eyeball the other hikers getting ready to take on the trail. "In that case," I say, "mind waiting outside while I layer up?"

Once he's out, he also very deliberately keeps his back to the car, giving me some privacy. I shimmy into the fleece-lined leggings I wore the first day of our trip, then check my phone. Ignoring Zoë hasn't discouraged her from sending numerous Sedona facts, including: It's named after a woman! Sedona Schnebly! And although we chatted earlier, there's an email from my mom; the subject reads "Shore do miss you" and there's a picture of my parents grinning around the mouthpieces of their snorkel masks—I feel too guilty to make fun of it. There are messages from others, but disappointment settles thickly in my bones. I didn't realize I was hoping for a call from Jade until I didn't get one.

A horn blasts—two short honks, followed by a long, drawn-out shriek—and tires screech as a dusty Subaru SUV comes to a quick stop a few cars away. A guy catapults out of it.

"K.O.!" Will bellows, and he's smiling as he lopes over to meet Kyle. Hearing Kyle's baseball nickname makes me smile, too. Guess that's a Sedona throwback.

They hug, slapping at each other's backs loudly, as their boisterous reunion sounds bounce around the lot. Arm and I share a look—*boys*—and I finish changing as demurely as possible before going over to join them.

When he sees me approach, Will's eyebrow pops up. I notice a slightly slanted tooth as he grins and clamps a hand on Kyle's shoulder. "Is this a new girlfriend?" He says it under his breath, and shakes Kyle playfully. Kyle doesn't budge. "Not the one with the black hair who's in all your profile pictures?"

I falter and skid for a second, my boots scraping across pebbles and blacktop. Kyle meets my eyes, which are fully open and dry. Clearly, Will hasn't heard about Ashlyn's accident. It's the sonic boom that's been reverberating in our everyday for months; that keeps echoing with memorials and vigils and bike safety seminars. Her death is how we live now, and it's a shock that there are people who have no idea. There are places in the world where Ashlyn is still alive. All these people who don't know.

How can people not know?

If I didn't foresee how embarrassed Will is about to feel, I'd knock the rest of his teeth crooked.

"Uh, no," Kyle stammers. "That was Ashlyn in my pictures." I watch his face, his shoulders, his fingers, every part of him for a sign that he can't say it—that I should. But he can. He is. "She died. Last year."

And there goes Will, all the blood draining from his face.

The tiniest of smirks clings to his lips, probably holding on to some prayer that Kyle's screwing with him. He waits a little longer, then: "Shit. Seriously?"

Kyle licks his lips. "Yeah."

"Oh, shit. *Shit*. I'm sorry, man." Will wipes at his face with both hands, groaning. "I'm such a dick."

"It's all right," Kyle says.

"I didn't realize; I swear it. I never saw anything about it online."

Kyle shuffles his feet, sneakers grinding stone against cement. "I sort of gave up on social media for a while," he says. "Ashlyn's name or photo would appear out of nowhere sometimes. It got too hard."

I want to grab his hand so he knows I'm here. Instead, I step up beside him. "Her parents had her page memorialized, so people go on there a lot to write messages. It's kind of impossible to miss."

And impossible to stomach. The notes have dropped off the past couple of months, but whenever one appears, I get queasy.

Will turns to me. His forehead is damp. "You're still Cloudy, though. Right?"

"Still Cloudy," I say. "But not Kyle's girlfriend."

Will exhales as if he'd like to restart the past five minutes.

Over his shoulder, I glimpse a map near the trail's entrance. How did we get here? A fantasy world where Ashlyn never died and I could be Kyle's girlfriend. Goddamn Candy Land.

SO FAR, ALL we've heard on the Teacup Trail are the sounds of our feet crunching over the rough dirt, and Will's apologies.

He's really, *really* ashamed of the Ashlyn confusion. It makes him easy to like.

Kyle finally got him to take a breath, and now they're playing catch-up while my attention drifts in and out. The part of the path we're on is narrow, so we walk single file. I'm up front with Arm—she's back in her duffel, draped over my shoulder, since we decided it's unfair for her to miss our first Sedona Event.

Navigating the stony terrain was tricky at first, but the trail smooths out in spots, and gives me the chance to gawk appropriately. Above us, the sky is still the same lively blue, streaked with wispy clouds, and the rock formations loom over us on every side. The ground is sprinkled with all kinds of plants to avoid touching: gorgeously fanned out—and impressively pointy—agave plants, and low-lying green bunches of cacti that are like the distant, mutated cousins of the tiny ones lined up along my windowsill. I wish I could bring some of this home with me, grow a little bit of Arizona in my backyard.

Once in a while, I spot something tall and spindly that might be a dead tree, but the thick spikes on its trunk tell me otherwise. And when I stumble on a patch of rotten cacti, it startles me. Everything here is so vivid, so vital and serene—the opposite of what I was expecting from the desert. The decay is out of place. Even the dirt is worth looking at. It's a rusted brown, like someone crumbled up an endless number of Butterfingers and scattered them here.

Behind me, Will and Kyle are talking about a girl named Hannah. Their conversation has eased into a comfortable rhythm. I'm jealous that they've been able to walk this trail enough that its beauty doesn't preoccupy them. But all the same, it's a privilege to be seeing this for the first time.

"So Hannah wants you at her birthday party tomorrow," Will is saying. "And she told me it's a 'special request,' which roughly translated means it's mandatory."

"Same Hannah," Kyle murmurs.

"Oh, yeah. Except she's kind of going through an *earthy* phase right now."

I smile at Will's phrasing. "What does that mean?"

"Is she, like, a vegan?" Kyle says, his voice curious.

"A hippie," Will blurts. "Or she's trying to be. The parts of the lifestyle that appeal to her, anyway. She's having us all drive out to Bedrock City."

Kyle chokes on a laugh. "No way."

"Bedrock City?" I ask, pushing my sleeves up to my elbows. The air is still comfortably cool, but all the walking has warmed my skin.

"It's sort of like an amusement park without the rides," Will informs me. "A rides-less Flintstones amusement park."

I should have guessed.

"Hmm," Kyle hums. "You up for it, Cloudy?"

"Depends," I say without turning. "What exactly goes on at a hippie birthday party?"

Kyle thinks about it before answering. "We'd be fighting the Establishment. I assume while eating cake."

"Definitely," Will agrees. "Damning the Man, till the break of dawn."

Idiots. Kyle and Will are so in sync, it makes me giggle. How did they ever lose touch?

Soon, the incline gets steeper, and the larger rocks have

arranged themselves into rough steps. The sun is dipping lower, its light reflecting on everything around us. My heart springs around in my chest at the sight of it. If this is a sneak peek, I don't want to miss a thing.

We trudge and climb, our breathing slightly heavier than before. And then the ground levels out and we're there, at the top of Sugarloaf. It's only just past six p.m., still a few minutes until sunset, and the wind carries a chill. I pull down my sleeves as I walk straight to the center of the summit and spin a lazy circle. Being the only ones up here makes it feel like we're the only ones *anywhere*.

We're still surrounded by the rock formations, but now, up higher, they seem closer. Kyle ducks his head to my height, pointing some out while he tells me their names: Chimney Rock, Coffee Pot Rock, Thunder Mountain, and the Fin, which actually does look like the fin on a giant fish. Silently, I hand him Arm's bag before peeking over Sugarloaf's edge. My eyes widen. Far below sit groupings of small houses—so we're not really the only ones here. There are people coming home from work, cooking dinner, and walking their dogs. They live normal lives in the middle of this.

Kyle hoists the duffel up on his shoulder, giving Arm a better vantage point. "So," he calls to Will, "is your mom okay with us leaving Arm at the house while we're out?"

"Definitely. She loves cats," Will answers. He's already holding the flashlight we'll need after the sun sets. "What else do you guys have planned? Aside from the mandatory hippie shindig."

Glancing at me, Kyle shrugs. "Nothing, really. We were thinking of heading to Oatman on our way out, though."

Will stiffens the tiniest bit. Kyle doesn't notice—he's turned sideways to show Arm a hawk perched high in a tree—but I do.

"Oatman?" he says quickly, sharply, and his eyes dart from Kyle to me. "What for?"

I step away from the mountain's ledge. "I promised a very small, very pushy person that we'd see the burros."

"Oh. Nice." Will nods. His abrupt weirdness disappears. "My parents used to take me there all the time when I was a kid."

This gets Will and Kyle talking about other places around town, stores that have closed since Kyle moved and new ones that have opened. But not too long after, the discussion ends, because sunset is beginning.

We stand in a line, our shadows growing longer. The sun blazes its brightest right as it sinks slowly behind a massive rock, and the sky around it radiates yellow and orange and pink. At our feet, the dirt begins to glow a deep, smoldering red—like I noticed on the way, but here, it's dialed up so many degrees. It sweeps across the canyon, coating the earth so it looks like magma, like it's absorbing heat and hot to the touch. We're suddenly on another planet, on Mars or Mercury—or someplace better that no one on Earth knows about. Where I'm not left behind or alone or completely absent, because those things don't exist here.

Kyle grins down at me, satisfaction on his face—my expression must be as dopey as I feel. He lifts his phone up, ready to take photos. "I told you so."

"I cannot believe you grew up here," I say to him again, but differently this time. And I grin back at him, while the last rays of sunlight spark along his face.

Kyle

By the time Cloudy and I are filling up on the strawberry-and-Nutella-stuffed French toast Vivian, Will's mom, cooked for us, it's almost eleven a.m. It sucks that we have only five hours before we have to meet up with everyone for Hannah's birthday thing, but I have to say, sleeping in was beyond necessary for me after the long day we had yesterday.

"Cloudy," Vivian says from the kitchen, "did you do all right in the Doll Room?"

"Any nightmares from having dozens and dozens of eyes on you while you were sleeping?" I ask.

Last night, I was on the living room Hide-a-Bed with Arm, but Cloudy was down the hall in the room Will calls "the creepiest place on Earth." It was a guest bedroom before Will's parents divorced about three years ago. Now, Vivian uses it to store collectibles and dolls to sell for her online business. She has boxes stacked to the ceiling, but she cleared a space big enough for Cloudy and an air mattress.

"I did fine," Cloudy says. "If the dolls came to life during the night, they had the decency to not murder me."

Vivian laughs. I hadn't realized how much I'd missed her and Will until I was with them again. My dad was around as much as he was able to be while I was growing up, but for a lot of those years, it was Vivian who took care of me when he couldn't. She drove Will and me to and from baseball practice and fed us snacks afterward. This table is where I did my homework three days a week.

Cloudy, having dug out every bite from her halved grapefruit, sets her spoon inside the bowl. "I had an email from Coach Voss at seven. Not my favorite wake-up alarm."

"Uh-oh. Was it a big lecture?"

"Could have been worse. She could have cc'd my parents. But I think she's trying not to dwell on what I've done and focus instead on fixing what I *haven't* done. Which is send snapshots of my best cheer memories and the answers to those preliminary questions for the *Cheer Insider* interview. Oh, and she also let me know the team's photo shoot is scheduled for next Friday, so there's that to look forward to."

It's odd how she treats this whole magazine thing like it's no big deal—like it's annoying, even. "If you need to get your interview stuff done, we can stay at the house today."

Cloudy shakes her head so hard her dangly earrings smack both sides of her jaw. "Be serious. I didn't come all the way to Sedona to *not* see it! I'll go through the questions once we get to Las Vegas tomorrow afternoon."

"Or I can drive and let you work on the questions then? That way, you'll have everything done before Sonia's wedding."

"Sure. And today, you can take me places. The places you've

been missing the most since you moved."

Vivian pokes her head into the dining room and grins at me behind Cloudy's back. I want to roll my eyes so Vivian might get the hint that she should cut it out. Instead I just tell Cloudy, "Works for me."

After our hike with Will last night, Vivian was waiting up with grasshopper pie. (It's the dessert she used to make on my birthday, with a crushed-Oreo crust and minty whipped cream filling.) Us four humans stayed up late eating and talking while Arm did cute stuff like hitting her face against Cloudy's chest, licking my hands, and batting at Vivian's hair. Cloudy then bowed out for bed at midnight, followed by Will, since he has school today.

While Vivian was helping me make up the Hide-a-Bed, she cleared her throat. "Will called me on his way home and told me about your girlfriend passing away last year. I'm so sorry. How are you?"

"I haven't been great. But I might be a little bit better since leaving town," I said, half surprised that it was the truth.

Knowing Vivian, there was a lot she wanted to say, but she kept it brief. "A change of scenery can make a big difference. I'm glad you're here." She gave me a long hug. "And that you brought Cloudy along. She's great. Sassy and smart and *so* pretty. You make a cute couple."

Embarrassed that these bigger feelings I'm having for Cloudy seem obvious to everyone else (three people mistook her for my girlfriend in one day), I told Vivian we aren't together. Her response was, "That might not always be the case."

Finished with our late breakfast, Cloudy and I take our dishes to the kitchen and then find Vivian in the living room with her laptop. Beside her on the couch, Arm stretches across the cushion.

"I'm going to show Cloudy around," I say. "You're sure it's okay if Arm stays with you?"

"Of course." Vivian smiles up at us with her red-framed reading glasses on the end of her nose. "I'll even give her food, water, and lots of petting. I'm *very* curious as to whose brilliant idea it was to bring a kitten on a road trip, though."

Cloudy giggles and points at me.

FIVE MINUTES LATER, I'm backing out of the driveway when Cloudy asks, "Is your old house far away?"

I swing around the corner and park in front of a tall terra-cotta house that almost blends into the massive red-rock formations right behind it. "Not far at all."

"This is the place?"

"This is the place."

I hadn't expected to make an event out of it, but Cloudy jumps out, so I kill the engine and join her on the sidewalk.

"It's like a Spanish mini-fortress," she says. "I know I keep saying this, but I really can't believe you used to live here."

In a weird way, it's almost as unbelievable to me as it is to her.

I wouldn't say I took Sedona for granted when I was growing up, but I truly didn't *see* it most of the time. When I'd visit my family in Oregon during the summers, I'd come home and Sedona would seem so much more vivid and interesting than it had been before I'd left. But it would be only a day or so before I stopped taking it in and everything here became the norm again.

Now, after nearly two years away, the haze has lifted. The house my dad had custom built probably isn't as impressive as Cloudy makes it sound, but there's nothing in Bend with Moroccan-style touches like the rounded brick archways over the windows and doors, and the stained glass window that makes the main stairway inside glow pink, orange, and yellow.

My chest kind of aches; the house I lived in since before I was old enough to have other memories is so unfamiliar in some ways.

"Do you think anyone's home?" Cloudy's smile is mischievous. "Or do we have to sneak around like ninjas?"

"My dad still owns it and rents it out as a vacation house. I heard him saying the next tenants won't be here until March, so we should be all right."

"Okay, good. Being ninjas would have been more fun, though."

I crouch low and creep up the driveway. When I glance back, she's smiling big and doing the same. I pause until she catches up, and then we tiptoe under the shadow of pine trees.

The back of the house is made up of huge windows and glass doors. All the curtains are open, revealing most of the rooms on the ground floor, including my old bedroom. Cloudy peers inside and makes her way slowly down the length of the house. "It's so different from where you live now. Has it always been this fancy?"

It takes a second to remember when and why she's been

inside my house in Bend. (Last winter a couple of times. To watch movies with Ashlyn, Matty, and me.) "It's always been exactly like this. This is our stuff. All of it."

Nothing has changed. None of the people who stayed here have repositioned one single thing. (Or if they did, the house-keeper changed it back.) When Dad and I moved out, we left behind the artwork, the electronics, every piece of furniture, even the dishes and silverware. Pretty much the only things we took were our clothes and a few boxes of keepsakes and books.

"In Bend you have such a *guy* house," Cloudy says. "Next to the river. In the woods. But it fits. Your dad seems like"—she puts on a Southern accent—"a fishin', skiin', boatin' kinda guy."

I imitate her fake accent. "An' he turns inta a Texan when he's doin' them thangs?"

She laughs. "I'm just saying *this* house doesn't fit either of you. It's like—"

"A yoga studio?" I suggest.

"A temple. I'd never have pictured you two with candles and tapestries and"—she leans closer to the glass door by the living room—"statues! There are actual *statues* inside."

"There's a meditation room, too."

"Shut *up*!" she says, grinning.

"It's true. Now, don't get your hopes up, but I might be able to show it to you."

"Oooh. Breaking and entering?"

"Just entering."

I motion for her to follow me down a trail away from the house. For the last ten feet, it's all tangled brush on one side and knee-high cacti on the other, so we walk single file. When we reach the stone wall and archway at the edge of the property, Cloudy bends to peek inside the outdoor fireplace. "Don't tell me this igloo thing has an underground passage to the meditation room."

"Not that I know of." I go around to the other side of the wall and run my fingers inside cracks between two of the rocks. "A spare house key might still be hidden here somewhere. I'll feel around for it."

Cloudy talks to me from the other side of the wall where I can't see her. "Matty once told me about some natural waterslides in Sedona. Are they close to here?"

"That's Slide Rock. It's, like, ten miles away."

"And we're going today, right?"

"If you want to, sure. The water's too cold for sliding right now, though."

"We'll see about *that*." Cloudy's smiling face pokes through a hole in the wall. "I'm still confused. Did your dad go through a major personality change when he moved back to Bend or what?"

"Nah. This was never him. He had this house built for my mother. She was one of those people who came to Sedona for New Agey reasons."

"They met in Sedona, then?"

I nod.

"Was that before or after he'd moved here?"

"Before," I say. "It's a convoluted story. You don't want to hear it."

More, I'm not sure I want to tell it. My entire family pretends I never had a mother, and I like to do the same. It's easier than trying to understand how a woman who, at times, made me feel very wanted and cared for could also walk away so callously.

"Now you're taunting me with this mystery." Cloudy skips around to my side of the wall. "Convoluted stories are the best kind. Come on. Spill it."

"All right. So, almost eighteen years ago, my dad was thirty-four." I continue feeling for the key. "He'd finished dental school and had a practice with his brother in Bend, but he was depressed. A patient told him the vortexes in Sedona changed her life—"

"Oh, yes. The energy vortexes. Zoë demanded that I have you tell me *all* about them."

"Of course she did. So vortexes one oh one. What do you want to know?"

"Not now. Go on about your dad."

"*Fine.* So after talking to his patient, he came here on vacation. First thing, he meets this waitress named Shannon, who offers to bring him to her favorite spot for spiritual clarity. He thinks she's probably too young for him, but she's pretty with long red hair, so he takes her up on it, obviously."

"Obviously."

Cloudy is smiling like it's all so romantic. Maybe I'd feel the same way if I didn't know my parents' last words to each other were "Grow up, Shannon" and "Fuck off, Ryan."

I continue. "As it happened, the vortex didn't have much

effect on him. But Shannon did. They figured out the first day that they had the same birthday and were exactly twelve years apart, which meant they had the same astrological sign *and* the same sign in Chinese astrology."

"That's a huge coincidence."

"Oh, not to Shannon it wasn't. She believed in everything there is to believe in *except* for coincidences. Not long after his trip was over, she told him she was pregnant with me. He moved to Arizona and married her. Just like that. Wife. Baby. He set up a solo dental practice and started a whole new life. And that's the story of how my kind of boring, nonspiritual dad ended up living in a house in the desert with a statue and a meditation room."

Cloudy bites her lip as if she's now remembering there isn't a happy ending.

"Ashlyn told you about Shannon leaving, right?" I ask.

"She said your parents got a divorce. That's all I know."

I'm not surprised Ashlyn didn't say more. She'd already been my girlfriend for a couple of months before I was willing to answer questions about why Shannon wasn't around. I'd worried that if she knew my own mother didn't think I was worth calling or visiting (much less sticking around for), she'd view me differently—as something less than before. Instead, Ashlyn had fiercely taken the same stance as my family: my absent mother wasn't worth talking about.

What I wasn't able to explain to Ashlyn (or to anyone) is that when Shannon lived with us, life was better. She laughed all the time, she didn't care what people thought of her, and she made everything an adventure. Maybe Dad would disagree, but

I always felt that when we had her, we were the best versions of ourselves. Without her, we're always going to be something less.

"Shannon's been gone since I was ten," I say to Cloudy. "She could be dead for all I know."

Her eyes go wide.

"I mean, I don't *think* she's dead. I'm just saying, she might be. I have no idea. And no way to ever find out." I focus on my search instead of Cloudy's concerned gaze. "Shannon disappeared a lot. It's what she does. She ran away from home when she was fifteen and never went back. Never contacted her family again. I don't even know who they are. When she was twenty-two, she married my dad, but she still kept running. She couldn't stop. Or she didn't want to. She left him the first time when I was a year old. Then she came back, like, six months later and said she wanted to work things out. So he bought the land and had this house built. She stayed with us until I was five, and then she was gone again. She'd visit maybe twice a year. For their birthday and mine, usually. When I was nine, she was ready to come home. For good this time, she said. But 'for good' turned out to be a few months. We haven't seen or heard from her since the day she walked out seven years ago."

"So they're still married?"

"No. When I started high school, my dad went through a special spousal-abandonment process to get a divorce; he could never find her."

My fingertips brush a jagged metal edge between two rocks. I've located the key. I'm about to pull it out to show Cloudy, but her eyes are so sad that I let my hand fall to my side without it.

"Kyle, I'm sorry." Her voice is gentler than I've ever heard it. "It must be hard for you, not knowing where she is."

I want to say it isn't hard at all, but I tell the truth instead: "I like to believe I don't care what she's doing, but I know I'm fooling myself." Cloudy waits, so I explain. "If I were indifferent, thinking about her would make me feel nothing. I don't feel nothing. And my dad. He really is a good dad, but we're too much alike. After Ashlyn's accident, he was giving me all this space, but maybe it wasn't what I needed? As pathetic as it sounds, I kind of started missing Shannon again."

"That's not pathetic," Cloudy says. "Of course you'd be thinking about her more when something like that happens. She's your mom."

People say I look like my dad when he was my age, and that's true, with my height, build, and coloring. But I went through pictures of Shannon when Dad and I were packing up to move and realized that my forehead, nose, mouth, and chin are all like hers. Biologically, she is my mother. I can't deny it. She isn't my *mom*, though. She's chosen not to be.

I sigh. "I pretty much avoid talking about Shannon, and then I get you out here and it's like . . . word vomit. Sorry about that."

"You're allowed. And I was asking. As long as it's words and not the other kind, you can vomit around me any time, okay?"

"Thanks." I touch Cloudy's arm. "Seriously."

She smiles. "Of course."

I no longer have the urge to go inside the house where Dad and I spent years surrounded by reminders of someone who didn't want to be with us. Reaching between the rocks again, I push the key until it wedges back so far I can't feel it anymore. "My entering idea's a bust," I tell Cloudy. "What should we do now?"

"SO THE PLAN," Cloudy says, pulling her hair into a ponytail, "is to jump, swim, slide. Right?"

I stare over the edge of a twenty-foot cliff and into the gurgling greenish water of Oak Creek, which I know from experience is achingly cold. (Especially now, since there are still scattered patches of snow on the property.) "We don't have to jump. We can climb back down and wade to the slides."

"No way. We'd get in ankle deep and change our minds like we did at the ocean. And that cannot happen."

After Cloudy and I left my old house earlier, we wandered Uptown Sedona and bought a necklace for Hannah's birthday, as well as cactus-print beach towels and clearance swimsuits from a sidewalk sale. Now we're at Slide Rock State Park because Cloudy insists she can't miss the natural waterslides Matty talked up.

The red-rock formations at Slide Rock follow the length of the creek on both sides. During spring through fall, they're covered with picnickers and people wanting to cool off, but it's only us here now. I spotted tourists heading through trees to the hiking trails when we arrived, but absolutely no one is in the water like we're about to be.

"Matty's only come here when it was, like, ninety degrees outside," I say. "Not sixty-five. Even then, he said this water was—"

She lifts her shirt over her head and drops it onto one of our towels, which she's spread over a level section of rock. Then, turning her back to me, she slides off her jeans. She's wearing her new two-piece swimsuit underneath the clothes, but still. Watching her undress herself has stunned me to silence.

As she faces me again, I look away quickly and focus on the water rippling below.

"Matty said this water was what?" she prompts.

If she has any idea I was checking her out, she isn't letting on. "Um. He said it's 'so fricken icy, you won't find your nuts for a week.'"

"That sounds like a potential problem for *you*, not me. Admit it, Kyle. You're chickening out. I'll be swimming to the waterslides while you're still up here."

"Please. I've been jumping in this creek since before you were born."

It isn't true, since she's about three months older than me, but it makes us both laugh anyway.

She lowers herself to sit on a towel. Her knees, thighs, and upper arms have bruises of every color like Ashlyn always had from doing cheer. "Immersing yourself in cold water is good for your body. It produces endorphins."

"And frostbite," I say.

"You're so paranoid. I swear, I'm going to push you in, if it comes to it."

"You can *try*."

While she unfastens her earrings, I strip down to my swim trunks and then sit on my own towel about two feet from hers, keeping my eyes on my clothes as I fold them.

Cloudy's phone goes off. "Oh, Zoë," she murmurs, glancing at it. "Do we honestly need a real-time play by play of each other's days?"

"Your sister does text you a ton. Is she lonely with you and your parents gone?"

"She'd be like this even if she weren't home alone. Ever since she started high school, she's been so needy. She snapped up the team manager position when Misty moved to Alabama, and she's my constant shadow."

"Did she at least pass along some Slide Rock fun facts to ponder?"

"If I'd told her we were coming here, she would have." She tips the screen toward me and cups her hand around it, blocking the sun's glare so I can read Zoë's message. Matty seems to think I'm your dog. He stopped by with Danielle and asked if I wanted to take a walk. I convinced them to take me to lunch instead.

Cloudy tucks her phone into her bag without sending a response. "You knew about those two, right?"

"Matty and Danielle? I kind of walked in on them last week. Inside an empty church."

"You went to church?"

"Let's just say I was having an off day and leave it at that."

Cloudy grins. "Interest fully piqued now."

So I tell her about last Thursday (leaving out most of the details that make me sound super-depressed). As I describe Danielle's head appearing from the front row followed by Matty's, Cloudy's grin gets bigger. "He has no shame. I mean, in a church?"

"Actually, he told me it was Danielle's idea. He didn't have a clue she liked him until, surprise! She's kissing him in front of a wooden cross."

"Ha. Now he knows what it's like!"

I side-eye her. "Do I want to hear this?"

She bursts out laughing.

"What?" I can't help laughing with her. "Why is that funny?"

"Your face! And the way you said it." She forces composure as she puts on a frown and speaks in an extra-deep voice. "'Do I want to hear this?'" She switches back to her regular voice. "What I was referring to is the important lesson I learned last year: when Matty Ocie catches your eye in the middle of an assembly, points at himself and then at you, returning his nod might set you up for something unexpected. Like, surprise! You've just agreed to be his date for Winter Formal."

I'd watched the whole thing and I interpreted Cloudy's nod the same way Matty had. "Why didn't you say something if you didn't want to go with him?"

"I didn't *not* want to go with him. Like I said, it was a surprise." She peeks down at her chest and tugs the triangles more toward the center. "But you think he really likes Danielle?"

I search her face. She seems more curious than anything, but I get a stab of jealousy at the idea that she might be jealous. "We didn't have a conversation about that part. She's the first girlfriend he's had in a while, though."

The first since he was with Cloudy in the fall, actually.

"Remember the Redmond High girl he was with last summer?" Cloudy asks. "She came to his first football game wearing cutoffs and that blue bikini top? Big support for Ocie number twenty-one! Except she painted the numbers on her cleavage in the mirror so they turned out as a one and a backward two instead of twenty-one."

"Breanna. Ashlyn couldn't stand her, for some reason."

"I thought Breanna was sweet in a puppyish way. But Ashlyn thought she was standing in the way of Matty and me. She refused to accept that we were never going to happen."

"Didn't stop you guys from trying, though. Twice."

I was in such a fog after Ashlyn's death that I don't know when, how, or why Matty and Cloudy got back together. I only found out it had happened at all because he showed up at my house in mid-October at two in the morning to tell me he'd just broken things off with Cloudy; he said he'd figured out they were better as friends.

"What can I say?" Cloudy snickers. "Matty's a magnet. Or, better yet, a rip current. He makes it easy to get pulled in and I was constantly losing my balance. I could never be still or get my feet on the ground."

"Ah, but isn't that how love's supposed to be?"

"I think that's vertigo," she says, tapping her chin. "The worst part was that I was *such* a disappointment to my best friend. I wasn't doing my part to make her big dream come true that our children would be second cousins."

Now it's my turn to laugh. "O-kay. That's quite a dream to have."

"*Very* specific." Cloudy rolls her eyes, grinning. "She came up with this whole plan. To start with, the four people who could make it happen needed to go to college together. Then we'd get these unbelievably great careers and settle down in the same amazing city. And obviously, you and Ashlyn would have kids, and Matty and I would have kids. They'd be second cousins and best friends and our lives would be perfect forever and ever. If only Matty and I could have stepped up for the sake of Ashlyn's dream. And for the hypothetical second cousins, of course."

Our lives would be perfect forever and ever.

"Yeah." My voice comes out in a croak. I clear my throat. "Anything for those rascals."

My attempt at keeping the joke going fails and both of our smiles disappear.

Every single day that Ashlyn was my girlfriend, I was in love with her. I never once thought about what would happen beyond high school. I never considered that we might get married, or break up, or (especially) that I could lose her in a sudden accident.

Cloudy traces her fingertips over her towel's cactus design. "I shouldn't have told you she said that. She'd be mortified."

I hate that talking about Ashlyn caused this heaviness to press down on us. Because she was funny. She loved being dramatic and saying off-the-wall things to get a laugh out of people. She also loved traditions and being surrounded by her friends. So whether she was teasing with this "dream" about the second cousins, or if it was her genuine wish that her favorite people would always be part of one another's lives, it's still a compliment.

"I don't think she'd be upset about you telling me. And it's cool that this perfect future she said she was imagining had me in it." I give Cloudy's leg a little jolt with my bare foot, causing her to glance at me. "That it had both of us in it."

"Don't forget your cousin," she says.

"As if I ever could."

Cloudy hops to her feet. "Come on. Let's do this now. Jump, swim, slide. Like you promised."

She reaches for my hand and I let her pull me up. Even after I'm standing, she doesn't let go. We walk to the cliff's edge. We look past our toes at the rolling creek beneath us. We count to three.

And together, we jump.

"HERE WE ARE at the cafeteria," I say, with a dramatic swoop of my arm.

Cloudy and I are wandering around my old school after having already stopped at the baseball field so I could say hi to the coaches and players I knew when I went here. (Sedona's season starts a month earlier than Bend's.) Now we're waiting for practice to end, so we can drive with Will for eighty miles to go to Hannah's birthday party.

Most people over the age of nine don't get too excited about a place like Bedrock City, but Cloudy was right about the endorphins; I've been on a high ever since we jumped into the creek two hours ago. I can hardly wait to show her the rides-less Flintstones park. I'm also excited about taking her to the Oatman donkeys tomorrow, and about us attending the wedding of Ashlyn's heart recipient, Sonia, the day after that. The only thing I'm not looking forward to is going home. I like getting to spend my days with Cloudy.

We slow our walking so she can look through the window. "I love it. This is the cutest school ever."

"*Probably* not what the architect was going for," I say.

"You don't know that. All these little buildings remind me of a college campus. Except scaled down to adorable proportions. And with these great views, who wouldn't want to go to school here?"

"You're right," I say as we continue the tour. "Every day of freshman year I was like, 'Three-sixty views? Heck *yeah*, I want to sit in these classrooms for seven hours.' I even tried coming in on weekends, but, you know. Locked doors."

Cloudy grins. "Your lack of breaking-and-entering skills is starting to become a problem. But speaking of skills, I thought for sure shit was going to go down when your friends saw you wearing a Lava Bears shirt in the 'Home of the Scorpions.'"

"Why would you think that?"

"You were one of their best players, right?" Cloudy asks. "And now you're wearing other colors. That has to sting. Scorpion pun not intended."

"*Not* intended?" I give her elbow a nudge. "Yeah, right. You've been waiting to say that since you saw it on the sign. Admit it."

"I admit to nothing," she says, elbowing me back. "You must have been Mr. Popular when you were here, being such a good ball player."

"Oh, yeah. *Every*one knew me." I chuckle. "By the way, there are only five hundred kids in the whole school, so everyone knows everyone. And it was just like Bend with baseball. It isn't the big-deal sport. There aren't cheerleaders at the games. Some of the guys' parents or girlfriends come, but nobody else. If people bother to think about ball players at all, it's that we're these dorky milk-drinkin', pledge-of-allegiance-sayin' good ol' boys."

Cloudy giggles. "And they put on South'un accents when talkin' 'bout ball playin'?"

"Ye-eah, they do."

We approach the outdoor commons, which is made up of budding trees, red sand, and a dozen or so backless benches arranged in a circle. She drops onto a bench and I sit beside her.

"Why did you even bother with it?" she asks. "I mean, everyone knows football and basketball are more exciting."

"That's a bold statement."

She crosses her arms over her chest. "Am I wrong? Why do people care about baseball? Give me reasons."

Cloudy knows exactly what it's like when people dismiss her sport, so I never would have thought she'd do the same to mine. "Because . . . it *is* exciting. Take the scheduling for the pro season. It's intense. Football fans can tune in to their favorite team once a week, right? And each basketball team plays two or three times a week. But a pro baseball team has games virtually every day. For over half the year, baseball is happening, and the more you follow it, the more you get addicted. And with the complexity of the rules and scoring, it turns into a puzzle. Plus, there's so much history. People grow up with it and teach their kids and grandkids to play. It's been trickling down like that for over a hundred and fifty years."

"Did you start playing because of family tradition?"

"Actually, no. My dad doesn't do sports. I got into it because Will's dad coached Little League. From when I was a kid, he said I was a natural. A true utility player."

"So you liked it because it was easy?"

I'm not sure where she's going with this, but the fact that she's smiling makes a tiny bit of my defensiveness fade. "At first. And there was the fun stuff. Getting a new glove and breaking it in, going to pizza parties, having my dad come to my games. There's also satisfaction in getting to hit this little round ball with a heavy bat. With solid contact and a sweet, long swing, you feel it through your whole body."

Cloudy nods: *Go on.*

"When I got older and playing became more competitive, that's when I really got hooked. I worked my way around the infield: first base, then third, then second. But shortstop was *it* for me. Because when you're in that position, the ball is constantly coming at you. You watch it leave the pitcher's hand, it hits the bat, you make the grab, you throw. It happens so fast. All these pops, like a string of firecrackers. When you're quick enough, when your body's positioned right, your weight's distributed, you have a good grip on the ball, your team gets the out, and there's nothing like it. You want to do it again and again. It feels so fluid and so right to be able to create perfection in this series of split-second catches and throws."

"I see."

"You're still thinking 'Why baseball?' Because every sport is about making those moments happen, right?"

"No, K.O. I'm thinking, I *totally* get why you don't want to be on the team this year. Clearly, trying to make more of those perfect six-four-three double plays than last year would mean nothing to a non-perfection-seeker like you."

She's watching me closely, like she wanted to catch the exact millisecond when I processed that she dropped position numbers into our conversation. "Six-four-three, huh?"

"Did I not mention my grandparents are big-time into baseball? And my mom went to college on a softball scholarship? And our family sometimes caravans for two and a half hours for the Eugene Emeralds on weekends?" She shrugs like she's trying to be casual, but a huge grin spreads across her face. "It trickles down like that sometimes, you know?"

"You were messing with me." I try to sound stern, but I'm grinning now, too.

She holds her finger and thumb a couple of inches apart. "Little bit."

"It wasn't nice."

"I'm a mean, mean girl. You took it well, though. Only three veins popped out of your neck. And one more. Right. Here."

She leans close and playfully pokes at my temple. I try to catch her hand, but she's too quick. She hops up and takes off running, and I go after her.

I'm within five feet of catching Cloudy when someone calls my name. At the edge of the nearly empty student parking lot ahead, Hannah is easy to spot—she's the one dressed like she belongs in the same era as the ancient Volkswagen bus she's standing near. Cloudy and I end our game of chase and Hannah's patchwork skirt brushes the concrete with every step she takes toward us. "Look at you, Kyle! You've gotten so tall. And buff. And *cute*."

"Um."

Hannah smiles. "But still shy, I see."

"Uh. Happy birthday." I bend to give her a hug, and she holds on tightly for maybe four seconds too many. As I'm pulling away, she plants a kiss on my cheek.

Hannah and I were never kissing-on-the-cheek friends (I've never had a friend like that, ever), but this must be part of her "earthy phase" Will mentioned. Friendly cheek-kissing goes along with the braided band circling her head and the incense that's saturated her clothes and curly brown hair, I suppose.

"I can't begin to describe how excited I am that you're here for my actual birthday." Hannah rests her forehead against my upper arm. "Of all the days in the year when you could have come, you showed up *today*. It feels so, like, fate."

We showed up yesterday, but I don't point that out.

Cloudy and I follow Hannah to join the others who are gathered between the van and the nearest parked car. They seem like an odd mix, but maybe being inclusive is another facet of Hannah's new personality.

Devynne and Natalie each give me a hug, and then I kind of nod at the rest of the group. "Hey, everyone. This is Cloudy."

I'm about to introduce them to her one by one, but Hannah interrupts with "Cloudy! Is that your real name?"

"It's actually Claudia," she says.

"Then why would you go by *Cloudy*?"

"My grandma was born in Italy. So she has an accent and—"

"William!" Hannah yells, cutting Cloudy off. "It's about time you finally got your bottom out here!"

Will meanders over. He never lets Hannah's impatience get to him. "I left practice as soon as I could. I told you to go on without me. I'm riding with Kyle and Cloudy."

"Well, we *didn't* go without you. Yamka took three people with her and so did Mason." Hannah does a quick head count. "There's still ten here now, so we can fit perfectly in two cars. Natalie, you have room for one more?"

"Yup," Natalie says. "Backseat only. Sergio called shotgun."

Hannah nods. "Kyle and William, you'll ride in my bus with Garrett, John, and me. Claudia, you can go with Natalie."

Cloudy says, "Sounds good."

She gives me a quick wave and starts toward the car before I've fully processed what's happening.

"No, wait!" I say. "I'll drive. We can take three cars. Then no one has to squish in, and Cloudy can come with me."

"But she gets to see you all the *tiiiiiime*." Hannah tugs on the hem of my sweatshirt. "We'll be there in two hours or less. William and I *really* want to hang out with you."

Hannah pushing Cloudy off onto strangers cancels out her friendliness toward me. "Then you two should ride with us."

Cloudy raises her hand. "Kyle, it's fine. Hannah's plan makes sense. You go with your friends." She puts on a big smile. "I'm sure you're dying for a break from me, anyway."

Hannah tosses her keys to Will. "Let's go, then."

While two engines start up and doors begin slamming, I stop at the Xterra and grab Cloudy's coat and Hannah's gift. As I'm setting the stuff inside the bus, I glance at Cloudy in Natalie's backseat. "Hang on a sec," I tell Hannah.

I hurry over and tap on Cloudy's window.

Lowering it as far as it will go (about halfway), she pulls her eyebrows together. "What's up?"

"To be clear," I say, resting my hand on top of the glass, "I don't actually want a break from you."

"Awww," Natalie and Devynne say in unison.

Cloudy doesn't acknowledge hearing them, but my face heats up anyway. "That's the Stockholm syndrome talking," she says.

I lean in closer so I can see her face better. So she can see mine. "It's nothing like that. Not for me."

"Come *on*, Kyle!" Hannah yells from her open side door.

"You're holding up the caravan." Cloudy uncurls my fingers from around her window, one at a time, looking into my eyes the whole time. "Go. I'll see you in two hours, okay?"

"Or less."

She smiles. "Or less."

Cloudy

"Sorry Hannah is so bossy," Natalie tells me from the driver's seat. "I'm sure you'd rather be with Kyle."

I'm watching the bus, half expecting Kyle to climb out and come over again. Half disappointed when he doesn't. My chest is warm from whatever's just happened. It felt dangerously nice to have Kyle look at me like he did, as if he didn't want to leave. "We've been apart for longer than this."

"Still." Natalie shrugs. She puts the Toyota in drive and follows the bus out of the parking lot. "Not that we mind having you. This is Sergio"—she jabs a thumb at the brown-haired guy in front of me in the passenger seat, then over her shoulder—"and that's Devynne and Charlie."

Beside me, Devynne and Charlie wave in unison.

"Thanks for letting me squeeze in." I turn, microscopically, to Charlie, whose bony arm is pressed up against mine. "I can sit in the middle if you're uncomfortable."

"Don't bother," Devynne says, shaking her head. "He always volunteers for the middle."

"It's the safest seat in the car." Charlie's voice is somehow equally gruff and squeaky. "If we get T-boned, I'm golden."

Sergio snorts. "Your scrawny ass would hit the roof if we rolled over a quarter."

"And we are not getting T-boned," Natalie says, giving me a swift, panicked look. "We're not getting T-boned."

Charlie plants a foot on either side of the hump dividing the footwell. "Repeat it all you want, that doesn't make it true."

"Well," Sergio grumbles, "I'd rather get T-boned than be going to Bedrock City right now."

Devynne puts a hand up. "Can we stop saying 'T-boned'?"

"Sergio, what are you talking about?" Natalie lowers the radio, keeping one hand on the wheel. "Bedrock City is a quirky pit-stop classic. It's retro Americana." She says it like Hannah would, with a fake sincerity that makes Devynne snicker.

But Sergio grumbles again. "It's yabba dabba dorky."

Devynne leans around Charlie, straining against her seat belt, to smile at me. "So are you and Kyle here for a few days?"

"Just today, really," I say, but I don't want it to be true. The closer we get to Sonia's wedding, the farther away I want to be. "I'd like to stay longer, though. It's so beautiful here."

Natalie bites her thumbnail. "You get used to it."

Charlie, who's been tapping on his knee for the past minute, whips his head around to Devynne. "Didn't you make out with Kyle at Bedrock City?"

Up front, Natalie groans and Sergio laughs.

"No!" Devynne yelps. "No. Oh my God, no. We were, like, thirteen. And it wasn't even at Bedrock City, *Charlie*." She punctuates her sentence by smacking his bicep.

The car has gone silent. Maybe they're all waiting for me to go full-on wildcat and tear Devynne's hair out because she kissed Kyle years before he was ever my not-boyfriend. It's tempting. She's all heart-shaped face and batty eyelashes and hazel eyes. Of course Kyle would want to kiss her.

But that's not her fault.

I feel myself smiling. "Then where did you make out with Kyle?"

Devynne has this delicate prettiness to her, a little like Ashlyn, where the points of her nose and chin seem like they could chip if she sneezed too hard. All this time I've never thought of Kyle as having a Type, but I guess I didn't have other girls to compare to.

"It wasn't even making out." Devynne sighs like she'd rather not go there, then covers her eyes. "I kissed him on the bus during a school trip to Tombstone."

"With tongue?"

"CHARLIE!" Natalie's glare practically melts the rearview mirror.

Devynne palms Charlie's face and presses his head into the back of the seat. "*Anyway*, you and Kyle are so cute together."

She's changing the subject with a compliment. There was totally tongue.

"Oh," I say, "we're not—"

"Eh," Charlie says, tilting his head to look at me. "I don't know. You're both blond."

I level a look at him.

"It's a little freakish," he continues. "Not creepy, like two redheads dating. But it's unsettling. Like *Children of the Corn*."

Sergio finally moves. He turns in his seat to punch Charlie on the leg. "*You're* unsettling."

They all laugh, like *Isn't it hilarious how unhinged Charlie is, but that's Charlie; what can you do?* The easy way they tease one another pinballs in my gut. It makes me miss home more than I thought I would.

Outside, road signs direct us to Slide Rock State Park. I realize we're doubling back on 89A, the same route Kyle and I took only a few hours ago. The familiar scenery passes by as I finger-comb my hair. It's finally dry after I jumped into the frigid water with Kyle.

My body buzzes, and it's definitely not frostbite. It's everything that happened before the jump. I don't know why I told Kyle about Ashlyn's family-planning fantasy. One minute we're discussing Matty, and the next, I'm remembering the dreamy expression on Ashlyn's face whenever she talked about our combined futures. The story came tumbling from my lips before I realized. And even though I'd swat at Ashlyn whenever she brought it up—Ashlyn with a goal and a plan, as usual—the reality of it not being possible anymore is outrageously cruel.

Two hours and zero T-bonings later, Natalie steers us off the highway and under a welcome sign that reads Flintstone Prehistoric Park. The sun has already dropped, and I feel a pang of regret that we're here, pulling into a narrow parking lot, instead of on top of a mountain.

The rest of the group is waiting for us, assembled by their cars. They're nearer to the entrance—a squat, green building with a Wilma Flintstone plywood cutout at the front door. That's where Hannah is, chatting with a tall guy in an apron.

As soon as I step out, my gaze swings over to the bus, parked on the other side of a dirty black sedan. Kyle straightens when our eyes meet, and he *looks* at me, like he's taking inventory of my face to make sure each part is where it should be. Was he that worried about being separated?

I give him a thumbs-up as I walk over, and Kyle returns the gesture with a small smile. Natalie and Devynne pass, *awwwww-ing* and giggling.

I come to a stop in front of him. "You know," I say, smirking, "being in a car without a black kitten in it? Overrated."

"So the ride was okay?"

"Charlie thinks we're hell spawn."

"Huh."

Over his shoulder, I see Hannah trailing her taupe-colored sandals along the dusty ground. She's playing with a square pendant hanging from her neck; it's the birth-flower necklace Kyle and I bought for her. "I guess Hannah liked our gift."

"We barely made it out of the school lot before she opened it—and everything else. And she made Will drive while I sat in back with her."

I laugh. "So much for all *three* of you spending time together."

"I'm not sure she knew the *two* of us were spending time together. All she did was talk about herself. But"—Kyle lifts his hand; in his palm sit two dark cookies bundled up in plastic wrap—"I did get snacks."

"I thought we were eating here."

"We are. But *we*"—he waggles a finger between us—"haven't eaten since this morning. I thought you might want one. Garrett and John brought them, and Hannah has a cooler full of stuff for later."

Garrett and John have perma-sleepy eyes and walk like they're trapped in Jell-O.

Grabbing a cookie, I turn it over in my hands, examining it in the egg-yolk-y glow of the streetlights. Then I sniff it through the plastic. I have no idea what pot cookies smell like, aside from pot, which these don't. "Minty."

A grin stretches across his face. "*Chocolate* minty."

"You are so predictable," I tell him, then place the cookie back into his palm. "Keep mine for later?"

"GUYS!" Hannah shouts, and we flinch. She comes up behind Kyle and gives him a quick cuddle. "It's time for my birthday dinner."

BIRTHDAY DINNER IS at Fred's Diner, a restaurant attached to the gift shop. The three-person staff—including Hannah's tall guy in the apron—has already cooked up a bunch of burgers, fries, and other selections from the menu. Technically, Bedrock City closed thirty minutes ago, but Tall Apron Guy is doing Hannah a Birthday Favor. The tiger-print chairs and dinner specials like Betty's Bowl of Chili should be a mismatch for Hannah's Mother Earth–like sensibilities, but she doesn't seem bothered.

"I think Hannah's drunk on Birthday Power," I whisper to Kyle while we're eating, and he laughs with his mouth closed

241

because it's full of a Bamm-Bamm Burrito. His expression pins me to my seat.

This is why I like you.

It snakes its way through my mind, in and out before I can trap it. I didn't say it at Slide Rock, but Kyle is a magnet, too. He's more careful about drawing people in, but he does, whether he knows it or not. And he doesn't throw me off center, not in the bad ways. With him I'm stable, unshakeable, like everything is real but colored-in more vibrantly.

Nothing has uncoiled Kyle like being in Arizona. It's been happening a little more every day since we've been on this trip, and now he's so slack. Content. I'm better here, too—different from my murky jumble of emotions in California. And what if being here is how to keep us that way? What if seeing Sonia is just like seeing Freddie? Or makes me feel how I did that night after Ethan? What if it's frustrating and discouraging and all the things Ashlyn would hate being associated with?

Tonight would be the perfect time to ask him to stay. We could forget the wedding and spend the rest of midwinter break in Sedona.

Minutes later, Hannah stands up in her seat, waving her arms. "The next part of the night is about to start, and you don't want to miss it. Let's go, friends!"

She hops down, then slips past our table, tugging at Kyle's shoulder. As she pulls him away, he grins at me. Our consensus is it's better to humor Hannah than defy whatever Birthday Gods might be on her side today.

Outside, I finally get my first real view of Bedrock City.

It's . . . certainly quirky. Natalie was right about that. On the way back down the Sugarloaf trail last night, Will and Kyle explained that the place was built in the early seventies as a roadside attraction between Phoenix and the Grand Canyon. There isn't much upkeep within the grounds, but people still stop here for its offbeat charm. Now I can see why. It *is* sort of like walking into a whacked-out version of the Stone Age. On my right is a clearing of dirt and patchy grass, surrounded by trolley tracks and overlooked by an incredibly fake volcano—but at least the pterodactyl attached to the top looks securely bolted on. Some squat buildings, designed to resemble the ones out front, are to the left. Even with the few strategically placed spotlights, it's too dark to catch the details from here, but I can tell they're evenly spaced. Farther in the distance, I make out a large brontosaurus-shaped silhouette.

The group is following Hannah's lead into the clearing. Once we reach the middle, I notice paper lanterns strewn on the ground. Someone's already arranged them neatly in two rows. They're pretty much like the kind people string up festively for parties and barbecues, except these are all cream-colored and more lightbulb-shaped than round.

As everyone gathers near Hannah, I sidle up to Kyle, who's standing off to the side.

"I want to thank everyone for coming tonight," Hannah begins. "I invited you all because birthdays are about celebrating the things that make your life special." Her hands are clasped together, perfectly displaying the multiple rings stacked on her fingers. "Every year, the Taiwanese hold a festival where people wish on lanterns and release them into the sky. I was so deeply inspired by that, and I thought, what better way to spend this magical day than by giving something back to *you*? So I'm sharing my birthday wishes." She hops up and down, adding, "And I brought a wish lantern for everyone. Come and get yours!"

Slowly, people begin shuffling forward. Before one girl bends to pick up a lantern, she looks skeptically at her friend. "The Taiwanese?"

The friend smooths her dark hair. "Please. She for sure got this from watching *Tangled*."

Out of nowhere, Hannah plants herself directly in front of Kyle and me. "I have some bummer info: I only brought one lantern for each guest I was expecting, and since you guys were last-minute additions, there aren't enough. But here's the lucky news! I packed two for me—one wish for now, one to grow on, naturally. And I'm more than happy to give my second lantern to Kyle." She turns to me and pouts. "Unfortunately, there still won't be one for you."

Kyle shrugs with one shoulder. "That's fine. Cloudy can have mine."

"No. Kyle," Hannah whines—*Ky-uuuhhll*. "You're an old friend, and it's important to me that you're part of this. Claudia understands. She gets why I want this moment for those dearest to me. And she doesn't have to feel totally left out. There are countless other ways for her to offer up a wish to the universe."

She looks to me for confirmation, and I say, "I'll rip out an eyelash."

Hannah is satisfied with this, and although he's reluctant to go, I nudge Kyle away to grab his inherited lantern. I stay behind and watch as everyone picks their own, putting lighters to the small squares at the base. The flames catch easily, puffing air into the lanterns' empty spaces, filling them up and out.

"You can take mine."

It's Will, holding out his unlit lantern. When I refuse it, he says, "You can't just stand here; it's not fair."

"I'm not much of a wisher lately."

His mouth bunches up to one side. "All the more reason for you to have it, don't you think?"

I consider that. "Let's share it, then?"

Will helps me straighten the lantern out and ignite the base, and once it's inflated, it's almost half my size. Finally, everyone is grasping one, the glow illuminating our faces and turning the darkened clearing to a flickering gold. Candlelit and ethereal.

Hannah steps forward again, raising hers up high. "Now, meditate on what you want the most. By releasing our lanterns up into the air, we're sending our wishes out, where they can come true."

"Or confuse the hell out of some birds," I hear Charlie mumble behind me.

"So," Hannah continues, "make it a good one! And when you feel the time is right, let go."

Kyle and I share a look across the field. *These are* your *friends* is what I'm telegraphing, and whether or not he gets it, he smiles at me. Hannah returns to him, redirecting his attention, and he says something that makes her laugh. They close their eyes— meditating on their wish, like Hannah instructed. Seeing them together, even though they're not *together*-together, sends a sea-sick current through me. Sometime, maybe even soon, Kyle will be ready to date again. He'll want to be in love with another girl. And that girl won't be Ashlyn, so I won't be able to cork shut everything I feel for him, and I won't be able to ignore it without hurting him all over again. It'll be more pain for me to wade through.

I've had enough wading. I don't want my stomach to churn at the thought of Kyle with a new girl. He deserves to move on, and I want to be good enough to let him. I want us to stay friends, just like this. And I want to move on, too.

So I press my eyes shut. I make all of that my wish.

"Ready?" Will asks.

When my eyelids flit open, Bedrock City is shimmering. Will and I are the last ones holding on to our lantern—the others have already been released, and they're rising from the earth at different heights, fireflies taking flight. They gleam against a night sky that's silky black, and make this space look bewitched. Like our wishes might really come true, despite how fairy-tale it all might be.

Will counts to three, and we both let go.

It hovers for a moment before leisurely lifting up and above us, higher and higher, to present my wishes to the universe. I find myself hoping with everything I have that it's strong enough to carry them all the way.

I KEEP WATCH of the lantern, tracking it among all the others, until someone drops down beside me on the sparse grass. I'm the only one left by the faux volcano. Kyle was, once again, steered away by Hannah, and everyone else has scattered.

Everyone except Will, it turns out.

"Kind of protective of that lantern," he says. It's too dim to see very much of him, but there's lightness in his voice. "You must really want your wish."

"I do," I say. "Don't you want yours?"

"Do I want a contained fire to take out my mom's doll room? Of course."

Laughing, I pull my knees up to my chest. "Is this how you celebrate your birthdays, too, *William*?" I'm joking, but even after only a day of knowing him, using Will's full name is strangely stiff and pretentious. How does Hannah stand it?

"To be honest, *Claudia*," he jokes back, "I prefer more solemn affairs."

"Then lots of chanting? Ceremonial robes?"

"It varies year to year. I bet you're a birthday bash person, though."

"No question. I am all about the bash. A solid gold dance floor. *Maybe* shooting someone out of a cannon."

"Please don't share any of that with Hannah," he chuckles. "So you and Kyle are still leaving for Oatman tomorrow?"

"Uh-huh." It's one more way to put off going to Vegas, and a slightly better plan than slashing Kyle's tires in the middle of the night.

Will swipes at his thigh once, then again. "When he mentioned it at Sugarloaf, I'd thought about saying something, but I didn't want to mess with his first day back. Especially not after bringing up Ashlyn." His voice is low, and the softness of it jangles me. "But if you guys really are going . . ."

247

I sit up taller. "What is it?"

"Kyle's mom is there. In Oatman. She works at some souvenir shop that has 'ass' or 'jackass' in the name. Nice, right? My mom saw her there a couple months ago when she brought some relatives to visit."

Will's strained reaction when Oatman came up yesterday is suddenly fresh. "You're kidding."

"Shannon's let him down so many times. And obviously, he and his dad are better off without her." He scratches his chin. "But I keep thinking about it, and if she was my mom, and she'd been gone for years . . . I'd want to know. Then at least it would be up to me whether I find her or not."

An image of Kyle standing in his old backyard flashes through my mind. It tore me up when he'd talked about his own mother that way—so unsure of her and where she was. She'd abandoned him, and he still missed her. Maybe even needed her.

If he knew she was this close, he might decide to go to her. If anything, Shannon should see him, see what a strong and good-hearted person he is now.

"So you're telling him?" I ask Will.

He clears his throat, nervous, and with all the worry for Kyle clogging the air, I could just as easily be sitting next to Matty.

I wonder if Kyle realizes how lucky he is to have both of them, Will and Matty; two people in two very different places who care for him in the same big way.

"Actually," Will says, "I thought he'd want to hear it from you."

248

"Me?"

"He trusts you, Cloudy. I know by the way you guys are together." When I start to protest, he adds, "I'm serious. Look at my face. I have an undeniably serious face."

Now that the lanterns are elsewhere in the stratosphere, the only light near us is coming from the spotlights and the tiki torches set up near the gas station. "Your face is a little hard to make out."

He pitches forward, grabbing my phone where it's perched on my knee. Holding it up to his jaw, he presses the on button. The backlight brightens his face, barely, and even the lit-up spots make him appear ghostly. "Check it out. I exude serious."

"Serious and undead."

He clicks another button and the area goes nearly dark again. "It's okay if you feel awkward about it. I can tell him instead. But I wouldn't have mentioned it if I didn't think it's what Kyle would want."

A lazy warmth goes through me like syrup. Believing Will—believing that Kyle would want me, of all people, to be there for him—is a comfort. More encouragement that Kyle's and my relationship is becoming something better.

"I'll do it," I say.

"You will?" He sounds relieved.

"I think he should know where his mom is."

Will's head bobs once in agreement, and we sit together until one of his friends calls him away. "You want something from the cooler?" he asks. As he stands, my phone begins a rapid-fire chiming, and he tosses it back to me.

"No, thanks," I mutter, waving good-bye without taking my eyes off the screen. The sound of multiple texts coming in is insistent and scary, but before I can visualize all kinds of nightmare scenarios happening back home, I notice they're from Kyle.

Meet me at the bronto slide in 5 seconds or your cookie bites it.

I mean I'LL bite IT.

You get what I'm saying.

Okay. Countdown. 5 . . .

4 . . .

3 . . .

I scramble to my feet and squint across the field. The brontosaurus slide is straight ahead, and in front of it, a tall figure brandishes his cell phone in the air. I don't care about the cookie, weirdo, I write to him. Have it.

Kyle brings the phone down and pauses for longer than it should take to read my text. Then, as I look on, he writes back: You'd be the worst hostage negotiator. Please meet me anyway.

My heart squeezes.

I break into a jog, my feet crunching into the gravelly dirt as I bound over the trolley tracks—still no sign of a trolley, by the way—and past an oversized yellow cement snake with its mouth opened wide enough to crawl into. And from the echoing shouts coming from inside it, it sounds like someone has. By the time I reach Kyle, both cookies are already gone, and he's shoving the balled-up plastic wrap into his pocket.

His face is as easy and unguarded as I've ever seen it. And I decide I'll tell him about his mother tomorrow, not now. Tonight he should stay like this.

Kyle's arms fling out at his sides. "I want to show you Bedrock."

There's a couple trying to climb the volcano, but everyone else is gathered by the coolers near the general store. There are thick, round tables set into the ground there, and Hannah has hooked up her phone to some portable speakers—some song about a white-winged dove has played about fourteen times. Beyond the lights placed there, it's hard to spot much else. "It's probably too dark to see anything, though."

His sigh is exaggerated. "Cloudy, it's nighttime in the Stone Age. It's supposed to be dark. Where's your sense of authenticity?"

I examine his gleeful face one more time. "I think the desert air is making you goofy."

We start with the brontosaurus slide. It's exactly what it sounds like, except sliding down the back of an actual brontosaurus might involve fewer safety violations.

After we clang up the metal staircase lodged inside the green dinosaur's belly, Kyle motions for me to go first. So I sit at the top of the tail, and he squats behind me as his hands come down on my shoulders. "Do you want to practice?"

"Hell no," I say. As it turns out, some attractions at Bedrock City come with instructions. And this one is the most important—and geekiest—of them all.

"Scream it," he reminds me, patting my back. "It's tradition. You have to."

I give him a quick glare. Then, gulping some air, I push off and yell, "YABBA DABBA DOOOOO!" The cool metal stings through my jeans, and my arms go vertical, and I feel like an ass the whole way down. But I'm also cracking up too much to care. When I reach the bottom, Kyle laughs and claps for me. A second later, he follows, and meets me on the grass.

We pick through the grounds and tour the buildings. There's a post office and grocery store, even a beauty parlor, and they're all tricked out with Bedrock amenities. Using the light from our cell phones, we find huge dinosaur eggs and watermelon slices on the store shelves, and stone benches and animal-print bedspreads at Fred and Wilma's house. When we pass a squat statue of Barney Rubble, Kyle snaps a photo of me kissing Barney's nose. It's only fair when I get one of him with his arm around Barney's wife, Betty. By the time we're done, we're both blinking hard from the too-bright camera flashes.

We're about to head into the barbershop when we spot it— some kind of prehistoric vehicle, the kind Fred Flintstone has to pedal with his feet. We take off for it.

"What do you think? New wheels for Vegas?" Kyle says, sliding behind the cement steering wheel. "Probably not as smooth a ride as the Xterra."

I point to the backseat. "But there's room for Arm."

"Nowhere for us to play our music, though."

I flatten my palm to my chest. "No more songs about people who hate fun."

"And no more songs that repeat the same three words over and over. And over."

We smile at each other, and this could be it. I could ask him now.

"I'm really glad we decided to come to Sedona," I tell him. "Aren't you?"

He looks mellow, but his eyebrows come together in a question. So I keep talking. "I've never been anywhere like it before. And I loved going to your old house, and meeting your friends—most of them." I run a finger along the stone dashboard. "I was wondering if we could stay."

"Forever?" He's still smiling, and I thwack him.

"For a few more days. Until we go back to Bend. You can spend more time with Will and Vivian, and I can learn to harness my chi. We can spray paint *Lava Bears Rule* on your old baseball field."

Kyle presses his lips together. "What about Sonia's wedding? We'd miss it."

I shrug even though my heart is beating hard enough to hurt. "We don't have to go. We saw Ethan and Freddie, right? And that was worth the trip. Maybe that's why we came to Sedona, because we're supposed to end it here. Maybe we've done enough."

Rubbing his neck, he says, "Vegas was always where we were headed, though. Plus, Matty already set up the time-share for us, and I've never been to a wedding. I don't think we can stop now. Unless you want to?"

He sounds disappointed that I might. It's really all the answer I need.

"I didn't want to rush the visit if you're not ready to go.

But I am if you are." And I drop the subject or else he'll know something's up.

"Oh, hey," he says a moment later, our previous conversation forgotten. "There's something else I want to show you."

The building where he leads me has a pretend pay phone mounted to the facade. Bedrock City Jail is what the sign out front says. Inside, the right half is set up as a common space with rough cement tables and chairs. Along the left wall, there are two jail cells. Kyle directs me farther into the rectangular room until I step up to the second cell.

"What exactly am I seeing here?"

Kyle tips his head forward. "His name's Wally."

The grizzled mannequin is life-sized, and crumpled on a bench inside the cell. He looks about as old as the Stone Age. His hair and beard are a dull white and matted, and inexplicably, someone's dressed him in a fisherman's slicker. "Wally?"

"I named him when I was a kid," Kyle says, slipping inside. "He didn't have the Hulk gloves back then. That would have changed everything."

There's a small window near the ceiling, and some ambient light from the parking lot trickles in. It lets me take in Wally's large green superhero fists. "What's he in for?"

"Illegal fishing, obviously." Kyle gestures at the ratty fishnet hanging above the poor guy; the decor in here is punishment enough, never mind the solitary confinement. "Possibly Hulk-smashing."

"So much for parole."

Kyle takes a seat beside Wally on the bench. He angles toward the mannequin as if straining to hear something, glancing at me slyly before nodding. I watch through the cell bars as Kyle takes the Hulk hand, pats Wally's chest with it, then extends the same floppy arm toward me. Bending it back, Kyle pats at the soft chest again.

A surprised laugh shakes my shoulders as my head falls back. "Oh, no."

Kyle smiles playfully. "Bet you didn't know that move's been around for three million years."

I move into the small cell, my arms crossed. "Just so we're clear, Wally, I am *not* going to any future school dances with you."

"Sorry, dude," Kyle says to him, frowning. "I thought she'd be into the bad boy thing."

This pulls me up short. "What?"

"Sure. I can see it." He scoots over, leaving a space for me between him and Wally, and waves his phone at me; it's our newly invented sign for requesting a photo together, more evidence that this friendship is getting solid. Friends use secret signs.

After we squish together and Kyle takes the picture, I say, "I must put off twisted signals. Boys don't really get me."

"We don't?"

I tuck a strand of hair behind my ear. "The boys that I do like think I only want to be friends, and the boys who I only like as friends think I want more than that."

Kyle fiddles with the strings on his hoodie. He loops one

tightly around his finger. "So what does it mean when boys think you can't stand them?"

"Depends." I smile. "If you mean Jacob Tamsin, I'd say my signals are working perfectly."

He lets the string fall loose. "And if I mean me? For the past year?"

One time at practice, Violet Porter accidentally elbowed me in the diaphragm after I lost my footing doing a Scorpion. That's what this feels like. When Kyle brought this up our first hour into the trip, I wriggled out of it like I always do. I can't do that again.

"I never hated you," I tell him, leaning back against the wall and staring through the cell bars. "You know that, right?"

"I do now," he says, his voice deep and quiet.

"I was just—"

What?

I was just trying to keep a secret. That I was just a little in love with you when I wasn't supposed to be. When any good thought I had about you was also a betrayal. So I hated myself and punished you for it, too. But I'm better now, you see? I wished on a paper lantern.

I don't say that.

I do say, "I'm just . . ."

Kyle's glance is razor sharp, curious. "You're just a vampire? And the smell of my blood consumes you with bloodlust, but you made a vow to your coven that you wouldn't drink from humans anymore?"

My groan is guttural and pathetic.

He keeps going. "You're just a time traveler sent from the future to assassinate me, but I was such a good lab partner, you haven't been able to make yourself do it?"

I jiggle my legs up and down before looking at him. "I humiliated myself at WinterFest, and then I made it worse by being a dick when you came over. It was stupid, but avoiding you was simpler."

"No, I get it." He moves back so our shoulders touch. "It sucked, though. I missed talking to you."

"Come on," I laugh, but his face is serious.

"I know our conversations weren't, like, deeply philosophical or anything. But they were fun. I liked being with you."

Everything about the way he says it and the kindness in his eyes makes me believe it.

Then he swivels, knocking his knees into mine. "And I am happy we came here, by the way," he says. "I was worried it would be too different, or that *I'd* be too different. But it's like nothing's changed. In a good way, I mean."

"Except," I tell him, channeling Hannah from earlier today, "you've gotten so tall. And buff. And *cute*."

His eyes spark. I'm paying for that.

I sense the movement a half second before he lunges, and I slide away, but I'm too late. My elbow bumps into Wally so hard his decrepit head rolls off his body and into my lap. I yelp and punch it to the ground.

Kyle's laughter tickles my ear, and he's shaking from it—I only know that because his fingers are curled into the sides of my coat. His laugh fills up the tiny cell like warm water, the opposite of the frigid, paralyzing stream at Slide Rock. His laugh is something I want to spend time in.

He's so close, I can see the spaces between his eyelashes. We're passing the same breath back and forth between us, and I'm smiling so big, my lips might crack apart. And then, somehow, impossibly, his lips are there against mine, and every other part of me might crack apart instead.

Our mouths press together gently; we're almost not kissing at all. But we are, and I can tell we are because this isn't our first. Our first was a mistake—my biggest mistake, muddled with alcohol and resentment. Even in the moment, it wasn't like *this*. Pure and certain and what real first kisses should be like.

Kyle pulls back slightly, and my stomach roils as I wait for him to politely shrug me off. Instead he watches me, his eyes dark, his hands still making fists in my coat. My wish lantern is floating somewhere above us now, and didn't I pack my feelings with it, sending them far from here? Some must have jumped overboard before the universe got to them. Or maybe the truth is I was kidding myself. You can't wish away what you want to keep. I reach up and put my fingertips to Kyle's brow like I've always wanted to, smoothing out the questions.

Our next kiss is not gentle. My lips part as he angles his mouth over mine. I hook my arms around him because it's all I can think to do: *bring him nearer.* My brain sizzles with the need to have more of him against more of me. Without breaking the kiss, Kyle pulls me up so his chest is against mine, and I crawl into his lap, facing him.

My coat makes swishy noises as Kyle runs his palms flat

down my back. When I tilt away to shrug the thing off, he moves with me and I grin against his mouth. With my hands free, we both pull at his hoodie. He helps me lift it up, but I'm too impatient; without waiting for it to clear his nose, I go straight for his lips. His arms are wrapped in the sleeves, and he's grinning as I help him break loose.

"Sorry," I say. My voice is thick and very not-sorry, especially when his fingertips dip under the hem of my shirt.

He smiles a swollen-lipped, dopey smile. My heart lurches, expands, makes even more room in it for Kyle Ocie.

I arch back as he presses his mouth to my neck, making our hips meet. His fingers flex on my waist, and we're kissing and breathing and moving together, holding each other tighter. The ends of my hair could singe from how strong his hands are, or the chocolate-minty taste on his tongue, or what his skin feels like through thin cotton.

I want Kyle to know. I want to rewind to earlier—how long has it been?—when I should have been honest about how I've always felt about him, because I can't lie to him anymore. For the first time, I can tell him.

For the first time, it might mean something to him, too.

Kyle

Of everything that's happened during the past week, Cloudy Marlowe and me making out in the dark next to a decapitated mannequin is, by far, the most unexpected.

I mean, *I* did this. I kissed her first. But I couldn't have predicted that she'd kiss me back so intently, she'd sit straddling me on this bench, or that, just like that, I'd become addicted to inhaling her coconut scent and feeling her body pressing against mine.

My hands are on her hips, holding her steady, pulling her closer, always closer. I have no idea how many minutes have passed since we started this (five? ten?), but our lips haven't taken a break for more than a second.

I've constantly been sneaking glances at her. I want to see her. I need to. And I'm hoping, just once, she'll open her eyes again and see me, too.

The Bedrock City Jail has holes cut out for windows and doors, so some of the talking and laughter outside is coming through, but as Cloudy rakes her fingers through my hair, the sudden *CRUNCH! CRUNCH! CRUNCH!* of shoes on gravel directly outside startles us both. We detach our mouths and sit frozen in place, listening. I keep my eyes on the doorway, but when no one comes inside after several seconds, I exhale and refocus on Cloudy.

She's finally looking at me, and I don't have to guess whether she's as glad as I am about what's happening here with us: her dreamy expression says it all.

As our lips touch this time, I don't close my eyes and neither does she. She cups her palms around my face while I slide my hands underneath her shirt and all the way up her back. We're looking into each other's eyes and touching each other's skin and kissing and shivering, and it's so intense that a tiny part of me is relieved when crunching gravel interrupts again.

Unfortunately, it's then followed by Devynne's voice getting closer. "Well, it's *ridiculous*, is what it is. We're all here to celebrate *her* birthday, and of course, she has to go and— Oh!"

One phone flashlight shines directly at my eyes, and is joined by two more. It's so bright I can't see the faces of the people holding them. Instead, it's three gleaming white circles cutting into blackness over three headless torsos.

As I'm blinking and squinting, Cloudy covers her eyes and hops off my lap, landing awkwardly on the bench between me and the other headless body in this jail. "That's kind of blinding," she says.

Devynne again. "Sorry!"

The lights jump to new spots in the jail cell: one shines on the fake bones and net hanging above us, another lights up Wally's body, and the last illuminates Wally's head lying beside the heap, which happens to be Cloudy's coat and my sweatshirt.

My vision adjusts in time for Devynne and Sergio to exchange amused glances. Charlie is taking in the whole scene with his mouth hanging open.

Devynne steps back. "Um, maybe we should—"

"Yes," Sergio says. "We definitely should."

The three of them scramble to the doorway, leaving Cloudy and me sitting in darkness once again.

"It would be better," I whisper, putting my arm around her, "if buildings from the Stone Age had doors."

Cloudy giggles. "Those won't be invented for at least a million years."

Outside, Charlie announces, "That was *utterly* macabre."

Sergio and Devynne burst out laughing.

"Hey!" From a distance, Will's voice cuts in. "Have you guys seen Kyle or Cloudy?"

"Both," Sergio yells back.

Devynne chimes in. "They're kind of . . . busy in the jail right now."

"You mean, *getting* busy in jail," Charlie says. "And now we do know someone who's made out with Kyle at Bedrock City. Next to a severed head!"

"Next to a *what*?" Will is much closer now.

Cloudy sighs, and then calls out, "Will, what's up?"

He answers from somewhere near the doorway. "We're getting ready to leave. In maybe ten minutes? I'll be driving Hannah's van back."

"Thank God," says Sergio. "For the leaving *and* the you-driving concepts."

Soon their voices grow faint as they migrate elsewhere.

Leaning in close, I kiss Cloudy's lips one more time. "To be continued?"

Nodding, she smiles back at me.

AFTER CLOUDY AND I have set Wally's head onto his neck where it belongs and slipped our discarded clothing items back on, we step out of the jail together, holding hands. I don't care what Hannah has to say about it; I'm riding back to Sedona in whichever vehicle Cloudy and I can be in together.

I'm about to tell that to Cloudy as we're making our way past a Stone Age police trike, but the ground shifts, pitching me forward. I catch myself, somehow managing not to fall.

She grips my hand tighter. "Are you okay?"

"Was that an earthquake?"

"If it was, I missed it."

I can't keep upright, so I sit on the gravel, bring my knees up, and hold on to my legs with my eyes closed.

"Did you get up too fast and make yourself dizzy?" Cloudy asks.

She doesn't feel it. How can she *not* feel that we're dice in a Yahtzee cup? That everything is too hot and too bright and too swirly?

"Kyle?"

I hesitate until the world rights itself. "I'm fine now. Sorry."

"It's all right. You kind of freaked me out." She takes both of my hands to help me up, but I can't do it yet. I let myself fall backward and she falls with me. *On* me. We both laugh and it's loud in my ears. I wrap my arms around her and shift our bodies until I'm flat on my back with her lying on top of me. Better. This is better.

Strands of her hair hang over my face, and I peek through them at the sky. Overhead, it's a black sheet with thousands of pinpricks of white light bleeding through. Her hair is making fine lines in front of it.

"So," Cloudy says softly by my ear, "what exactly are we doing on the ground?"

I don't know. I don't know what I'm doing. All I can think at this moment is: *I need you so much closer.*

It's the truth. I don't know why it became the truth, but it is now. I hold on tighter. "I don't want to go back."

She lifts herself up and kisses my cheek. "Now *you* want to stay forever?"

What I meant is, I don't want us to go back to how we used to be. I don't correct her, though.

As she settles down again and rests her face against my neck, the sky—it winks at me. It goes entirely black, then flashes bright white. *Too* bright. The stars become . . . superstars. Bigger than the sun. All of them. All at once. Then they contract so they're sparkling flecks, as small as dust.

They turn big again.

Then medium-sized.

Huge.

Tiny.

Then all the sizes, all at once.

"The stars are weird tonight," I say.

"How so?"

"I don't know. They're . . . shiny."

She laughs. "Okayyyy."

"Sorry if I'm not making sense. I'm a little"—I don't know. There's a word for it. For what I am right now. I'm pretty sure there is. I can't remember it, though. I'm trying. The word. The word is—I'm . . .—"tired," I finish.

"We've had a busy week."

I've felt like this before. Silly like this. I was twelve and my dad took me to Las Vegas for the weekend—

"When you were *twelve*?" Cloudy asks.

I hadn't realized I was speaking aloud. "We did kid stuff. Riding roller coasters. Buying candy and T-shirts at the M&M store. A magic show. Have you ever been to Vegas?"

"No."

"Well, on the Vegas Strip, everything seems so close. But once you start walking, you realize it isn't. It's like a—like that thing in the desert when people think they see water, but it isn't water?"

"A mirage?"

"Yes. A mirage." I pause. It's so hard to remember words. "Except it's like, you keep heading toward a place and it stays the same distance away no matter how many steps you take. So my dad and I were walking back to our hotel late. I don't know why he didn't get a cab, but he didn't and I was exhausted. There was this picture I saw later. My dad had taken a picture of me in front of a statue. This winged horse. So I'm in the picture. I'm standing there. But I could swear I've never seen this

Pegasus statue in my life. I don't remember posing. And it was like. It was *crazy*."

I wait for Cloudy to say something. I wait a long time. Finally, she does. "Is there more?"

"More what?"

"You were saying the Vegas Strip is like a mirage."

"Yes."

"And then . . . did something specific happen?"

I blink a few times. I already told her. I told her the whole story. "The winged horse picture!"

"The what?"

Did I not say that part aloud? Did I not say *anything*? What the hell is wrong with me? "I'll show you when we get there. You're going to like it."

"Okay."

She strokes my cheek. This is so confusing. Why did I tell her she'll like a statue that I don't know how to find? I should stop talking. And thinking. Just stop.

S-T-O-P spells *stop*.

Stop. Spot. Tops. Opts. Pots. Post.

Four letters. Six words.

S-T-O-P.

S-P-O-T.

T-O-P-S.

O-P-T-S.

P-O-T-S.

P-O-S-T.

S-P-O-T.

S-T-O-P.

It's *Sesame Street* in my brain. I'm Elmo. Or Melmo. That's how I said the puppet's name as a kid. My parents thought it was hilarious.

Melmo!

I stifle a laugh and keep watching the sky. Every single one of those stars is about to fall. Fall onto my fingers running through Cloudy's hair. Fall onto my face. It's going to happen and all I can do is watch and wait for it.

Wait for it.

Wait.

What am I waiting for?

I'm waiting for . . . something.

My thoughts are slipping, slipping, slipping, slipping thoughts. Thipping sloughts.

Thipping sloughts?

Cloudy whispers, "It's always been you."

It has?

What has?

Is this her answer to my question? Did I ask a question?

She's still saying words, but I catch only the last four: "And I love you."

That isn't what I asked. I would never even think to ask her something like that.

"Cloudy—"

"You don't have to say anything." She props herself up so her chest, her warmth, is no longer pressed against me. I miss it. I miss her. "I thought you should know the truth."

"That you . . . love me?"

She nods.

Her face. Is mesmerizing. Her mouth is so. Pretty. And her nose. Her cheekbones. They're so—

Today she held my hand. I kissed her. I wanted to kiss her, so I kissed her. We kissed each other. We kissed a whole bunch of times.

And now. We love each other?

Maybe.

It makes sense.

I think it does.

Her lips are so perfect. And her eyes. They're so . . . big. I place my hands on either side of her face. It's the regular size, I think. I mean, it feels normal in my hands. But it looks—it looks like— "How are you doing that?"

She smiles down at me. With her huge mouth. So. *Huge.* "Doing what?"

"Your face. Your whole face. It's so— It's like— Expanding. How? How can you make it that big?"

"What?"

Her screeching voice makes me laugh. And laugh and laugh and laugh and laugh and laugh—

"For real, Kyle." She climbs off me and plops onto the rocks. "Are you drunk?"

—and laugh and laugh and laugh and laugh and laugh and laugh—

"Kyle!"

"Sprite!" I explain, forcing my laugh to be small. To be tiny.

Tiny giggles piled on top of tinier giggles. Like soda bubbles. I try to sit up like she is. I fall back again. "I only drank Sprite. I ate a burrito. Remember? And a cookie. No. My cookie. Your cookie. *Two* cookies." My tiny giggles turn into big ones. They clog my throat. I can hardly breathe. "I'm not Melmo. I'm Cookie Monster."

"Oh. My. God," Cloudy says. "It's the *cookies*."

Cloudy

No no no no no no no no no no no no no no no no no no no no no no no no no no no no no no no no no no no no no no no no no no no no no no no no no no no no no no no no no no.

The cookies.

THE COOKIES.

I drop my head in my hands. I'm hollowed out and overflowing at the same time. Empty and bursting. Every emotion courses through me at once, ribbons that are too tangled to separate and pick apart.

Gutted. Charged. Lost. Hopeful. Terrified. In love. Alone.

And angry. That one stands out in the balled-up mess of my insides, prominent and familiar, easiest to grab on to. A flush spreads through me, burning so hot that I'm sure I'll leave a scorched imprint on the ground.

Rolling forward onto my knees, I bend over Kyle. He's outstretched on the dirt, still laughing and beaming up at the sky. "Kyle, there was pot in those cookies." My voice quakes, so I hold my breath to steady it.

"Ohhhh."

"That's why you're . . . like this." I can't be mad at him; I shouldn't be. But why couldn't he have forgotten he had the cookies?

Why did he kiss me?

Kyle's dazed stare meets mine, and he reaches up to softly tug at my hair, coiling it clumsily around his fingers before letting his hand slip away. "Your eyes, they're so dark. But blue. Like that," he says, pointing up. "But without the stars. Your eyes don't have stars."

"Kyle, we're leaving. Can you stand up?"

He doesn't answer, just keeps blinking at the stars.

"You can sleep it off at Will's, okay? But we need to get out of here."

Blink, blink. Blink.

"Kyle," I repeat, pleading, a sob in my throat. "Please."

He grins wide, so wide that his eyes stretch into a squint. Those are the only parts of him that move.

My teeth clamp together to smother a scream. There's no chance of getting him up and to the parking lot by myself. I pat his pockets for his phone so I can call Will, and he cackles and twists away like I'm tickling him. But even when I find it, I can't think straight enough to tap in a security code that makes any sense. Numbers flash briefly in my brain but don't stick around to make an impression.

Panic swarms and, for a split second, I'm sure we've taken too long. Everyone's left us here and we'll have to spend the night and what do I do? I can't take care of Kyle like this; I can't make things better when all I want to do is curl up somewhere, be small enough to disappear.

But then I spot a shadowy movement between the beauty parlor and post office, thirty feet away, and I do the opposite. I stand on trembling legs, jumping and waving my arms, making myself bigger so whoever that is will notice me. The figure gets closer and its—Will's—jog falters when he sees Kyle sprawled out. Then he speeds up into a sprint until he's right in front us. "What's wrong with him?"

"Will, Will, Will," Kyle mumbles. He's calming down some, but his fingers flex and claw at the dirt underneath him.

I start pacing. "He's high or something. He ate some cookies that Hannah's friends gave him."

Will's eyes go round as he squats down near Kyle's head. "How many?"

"Two." A pain twists around my stomach. If Kyle had been aware of what those cookies were, he never would have eaten them—never would have offered one to me. I'd suspected and didn't say anything. No one said anything. The thought snaps at me like a rubber band. "Did you know?"

Will's hand is flat against Kyle's forehead. "That he ate some?" Will says. "No. Garrett mentioned bringing them, but I didn't realize Kyle had any."

"You rode over here with him." A cold sweat beads on the back of my neck as something that's close to hysteria builds inside of me. "Are you saying you didn't see anything?"

"I was driving," he tells me, his tone clipped. "I couldn't pay attention to everything that happened, Cloudy."

I swallow a deep breath. An hour ago, I believed Will was a good guy—a good friend. I know this doesn't change anything. You can't watch over your friends all the time. I know that, too.

I shake my head, feeling even worse now for barking at him. "Can you help me get him to the parking lot?"

Without a word, Will props up a boneless Kyle. "We're taking you back home, buddy," he murmurs.

I'm certain Kyle is too out of it to process this, let alone respond, but as I stoop to help lift him, I hear his lilting whisper. "Not home. Here. Forever."

It goes through me like a lightning bolt, and it aches all the more because he doesn't know what he's saying. It means nothing to him, like repeating a word in a foreign language. Everything he said after eating those cookies means nothing.

Will takes on most of Kyle's weight, but I shoulder what I can. We totter past buildings and character cutouts, Kyle's toes dragging through the gravel between us. I don't notice the parts of Bedrock City we were so eager to discover earlier—all I want is to get to the car, so we can get out of here. I focus on leaving instead of having Kyle pressed against me once again. This time, it's like a parody, and totally unfamiliar to how being close to him felt only minutes ago.

Finally, we make it through the gift shop and into the brightly lit parking lot. The other cars are gone except for Natalie's Toyota and the bus, which has all of its doors splayed open. My eyes fix on Hannah, listless, draped over the van's front seat. My spine stiffens at the sight of her.

Will walks Kyle over to the bus, guiding him inside the large cargo area, and I take off like a torpedo—rapid-fire, roaring, unstoppable. *"What the hell is wrong with you?"*

Hannah must be stoned, because she chooses to smile at me. "Clauuuudiaaaa. Sooooo serioussss—"

"How could you let Kyle take those cookies without telling him what they were?"

She looks at me with a dreamy fuzziness. "He didn't know about the pot?"

The height of the bus forces me to glare *up* at her—it makes my blood rage past boiling. "Do you think he would've eaten them if he did?"

Her head bobs around as she puzzles this out. "I thought he was up for some fun. Despite his choice in dates."

Snickers skitter out from behind me, and that's when I notice Garrett and John huddled together on the ground near the front bumper, holding each other up, but not really.

Turning to Hannah, I raise my chin. "I'm riding back to Sedona with Kyle. So don't bother assigning seats again."

She attempts a sympathetic, sulky noise, but it bubbles into a giggle. "There's not enough room, remember?"

"You'll make room."

"Oh, Claudia, you need to unclench and give Kyle some space." Hannah's know-it-all teacher tone sounds sloppy. "Will told me what happened to his ex. And, like, it's sad and stuff, but pretty lucky for you. No ex-girlfriend for you to worry about."

I've been dropped into a black hole. I'm turned inside out. Maybe my senses have stopped functioning. But all I need is for my hands to work to slam Hannah's wasted, condescending face against the bus.

"Hannah!" The world refocuses and it's Devynne, rushing up before I can make a move. "Why don't you ride back with us?"

"You should," Natalie says, somewhere to my right. She, Charlie, and Sergio, they're all out of the car; our audience. "We can switch you with Cloudy."

"Yeah," Sergio monotones.

"Noooooooo," Charlie whisper-yells.

Hannah grimaces with whatever muscle control she has left. "Why?"

Devynne clenches her jaw. "Because it's a good idea."

". . . What about my bus?"

"First," Devynne says, gesturing at Natalie and the others, "we'll drop everyone off at the school. Then Will can follow Natalie back to your house, and she'll drive him back to his car."

"Sounds like a plan to me," Will adds, clapping his hands once. "Let's get out of here."

"Perfect," Devynne says.

Once Hannah is safely—if a little wobbly—on her feet, Devynne reaches behind her to squeeze my elbow. She gives me a reassuring smile, and instantly, my eyes well up, ready to spill over. Maybe this was all for Kyle's benefit, but I am so, so, so grateful.

Devynne tows Hannah away, and their doors slam shut before I can say that.

The Toyota pulls out of the lot, and I climb into the bus before collapsing onto the floor. My shoulders fall against the backseat, near Kyle's head as he dozes. The middle bench has been ripped out, so the bus has a large, empty space between the front and back. That's where Garrett has crashed, on a mattress and pile of blankets that serve as cushioning. John is up front with Will, who's already gunning the engine.

"I'msosorry."

It's the slightest of moans, but it's clear.

"Kyle," I say. "Just try to sleep."

He's lying on his side, eyes slitted. "I screwed up."

"You didn't."

"I'm such an idiot."

"Shhhh." I lift my hand to stroke his hair, but he grabs it with his own first. "You're okay. You'll be better soon."

"You're staying with me?"

"Yeah," I say on a breath. "I'm here."

With a tired grunt, Kyle tips over so he's on his back. He takes my hand with him, holding it to his chest. His strained eyes flutter shut and I want to nestle in beside him, wrap my arms around his waist, and gather him together.

Immediately, I force the image from my mind. Kyle might want me here as support, but that's all he wants—a familiar face to cling to while he's miserable. To him, what happened in the jailhouse will be some foggy drug-induced hallucination. It'll sit hazy at the edge of his memory, never real or meaningful enough to remember.

Or maybe not—maybe he *will* remember, that I kissed him back with everything I have, that I said the word "love" to him, that I meant each touch when all of his were false, orchestrated by something outside of himself, like those puppets with the strings. And this time, maybe he'll be the one who asks me to forget.

But won't I want that, too?

Hannah's words play on repeat: *No ex-girlfriend for you to worry about.*

As if it's a relief.

I am disloyal and deceitful and, worst of all, guilty. Because not only did I let Kyle kiss me tonight, I wanted to kiss him, despite all I wished for in that clearing. I couldn't let him go, not even for her. No matter what happens tomorrow, whether Kyle remembers our kisses or doesn't, there will always be that. I will always know that I betrayed my best friend while on a trip meant to celebrate her. A trip meant to keep her alive.

Once in a while, the orange light from a streetlamp streaks by the half windows that run around the bus, and the only sound inside is Garrett's faint snoring, and the classic rock radio Will is listening to. Half an hour out of Bedrock City, we hit a bump that rattles the undercarriage, and Kyle whooshes out a cough. I pat his chest to reassure him, but his lungs heave under my palm.

"Hey," I say, bending over him. Even in the dim light, it's obvious how washed out he is. "Do you need something? Water?"

Weakly, he pushes himself up onto his elbows. "Air."

"Will!" I call out. From behind, I see Will tense. "Pull over!"

He doesn't waste any time. Though I can't tell where we are, Will guides us to the right side of the road with a sharp jerk of the steering wheel. As soon as the bus brakes, he hops out of the driver's seat, and he's gone until the side door rumbles open. Before Will can step inside, Kyle shoots past us, stumbling into the darkness.

I scurry out and use the light from my phone to find him on all fours, crumpled on the shoulder of whatever highway this is. Kyle is shaky and whimpering—and then suddenly, he goes rigid. A second later, he retches in the dirt. I dig inside my coat pocket for a tissue, and he apologizes to me over and over, again and again, as a tear drips from the corner of his eye, down his nose. I click my phone off. Aside from the bus's headlights and the occasional car passing, there's not much to see by.

Stooping beside him, I rub his back in lazy circles. I turn away from him. Not because he's sick, but because I can't stand how it's written all over his face, how today has turned out, with us crouched and broken under stars not worth wishing on.

But there's tomorrow—there's Oatman and his mom to tell him about. I can do something for Kyle, something that Ashlyn would be proud of. The idea of it ignites a light inside of me brighter than headlights, brighter than stars and lanterns saddled with wishes.

Kyle

A door slams not far from my head.

The Xterra is stopped, the engine is off, and Cloudy's shoes are shuffling farther and farther away. Without opening my eyes, I know it's too soon for us to be in Las Vegas. She must have needed a rest stop.

I was supposed to do all the driving to Nevada, but instead I've spent the past fifteen hours as this blob of groggy, dehydrated, embarrassed uselessness. We left Sedona after lunch and ever since, Cloudy's been driving and I've been lying across my backseat with seat belts twisted around me in an uncomfortable configuration with her pink cloud-print pillow under my head as I sleep, jolt awake, sleep, jolt awake.

I'm drifting off again when, somewhere up front, comes insistent rustling and . . . hissing? I open my eyes in time for Arm to launch herself over me from the front center console, land at the top of the backseat, and then disappear into the cargo area behind.

"What the hell?" Untangling myself from the seat belts, I wriggle to sit up.

A donkey has forced its head in and is nuzzling a large, open bag of pretzels on the front passenger seat.

"Hey! Get out!"

I lean over the console to pull the bag away. The donkey grabs on using its teeth, and pretzels rain down as it hurries to slip its head back out the window. It runs about ten paces, glances back, sees I'm not chasing it, adjusts the half-empty bag in its mouth against the ground, and then traipses off with what used to be Cloudy's snack.

"So that just happened," I announce to Arm.

I can't see her, of course. What I can see is that the dirt and gravel where my car sits isn't a rest stop or gas station on Highway 93. Instead, I'm near a white-and-red-painted sign, which reads: Parking Lot.

I swivel my body. In the distance, clusters of donkeys and humans wander the street, which is lined on both sides with Wild West–style buildings.

Cloudy's brought us to Oatman. After the Drugged-Cookies Incident, I'd assumed we'd take the shortest route to Vegas, but now that we're here (an hour out of our way, with at least a couple more hours of traveling to go), I am glad to have one less thing to feel crappy over; my mistake last night didn't end up causing her to miss this detour she's been excited about.

I'm not feeling 100 percent, but I put the windows up, grab the keys from the ignition, and head back to make sure Arm is okay after her donkey scare. Once I lift the hatch, it takes a moment to spot the black kitten in the corner; whenever she's on dark-colored objects or in shadows, she tends to blend in.

"You okay?" I put out my hand, which, after several seconds, lures her over.

Her green eyes are open wide and the fur on her back is spiking up, but she's uninjured. She gives a growly meow, which I've figured out is her way of saying, "Pet me now!"

"You want to come with me?"

Breathing in the farmlike smell of donkey poop and dust being kicked up by passing cars, I chug a water bottle and then lift the bottom of my sweatshirt. With my help, Arm climbs up so she's nestled against my T-shirt underneath. I'm not sure it's the best idea to walk around with a cat hidden in my clothes, but if I keep one hand cradled underneath her and steer clear of her enemy the donkey, we should be fine.

After locking up, I follow the wooden sidewalk, stopping at the first shop. Most of what they sell is shirts and hats, which (like everything in this town) feature mining, donkeys, or ghosts. Cloudy isn't inside. I move on—popping into each store I approach, scanning, and then heading out. Finding her would definitely be easier if her phone wasn't still in the car, hooked up to the car charger. Did she leave it behind for this very reason? She has seemed concerned over my health and comfort today, but she's also avoided most conversation and all eye contact with me.

At the center of town, I finally spot Cloudy's rusty-blond hair across the street as she's about to walk into a gift store.

"Hey, Cloudy!"

She waves and waits for me to cross. While I'm approaching, she wrings her hands and steals a glance at the store window. I understand her nervousness because my first thought when I woke up was: *I kissed Cloudy.*

It was immediately followed by: *I kissed someone other than Ashlyn.*

I will always be Ashlyn's last kiss, but she isn't mine anymore. On some level, I've known since she died that this would happen eventually. It still didn't prepare me for the thunderbolt of guilt or my pinwheeling emotions this morning after it had become a reality.

I have no regrets about Cloudy and me, though.

Well, not about what happened between us inside the jail cell, I should say. Once we got back outside and the effect of the drugs hit me all at once, everything became so confusing. I remember lying on the ground with her on top of me. I remember the stars and telling her about the Pegasus statue in Vegas. I remember her saying she loved me, but that doesn't make sense. It must have been me. I was rambling about nonsense. I told her I loved her. I told her that her head was expanding.

What a dumbass.

"You're awake," Cloudy says. "Feeling better?"

"A little hazy still, but yeah, much better." She's become transfixed by my feet, so I quickly add, "I know I ruined everything at Bedrock. I feel like—"

"No. None of that was your fault. They tricked you, and I should have realized it sooner."

I'm not sure how she could have; by my recollection, she figured out the cookies were the problem right away. But my memories aren't reliable. At some point last night, I stopped being able to comprehend words. Then there was relentless shouting in my head. And the nightmares—so many terrifying dreams, for so many hours. I truly believed I was dying, and I'm still shaken up by it.

"I don't think those guys were trying to trick me," I say. "Garrett said the cookies were 'an extra-strong batch.' I thought he was talking about the overpowering mint flavoring. I then ate two of them for a double extra-strong dose."

"You'd never heard of edibles?"

That's the same question my dad asked when I called him. The way he said "Oh, *Kyle*" after I explained that I'd puked and spent the night hallucinating was worse than if he'd yelled at me. Then he told me marijuana usually has an *anti*nausea effect, which is why some chemo patients use it. That made me feel extra worthless, like I can't even react to drugs properly.

"I'd heard of hash brownies and space cakes," I tell Cloudy. "Not pot cookies, though. In other words, I was an idiot."

"Naïve, maybe, but not an idiot."

Those two words sound identical to me. I give her a small smile. "Then will you please forgive me for the multitude of *naïve* things I did and said last night? And for throwing up in front of you. Talk about humiliating."

"You've done nothing that needs forgiving. We never have to talk about this again, okay? But misunderstanding or not, it still wasn't your fault. If a friend gives you something with drugs in it, that friend should say, 'This has drugs in it!' They didn't and that sucks."

I nod because Cloudy's right. Of course she's right. My tension is easing, too, because whatever else she might be thinking right now, at least she isn't pissed at me. "Jackass Gifts." I gesture at the sign on the door. "Oatman sure knows

283

how to name their stores."

"No kidding. I saw an antique shop called Glory Hole. How can they allow children into this town?"

Keeping a straight face, I scratch at my cheek. "Glory Hole. That's a mining term, right? I wonder what kind of souvenirs a person might find there."

She squints, like she's trying to work out if I'm aware of the double meaning. "You know what *I'm* wondering? Why you're holding your stomach like a pregnant woman."

"Oh, this? This is because of a thieving donkey, a bag of pretzels you'll no longer be eating, and a certain black cat who wanted to be comforted as a result."

She laughs, and I want to believe we'll bounce back from this, that we didn't finally fix our friendship after a year only to have it fall apart because I chose the wrong dessert. But I can tell by the way she's fidgeting that she's still uncomfortable. I'm not sure what more I can say, so I go for a Matty-style approach: cheerful distraction.

I push open the door of Jackass Gifts with a flourish and step inside, where racks upon racks of items with names printed on them are spread out before me. "We've arrived," I say, my voice mock reverent. "Personalized trinket heaven."

Cloudy yanks me back outside and slams the door behind us.

"What's wrong?" I ask. "I thought you wanted to go in there."

"There's something we have to talk about first. It's really important."

I'm suddenly getting the feeling she's about to give me another "I shouldn't have kissed you, so let's pretend it never happened" speech. It's the opposite of what I want to hear, but I shrug as if I'm unbothered. "All right."

She loosens her grip, but still holds on to my arm as she leads me down the sidewalk and past the old Oatman Hotel. We stop at a bench mounted to the building, and sit beneath flyers advertising Oatman's staged gunfights. To calm myself, I peek down my shirt at Arm's eyes glowing up at me.

"There's something I was planning to tell you earlier," she says. "But you were out of it, so I decided to wait."

And here it comes.

I lift my face and meet her gaze. "Okay?"

"Last night, Will and I were talking. And he told me Vivian recently saw . . . your mother."

My body snaps to attention, but my brain can't catch up. "Wait. She *saw* her? Where?"

"Here. In Oatman."

Real words escape me, and what comes out instead is: "*Whuh?!*"

"Your mom was working as a cashier," Cloudy says in a rush. "Will wasn't sure at which gift shop, though, so I was asking around while you slept. Someone told me there's a redhead named Shannon who works at Jackass Gifts."

I've become hot and cold at the same time, and it's entirely possible that I'm going to be sick again. "You're telling me Shannon's inside the store you just pulled me out of?"

Cloudy puts up her hands and lowers them again, like she can calm me with a simple gesture. "I'm not sure. But I can go in and check, if you want—"

"No! Why would I want that?" Six people on the street

crowded together to feed three donkeys all glare at me, so I lower my voice. "*Why* would you bring me here?"

"I agreed with Will that you should know the truth. And because you said you might miss her." Her eyes are filled with concern and worry. "I decided to scope things out to make this as easy for you as possible. I was never going to tell her you're here, though. Seeing her or not is your decision, obviously."

Still holding Arm gently, I close my eyes and lean back until my head is pressed hard to the building. I have to suppress the urge to bang it against the wood.

When I was a kid, I had theories for why Shannon kept leaving us. She was a spy sent on dangerous missions. She was in witness protection for putting away a crime lord. But I had to let the fantasies go. Since then, I haven't imagined what it would be like to see Shannon because I've had no intention of looking for her.

Now there's a chance she's a mere thirty feet from where I'm sitting. In the years to come, will I regret not going back in? Will I regret it more if I do?

"We can get in the car and leave right now," Cloudy says. "If that's what you want. But maybe it could be therapeutic for you. You can show her exactly how well you've been doing without her."

I choke out a laugh. "Today, of all days, isn't the best proof of that." Pretty much none of the days during the past almost six months have been. "I don't know what I would say."

"Something will come to you. Or you can see what she has to say and go from there."

Cloudy thinks I should do this, but I can easily come up

with fifty reasons why I shouldn't. Yet there's that regret thing. I might not get this chance again. "Can you check for me? If she's there, I'll have to decide what to do. If not, there's no decision to make."

"Okay. You want me to go now?"

I nod.

Cloudy squeezes my shoulder before starting back toward Jackass Gifts.

As she walks away, there's no relief for me that she's taking care of it; I'm acting like a little boy who's scared to find his own mother. I'm not a little boy anymore. I can handle this.

Pushing myself off the bench, I sprint to catch up with her. "Never mind. I'll go in."

"Are you sure?"

"I'm sure." We reach the door, and I smile at her. "This is becoming a bad habit of yours, you know. Taking me to people without telling me first."

"I know." Cloudy chews her lip. "Do you want me to come with you?"

"Of course. Do I look all right?" I ask, skimming my free hand over my hair.

"Of course," she echoes. "Even if you do have a kitten-sized growth at your midsection."

THERE ARE NINE people inside Jackass Gifts: Cloudy, me, a middle-aged couple in matching Grand Canyon T-shirts; a very short man wearing a very large cowboy hat; a young woman with a baby in her arms, along with her little boy, who keeps asking, "Mama, can I have this? Can I have this, Mama?" And the cashier, a woman with a silver Afro.

The tension inside me eases. "Looks like she had a premonition I was coming and skipped town."

"Let's ask the woman at the register. It might be her day off or her lunch break."

I forced myself to walk into this shop, but now that I know Shannon isn't here, I'm not in the biggest hurry to ask questions. I motion at the display in front of me. "Don't you want to find an Arizona key chain with your name first?"

"Unfortunately, there's no such thing as a 'Cloudy' key chain. Here's 'Kyle,' though."

Arm's tail curls out from under my shirt in a way that's kind of obscene; I tuck it away in a hurry.

Cloudy giggles. "You should have brought her in my bag."

I sneak another peek at the cashier as she leaves the register to tidy up a display. "What about 'Claudia'? Would they have that on a key chain?"

"I've never come across it. But there was one Christmas when my dad got each of us coffee cups with our own names on them. They say, 'I heart Zoë.' 'I heart Nina.' 'I heart Claudia.' I was like, 'Dad, what kind of narcissists do you think we are?' So on any given morning, Mom and Zoë and I might be using one of those mugs, but never the one with our own name."

"Well, since your dad has proven that such a thing exists, somewhere in this store filled with personalized souvenirs, there's has to be another 'Claudia.' I'm going to find it and buy it for you."

And *that's* when I'll talk to the cashier about my mother's whereabouts.

I start the hunt, checking through the *C*s at each display. It calms me, focusing on something other than what I ought to say to this woman who might or might not know Shannon. I spend ten minutes poring over stickers, door signs, bracelets, barrettes, necklaces, toothbrushes, combs, jewelry boxes, back scratchers, pocket knives, mini flashlights, and more, but I turn up nothing.

Until . . .

"Aha!" Beneath my sweatshirt, Arm startles at my outburst. I grab a five-sided silver star. "CLAUDIA" is in the center, encircled with the words "SHERIFF—OATMAN AZ." I hold it up for Cloudy. "Found it! *This* is what you've been missing out on your whole life."

"Yes. A 'Claudia' sheriff's badge. It might not be functional, but it's certainly fashionable." Cloudy turns the display and taps her finger on a "Kyle" badge. "Here's yours."

"Sweet." Snatching it from the rack, I take a deep breath and let it out slowly. Then, carrying a badge with each of our names, I head up to the register with Cloudy beside me. We glance around as I set my purchases on the counter. Now that I'm ready to casually interrogate her, the cashier seems to have disappeared into the back room.

"I can never wear this in front of my parents if I don't want them wondering how I got it," Cloudy says.

"What? How can we be the best sheriffs if we don't have our badges on at all times?"

I'm not doing it on purpose, but my voice is coming out extra loud, like, *I'm a happy person who loves corny gifts!*

"We can't both be sheriff, anyway," Cloudy says. "Someone has to be deputy."

Arm wiggles. I adjust her positioning, but she doesn't like it. "Is that how things work? Fine. You can be my deputy."

"No, you can be *mine.*" The movement under my shirt grows frantic, and there's more than a hint of I-told-you-so in Cloudy's smile. "Uh-oh."

Arm catches her tiny claws into my T-shirt, climbs up my chest, and pops her head out the top of my sweatshirt. I burst out laughing, and Cloudy moves in close enough that I could kiss her forehead. (I don't.) She's laughing, too, as she slides her hand up the front of my shirt to help with the flailing kitten. Arm has no interest in leaving through the bottom, though; she kicks her feet as Cloudy tries to get ahold of her.

"It's okay. I've got her," I say, still chuckling.

I free Arm's squirmy body through my sweatshirt's neck hole, somehow managing to avoid getting scratched. Cloudy takes her from me, stroking and calming her while I straighten out my clothes.

At the sound of a woman's voice, my body turns ice cold and my heart beats so hard, my veins might explode. The new cashier who's just stepped behind the counter is saying, "After what I read in my horoscope, a black cat crossing my path is the last thing I need today. It's all good, though."

Involuntarily, my head jerks up and my eyes take in her face, her hair, the name on her copper necklace: Shannon.

Of course it's Shannon.

Seeing my mother shouldn't be such a violent shock to my system, but it is. I do a double take, a triple take, a quadruple take. I came into this store for her, but she wasn't here. That was better. She shouldn't be here now. Not now, not here, not in Arizona.

And yet, she is. And a part of me knew it in an instant. Even though my conscious mind still can't comprehend this, my adrenaline was already pumping from the first syllable she spoke.

"She's a gorgeous cat." Shannon scans the bar code on each of the badges. "And her green eyes match her aura."

She still has red hair; it's chin length now instead of down her back. She still wears embroidered sundresses and beaded earrings. She's still taller than most women. Poised and graceful. She still has a dandelion-seed-head tattoo on her wrist with "Wish" below it in cursive. She still has a forehead, nose, mouth, and chin similar to what I see in the mirror every day.

Now she's looking back at me. Right into my eyes. Impossibly, my already off-the-charts heart rate ramps up even higher. My mother smiles, and I can hardly breathe as she opens her mouth to speak.

And then she tells me my total.

I keep watching, waiting for something to spark for her.

Nothing happens.

With my eyes, I beg her to not just look at me, but to *see* me standing right here.

She turns away, saying something now about Cloudy's aura.

I open my wallet. Drop it to the floor. Pick it up. I fumble through the bills with shaking hands. I pass her what I'm hoping is the one she needs.

It's as if my chest is being kicked over and over again while she works the register, turns to me again, and gives me change along with a small bag containing souvenirs, including one with my first name engraved in it.

She aims a smile at Cloudy, at Arm, at me. "Have a blessed day, you three."

"Uh, sure," I say.

I head out the door of Jackass Gifts, increasing my speed until I'm full-on running.

Putting one foot in front of the other, all I can think is that my mother has told me she's an empath, she can channel nature spirits, she harnesses mystical energy. Now she's claiming she can read my kitten's aura.

And yet, somehow, she looked her own son in the face and she didn't fucking recognize me.

NEVADA

Dear Paige,

Ever since I received your letter, I have been so anxious to contact you. I am so sorry for your unfathomable loss. Nothing I say can possibly alleviate your grief, I'm sure, but please know that Ashlyn is always in my thoughts. I feel so much closer to her after reading the wonderful things you've written about her. She sounds like an incredibly spirited and special girl, and she must be deeply missed.

Is there any way to adequately express my gratitude? I am alive today when two months ago, I never believed I'd make it to my twenty-ninth birthday. In the days before my transplant, my condition, hypertrophic cardiomyopathy, left me confined to a bed, sometimes too dizzy to stand up on my own. I wasn't sure that I'd ever leave the hospital. I did, though. I'm writing this from the kitchen table in my tiny apartment, my dog Flynn sitting at my feet. (I hope Ashlyn liked Samoyeds.) And in a few weeks, I'm leaving for a short trip to the lake with my boyfriend.

I suppose I'm answering my own question here, but I'm going with no. I won't ever be able to articulate how much this means to me. Maybe the only way I can is by living the joyful, meaningful life you wrote about.

Ashlyn is my miracle, and I promise to do her heart justice.

With all my love,
Sonia

Cloudy

The lobby of the Ocies' time-share matches up with everything I've seen of Las Vegas so far: it's gigantic.

"*Whoa*. No wonder what happens here, stays here," I say to Kyle, gaping at the vaulted ceilings and skylights. "It can't fit anywhere else."

The joke falls flat, just like my other attempts at conversation since we left Oatman. Kyle's face is blank as we make our way to the front desk, and he remains silent while the concierge taps on her keyboard and hands each of us our own room key—thankfully, it's a smoother check-in than our attempt in Sacramento. He's a zombie while we move through the lobby, past overstuffed armchairs and potted palms, into the breezeway that'll lead us to the suite on the second floor.

I want to say the magic phrase that'll *shazam!* today better, but my tongue is too clumsy from worry, and nothing is coming out right. And anyway, there are no words right enough for what went down with Shannon. On what planet does a parent not remember what her own son looks like? It's animal instinct or genetic or something that happens at a soul level. Shannon should have carved permanent room in her heart for her kid, and it should be forever, no matter what.

Kyle spent the two-hour trip to Vegas just as distant, flopped on the backseat of the Xterra, and nodding in and out of sleep with Arm snuggled to his side. As the sun set, I crafted apologies for him in my head while drumming my anxious fingers on the steering wheel. It kept me from checking the odometer and the clock. Every mile and every minute brought us closer to Sonia's wedding. At eleven tomorrow morning, she'll be walking down the aisle in a chapel at the Bellagio Hotel. Kyle and I will be there somewhere, hoping to go unnoticed, but angling for a clear view of the bride.

My nerves rattled like maracas as soon as the car crossed over onto the Strip, as if there were some invisible force field at the boundary.

Not that the scenery didn't offer any distractions.

It's as glitzy as the movies promised. Hotels and casinos and shops rise up on either side of Las Vegas Boulevard, enormous and spectacular—emphasis on the spectacle. Electronic billboards flash from everywhere, relentlessly teasing shows and restaurants. There's a castle with blue, red, and gold turrets capping the white building, and on the next street over, every New York City landmark—the Statue of Liberty, the Empire State Building—is crammed onto one corner. Farther up, a glowing replica of the Eiffel Tower points to the night sky. It was like we'd been dropped onto an oversized, interactive game board. After this long, longer, *longest* day, driving up the Strip felt like riding on the city's pulse—even though traffic was moving at a crawl.

Kyle finally sat up when we were stopped at a red light on

East Harmon Avenue. I wanted to point out the hotel that's shaped like an Egyptian-style pyramid, but one look at his face and my mouth stayed shut.

Bedrock City seems like ages ago, and that all doesn't matter, anyway. What I need to do is make sure he's okay after seeing his mom. He shouldn't carry any of it; it's Shannon who deserves to be depressed, because she's the one who's losing out.

We swing through the back doors, into the breezeway. The entire complex is sprawling, surrounded by multiple open-air parking lots and framed by black metal gates. It's made up of two buildings, both five floors high, that interconnect with the main lobby. The lazy river pool sits in the middle, ringed with lounge chairs and fire pits. When I checked the Xterra's dashboard earlier, the temperature had already dipped into the forties—similar to our past couple of nights in Sedona. But despite the chill, there are people bobbing along the heated water.

Kyle reaches the bottom of the staircase before I'm halfway there. I have this vision of him drifting up and disappearing, never making it to the room. If he gets away from me now, I won't be able to pull him back. When he lifts his foot to take the first step, there's a panicked flurry in my chest.

"Hey, wait!" I rush to him and blurt, "How are you feeling?"

His fingers clench around the strap of Arm's duffel. He's carrying her by the smaller handles, not the longer one that loops over his shoulder. "I'm tired," he tells me, and he sounds it. Drained.

"I bet. But how are you? Really? About everything that—"

"I can't do this right now," he says, tromping up the stairs.

"Okay," I call after him. "It's okay."

He doesn't wait for me at the landing, or hesitate before turning down the hallway. He moves as if he knows where he's going, or doesn't care where he ends up. I race up, my heart pounding, and I hustle until I'm at his side again. "Listen, Kyle. I'm so sorry about Shannon. If I'd had any idea—"

"That she couldn't tell me apart from any other random teenager?"

"You know there's something majorly wrong with her, right?" I stumble over my feet and realize I can't catch my breath. "That is not normal."

"I said I'm not in the mood to do this right now."

"Whenever you are, though, you can talk to me." I scuttle ahead to face him, so he can be sure that I mean it. "You can tell me anything."

His footsteps remain steady. "Yeah, thanks."

"I feel so awful," I say. "Like it's my fault."

"It is your fault!" It explodes out of him, an eruption of pent-up noise that blasts through the quiet hallway, rocking me to a shaky stop. He's breathing through his nose, and while his next words are more hushed, they're no less seething. "Why did you have to tell me she was there?"

My instincts are clamoring like an alarm, compelling me to get out of there. I don't need to explain myself. But now that he's actually looking at me, I glimpse something beyond anger in his eyes, something like desperation. It hits harder than the sight of him running away from Jackass Gifts, and it tugs the words from my lips. "You said you missed her. I couldn't keep it from you when I knew that."

"Will shouldn't have gotten you involved in the first place."

"He wanted you to have the choice."

"What kind of choice did I have, Cloudy?" he snaps. "Did you really think I wouldn't go see my mother after you practically walked me up to her?"

"I didn't know it would end up that way. I was only trying to help."

Kyle inhales a hiss. "Help? It seems a lot like control. Everything you do is on your terms. The rest of us just follow along."

My mouth is full of battery acid. "That's not true," I say.

He's entirely still. Maybe it's so he won't jostle Arm in her duffel or maybe he's *that* angry at me. "*You* decided to stop talking to me last year. *You* decided not to tell me about the organ recipients until we were already in Sacramento. And *you* decided to bring me to Oatman with no explanation. By the time I'm allowed to have an opinion, it's too late for it to matter. It makes me feel useless, like I have no say in my own life."

Everything inside and out of me becomes solid and heavy, and all I can do is stare wide-eyed at Kyle. Taking him to Oatman was supposed to be a favor—to him and to Ashlyn. A way to make up for last night and prove that I'm a good friend. That I'm not selfish. Instead, I led him straight there without asking, waiting to tell him the whole story until it was absolutely necessary. It's exactly how I got him on this trip.

But I don't need him to remind me.

I don't need him throwing it in my face. Not when I did it all for the right reasons.

Backing away, I say, "Maybe if you stood up for yourself, I wouldn't have to make decisions for you. You don't know me. You don't know what I'm thinking, and you don't know why I do anything." Then I storm off in the opposite direction.

"I knew you were going to do that," he says, his voice a low growl. "I knew you'd walk away first."

It's an arrow right to my back.

Bull's-eye.

Kyle

Solitary confinement is the one torture method I always thought I'd survive with ease, but only two hours alone at this condo is making me rethink that assumption.

Despite the exhaustion and emptiness that set in after Cloudy left me in the hallway, I somehow managed autopilot. First, I found our room and dropped off Arm. Then I went back to my car and grabbed the rest of our stuff. I called for pizza delivery from a place off the Strip. I set up Arm's food and water dishes in the kitchen, her litter box in the bathroom, her panda pillow in the living room. I washed my face. I sat on a wrought-iron chair under the dim lighting on our second-floor balcony. I answered a knock, signed a receipt, and brought a hot cardboard box inside. Lastly, I turned on the TV and put it on the Las Vegas visitor's channel, where some old guy wearing a flashy suit and fake-looking hair enthusiastically talked up the Very Best Shows in Vegas while I ate pizza on the couch.

By myself.

I never wanted to ruin, in an instant, everything good that's been building between Cloudy and me. If I could have handled it differently, we'd be hanging out on the Strip together right now. Then we'd have come back and had this whole condo to ourselves.

And the thing is, Cloudy didn't deserve to have me go off on her the way I did. I know that. But she'd witnessed the entire humiliating encounter with my mother, and she pitied me for it. It was all over her face. Worst of all, she wouldn't stop pushing me to talk—even when I kept telling her I didn't want to. So I needed for her to leave. Because now, more than five hours after I ran away from Jackass Gifts, I'm still not sure how I can get through this day without breaking the promise I made to myself on my fourteenth birthday to never cry over Shannon again.

Shannon used to tell me she and Dad were lucky because, according to one of her astrology books, the certain period when their shared birthday falls (Pisces, Week I) matches up with mine (Aquarius, Week II) to make for the best possible parent-child relationship they could have hoped for. After she left when I was ten, I got it in my head that since birthdays had always been a big deal to her, she'd be back again on February fifth for mine.

When I turned eleven, twelve, and thirteen, I hoped and I waited and I used my birthday-candle wishes on her. She always failed to show up.

Finally, on my fourteenth birthday, the day dragged on with no sign of Shannon (just like every other day of my life) so I used my wish on myself: that I'd get to play shortstop for my last season in middle school. (Tryouts were two days later, and it turned out to be my first birthday wish to ever come true.)

That night, after I'd eaten my grasshopper pie from Vivian and taken my gifts to my room, I sobbed in bed at the realization that I'd been born during the one week of the year that should have made me the perfect son for Shannon, but she still didn't care about me.

That's when I decided I was done. I'd never get my hopes up that she'd come back. I'd never think of her, talk about her, or cry over her. I've slipped up on the thinking and talking, but the last part—I'm not going to let it happen. My face is aching from my efforts and my head might split open at any second, but I will not shed a single tear over that woman. I refuse.

Flashy-Suit/Fake-Hair Guy on the television is now raving about the Very Best Buffets in Vegas. I can't stand his grin for another second, so I press the power button on the remote. The screen goes black. I close my eyes and the whole room disappears.

Something Cloudy said keeps nagging at me—about how Shannon not recognizing me "is not normal."

There are logical reasons for it. Like the fact that the changes in me from age ten to seventeen are more extreme than in Shannon from age thirty-two to thirty-nine. There's also the fact that Shannon had no warning I was in town, while I'd had a heads-up she might be.

Both of those excuses fall apart, though, because 1) she didn't have to recognize *me*; she only had to notice her own features (combined with a couple of her ex-husband's) on my face. And 2), even if I *hadn't* been warned, encountering a random red-haired woman in her late thirties wearing a "Shannon" necklace would have grabbed my attention no matter what. The reverse clearly wasn't true. She didn't read my name on the sheriff's badge, look at me, and think: *My son's name is Kyle, and this kid seems like he's the same age, and wow! He looks like Ryan and me. Is it possible—?*

Shannon works in a gift shop where she's constantly surrounded by dozens of items with my dad's and my names on them. When she's ringing up purchases or restocking the racks, does she come across "Ryan" and "Kyle" and just *never* think about us?

And what is she doing in Arizona? Has she been in Oatman all these years? Or did she find out we'd moved to Oregon and decide she could go back? Either way, it isn't all right with me. I can handle the thought of her in Morocco or Zimbabwe or some other faraway place, but not in the state where my dad moved to be with her, the state where she left us both behind. If she couldn't stand to be in Arizona with me, if she couldn't even visit me there, she shouldn't get to live there at all.

My breathing is becoming quick again and my eyes are stinging. I kind of want to call my dad, but I'm not capable of telling him about Shannon right now.

What I need to do is get out of here. I need to do something to get her off my mind.

I push myself up from the couch. One of the French doors leading to the balcony is open about five inches. I peek to make sure Arm didn't sneak out there, and am relieved that she didn't . . . until it dawns on me that I haven't seen her since I was sitting down with my pizza.

My first thought: *She's exploring the condo.*

I search every inch of every room. She's nowhere to be found. A new thought takes hold: *Arm fell or jumped from that balcony.*

There's no other explanation.

With my heart battering my chest, I step outside one more time, staring down the twelve-plus-foot drop. I see nothing below. I hear nothing.

I run from the unit and down the stairs. I throw open a gate. The sky is black, but there's a soft glow from the swimming pools, as well as from lights hidden in the landscaping. I hurry over and poke through the shrubbery beneath our balcony.

She isn't here.

With my phone's flashlight switched on, I go through every cluster of plants near where she would have come down.

I dash to each of the pools, peering into them in case she slipped somehow.

I jog to the first parking lot, then the second, checking every car.

I sprint down the halls of all five floors at both buildings.

I trample the property's perimeter, call out her name, and question every person I encounter. And I do all of this without stopping, until I'm sweating and on the verge of delirium.

The minutes have turned to hours. Panting, I make my way back near the pools and check beneath the balcony once again—just in case I missed her the last five times I was here.

That's when my flashlight winks out.

Stumbling to a lounge chair, I collapse onto it.

My battery is dead. I don't know where my cat is. I don't know how to find her. I don't know if she's okay. I don't know anything—except *I* am not okay.

I've been trying so hard to keep from crying for the past two hours. The past four hours. The past nine hours. The past six months. The past three years, seven years, twelve years. Because Shannon left. Because Ashlyn left. Because Cloudy left. Because Arm left.

I don't want these tears to fall from my eyes. I don't want my shoulders to shake uncontrollably. I don't want to curl up on this uncomfortable chair and hold my stomach and sob and sob and sob.

It's happening, though, and I can't stop it.

Because I am completely alone.

Cloudy

I stare at Kyle's name on my phone's screen. It's the second time that he's tried me, and the second time I've ignored him.

If I felt like talking, I'd still be at the suite instead of roaming the Paris Las Vegas at ten a.m. But Kyle wants me to go to Sonia's wedding. We were texting only minutes ago—him asking if I needed a ride to the Bellagio; me saying that I was very much *not* going.

I don't know why he's suddenly okay with us being on speaking terms. Whatever his reason is, I'm not feeling the same. I'm finished getting into Kyle Ocie's business.

After stomping off last night, I took the time-share's free shuttle to the Wynn, then hopped another to the Venetian, then jogged across the street to see a fake volcano erupt at the Mirage. I window-shopped at high-end stores I could never afford, ate Tater Tots topped with melted brie, and watched nightclub bouncers turn people away at their doors. I did whatever I could to distract myself, so I wouldn't obsess over Kyle and Shannon and Sonia. And I did it until my eyes drowsed shut and my feet went numb. Sometime in the middle of that, I'd decided to skip the wedding—I didn't want to go, and I absolutely did not want to be there with someone who didn't want me with him. By the time I slunk back into the suite, Kyle was holed up in his room. I set my alarm for early enough this morning so I could leave without running into him.

I hadn't counted on him trying to track me down hours after I left.

And he's texted me again: I think we need to talk. I can meet you outside the chapel.

I tap out a reply and send it: We'll talk later. I meant what I said about not going, but have fun.

I'm not sure I do mean it—the talking to him later part. Maybe the having fun part, too.

That over with, I wander slowly down Le Boulevard, the Paris's indoor shopping area designed like a quaint French town. Even the ceiling is painted a bright blue to make it seem like we're all walking under a real sky. I'm peeking into a store called Les Eléments when my phone goes off.

Again.

The vibration zings through my bones. Kyle can blow up at me, but now that he's ready to be buddies, I should be—what? Available? Grateful? Not after what he said to me. I know that he was hurting, but so was I. Why are his feelings more important than mine?

My eyes graze the screen, and it isn't Kyle's name that's popped up.

"Zoë," I say into the receiver.

"Cloudy!" She's hyper, like she had a bowl of caramel for breakfast. "Are you at the Bellagio yet?"

Shit. I was so relieved the call wasn't from Kyle, I forgot Zoë's been waiting for this day all week.

"Yeah, I'm—I'm here." The lie is the first thing that comes out of my mouth, but telling her that I won't be seeing Sonia feels bigger than disappointing Zoë on the information front. Admitting I won't be following through on the wedding would be admitting total failure. Kyle and Jade already believe I'm screwing up. I can't let Zoë think the same.

"Awesome!" she says. "I was worried you'd be late."

"There's still forty-five minutes to go." That's the truth. Despite how hard I've tried, I haven't been able to stop myself from checking the time.

"So where are you?"

"What?" I plug my other ear with a finger, straining to hear her. *Les acoustics* in *le corridor* make it difficult. "Why?"

"I'm looking at a map of the Bellagio online. If you tell me where you are right now, it'll really give me a visual."

"Seriously?" I rub my neck, weaving between groups of shoppers, rushing to get nowhere. "I'm not really sure, Zo. This place is pretty big."

"No kidding," she says. "You can land a plane in the pool area."

"I know. It's wacky." I break away from the crowd, next to a small fountain set into one of the buildings, and wipe sweaty fingers on my jeans. "I should probably figure out where I'm going before I actually am late."

"The South Chapel."

"Right, thanks," I tell her, a breathy laugh. The location was in Sonia's email, and I'm not surprised Zoë would have it burned in her memory. "Anyway, I'll call you later, okay?"

"Wait, hold on, isn't Kyle—"

I click off, then sandwich my phone between my palms, as if squeezing it will prevent another call from coming through. I wait five seconds, and another ten . . .

Nothing.

I'll have to make up some satisfying details for Zoë, but at least she's convinced at the moment. My shoulders are loose, but I feel like there's an avocado pit in my throat.

Old-fashioned signposts direct me to an information kiosk in the middle of the pathway. There's a middle-aged woman sitting behind it, flirting with a guy in a black fedora. Instead of interrupting, I study the brochures that are hanging around her booth. I grab one for Mandalay Bay and Planet Hollywood, and I read up on this place called the Downtown Container Park. While I'm reaching for a flyer for the Neon Boneyard—where classic Las Vegas signs go to die—I spot a pamphlet from the Mob Museum. All that crime and punishment under one roof sounds satisfying at the moment, so I pluck it from its plastic holder.

I stroll away from the booth, flipping through the first few pages. There's a quote scrawled up top that halts my steps.

"I never lie to any man because I don't fear anyone. The only time you lie is when you are afraid."

John Gotti said that. According to this, he was the head

of this insanely powerful New York crime family back in the 1980s. And he was convicted of a shit-ton of awful things, but his bold words make my blood pump furiously.

My chest aches, and my skin is searing hot. It's like being exposed, like someone poked through my dresser drawers and found the things I'd folded away in secret.

All the lies I've told. Today. Yesterday. Last week. Last year.

But that doesn't mean I *fear* anyone.

I'm not afraid of anything.

Any lie has been to protect other people, or help them—not myself.

Does that make me a liar? Lying to make someone else's life easier?

I glare at the paper in my hands. I'm not a liar. I'm not afraid.

And with my pulse still surging in my ears, it's time for me to prove it.

THE BELLAGIO'S MAIN lobby glows warm and hospitable, thanks to dozens of lamps and recessed lighting. I walked here from the Paris, six minutes up Las Vegas Boulevard, and maybe it's my mood, but the glamour of Vegas after dark seems dulled during the daytime. Everything that glittered last night is so ordinary in the sun. Bizarrely, the Bellagio's extravagance soothes me momentarily, as if it's restored the balance.

I stalk past the low counters that line the left side of the room, following the vines that are painted in a crisscross pattern on the floor tiles. There's a group of guests there, probably waiting to check out, but I only notice each of them long enough so I can brush by without crashing into someone. The rest of the room is a full spectrum of blended colors as my ankle boots *tap-clack* against marble.

I'm not thinking of what I'll do when I see Sonia or Kyle, but it's going to be fine. I'll sit in the back row, watch two strangers get married, make small talk with a boy who now hates me, and leave before lunchtime.

When I zip to the lobby's other side, I concentrate on a large butter-yellow sign without breaking my stride. It hangs from an archway, arrows pointing out directions to possibly everything in this zip code—even something called a Spa Tower—but not the chapels. It doesn't matter. If I keep moving, I'll find the South Chapel eventually. So I continue forward, passing thick pillars into a sunny courtyard, and that's where I skid to a stop. The whole area is filled with all kinds of flowers and plants, orange mums and red snapdragons, citrus trees and bright pink bromeliads. Above the room, the high domed skylight completes the greenhouse illusion, and I drink in the familiar aroma, let it fill me up.

"Cloudy?"

A chill trickles down my spine.

But I'm imagining it. It's completely and utterly, wholly and entirely impossible that my sister is calling out to me in a Las Vegas hotel. Not when she's in Oregon, locked securely in our house, and responsibly watering the plants.

"Cloudy!" The person who is not Zoë is still talking. "Over here!"

Behind me, I hear the thumping of feet. "A week away and she's already forgotten us."

That second voice—the one with the grin in it—makes me spin so fast my hair whacks against my cheek. The two of them, Zoë and Matty, standing only steps away from me in between the large flowery displays, can't be real. Am I hallucinating from all the pollen?

"Surprise," Matty—definitely Matty—sings. He's wearing a light gray suit that's tailored perfectly to his body, and the straps of a backpack are slung over his shoulders. He gives me the once-over. "Is that what you're wearing to the wedding?"

His smirk flattens when he sees my expression.

I absorb the sight of Zoë in a chiffon dress, the one she bought for our grandparents' anniversary party. She's holding an old-fashioned, boxy piece of luggage by its handle. Mom brought it home from a yard sale as decoration, but Zoë's been eyeing it for its intended use ever since. If blood wasn't pooling in my brain, I'd laugh.

"Remember when we talked on the phone fifteen minutes ago?" I say to her, keeping my voice low. "Did I black out during the part when you told me we're in the same city?"

Zoë throws Matty a stunned look. Perhaps she was expecting a group hug instead of a crazed girl ready to breathe fire. "We wanted to surprise you," Zoë tells me.

I glance between her and Matty. "We?"

"Technically, it was my uncle's idea," Matty says. "He even persuaded my parents—the guy is shockingly charming for a dentist. And when I checked in on Zoë yesterday, I told her about it, and she jumped on board. Long story short: we got here a couple hours ago."

Two women slip between us to ogle a tall arrangement of feng shui coins mounted on bamboo stalks and cinched together like a bouquet.

"How?" I ask him. "You don't have your car back yet."

He clears his throat. "We rode the bus."

When I glance at Zoë, she stops fidgeting with the small silver digital camera in her hands and gives me a perky nod. "It was so fun, Cloudy. We drove through this big chunk of eastern Oregon, and then through Nevada, and maybe even some of Area Fifty-One. The driver wouldn't tell us, though."

Matty props his hands on his hips, so at ease wherever he is. "Zoë questioned him about it until, like, two in the morning, too. Persistence must be a family quality."

"You took my little sister on an overnight bus ride to another state? I could have you arrested!"

He shrinks away from me. "She wanted to come!"

"I did," Zoë tsks. "God, you're acting like he kidnapped me."

Moaning, I rub my temples. "You are so lucky I can't tell Mom and Dad about this."

Her glance swings over to Matty, and he raises his eyebrows at her, some kind of signal.

"There's something else I should tell you," Zoë says.

A ripple zigzags through my stomach. "What?"

She chews her lip, inhaling deeply. "I told Ashlyn's mom about the trip. She knows you and Kyle have been seeing the recipients."

315

I rock back as if the news is a physical force. *"What?"*

"The dishwasher started leaking all over the kitchen floor." Zoë's voice wobbles when she's panicked, and it's doing it now. "I was scared it would ruin the wood, and I didn't know what to do. Mrs. Montiel was the only adult I could think to call."

My mind is on overload. Thoughts are racing through it like a news ticker, and I can't keep up, so I cover my face with my hands to force it still. But it's already a fight for me to breathe. "So?"

"So when she came over, she asked me where you were."

Heat slashes through me, and I let my arms fall. "You couldn't come up with some excuse?"

"I couldn't lie to her, Cloudy." She shakes her head. "Not about this."

Matty is nodding at her side. They're teammates and I'm playing defense. "When did this happen?"

She watches the toes of her ballet flats on the shiny floor. "Sunday."

"And after texting me a thousand times this week, you're only telling me this *now?*"

"I was afraid you'd come straight back if you knew. And Mrs. Montiel's not mad at you or anything."

"How could she not be mad at me?"

"She wishes you'd been honest about it. She said it could've gotten her into a lot of trouble—not to mention you, too. But she was also kind of proud that you're doing this. She didn't think you seemed all that interested in the recipients last week. She didn't think you'd go *see* them."

My chest tightens. "Is she going to say anything to Mom and Dad?"

"Maybe. But she'd probably rather have us tell them." Zoë pats me softly on the arm. "She does expect you to give her all the details once we're back."

I just want to be back now.

No. I just want it to be last week, when the biggest thing on my to-do list was putting together that stupid gift basket. Way before Mrs. Montiel ever told me about the recipients and those emails.

And she's known about us since Sunday, when we were driving out of Sacramento and down to LA. She's had five days to believe the worst of me. To imagine all the ways I've invaded her privacy and taken advantage of her kindness. I may have had a noble excuse for doing it, but it doesn't change the fact that I went behind her back to get what I wanted.

I guess I'm doing that a lot.

"And now," Zoë chirps, "I can also give her details! Of the wedding, anyway."

Suddenly, the floral scent is too much. It makes my head soupy and my stomach queasy, so I focus on one thing: Zoë. Here. The suffocation presses at me from all sides.

"You have to stop."

Zoë's skin is a little pale. "Stop what?"

"You can't be here," I shoot back. "You have to leave."

"Cloudy?" Matty says it like he's not sure I really am Cloudy.

"And don't text me anymore," I tell her. I don't know where that came from, some dark pit inside of me, but it feels sharp enough, so it feels right.

"What's going on?" she asks.

"You keep texting me, and you expect me to be there all the time to give you attention. But *you're* always *there*. You're at home, and at school, you're even on the cheer team. And now you're here, too? You're like one of those fruit flies that won't get out of my face, and all I want is for you to leave me alone!"

We're both too quiet. Then: "Screw you, Cloudy."

"Zoë—"

"I'm only trying to be a part of your life. Being in your face is the only way you'll pay attention to me—and that doesn't even work. I'm the one who gave you the idea for this trip, and you didn't ask if I wanted to come! But I'm doing the best I can. And maybe if you'd be honest with me for once, instead of pretending everything is perfect, I'd know what to do. I'm trying so hard, and you don't care."

I've started moving, doing the only thing that's been keeping me from falling apart so far: getting away.

Behind me, Zoë calls out, "Where are you going?"

I follow along whatever wide hallway I find first, blowing by a salon, and a restaurant, and windows overlooking the enormous pool area. Air clatters around in my chest, and I press a hand to my stomach. When I blindly round another corner, what I see in front of me freezes my struggling lungs.

A young bride—not Sonia; I tell myself she's not Sonia—and another girl are standing, huddled together, in front of a large, gilded mirror on the wall. The bride is in a floor-length, eggshell-white dress with lacy cap sleeves; her friend's is navy blue, the hem hitting at midcalf. Instead of passing them, I scuttle backward, farther into a corner. The bride's face tightens in worry while her friend fiddles with the neckline of her gown. When the friend leans away, brandishing a pair of cuticle scissors, they giggle.

"I guess you get what you pay for," the bride says, smiling and shaking out her skirt.

Her friend dismisses that with a wave. "It was just a stray thread. Besides, you are so not self-centered enough to truly believe today would go a hundred percent smoothly."

They both laugh again, working jointly to smooth out the delicate embellishments on the bride's bodice. Their closeness is as tangible as anything else in this hallway. I feel it like bulky hands on my shoulders; I feel it until it wraps around my throat and squeezes.

I'll never stand like that with Ashlyn on her wedding day.

I'll never know what dress she'd wear. Satin, organza, lace, cream, ivory, blush—I'll never be with her when she chooses one.

I'll never room with her at college, or help her move into her first apartment, or sit next to her on a plane. I'll never snip a thread from her clothes. I'll never laugh with her again, or talk her down from a freak-out, or look in her eyes.

Or belong with anyone as much as I did with her.

And the rest of my life will be one never-ending reminder of that.

My brain is doing the news-ticker thing again, and no matter how many breaths I take, it won't stop or slow down. I'm off-kilter and the ground is spongy under my feet and nothing is stable or right side up.

I double back the way I came, getting far from the two friends. My legs pump, and my strides get shorter and shorter as a bitter taste crawls up my esophagus and my eyes begin to burn. I make a right and find myself in a dead end—but then I spot the door to the ladies' room. I burst inside and hurry by the row of sinks, straight into a stall. There's a loud metallic *clink* as I slam the lock shut.

My spine presses against the door as I fan my face with my hands. But it's too late. The tears are hot tracks running down my cheeks, singeing proof that I am weak. That I am a liar— not only because of the things I've said to other people, but the things I've told myself. Because I'm nothing but afraid.

I am. I'm terrified of this—of feeling all of this. I'm afraid of the things I walled away so I wouldn't have to deal with them. I'm not sure if I can survive it, if I'll come out the other end. So I've shoved it somewhere, cramped and neglected, until I didn't miss Ashlyn anymore.

But I miss her. I miss her. No matter how much I force myself not to, I miss her.

The stall goes blurry and my lips part in a sob. My shoulders push back into the stall door once more; it makes a shaky noise but barely budges. After all the escaping I've done, I've managed to end up here. Trapped. And now there's only me, alone, with nowhere else to run.

Kyle

Back when my dad brought me to Las Vegas, we watched fountain shows at the man-made lake outside the Bellagio but never came inside the hotel. Now, as I'm stepping into the Bellagio's lobby with my nerves rattling, I'm hit with the scent of fresh flowers, and all I can think is that Cloudy would love it here.

Aunt Robin and Uncle Matthew's time-share is nice. But this? This is so far beyond. It's gold and cream and white and marble as far as I can see. It's hundreds of blown-glass blossoms in every color of the rainbow mounted to the ceiling. It's pillars and archways and extravagant floral arrangements and potted plants taller than I am.

This is the very definition of *whoa* and Cloudy has chosen to miss it.

When I woke up this morning, I'd wanted to explain why I lashed out about Oatman. I'd wanted to tell her that I know she took me on this trip and to Shannon only because she was trying to help me. I'd wanted for us to head outside, find Arm together, and bring her safely back to the condo. Basically, my intention was to try to reverse everything I did wrong yesterday before the wedding at eleven o'clock today.

None of it ended up happening. Cloudy left before I dragged myself downstairs for the breakfast buffet at eight a.m. (The only reason I know she slept in our suite at all is because the clothes she wore yesterday are in a pile and her bed's unmade.) Cloudy has no clue Arm is lost; she never came back during the two hours of my (once-again failed) search during daylight hours, or while I was ironing my shirt and slacks and getting ready.

Obviously, she's avoiding me and I deserve it. I wish I hadn't shut her out. But for her to text that she's not attending the wedding? To refuse to pick up when I call? Why would she be like that? We don't know the soon-to-be-married couple, but truthfully, us coming here was more about Ashlyn than them anyway. And Cloudy *not* coming here shouldn't be about her and me.

Even though it feels impossible, I have to accept that Cloudy made her own choice. I have to stop thinking about Shannon. I have to get through this alone.

Keeping in mind the directions to the chapel the Bellagio valet listed off when he took my car, I make my way across the lobby, spotting people wearing business suits, tank tops and shorts, and everything in between. The sign I'm supposed to keep an eye out for is "Convention Center." (I'm guessing they don't have a "Chapel" sign in the main lobby so fewer random weirdos will try to sneak into weddings.)

I'm not sure if there's going to be a guest check-in for the ceremony, or if attendees will have to show invitations to be allowed in. No matter what happens, though, whether I'm able to witness the wedding or not, I just want to catch one glimpse of Sonia. I want to know without a doubt that she's happy on this day, which was made possible with the help of her seventeen-year-old heart.

As I approach the far end of the lobby and walk past a fountain designed with cherubs on pillars, the fragrance in the air becomes even more noticeable, and strong incense now competes with the flowers. I slow my steps to stare ahead into the huge indoor garden spread before me. The theme is entirely Asian, with a gazebo, paper lanterns hanging everywhere, bamboo stalks shooting toward the domed-glass ceiling, and . . .

Two life-sized panda bears constructed from flowers and leaves!

I don't believe in fate, but coming across plant sculptures of Ashlyn's favorite animal at this time when she's so very much on my mind makes me glad I'm here.

Stepping into the garden for a closer look, I breathe deeply and stand perfectly still, taking it all in.

Beside me, Matty says, "Ashlyn would have loved this."

My words come without thought. "I know."

Then I turn and gape at my cousin.

"It's rad that they have the Chinese New Year decorations up." There's worry in Matty's eyes, but his lips are upturned. "Except, I don't know about you, but I'm fighting a *serious* urge to hug that baby panda. I don't even care that it's made of flowers."

And just like that, I'm fighting a serious urge to hug him. "Matty. Holy crap!"

"I know, I know. I get that this is yours and Cloudy's deal and you're pissed that I'm—"

"No!" I shake my head. "I'm not pissed."

He drops his hands. "You're not? Because I have, like, a whole argument ready if necessary."

"Not necessary."

"Really?"

"Really."

Of all the places in the world that either of us could be right now, we both ended up in Bellagio Las Vegas. Somehow, he managed to show up when I needed someone. And now I'm not alone.

Matty breaks into a grin. "I'm tempted to check you for a fever, but I'll just go with it instead." He lightly punches my arm. "Hey, Zo! Look who I found."

Ten feet away, Cloudy's sister has on a red ruffled dress and is resting her elbows on a fence. She glances up and, spotting us together, grabs the very old suitcase at her feet. The way her shoulders are hunched gives me a clue that either it's much heavier than it looks, or she's not as enthused as Matty.

"This is such an amazing surprise," I say as Zoë comes to stand beside us.

"Aaaand we've officially arrived in Backward Land." Matty is still grinning as he bounces on the balls of his feet. "It's a magical place where my cousin is happy to see us, and your sister wants to cut our hearts out with a spoon."

Zoë gasps and looks around, as if Matty was shouting curse

words in front of the three little kids running past. Her voice is hushed and urgent. "You shouldn't say stuff like that where Sonia or her family might hear you."

For a second, Matty falls silent, mulling it over. Then: "Oh, shit! I wasn't even thinking about"—he lowers his voice—"*the heart thing*. I was quoting a movie."

She lifts her eyebrows high over the top of her glasses.

"I swear!"

I want to grill Matty about when it was that he talked to Cloudy and what she told him, but he isn't ready to let Zoë's scolding go. "You've seen the Robin Hood movie that's always on TV, right?" he asks us. "*Robin Hood: Prince of Thieves*? It takes place in England, but Robin Hood sounds American because Kevin Costner couldn't get the accent right."

Zoë shakes her head, but I nod.

"Well, there's this one part. It's classic. Professor Snape—as the evil Sheriff of Nottingham—gets slashed across the face with a knife by Robin Hood. So he yells, 'I'm going to cut your *you-know-what* out with a spoon!'"

"'You-know-what'?" Zoë asks. "That's what he yells?"

Matty heaves a playful sigh. "No. It's that one word, which starts with an *h* and rhymes with *dart*. Can you please try to keep up?"

She giggles, almost against her will, it seems. "I read somewhere that modern American accents are more similar to Old English than modern English accents. So it's possible Kevin Costner was the actor in that movie who spoke most authentically."

Matty's jaw drops and he turns to me. "Wow. This is what

this girl does. Turns a person's whole world upside down. We were by the little pond around the corner and she told me 'koi' *isn't* the Japanese word for *goldfish*. They're two totally different kinds of fish. Who knew?"

I clear my throat, anxious to steer the conversation back to where it started. "So, you were saying you talked to Cloudy?"

Zoë deflates again, and Matty shoots me a look, like that's the one question I shouldn't have asked.

"What's going on?" I ask.

"Cloudy isn't the best at handling surprises. That's *all* that's going on," Matty says, firmly. "It's something we'll need to keep in mind the next time we take a Greyhound bus adventure behind her back. I do have to give her credit for the dramatic exit, though. The flowers wilted in terror."

"Are you saying you saw her? Here in the Bellagio?"

"Here in this very conservatory," Zoë says. "Five minutes before you walked in."

"Don't you love being able to say we're *in the conservatory*?" Matty asks. "It's like the game of Clue, except it's our lives. I accuse Miss Cloudy Marlowe of committing the crime. In the conservatory. With the spoon."

Zoë rolls her eyes, but a hint of a smile has returned.

"And Cloudy's coming to the wedding now?" I ask.

"What do you mean, 'now'?" Matty rests his hand on Zoë's shoulder. "Isn't that the whole point? We're *all* going."

Behind them, a streak of white catches my eye. A woman in a long wedding dress is walking beside a man in a navy-blue tuxedo. While their wedding party (three women in matching navy-blue dresses and three men in tuxes) stays out of the way, a photographer directs the couple to pose in front of the bridge.

I nod in their direction. "Hey, you don't think that could be *them*, do you?"

"It isn't," Zoë says, shaking her head. "Mrs. Montiel showed me a picture the other day, and Sonia has a darker complexion."

Matty lifts his sleeve to peek at his watch. "About twenty-five minutes until the wedding. We should check out the seating situation at the chapel."

"You guys go ahead." Zoë gestures toward the outer perimeter of the garden. "The World's Largest Chocolate Fountain is over there, and I want photos of it."

"And you'll come find us right after?" Matty asks.

Tracing a curlicue on the floor with one of her glossy black shoes, she shrugs.

"If you're not there in fifteen minutes, I'm hunting you down. In fact"—he holds out his hand—"give me one of your dirty socks, so I'll have it ready for the hounds."

She snorts. "I'm not giving you a sock, you sicko. But I'll be there."

Then, swinging her suitcase, she walks away.

MATTY AND I set out together, and start down the long hallway I was preparing to take before I got distracted by the pandas in the conservatory.

About a minute into our stroll, Matty says, "I've only ever seen Cloudy go off on, like, soccer players and miscellaneous douchebags the way she was going off on poor Zoë. And she's wearing jeans. To a wedding. What is *up* with her today?"

"Not sure. What was she saying to Zoë?"

"'Go away!' 'Stop texting me!' I had to avoid eye contact so she couldn't turn me to stone." He shakes his head like he's undoing the memory. "Why did you guys come here separately?"

I want to explain everything, but since we're going to be running into Cloudy at the chapel soon, this isn't the time to get into it. "I actually haven't seen her since last night. She needs space from me, I think. Anyway, how was *your* week? Why'd you take the bus instead of driving?"

Halting abruptly, he lets his head fall back so he's staring at the elaborate light fixture above us. "Either because my parents love me, as they claim, or because they curse the day I was born. I'm leaning toward option two."

"Meaning?"

He expels a half sigh, half groan and resumes walking. "Meaning, I got a ticket on the pass on Sunday for 'driving too fast under the conditions.' It was completely bogus and I'm going to fight it. In the meantime, my car's in purgatory. *Again.* I'm sure Danielle's going to get sick of driving me around."

We continue following the signs, and turn down an even longer hallway where sections of marble flooring now border patterned burgundy carpeting. "Danielle didn't mind you taking off with another girl for a few days?"

"Of course not," he says. "I mean, I didn't ask her permission, but everyone knows it would never be like that with Zo and me."

"Because she's Cloudy's little sister?"

"Because she's practically mine. But sure, there's that, too." Matty laughs. "Oh, man. Can you even *imagine* the many ways Cloudy would murder me if I ever did anything with Zoë?"

Maybe in as many ways as he'll want to murder me when he finds out what I did with Cloudy?

After the accidental kiss at last year's WinterFest, I would have been okay with telling Matty. I figured he'd understand that Cloudy had had way too much to drink and got confused. But the kisses with her the other night *did* mean something, which is a different situation. Even if Matty thinks they're better as friends, that doesn't mean he'd ever want me to be with her.

The Wedding Chapel sign is now in sight, as well as dozens and dozens of people all dressed up and chatting in small groups outside the closed doors.

"It's our lucky day," Matty says, rubbing his hands together. "Blending into this mess is going to be *cake*."

I follow him to roughly the center of the action and scan the area for Cloudy. Then the doors push open from the inside. A woman wearing a pink dress and a name tag steps out and projects her voice to announce: "Welcome! The invited guests of Sonia Jimenez and Francisco 'Paco' Peña Rivera may now be seated in the South Chapel."

Adrenaline floods through me, like the moment when Cloudy and I saw Ethan walking toward us after his play. This is real. *Sonia* is real. It's all about to happen, but there's no sign of Cloudy.

The crowd trickle through the entrance, so Matty and I shuffle along with them. Inside the first set of doors is a waiting room with glass tables and cushioned chairs arranged against the walls. In the center of the room sit two upholstered couch-type pieces, which remind me of four-leafed clovers. At the next set of doors, which leads to the actual chapel, three guys in black tuxes and coral bow ties are greeting each and every guest with handshakes, hugs, and conversation while harp music plays through the sound system.

Matty and I wander to a table at the corner of the waiting room. He slides off his backpack and we sit across from each other. Here, we have a good view of everyone coming in, but no one will pay attention to us. Or so I hope.

"Which one is marrying Sonia, do you think?" I ask.

"Hmm." He studies the tuxedoed men. "I'm guessing the older guy must be his dad. Or her dad. The one on the left has to be the best man; no woman's going to marry a dude with that mullet. So that leaves the nervous-looking one everyone keeps congratulating." He pokes my arm. "Imagine how much more nervous he'd be if he knew you were here."

"Me?"

"Come on. You've heard people say there's a connection between a person's heart and their soul, right?"

"So?"

"So, his fiancée's heart was *in love* with you, Kyle." He grins. "Maybe he'd be afraid it still is."

"Oh, jeez. I doubt that."

Matty clasps his hands together and sets them on the table-top. "Are you going to tell me the truth about what happened with you and Cloudy?"

"What did she say happened?"

"You made out and now things are weird."

My mouth falls open. "She told you that?"

"Nah. That was just my theory. Which you've now proven. Cloudy said nothing about you. It was as if she's suddenly taking this trip by herself and you don't exist. What's that about? Why did she need space?"

I survey the room. A number of guests are milling around, and the presumed best man is helping an elderly woman into the chapel, but there's still no Cloudy. "We had an argument last night," I tell Matty.

"And?"

"And I don't know. Everything's messed up." I try to make sense of the misshapen brown-circle pattern on the carpet. There's no sense to be made from it. "Maybe this is too weird and you don't want to hear about . . . stuff with Cloudy and me."

"Sometimes it's like you don't know me at all," Matty says. "Zoë and I were talking and she told me she's suspected for a long time that Cloudy has feelings for you. And suddenly, a whole lot of things became a whole lot clearer."

I flash back to Bedrock City, to me lying on the ground with Cloudy. I was saying strange things. I imagined she was saying even stranger things. Maybe I wasn't imagining it? "Matty, I don't think—"

"It's *okay*. Whatever's going on, I can handle it, all right? You talk and I'll listen."

So I do. I sum up Sacramento, Los Angeles, Santa Monica, and Palm Springs. I tell him about Cloudy and me in Sedona and Bedrock City. About kissing and cookies and hallucinations. The more I say, the wider his eyes get and the closer he leans in to listen.

When I get to the part after I woke up in Oatman and Cloudy confessed the reason she'd taken me there, he can't keep quiet anymore. "Are you serious? Was Shannon really there?"

"She really was."

"Holy. *Fuck*." We both check that no one's paying attention to us. "What did she say when she saw you?"

"She . . . didn't recognize me. She had no clue. And I didn't tell her. I just wanted out of that store and away from that town."

"Seriously?"

"Yeah." I hurry to give him the details about my argument with Cloudy, and wrap up the story with, "And now I haven't seen or heard from Cloudy since then—except for texts saying to have fun at the wedding without her."

"Shit," he says.

I set my elbows on the table and rub my temples. Telling him has sucked the life out of me.

"Does Uncle Ryan know about your mom yet?" he asks.

I shake my head. "It's too humiliating. I should have seen it coming. I should have known Shannon wouldn't know me. That she wouldn't care. There's something about me that makes people want to leave. I think karma is real and I have the bad kind. My mom. Ashlyn. Cloudy. Even my cat. Last night, she jumped off the fricken *balcony* and disappeared."

Matty shifts so his back is very straight. His voice comes out quiet yet fierce. "Okay, I'm going to call bullshit right now.

Ashlyn had no choice and Cloudy needed a break for a few hours. That leaves Shannon and your cat. There's no nice way to say this part: your mom walked out on you. She did. She's the worst."

"Is she, though? I mean, she was perfectly polite to me. Friendly, even. Maybe she's a good person."

He lets his shoulders slouch again and softens his tone. "Maybe. Maybe she's a *great* person. But she is neither good nor great as your parent. You know who is, though?"

I do know: my dad, who has never left me and who never will—not as long as he has the option.

Matty answers his own question. "You're always going to have your dad, Kyle. And me. And the rest of our family. Cloudy, too, once you work things out. None of us are going anywhere. Got it?"

I nod, even though him throwing Cloudy into the mix might weaken his argument. Still, it's comforting and I hope it's true. "Thanks."

"No problem. Plus, I'm totally the Cat Whisperer. Hercules jumped down our chimney once as a kitten and I managed to find him all on my own. So don't worry about your cat. When the wedding's over, we'll head back and I'll find her. Now, can I have your phone?"

"Why?"

"Because I want to check something. Unless you have a bunch of dick pics. In which case, never mind."

I fish the phone from my pocket and hand it over.

After several seconds of tapping, he says, "Just as I suspected."

He turns the screen to reveal the picture he's pulled up of Cloudy and me in Bedrock City Jail, laughing like dorks beside Wally the mannequin. "You're happy here. You and Cloudy were having actual fun. Do you have any idea how long it's been since I've seen either of you like that?"

I don't respond, but we both know it was shortly before Ashlyn's accident.

"What this past week helped me figure out," Matty says, "is that me sending you links to life-coaching seminars and trying to force you to be happy doesn't work. It's never going to work. I want us to hang out and play on the team together, but me wanting it isn't enough. You have to want it, too. And I get that you need time to do that."

I look down at my hands on the table. "I haven't been able to figure out how to get back to my normal self. But I want to. When you saw me at Danielle's church, it was because I was looking for a sign that Ashlyn still exists in this world somehow. The kitten with black fur and green eyes sleeping on my car seemed like an answer from the universe."

"Dude. Those might be the most un-Kyle-like words you've ever spoken."

Hearing the smile in Matty's voice, I lift my head. "I know. It's bizarre." I run my hand over my hair. "And now I've seen three of the people who have parts of Ashlyn living inside them. It's really cool. I still wish she was with us, though."

There's a pause. "I know you've heard this before," Matty says, "but Ashlyn *is* with us in a way. She'll always be the girl who could beat me at Horse with tricky under-the-thigh shots.

Who always ordered double cheeseburgers without the burger, which confused the crap out of the people working drive-through. She'll always be the first girl you loved. Just because she isn't here now doesn't change the fact that she *was*."

He's right; I've heard it before. And like "She's in a better place" and "She's looking down from heaven," it always pissed me off. It doesn't today, though. Maybe I'm finally ready to accept that while memories aren't everything, they aren't nothing, either.

Matty murmurs, "Uh-oh."

I turn to follow his stare.

Sonia's fiancé's eyes are locked right on us. And with a determined stride, he's coming our way.

Cloudy

I forgot that crying for five minutes straight feels like getting beaned between the eyes by a volleyball. It's been a while, I guess.

Tearing off some tissue from the roll, I blow my nose. A good, intense weep is supposed to be cathartic, but it just seems like that hole inside me—the one I've been stuffing with other things to dull the pain of losing Ashlyn—is now drained and dusty and hungry for more space.

Through the stall door, I hear the clacking of heels on the ceramic tiles and straighten up. Somehow, miraculously, the bathroom stayed empty while I was falling apart. As if Ashlyn arranged it that way. Like she was up there thinking *Finally*, and pulled some strings to give me privacy. The thought of her being anywhere other than with me makes my eyes fill again. I don't bother wiping the fresh tears away.

But I do get to my feet and unlatch the lock and step out. I'm not sure anyone will come looking for me after how I acted in the greenhouse room, but I need to clean myself up. I walk past the other stalls to where the sinks stand parallel to each other on either side. The woman with the clacking heels is at one of the granite counters. She's a bride. *Another* bride. Not the one I saw in the hallway, thankfully, but this place must be swarming with them. This bride is on her own, her white A-line dress skimming the floor as she carefully adjusts a headband made of crystal garland in her thick, dark hair.

When she spots me, she stiffens and blinks at me. She probably didn't expect to find another person in here.

"I'll be out in a minute," I mumble, in case I've barged in on her pre-wedding ritual, moving to the row of sinks opposite her.

I glance into one of the oval mirrors, and it's confirmed: I also *look* like I got beaned with a volleyball—maybe one that was set on fire first. The area around my eyes is swollen, and the rest of my face has the unmistakable blotchiness of someone post-meltdown. Fantastic.

On a sigh, I swipe my fingers under the faucet to activate the motion sensor, then cup my hands to gather the water gushing out. I bend over the basin, ready to splash my face.

"Wait!"

I startle as the bride rushes to my side. "If I've learned anything this past year, it's how to freshen up without washing off your makeup." She smiles and grabs a paper towel, folds it into a neat square, and places it under the running faucet for the briefest moment. Holding it up to me, she says, "Use this to dab at your skin. The cold water is supposed to constrict your blood vessels and stop the redness."

Frowning, I do as she's instructed, blotting the wet paper against my face. "No offense, but judging by your ensemble, I'm sure you have somewhere better to be right now."

She laughs, her brown eyes crinkling at the corners. "I finally got to sneak away. The bridal dressing room was getting a little too crowded, and I needed a minute to myself."

"I didn't mean to interrupt."

"Hardly." Her mouth curves up into another kind smile. "You're Cloudy, aren't you."

It's not a question.

I wobble on unsteady legs. "How—?"

"I'm Sonia," she says.

Now I can't move at all—my muscles are clamped tight, my knees don't bend, my toes don't even wriggle. I'm suctioned to the floor, paralyzed, and Sonia—*Sonia*—is still talking. "Paige Montiel sent me some photos of Ashlyn with her friends. And she told me that you might be here today." She scrunches her nose. "Well, not *here* here, like the women's bathroom. Here as in the Bellagio. Coming across you right now is just a coincidence."

The room tilts, and nausea churns like storm clouds in my stomach. "We can leave," I tell her, shaking my head. "We didn't come to cause any trouble."

"Oh, no." Sonia's hands come up in an appeasing gesture, and the jewels on her bracelet glint in the fluorescent lighting. "Please don't go. I'm so happy you and Kyle could make it."

I gear up to propel myself out the door, when Sonia shifts one hand to brush the collar of her dress. It comes flush up to the bottom of her throat, too high to see any scars—but I know they're there, under the sparkling fabric of the bodice. Proof that Ashlyn's heart is alive and pumping only inches from me. And that is hypnotic, pulling me closer, rooting me in place.

"How do you feel?" I blurt it out so I don't lose the courage. "Since the operation, I mean."

Sonia purses her glossy pink lips, thinking about it. "I'm good," she says. "Some days are better than others. I still have these moments of total weakness—physical and emotional. I'll get really tired out of nowhere, or I'll have to force myself out of bed to get anything done. It's like learning to live a whole new kind of life. But I'm so grateful for all of it. Every single second of it."

I inhale a deep, shaky breath and turn back to the sink, tossing the now-crumpled wet paper towel onto the counter. I'm waiting for the same resentment I felt after Ethan and Freddie— the tightness in my jaw, the expected, comfortable anger—but nothing happens.

How can I resent Sonia—or any of the recipients? They've each had their own struggle. They've all been close to dying— and would be dead if not for the transplants. And maybe they're alive because Ashlyn died, but they didn't steal anything from her. She gave it to them. She gave them so much. They're living these different lives, with different kinds of limitations, but they're still lives full of possibilities.

"And talking to her helps a lot."

"To Ashlyn?" I say.

Sonia nods at me in the mirror as she continues to adjust her headpiece. "I'll be doing something like chopping an onion, and I'll say, out loud, 'I can't believe I fell while doing the downward dog pose in yoga today' or 'I'm definitely getting that dress even though it's not on sale.' Whatever pops into my head . . . She'd probably hate that, huh?"

My throat is sore. "No. She wouldn't."

"I know she's here"—Sonia brushes her chest so tenderly—"but talking to her makes her more real. It's like we're in this together."

The guilt funnels through me before I can brace myself for it. Sonia wasn't fortunate enough to have met Ashlyn, but she's honored Ashlyn's memory more than I have. All I've done is missed out on almost half a year with her. And yes, of course it's because Ashlyn's not *here* anymore. But I shut her out. I was so afraid of living without her, I chose to pretend that I didn't need her—that everything hadn't turned upside down without her. But I didn't have to ignore Ashlyn in order to heal; I only had to let her in. Losing her doesn't mean leaving her behind. It means finding new ways to keep her with me.

Sonia steps back from the counter, her arms thwacking against her skirt as they drop down. "This is as good as it gets, I think."

"You look beautiful," I say.

And she does. It's not the shimmering dress, or the intricate hairstyle, or her makeup. It's Sonia. What she must have been like before the transplant. What she's like now. The better days and the difficult ones. No matter what she's said, none of the words I'd use to describe Sonia is "weak." She is radiant and resilient. She's a fighter. And I'm electric with pride for Ashlyn that Sonia is so deserving of her.

"You look beautiful, too," Sonia tells me, winking.

"Right," I laugh, sniffing back more tears; I must resemble a ripe tomato by now.

Sonia's eyes spark. "I'll never be able to thank Ashlyn enough, but I damn sure do it every day. And I want you to know I won't ever forget it."

I can't think of what to say, the proper words for what meeting her has meant. But that's beside the point when Sonia's arms come around my back, gingerly pulling me against her. I don't hesitate—I rest my head on her shoulder as my eyes squeeze shut and my chest presses to hers.

I feel it instantaneously, as if this is what I've been waiting for all along. A steady thumping. A rhythm that is all Ashlyn's. My best friend's heart beating against mine. Again.

Kyle

By the time Sonia's groom reaches the table where Matty and I are sitting, I've already come up with (and dismissed) five different explanations to give him for why we're here.

Matty stands, so I hop to my feet as well. Are we going to bolt?

"Big day for you," Matty says. "Congrats, man."

Okay, then. He's decided to fake like we already know this guy, so I don't even have the option of pretending we've shown up to the wrong wedding.

Paco smiles. "Thank you. I've seen both of you in pictures, but I'm so bad at names." He wags his finger and squints a little. "You're . . . Ashlyn's boyfriend. Kyle, right?"

I'm too shocked to speak; I just nod like a bobblehead doll.

Paco turns to Matty. "And that means you are . . . ?"

"Matt." He puts out his hand, which Paco shakes. "I lived next door to Ashlyn. I'm also the cousin of her boyfriend." He nods toward me. "And the ex-boyfriend of her best friend, but we're only friends now."

"Gotcha." Paco exhales a laugh. "Very tangled relationships."

"You have no idea," Matty says, grinning.

Paco glances over his shoulder. "Her best friend is here, too? Stormy, is it?"

"Cloudy," I say.

"That's right! I knew it was something to do with the weather—"

"Excuse me." The woman in the pink dress (whose name tag reads "Bernadette—Wedding Coordinator") sets her hand on Paco's arm. "Sonia is going to be coming through the main doors here any minute. We need to get you down the aisle before you and your bride accidentally bump into each other."

"Sure, sure," Paco says, smoothing down the front of his jacket. "But I thought she was hidden away somewhere."

"She was. Then she took a field trip. But we can work around it, no problem. Are you ready?"

"Very ready." Paco nods at Matty and me. "Great to meet you both. See you in there."

We wish him luck as he follows the wedding coordinator to the open chapel doors, where the minister, best man, assumed dad, and a bridesmaid in a flowing coral dress are already gathered.

"Should we get our seats now?" I ask Matty.

"Let's wait a minute." He grabs his backpack from the floor and pulls his phone from the front pocket. "I'll find out where the Marlowe sisters are."

Cloudy

I left Sonia by the sinks, giving her the alone time she'd come for, and told her I'd be waiting out in the hallway. And I am. I want to be. No more running away.

Hearing Ashlyn's heartbeat was astonishing. It isn't an instant fix, but pieces of me are mending together—starting to, anyway. So I'm hoping Zoë will answer my text, or meet me here like I asked her to. Her words are on repeat in my mind, and they're a deeper stab on each replay. Zoë was only being Zoë, and instead of meeting her halfway, I faulted her for it. Her help wasn't good enough for me.

I'm not sure I deserve it, but all I need is a chance to tell her that.

My phone beeps, sending a jolt through me, but it's playing "I Touch Myself." I jab the ignore button without checking the screen.

The dead-end corridor outside the ladies' room is perpendicular to a larger hallway that connects ballrooms and conference rooms. I'm sitting on the cool floor, slumped back into the wall, watching a stream of people walk by. Some are in casual business attire, some in T-shirts like me, but it's the ones in dressier clothing who put me on edge. Sonia is set to glide down the aisle in minutes and I don't know what I'll do if Zoë refuses to see me before that. She's never been this pissed at me.

I tilt my face up to the ceiling, my palms rubbing nervously along my jeans. I shut my eyes so tightly that when I open them, I'm dizzy and my vision doubles.

Double Zoë.

I shoot up from the floor. "You came."

She shrugs.

"Where's your suitcase?"

"I checked it."

This is painful. I don't ever have to tiptoe around Zoë. "I'm sorry for what I said to you. I was horrible, and I didn't mean any of it."

"Cloudy."

"*Fine.* I meant it when I said it, but I was wrong." I bite my lip and cross my arms over my chest. Then uncross them. "I've been having a hard time since Ashlyn died. And I don't think I knew it, but I was floundering a little—a lot, actually. That's not an excuse," I rush to add. "But it's the truth. And I'm really, really sorry."

Zoë toys with the thin chain of her gold necklace as she examines me. I'm sure my puffy, discolored face is one big confirmation of my breakdown. "It wasn't fair of Matty and me to blindside you by coming. I should have mentioned it."

"I shouldn't have exploded like that."

She fixes her glasses. "I didn't realize I was, I don't know, *fruit-flying* you."

I exhale. "I felt like you were invading my space. I mean, you used to tease me about cheerleading, and then one day, you're on the team—without even telling me first."

Zoë's hands fall to her sides. Then in one swift motion, she turns and drops to the floor, leaning into the wall where I've just been. When she hits the marble, she winces from the chill against her bare legs but tucks her dress underneath her.

When she yanks at my arm, I know I'm forgiven.

I settle in beside her, but it's more of a full-body collapse.

"I only joined the team because it was a chance to be around you more," she says. "You've been impossible to reach lately. I wanted to make sure you were okay."

The muffled sound of Matty's ringtone comes from Zoë's purse. She plucks out her phone and hits a button, cutting it off. "But I wasn't trying to invade your space. I guess I hoped that if I was around a lot, you'd talk to me."

I hug my knees to my chest. "Sometimes talking is the easy part. If I focus on when Ashlyn was alive, I can trick myself into believing everything's fine. For a little while, anyway. But talking about her dying is like accepting it. I couldn't admit that it really happened."

"It did, though," she says softly, kindly.

"It did."

"I used to be jealous of her."

I smother a surprised laugh. Zoë is so secure; I didn't think she knew what jealousy felt like. "Of Ashlyn? Be serious."

Zoë sniffs. "You two could spend, like, infinity together and you never got sick of her. You got sick of me all the time," she says, throwing me a pointed look.

"That's not true. Ashlyn and I fought sometimes; you know that."

"Not like you and me. Once you didn't speak to me for a week."

Now I do laugh. I was twelve and I had this gorgeous pink-and-white scallop shell in my room. I hadn't even found it on the beach—I'd bought it with my allowance at a shop on the Cannon Beach boardwalk—but I'd decided it was my favorite charm. Zoë had smashed it after reading that seashells in the house bring bad luck.

"We're sisters," I say. "Our relationship is different. We say shitty things to each other because we know we'll get away with them."

"So, what? Sisters can be jerks to each other because they're related?"

"No. It means that no matter how much of a jerk I'm being, I still love you the same. And I still want you around. Even when I don't want you near me."

She presses her lips together, squashing a grin. "Okay."

I make the tips of my fingers touch, thumb to pointer finger, thumb to middle finger, and so on. "Did you really want to come on this trip?"

Zoë opens and shuts the clasp of her bag. "I was glad you and Kyle were taking it. But it would've been nice if you'd asked. Ashlyn wasn't my best friend, but I miss her, too." She cuts me off by holding up her hand. "No more. You apologizing so much is kind of unnerving."

God, how out of it had I been to disregard Zoë's pain? She knew Ashlyn for as long as I did. They'd met when Zoë was only six years old.

"So how do you handle it?" I ask Zoë. "Missing her?"

"I let it be sucky."

My head jerks up. "What?"

She carefully repositions her legs, crossing them at the ankle. "I let myself be sad and angry and confused. And then, before it's too much, I swap it for happier thoughts of Ashlyn. That's how I want to remember her."

My body seizes at the idea of feeling all of that. Misery and rage and regret. Lightness and acceptance. Going through an obstacle course of emotions and making it through in one piece.

But I had, hadn't I? I'd let the pain push me down and then, with Sonia's help, I'd crawled my way out of it. Maybe the more it happened, the more I recognized the grief instead of stifling it, the less crawling it would take to get out.

"Eventually," Zoë tells me, "the happier will come easier than the suckiness. It has to."

I smile. "I'd like that."

I don't know when that'll happen. But I know that right now, I'm sitting with my sister, on the cold floor in a hallway in Las Vegas, staring at the opposite wall's white plaster molding. I know I had a best friend, who I love so much it's stamped into my DNA. And I know that I can exist in a world where she doesn't, because having her in my life gave me all the courage I need to go on. She wouldn't expect any less from me.

A few feet away, a door swings open.

I grab Zoë's wrist and squeeze. "You are never going to guess who I met in the bathroom."

Kyle

According to the wedding coordinator, Bernadette, a wedding doesn't truly begin until the bride is ready. By that measure, even though the benches are filled with guests, the sound system's harp music was switched out with an energetic instrumental, and Paco has already made his way to the front along with his best man and the minister, this wedding has not yet started.

Beside me in the last row, Matty keeps bouncing his legs and alternating between staring at his silenced phone and the closed door. Cloudy and Zoë didn't answer his calls. He was debating whether he should go looking for them when Bernadette coaxed us to please take our seats in the chapel.

So we did. And here we wait.

As the minutes pass, anxiousness is increasing for us both. He's concerned over whether the Marlowe sisters will make it in time. I am, too, but I'm also wondering what it will be like to see Sonia, who will be walking through the doors at any moment. During this past week, I'd envisioned myself blending into the crowd without her ever knowing I'd come. That isn't going to happen now, since Paco knew me on sight.

The double doors open. Everyone in the room rotates to stare. Holding my breath, I do the same.

But it isn't a woman in a wedding dress who steps inside. Instead, it's a blonde in jeans and a brunette wearing glasses and a ruffled red dress.

Matty lets out a loud, relieved sigh and waves to them. Zoë slips into our row beside him, and Cloudy follows, making eye contact with me over Matty's and Zoë's heads. I can spot even from here that her face is red and her eyes are puffy because she's been crying, which makes the smile she's aiming my way even more of a surprise.

Cloudy takes her seat and disappears from my view—blocked by my cousin and her sister, who are now whispering together. After thirty seconds or so, Matty turns away from Zoë and says in my ear, "They ran into Sonia a few minutes ago. Cloudy was able to hug her and feel Ashlyn's heart beating."

"Wow! Really?"

Bernadette opens the door again and everyone swivels with even more urgency than before. This time, Sonia's bridesmaid walks through and slowly makes her way to the front. Cloudy leans across Zoë and mouths, "Coral!"

We grin at each other; Ashlyn's hatred of the color didn't stop Sonia from choosing it for her wedding.

The music changes again and the minister speaks. "Please stand for the bride."

Now the wedding is officially beginning.

We hop up simultaneously. All eyes in the room are aimed

down the center aisle at Sonia and her father. All except for mine, which are seeking out Cloudy.

Matty glances at me over his shoulder. "Will you just go *sit* with her? I know you want to."

He steps back and stands extra straight to make room for me to walk in front of him. Zoë notices his movement and does the same. I hesitate, but then Matty gives my arm a yank. I ride the forced momentum and stumble past them both. As I come to a stop beside Cloudy, she looks up with a smile, and I become warm all over.

"Hi," I whisper to her.

"Hey," she whispers back.

"How are you?"

"I've been holding in so much. But I need to deal with it."

I nod. That's something I need to do, too. Deal.

Sonia's father delivers her to her groom. We all take our seats and I'm hyperaware of Cloudy beside me. There's so much I want to ask her and so much I want to say, but I have to wait.

The minister goes into his speech, which has a lot of flowery phrases about the gift of love and the sanctity of marriage. It reminds me of every wedding I've ever seen on TV. Maybe this is how all traditional weddings go.

When my parents got married, it wasn't like this. Their ceremony was at sunrise near a Sedona vortex. It included eagle feather blessings and Native American drumming. (And technically, Matty and I were there, since Aunt Robin and Shannon were pregnant.) On that day, Shannon promised to be with my dad for the rest of her life. I assume she meant it at the time.

But whenever things got hard, she couldn't deal with him. She couldn't deal with either of us. She wanted to be out of our lives and now she is. That might change someday, but I doubt it. Regardless, I have other people who have always been there for me, and who always will be, in whatever way they can. My dad offered to see a counselor with me, and I think I'll take him up on it. Maybe we can finally talk about what we lost when Shannon left us.

Beside me, Cloudy's eyes are bright with tears. Sonia and Paco finish their vows and the minister recites a prayer. He prompts Paco to slide the ring onto his bride's finger and to speak another set of poetic phrases.

It's possible every wedding at this chapel includes these words, but they have a deeper meaning for Cloudy, Matty, Zoë, and me. These certain words make the four of us sit up straighter and exchange smiles. These certain words remind us of the girl we love, whose too-short life helped make it possible for this couple to say them to each other.

When it's Sonia's turn to repeat those same words to her groom, I take Cloudy's hand and squeeze it. She squeezes back.

"With this ring, I give to you my heart. I have no greater gift to give. . . ."

Cloudy

"For wedding crashers, we're very popular."

I smile. Across the small ballroom, next to the bar, Sonia's relatives are chatting up Zoë and Kyle. They're crowded together in a tight group. Everyone wants to meet Ashlyn's friends.

Matty and I are sitting together, the only ones left at Table Six. Our accommodating tablemates—who didn't grumble once when the hotel staff had to squeeze in four extra seats— are back in the buffet line. I scour the room and find Sonia and Paco in the middle of the dark-wood dance floor, their arms wrapped around each other, even though the song coming from the speakers isn't a slow one. She's been so focused on making sure we're comfortable, it's nice to see her enjoying her own reception.

Maya, Sonia's sister, rushes by us in a splash of coral satin, eagerly waving hello on her way.

Matty beams. "They love us!"

"Is that why you started the conga line?" I ask, scraping the last bit of mashed potato onto my fork.

"Hey, I'm just living my life to the fullest while I can. Before, you know—" He clanks his wrists together as if they're handcuffed.

I roll my eyes. "I wasn't serious about having you arrested."

"*Smoke* came out of your *ears*, Cloudy. You meant it."

A surge of laughter by the bar swallows my sigh. This guy in a checkered bow tie has his hand clamped on Kyle's back, while Zoë hides a grin behind her glass of lemonade.

"Look," I tell Matty, "I'm incredibly annoyed that you took my sister anywhere without telling me first. But I do appreciate you keeping an eye on her. And I'm really happy you guys are here for this."

"Me too," he says, slapping his palms against the tabletop to the beat of the music. It makes the tiny brown-and-orange boxes of chocolate that were next to each plate jump—especially Kyle's, which is already empty. He traded his dark chocolate truffles for Sonia's aunt's chocolate mints. It's a miracle that not even puking up those cookies could sour Kyle's love for chocolate mint.

"Matty." I stare at the centerpiece—a square vase filled with coral roses and hydrangea—and shore up my nerves for what I need to say next. But it's about time. "I'm sorry for what happened after Ashlyn died. With us. I was so lost and you were—"

"Willing?" he says, his hands going still.

"You made me feel safe again. Everything was so shitty, and being with you helped me forget about her. I was using you to deal with stuff I had no idea how to handle. You were always good to me and I took advantage of it."

He groans softly, bending his head back, his eyes on the brass chandelier above us. "It wasn't only your fault. I should have known something was going on when you wanted to start hooking up again. But I guess it felt right, or comfortable, or something. So I didn't want to ruin it. That's on me just as much."

"You did end it first," I say.

"Well, I am the better person."

"Clearly."

"So," he says, lifting one eyebrow, "are things back to normal with you and Kyle?"

"'Normal' is a thorny word."

Matty nods, scratching the top of his head. "It's cool if you're into him."

My skin flames, but I don't deny it. Hiding has been exhausting, and I'm done pretending with him. "We don't have to talk about this."

"I think Ashlyn would be okay with it, too."

I arch forward, curving over my plate. It's rimmed with gold lines, and underneath, the tablecloth is the color of champagne. "I'm not so sure."

"Let's consider this." His tone has me shifting to watch him. "The tables are turned, and you're . . . on the Other Side. If Ashlyn wanted to go out with me—and, *duh*, of course she would—would you be mad?"

The image of Ashlyn ever thinking of Matty *that* way ignites a grin on my lips. "I'd muster all my paranormal mojo to spell out 'Think it over' in her Cheerios."

He bops my forehead with his knuckles. "Come on, Cloudy. Aside from her family, you and Kyle are the people she loved most."

"Doesn't that make it worse?"

"The way I see it? I'd want my favorite people to be together." He shrugs. "I'm not trying to speak for Ashlyn, but if I know anything, it's that she'd want you to be happy. Like, out-of-your-mind happy. And if any of that happiness involves Kyle, she wouldn't expect you to sacrifice it."

I fold and refold the napkin in my lap to make it go away. "And that's how you feel, too?"

"Don't flatter yourself, Marlowe," he says, his expression all mock sympathy. "You're not that hard to get over."

I laugh, bumping his shoulder with mine.

"KEEP THEM SHUT." I wriggle my fingers in front of Kyle's face as a test.

He doesn't flinch, but he must sense the movement because he smiles. "I won't open them until you tell me to, I swear."

Satisfied, I grip his elbow, leading him forward. "You'll ruin the surprise if you look, and then you'll only have yourself to blame."

"As long as you promise not to walk me off a ledge."

Even though he can't tell, I smile back. "I promise."

Kyle's already caught a small glimpse of the Forum Shops at Caesars Palace, but the reason I wanted to bring him here, of all places, is still a secret. After Matty and Zoë dropped us off out front, Kyle followed me past a replica of the Trevi Fountain, inside the ornate, Ancient Rome–inspired entrance and up a curved marble staircase to the second floor. That's when I ordered his eyes closed.

Shoppers part to give us space as I guide Kyle through the most lavish shopping mall I've ever been in. The stores are modern, but the setting is totally old-world imperial. Granite pillars are sculpted in the shapes of striking women, and the tall, rounded ceiling is painted like the one at Le Boulevard, a serene blue with filmy white clouds.

I'm a little sorry that Kyle can't see any of it yet, but more sorry that Zoë and Matty might not see it at all.

Once we'd said our good-byes at the reception, finding Arm became top priority. I couldn't believe it when Kyle told me she'd taken off. Arm had been totally obedient this entire trip, and she'd chosen last night to start a rebellious phase? The thought of her out there, tiny and on her own, sent bolts of anxiety through me. But Matty insisted that Kyle and I stay out of it while he and Zoë worked up a plan. He was confident that, between the two of them, they would have Arm back to us in no time. Considering what they'd pulled off this weekend, I couldn't disagree.

I guide Kyle carefully, steering him into another section of stores.

His eyelids are still shut tight when he stops. "Cloudy, can we talk for a minute?"

Over his shoulder, the pathway opens up to a more expansive space. "We're almost there."

"There's something I have to tell you."

My pulse pounds as I tow him past a fancy jewelry store

and into a corridor off the main hallway. Despite the matching glossy floor, it lacks the grandeur of the rest of this place, so at least it won't him give any hints about where we are.

Positioning Kyle against a pale yellow wall, I say, "What's up?"

His eyes blink open, refocusing in the light. "You brought me to a mall?"

"You interrupted the surprise." I plant my hands on my hips. "So get on with it."

He straightens up, his gaze locking on mine. "How I acted yesterday was so out of line."

"You were upset about Shannon."

"That's no reason," he says, shaking his head. "It was like I was gasping for air. I needed to get out of that moment, and it turned into me shouting at you. I suck."

It would be easy to change the subject and minimize this, but avoidance has gotten me into too many messes. And Kyle's already reached out to me on this trip—it's my opportunity to return the favor. So I inhale deeply and go for it.

"I miss Ashlyn. *Monumentally*. Except it turns out I've been doing a pretty crappy job." I twist my hands behind my back. "I guess what I'm saying is . . . I know what it's like—doing stuff you don't mean because it feels like the only way you'll pull through."

He nods. "We'll get better at it, though. Right?"

"Yeah," I say. "I think so."

With another nod, Kyle slams his eyes shut again and lifts his arm out. "I had to say that before you do another nice thing for me."

I purse my lips. "I could be trading you in for cash to pay for an all-you-can-eat buffet."

"I'll take my chances," he says, grinning.

He trusts me. The thrill of it flurries in my belly.

"You can keep them open," I tell him, walking backward.

Together, we turn the corner, and only a few steps later—finally—we're here. The Fountain of the Gods.

It stands, imposing, in the middle of a large courtyard, the focal point among more shops. Four separate, rounded archways circle the fountain, supported by pillars. Closest to us, a marble armored soldier holds a shield and a spear, and behind him, the god Neptune stands even taller. Streaming water flows noisily and bubbles around the whole thing. It's Vegas in a nutshell, straddling the line between lavish and tacky, high-end and gaudy.

Kyle studies the area, searching for some clue as to why I'd bring him here. When his eyes latch on to something, I know it's clicked.

"Pegasus," he murmurs, his head tilting in every way to take in the whole structure. "And there's more than one . . . *Pegasi.*"

Without another word, he takes off for one of the winged horses.

"I found it by accident," I say, following him up to the fountain's base. Pegasus looks ferocious—way different from the Disney version I grew up on. He's rearing up on his hind legs, his mane wild and his wings outstretched. "When I was Googling things to do in Vegas last night, this popped up in one of my searches."

He reaches out to stroke Pegasus's granite muzzle. "And you wanted to bring me here."

"You mentioned it in Bedrock City. You said—"

"I remember."

My head pulls back. "You do?"

"It's foggy," he says, sitting below Pegasus on the lip of the fountain, "but yeah."

"What else do you remember?"

The uplighting is dim and has turned the faux sky above us a dusky blue. Nevertheless, Kyle squints up at me. "More than you think, probably."

I sit beside him so I won't have to raise my voice over the fountain. "So you know that we . . . kissed."

"Oh," he says, his face blank. That's it. *Oh.*

I'd panic if my body wasn't flooding with adrenaline.

I drop my phone onto my lap, knotting my fingers together. "It must be something about illegal substances. One of us gets intoxicated and the other is suddenly irresistible."

Kyle's expression sharpens. "But I wasn't intoxicated."

I choke and cover it with a laugh. "What are you talking about? You couldn't even stand up on your own."

"The cookies didn't kick in until after we left the jailhouse." His lips part slightly. "Everything before that . . . I was sober. It was me, Cloudy."

"Oh."

Oh.

He smiles, bashfully, at a spot between his feet. "So you really were that irresistible."

"I wasn't exactly resisting, either."

"I do also remember that."

I blush fiercely.

We sit there, quietly staring straight ahead. A family with two small girls stops beside us. Turning their backs to the fountain, they each toss something over their shoulders, into the water. I swivel to peer inside and only then notice the glinting of hundreds of coins resting at the bottom.

When I spin around, Kyle is holding out two pennies. I grin and pick one, before closing my fingers into a fist around it. I guess I was mistaken about not being the wishing type.

And there's so much to wish for.

But only one thing I want: the chance to get it right. To live without all the heaviness and guilt I've been carrying since Ashlyn died. To make sure her memory is a comfort I keep nearby, not something I hide from.

I press the coin into my palm, then fling it into the fountain.

A second later, Kyle does the same. "You know what I wished for at Bedrock City? When we set those lanterns loose?"

"No," I say.

"That things won't go back to what they used to be between us. That we'll be more than ex–lab partners when we go home." He ducks his head. "I still want that, whatever it means for us."

He said as much to me on the ground outside of the jailhouse— or something close to it. I figured it was the pot twisting his brain, making him repeat what I'd said to him earlier that night. But I was wrong.

I have never, ever been so relieved to be so wrong.

"So do I," I tell him. "But isn't there a rule about wishes? If you tell someone about them, they won't come true?"

Kyle's hand slides a microscopic amount along the fountain's base. As his pinkie wraps around mine, he says, "I think this one will."

I TUCK MYSELF into a tighter ball so I'll fit in the armchair, then go back to explaining why I kick ass at cheerleading.

Well, not exactly. So far, most of the preliminary questions for the *Cheer Insider* interview are basic: my GPA, my favorite stunts, any individual honors I've received, things like that. The tougher questions, the ones that ask for my favorite competition stories and how I started cheering, they all include Ashlyn. While I'm certain I'll be able to face those, I assure myself not everything has to be done tonight.

Across the room, Zoë snuggles under the bedsheets, fast asleep. Unfortunately, she and Matty had no success finding Arm this afternoon, so all four of us kept at it until it got too dark outside. After hitting the buffet at the Cosmopolitan, Zoë passed out, but not before claiming she'll implement Plan B in the morning. Whatever that is.

Folding my legs underneath me, I close out of my phone's email app and tap on the text message icon. The Claudia Marlowe Apology Tour, as Matty so sympathetically called it, rolls on. But I have things to own up to, and I don't want to waste a minute.

And Jade is at the top of my list.

You were right. I was pushing everyone away, including you, I type out to her. Let's talk sometime?

A minute after hitting send, my phone buzzes. There's an edgy tremble in my fingers as I read her reply.

Anytime. Whenever you want. xo.

Smiling, I answer back. And I remember something I thought about in Bedrock City. How fortunate Kyle is to have two people—Matty and Will—who live such separate lives, but care about him so much. I'm feeling pretty lucky tonight, too.

I pad over to the queen-sized bed and carefully slip under the covers. Zoë doesn't stir as I sit up against the headboard. I reach over to dim the lamp, then pause. There *is* one more thing I want to do before today ends.

So I open the internet browser on my phone and pull up *Cheer Insider*'s website. After keying the correct information into a tiny search box, the result I'm looking for shows up first thing. I press my thumb to her name, wait the three seconds it takes to load, and hold my breath as Ashlyn's essay appears on the screen.

It shouldn't have taken me this long. But I'm ready now.

Mostly.

Her words are waiting patiently, as ever, for me. Right there in my hands.

It's time to go through this.

My eyes sting as soon as I begin. Ashlyn starts by introducing herself, explaining where she lives and what team she cheers for. She describes moving to Bend when she was eight years old, and meeting me in school. That summer after, when we joined a cheerleading program at the Juniper Swim and Fitness Center.

The first time I stepped onto the mat, I was so nervous. I looked over at Cloudy, and her little face was determined and focused. She must have noticed how scared I was, because she nodded at me, as if saying, "You can do this." And I did do it, kind of. I still tripped over the words in V-I-C-T-O-R-Y for that entire practice, but with Cloudy shooting goofy smiles at me, I knew I'd get better. Not to brag, but I did, and only because Cloudy was there with me the whole time. Now, whenever I'm edgy before a game or competition, I do the same thing. I look over at my best friend. With her at my side, I feel like I can do anything.

I guess that sounds dramatic, but I think that's what cheering with your best friend is all about. You complement each other so perfectly outside of the gym that when you're inside, you feel complete and invincible.

More than anything, though, I've learned that, just like in cheer, life is all about support. Being capable on your own is important, but big or small, having the right team makes all the difference. Cloudy's my team. My support. My family. She gives everything one hundred percent; she never backs down from a challenge; and she's always there to motivate me. Because of her, I'm strong enough to get through things on my own. But also because of her, I don't have to.

Cloudy will always mean more to me than cheer. Our friendship is bigger than all of it. And she's shown me that no matter what I do, I have to give it my all.

Persistence and commitment will get me everywhere. And I definitely want to go everywhere, especially if my best friend is right there next to me.

I wipe at my cheeks.

Kyle was right. She could have been reciting the words in my ear, or sitting at the foot of the bed.

This is what it can be like now: I can make it through the day, even when it sucks. *Especially* when it sucks. Just like Sonia and the others, I'll fight for this new kind of life. And I'll face what's up ahead because Ashlyn is on my team, too—my support. My best friend. Knowing her gave me everything I need. And wherever I do end up, I'll take her with me. Love like that doesn't get left behind. Maybe it's not the future we imagined for ourselves, but it's a plan. Something to hold on to and look forward to.

Before I read her essay again, I lower my phone onto my knee. I breathe in quietly. "So that Snow White play," I whisper to Ashlyn. "It's not as boring as I remembered."

Kyle

"Don't get your hopes up." Zoë sets her phone on the table between us. "But we might have a lead."

"We *might?*" I ask.

"Well, unlike all the other animal shelters we've called, this one can't tell me they *don't* have a shorthaired female black kitten with green eyes that's arrived in the last two days. So we need to go see for ourselves."

"Are there more places to call?" Cloudy asks.

Zoë shakes her head. "That was the last one."

"We should do this, then," Cloudy says, throwing her duffel over her shoulder.

Matty already took a couple of loads out earlier and sent a text five minutes ago that he officially checked us out with the front desk and is waiting at the car. I grab the shopping bags with my clothes and things stuffed inside while Zoë does one last walk-through to make sure no one's forgotten anything.

Whatever we learn at the animal shelter, we have to leave Las Vegas today. The drive home will be over thirteen hours, and the plan is to do it with as few stops as possible so we'll for sure beat Cloudy's parents home. I'm trying to stay positive like my cousin is, but the thought that we might have to leave without Arm has my stomach in knots. (Although one thing my dad pointed out on the phone last night does help a tiny bit: Arm survived the coldest time of year in Bend on her own, so she could be all right in Nevada.)

As we're about to walk out, Zoë's phone (which she was ignoring while making calls) goes off once again.

"It never ends, does it?" Cloudy says with a laugh. "What's the scoop today, Team Manager?"

"Let's see. Jenna's oversharing about what she did last night after WinterFest." Zoë pauses to read more. "Also, Lita says Jacob was just talking trash about a couple of baseball players with the last name 'Ocie,' and she told him to shut his mouth. More importantly, she can't decide how to style her hair for the *Cheer Insider* photo shoot next week, and she wants opinions."

I chuckle. "Tell Lita thanks for having our backs. And I say, go for the ponytail. It's classic."

"Will do." Zoë opens the front door and steps outside. "Cloudy, on a scale of one to ten, how much trouble do you think we're going to be in when Mom and Dad get home?"

"For you? Probably a four." Cloudy goes after her. "But for the irresponsible older sister? At least a nine. It was worth it, though."

"Totally worth it," Zoë agrees.

As the last one out, I pull the door shut behind me. I follow the girls through the breezeway and down the stairs to the parking lot. When we're about twelve feet from my vehicle, Matty comes rushing over with his hands up, motioning for us to wait.

"Quick question, Kyle. You said yesterday you *wanted* to believe your cat was Ashlyn reincarnated, but deep down, you don't. I'm wondering, though, do you think you'd be able to accept that she was an angel, sent to help you?"

I stare at him. "An angel?"

"Yeah. And maybe the reason she disappeared is because things are better, you're ready for ball season, and her work with you was finished?"

Cloudy and Zoë are exchanging glances like *Has Matty lost it?*, which is exactly what I'm wondering.

"Um, no. I didn't suddenly start believing in . . . cat angels."

"Okay, just checking!" He sets my bags in the back of the Xterra, and then grabs ahold of my wrist. "Now, I need to show you something."

I let him drag me away, shooting a confused glance at Cloudy as I'm pulled along the white line between my vehicle and the truck beside it. We reach the front, and he throws out his arm magician style. "Ta-da!"

There on my hood, the kitten I've been worrying about for the past thirty-six hours is curled up asleep on her panda Pillow Pet with half-empty dishes of food and water beside her.

"What did I tell you?" Matty's grin is triumphant. "Cat Whisperer, right?"

"I can't believe it!"

Zoë and Cloudy catch up. "Oh my God," Cloudy says, putting her hand to her chest.

"You lured her out of hiding," Zoë says. "Pretty smart."

"Danielle told me she likes warm hoods," Matty says. "So I

ran the engine for a while this morning. Not sure if it was that or the food that got her to jump up here, but I'm guessing the comfy pillow is what made her stay. She must have been touring Vegas on her own in the meantime, or at least the courtyard."

I reach out slowly, cautiously. As my fingertips touch her fur, her eyes open. "Hi, Arm. We've been looking everywhere for you. Are you okay?"

She responds by stretching and letting out a low, scratchy, "Mrowww."

"Whoa," Matty says. "That voice. So I *think* what she said is, 'I'm fine, dickhead. But I'm not coming home with you unless you give me a new name.'"

While Matty and Zoë get us situated for the trip, I carefully scoop Arm up and take my seat in the front beside Cloudy, who's volunteered to drive first.

I'm pretty sure I'll never be a person who believes in rein-carnation or heaven or mystical things. And that's all right with me. Because, really, whether this cat is *just* a cat or not is beside the point. What matters is that she's found the way back. Just like we're all trying to do.

Cloudy starts the car, and as she turns onto Dean Martin Drive, Matty speaks from the backseat. "I'm serious about your cat's name. If you want something to honor Ashlyn, why not call her 'Ash'? Or 'Lyn'? Or 'Rose'? Or even 'Montiel'? Those are actual *names*. Arm, leg, rib, ear. Those are body parts. See the difference?"

"This from someone who named his cat 'Hercules,'" Cloudy says.

"That name is *legit*. And it isn't an appendage."

"'Ashes' is cute," Zoë chimes in. "It would work better for a gray cat, though. Another option could be to name her after one of the places she visited. You could call her 'Angeles' for Los Angeles. Or 'Monica' for Santa Monica. Maybe 'Vegas'?"

"I've got it!" Matty says. "'Sedona.' She spent a few days there, and it's also where Kyle was born." His tone is just daring one of us to challenge him. "'Sedona' is perfect."

I force myself to keep a straight face. "I'd rather call her 'Bend.' Since that's where *she* was born."

Matty and Zoë groan in unison, but Cloudy laughs. She stops for a red light, and I ask, "What do you think her name should be?"

Tilting her head, Cloudy takes a moment to study the tiny black kitten on my lap. "I don't know," she says, aiming her smile my way. "She really just looks like an 'Armadillo' to me."

ACKNOWLEDGMENTS

We were first inspired to write *The Way Back to You* because of someone else's story—many someone elses', actually. Francisco "Paco" Rodriguez was a boxer who died in the ring, and whose wife, Sonia, corresponded with and met the recipients of his organs. Paco's family, and the recipients and their families, participated in ESPN's *E:60* and shared with the world how love and selflessness can bring hope after tragedy.

While working on this book, both of us lost significant loved ones, and what already felt personal became even more so. This story was sparked by people we've never met, but it was shaped and deepened by the people we knew and cared for. The people we still miss.

Endless gratitude to:

Our editor, Alex Arnold, whose vision, guidance, and passion helped bring our book to life. We couldn't have hoped for someone who loved Cloudy, Kyle, Ashlyn, and Arm as much as you do. xo

Our agent, Jim McCarthy, whose optimism, persistence, and after-midnight "Fair enough!" emails always keep us going. You're our shining star, and we appreciate you sticking with us through the years.

Dwayne Scott, who faithfully read every version of every scene and (almost) never complained. These characters wouldn't be who they are if we hadn't had you to bounce our ideas off of

24/7, and we're so grateful.

Liesa Abrams, who connected with our writing—and connected us!—during that long-ago MediaBistro class. A million thank-yous for your friendship and for encouraging us to write this book together.

Everyone at HarperCollins and Katherine Tegen Books for taking such good care of our book! Special thanks to Katherine Tegen, Kate Engbring, Stephanie Hoover, Risa Rodil, Kathryn Silsand, Jessica White, Alana Whitman, and Christine Cox.

Ruth Gallogly, Kari Olson, Laura Walker, and Gina Wimpey for your thoughtful critiques; Doris Berthiaume, Adrienne Fox, John W. S. Marvin, Josh Moon, Sarah Moon, Beth Scott, Julie Slawson, Katherine Smith, Jesse Stewart, Sedona Red Rock High School, and Google Maps for assisting with our research; the Sweet 16s and Sixteen to Read; and Bethany Larson, for talking about a certain documentary on the drive to work one day.

And finally, thank you to our friends and families—particularly our parents and siblings—for taking this journey with us and accepting our writerly quirks. You talked us down and cheered us on, and we love you for it.

The Chinese Ginger Jars

Myra Scovel

With Nelle Keys Bell

The Chinese Ginger Jars

Harper & Brothers · New York

117

For the six of them, lest they forget

Contents

The Chinese Ginger Jars

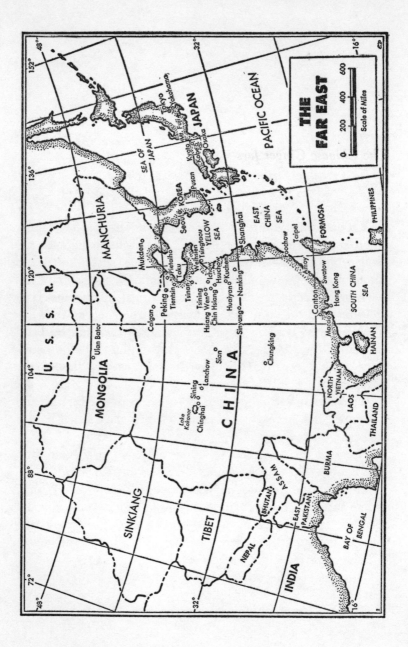

The Prologue
The Ginger Jars

We found them, quite by chance, this afternoon in the junk shop kept so carelessly by the old Sikh gentleman with the long white beard—two Chinese ginger jars, sitting squat and proud among the empty bottles and the broken tins. The jars were not a perfect pair, although identical in size and both covered with the same rich, jadelike glaze.

We looked at them for a long moment; then my husband smiled and put his hand in his pocket, pulling out the necessary coins. He carried the jars carefully as we climbed the steep hill back to the cottage.

They are green, the color of quiet water. My husband crumples the newspaper wrapping from the second jar of the pair.

"Look at it," he is saying, as he puts one of the jars into my hands. "Do you remember . . . ?" I turn it slowly, contemplating the plaques embossed on its six sides. China, home to us for more than twenty years! There is a memory of that home in each design—the gourd, the grape, the chrysanthemum, the peach, the flowering plum, the bamboo.

The glaze feels like cold stone.

"Let me see the other," I say, and I give him the one I have held.

This one has three scenes, once repeated—the Jade Pagoda;

the poem written in brush strokes in an ancient script; Lao Shou Hsing, the birthday fairy. Yes, the memories are all here.

We look at each other across the ginger jars, across the years.

One
The Jade Pagoda

Peking in 1930! It was a city straight from the pages of Marco Polo. The Temple of Heaven still retained its patina of age, unaware of the desecrating renovations that were to come. The whole city seemed steeped in the culture of its people, mellow as the smooth cream ivory of its curio shops, wise with a wisdom drawn from the deep pools of its clearest jade, relaxed as the curve of a temple roof against its sky. How did I, born and brought up in Mechanicville, New York, happen to be walking its streets?

Events had exploded one after another since that morning, a little more than two years before, when Miss Montgomery, the director of nurses, called me into her office in the Cortland County Hospital, in New York State. I was young, proud and confident in my new status as supervisor of the maternity ward, but I flinched at the summons. What had I done or what hadn't I done? I can still feel the panic beneath my starched white as I hurried through the corridors.

Miss Montgomery rose from her desk as I came in. This was worse than I had thought. "Miss Scott, I understand you are seeing a lot of Dr. Andrews." (I am, but what is that to you? I thought, a little resentfully.) But the cool blue eyes were twinkling. "Just don't give your heart away until you've met Frederick Scovel. He's the new medical student up in the lab. That's all."

Frederick Scovel indeed! If he had *that* effect on the director of nurses, he was probably handsome—and knew it. He was bound to be conceited, and pompous, and—and icky! I seethed all the way back to the ward.

Naturally I found an errand to take me to the lab. I had to see this paragon. The first thing I noticed about him was his ears. They were slightly reminiscent of faun's ears. He was tall; I had to look way up to see the light brown hair, brown eyes, and a Roman nose. Unbelievably, he was shy. Of course, nothing about this man was of the slightest interest to me. I picked up my test tubes and went back to the ward.

"Shy" was hardly the right word.

A week later, after eight hours on the ward, I hurried off duty to keep my third date with him. I remember that, as we sat in the living room, he bent to remove my shoes and gently rubbed my tired feet. Then he smiled, amused at something.

"What's so funny?" I asked.

"I was just wondering what that Dr. Andrews would say when he finds out that I'm going to marry you," he replied.

Before I could think of anything else to say, he'd risen and walked across the room. He sat down in the chair farthest away and said quietly, "I shouldn't have said that. I can't ask you to share my life. I'm going to be a missionary."

A *what?* This mild, disturbing man who had so quickly become the center of my existence did not look in the least like my mental picture of a missionary. And I couldn't, by the farthest stretch of the imagination, see myself in the role of what I supposed was the typical missionary wife—high-topped shoes, umbrella firmly clutched in the middle, straw suitcase tied together with twine, hair snatched back in a bun. Me? Well, hardly! But he'd probably change his mind.

It was natural for Fred to be drawn to such a calling. His

father was a minister; his mother, the daughter of a minister.
Both grandfathers had been ministers, for that matter. Missionaries had been in and out of Fred's home for as long as he could remember.

I forgot all about missionaries in the whirl of happiness that followed.

It was a beautiful wedding with peonies everywhere. I wanted to wear a mantilla, because the comb would make me look taller. "We'll look silly standing in the front of the church," I had said, "you six feet one and a half, and I five feet and half an inch."

"If I'd wanted a tall wife, I could have had one," he had answered conclusively.

There was a halo around life together, around our planning for the future. We talked of the day when we would go to China as missionaries, but that seemed like another age to come. I knew that Fred was in correspondence with what we always spoke of as "the Board," meaning the Presbyterian Board of Foreign Missions. But the joy at hand wrapped us in a cloak that shut out the winds of the world. We did not see each other often enough or long enough at a time to discuss anything at length. Fred was interning at Memorial Hospital in Syracuse, New York, and I was still working in Cortland, some forty miles away.

All other considerations were temporarily put aside when we knew we were to have our first child. During the last two months I went to live with Fred's parents in Cortland. "Just see how God answers prayer," said Father Scovel, who was more like Christ than any man I have ever known. "For twenty-six years I prayed for a daughter, and now God has given me one who even looks like me."

How Father's black eyes would shine when someone would mistake me for his own daughter and think Fred the son-in-law! But both men were cut from the same pattern, the tall frame, the slope of the shoulder, the "Scovel" nose. It was only that Father and I had the same black hair and dark eyes. And, as one friend put it, "I thought she must be your daughter because you look as if you loved each other so much."

Mother Scovel was a tall, queenly, cultured lady of the old school, with golden blond hair. She was a perfect minister's wife—kept a beautiful home, was an excellent cook, could lead a meeting with sparkle and verve and never fail to give you something that you could take home and live by. It might have been a difficult position for me, being the wife of an only son, but never in that home. I was accepted and loved.

Father Scovel wanted us to have a little girl. He always spoke of the baby as Carlotta. (Father's name was Carl.) But when our little son was born, we named him James Kiehle Scovel. "James" because he looked as if he should be called Jimmy and "Kiehle" because it was Mother Scovel's maiden name. China didn't exist.

Then, in one moment of time, the vague future became the crystallized present.

Young James Kiehle Scovel had been delivered in the Syracuse hospital where his father was interning. I was lying in bed that morning, a few days after the confinement, when Fred came into the room with the day's mail in his hand. He kissed me and sat down in the wicker chair beside the bed to read aloud the congratulatory messages from friends.

" '. . . so delighted with the news . . .' 'How lovely for you . . .' Um, here's one from the Board."

What was he saying? "We are looking forward to your sailing in August and have booked passage for you on the *President McKinley* from Seattle. That will get you into Peking in time for language school. . . ."

Peking? Language school? August? This was April! I looked at him, incredulous. But he had picked up another letter and was reading.

". . . We are so happy to hear of the birth of . . ."

I couldn't believe it. Our safe, comfortable world was crashing down upon our heads, and to him this bombshell was just another letter. After what seemed like hours, he was called to see a patient and I was left alone to think.

It was high time I did some thinking. I hadn't looked ahead to anything except the birth of our baby and a comfortable little home of our own somewhere nearby. Now, while I was still exhausted from a sixty-hour labor with complications, life in far-off difficult China was laid in my lap. I hadn't seriously considered Fred's call to a lifework.

There was little in my background to prepare me for a missionary life. My practical father would snort at the idea. "Aren't there enough heathen in this country?" I could hear him say it. Mother would know that I must live where my husband wanted to live. All that I knew of such a life in a foreign country had been learned from a few stories told to us as children when the mite boxes had been passed out in our beautiful gray-stone Episcopal Church. China was the picture of the sampan in our geography books, and my father's detective stories of the Mandarin with the slim silver knife hidden in his sash, Dr. Fu ManChu. My father called him Dr. Fume and Chew.

But did Fred really *want* to be a missionary? Perhaps he was doing it to please the parents he loved so much. It would certainly be gratifying to them to have their only son give his life in full-time Christian service. But surely they would understand if he changed his mind now.

"If you could do anything in the world that you wanted to

do, what would it be?" I asked him when he came in that evening.

"Why, I'd be a medical missionary and go to China," he said casually, folding his six-foot-one-and-a-half into the wicker chair. "You know, I can remember wanting to be a medical missionary before I knew that 'medical' meant doctor. Why do you ask?"

"Oh, I was just wondering," I replied.

He is so *sure*, I thought. Yet how can I bear it? How can I take this beautiful baby halfway across the world to a strange, germ-infested country? Is it fair to this child of ours? Suppose something should happen? How can something not happen?

I thought of the new nursery furniture which our son would probably never get to use, and came near to tears; but suddenly a new picture began to form in my mind. I saw our home in China—neatly plastered mud walls, a thatched roof, curtains at the window, the black, wrought-iron candlesticks upon a shelf.

Then it came, the Voice of Gentle Calm: "How little you trust Me who have brought you all the way."

I would take that nursery furniture to China.

Father and Mother Scovel went with us across the country to see us off at Seattle. Difficult as the parting was, for us it was colored by our starting out on a great adventure. What must it have been for the two on the dock as they watched their only son sail away to be gone for five years!

We left the *President McKinley* at Kobe and boarded the *Choku Maru*, a tiny Japanese ship that carried us through the Yellow Sea to Taku in northern China. We had a very rough crossing; even the captain and the purser were seasick. I turned out to be the world's worst sailor, a great disappointment to Fred, who loves a heaving deck. The voyage to Taku was memorable for one great event—the discovery of our baby's first tooth.

China didn't look like the picture in the geography book but it didn't feel like a strange country, as I had expected it would. I was not frightened by the jostling coolies on the dock, nor by the rickshaw-pullers haggling for fares, nor by the crowds on the third-class train during the journey of several hours from Taku to Peking. The sights and smells were different from anything we had ever known, but from the moment of our arrival in China, we felt at home. How does one express that quiet quality of friendship with which a Chinese reaches out to you? People were so good to us. A wizened old man moved over to make room where there was no room; a tiny, bright-eyed woman offered us chunks of chicken with a bright-red glazed sauce. The flies were thick and we didn't dare accept it, but we smiled our thanks as best we could.

We were thankful that we were not making this first train trip alone. Knowing how difficult travel with a small baby would be for newcomers, sandy-haired, salt-witted Tex Eubank had taken the trouble to come down from the language school to meet us; so my first Chinese words were flavored with a Texas drawl.

"How do you say, 'Please don't touch him'?" I asked Tex when the first passengers pushed and shoved to handle the white carrying-basket that held the baby, to feel the soft wool blanket and, horrors, to pinch his fat little cheeks!

"Pia tung," said Tex.

"I don't hear the 'please,'" I said.

"Never mind. You just use the words I give you and smile. They'll understand."

I was kept so busy with my first Chinese sentence that I

had no time to learn another before the train chugged to a stop in the Peking station.

We had talked about riding in rickshaws before coming to China. We had agreed that we could not let another human being pull us around behind him. I do not know what we have done to our moral standards, but we both think now that of all the modes of travel there are in the world today, travel by rickshaw is by far the best. There is a snapshot in our album, showing my first attempt at sitting in one. There was no other conveyance to take us from the railway station to the language school. There I sit, bolt upright, the baby held stiffly in my arms, protest written in every line of my face.

"Relax, gal," said Tex.

The streets were wide. I had pictured them as narrow lanes. And oh, there was so much to see! There were shop signs with huge gold characters in bold relief against black lacquer; there were chubby, pig-tailed children playing a game with short sticks; there was a wedding procession coming down the middle of the road with sedan chairs of bright red satin heavily embroidered in gold. Three or four black-bristled, scrawny pigs scurried into the street, their sagging bellies dragging the ground. And there was a camel! Our eyes were tired and we were sootier than we had ever been in our lives when we pulled up at the gate of the College of Chinese Studies on the street called T'ou T'iao Hut'ung.

The smooth green lawns of the interior courtyard with their potted evergreens and pools of quiet, chiffon-tailed goldfish were a welcome we will not forget. A smiling house-boy in a long white garment took us to two comfortable rooms overlooking the courtyard. It was our first home alone.

Such a new young family from such a new young world! It was appalling how little we knew. But we were there to learn and we took our places in the classroom the morning the language school opened. Our First-Born was left in his basket at the hostel to learn Chinese as it should be learned. We found a little old amah (almost entirely bald) to look after him during school hours. We thought En Nai Nai was perfection until we found her poking holes in the rubber nipple with the silver pin she wore in her hair.

There must have been a hundred and fifty of us in the classroom that first day of school—businessmen, consular officials, Catholic priests, men in army uniform, Protestant missionaries. All of us had our eyes on the door through which our first Chinese teacher would come. Someone had passed on the incredible information that no teacher in the school could speak English. This, we felt, was a serious mistake on the part of the administration. If Chinese were anything like what the laundries at home had led us to believe, these teachers were going to need a considerable command of our native tongue.

The door opened to admit one of the most charming gentlemen I have ever seen. He was wearing a long black gown with a sleeveless jacket of heavy brocade. His smooth young face beamed happily as he approached the desk. Someone murmured, "Dearest," and from then on we never spoke of him as anything else. Dearest wiped his heavy horn-rimmed glasses, and the lesson began.

"Wo," he said, pointing to himself; "Ni," with a long singing upward tone, pointing to us.

"What does he mean?" We looked at one another. Dearest repeated the words and the gestures. Light broke—"I," "You."

With a gesture that included us all, he continued, "Wo men, ni men."

"Ah, the 'men' sound means plural," we guessed.

We were learning the language as First-Born was to learn it after all. First we listened. We listened to the same thing

over and over for days. We heard old teachers and young
teachers, men teachers and women teachers, teachers who
spoke crisply and distinctly, and teachers who insufflated their
words through a fringe of mustache. Only after many days
of listening were we allowed to speak the words ourselves.
Finally we were shown the printed character. We were not
surprised when we heard that John Dewey, the great educator,
had called Dearest the best teacher he had ever known.

The unfolding of the language revealed the beauty of this
ancient culture—the calligraphy, the poetry, the wise old
sayings handed down since the time of Abraham. Every Friday
was Proverb Day. We were taught the sayings and the proper
time to use them: "A fat man is not made so by one mouth-
ful"; "The husband sings and the wife follows."

"Doctor," said the teacher one Friday, "what proverb comes
to your mind when you think of your wife?"

Obviously the answer should have been, "The husband
sings and the wife follows."

I was a long time forgiving Fred for his reply: "If the old
doesn't go, how can the new come?"

Language study continued after school hours as we tried out
our new words on long-suffering shopkeepers and the rickshaw-pullers. What companions they were, those rickshaw
men! Even small shopping expeditions became personally
conducted tours. They would tuck the fur robe cozily about
our feet and start off on a jaunt to a side street to show us
the amusing shop signs—"False teeth and eyes, latest Meth-
odists," "Tailor Shop. Ladies have fits upstairs." If we gave
directions in a brand of Chinese that was almost beyond com-
prehension, they were quick to sort out the meaning.

Best of all we liked the ride to church on Sunday morn-
ings. Then the streets were hushed and quiet. The fronts of
the shops were closed and boarded up. The air smelled like

orchards in the fall, and the sun spilled long shadows over the pavement of rut-worn stone. The pat-pat-pat of the pullers' feet echoed in the empty lane. Occasionally a slower pat—pat—pat would be heard, and a caravan of camels would appear. What a picture they were, their proud noses in the air in spite of their ragged coats! Some of them would be laden with coal and some would have flung over their backs large burlap sacks containing hand-woven Mongolian rugs. The whole caravan would move along the street like a stately, rhythmic poem.

These were thought-provoking days and I was troubled. Before we had left America, there were those who asked, "Why do you want to go way out there and impose your Western religion upon the Orientals?"

I had been very sure of the answer then; now I wondered. What did I have that these wonderful people didn't have? And (did I dare whisper it, even to myself?) what did Christianity have to give them? I had thought that, seeing how happy we were and how well we did everything, the Chinese would flock to our gates to find out more about the God we worshiped, the Christ we loved. So far no one had asked me a question. The only Chinese we had even met—aside from the faculty of the school, who did not seem particularly impressed with the benefits we had to offer—was a young student who came to practice his atrocious English and who invited us out to eat impossible things like sea slugs. (Fred loved them.)

As I stood looking out across the quadrangle one day, Fred said, "Something is troubling you. Are you homesick?"

"Isn't it strange that in this strange country I have never felt a moment of homesickness? No, it is something deeper than that," I replied. "*You* never seem to have had a doubt in your life. Will you understand if I tell you?"

He has always understood, usually before I can voice my thought.

"Why don't you take this Weymouth translation of the New Testament," he suggested, "and imagine you are a Confucianist or a Taoist. You've never seen a church. All you know of religion is the dusty temple where you go on feast days to pray for a son without which you will be a disgrace to your husband and mother-in-law. Read it through as if for the first time. Don't even try to make any decisions. Just read it."

The Bible suddenly came alive. Here, in this very city, sat the beggar at the gate; here two women were often seen grinding at a mill; here one had to know which were the high seats and which were the low seats at a feast. I began to wonder how such an Oriental religion as Christianity had ever taken root in the West.

Then Christmas came, and like turning on the lights of the tree, all the little lights turned on inside me and I knew what I had to share. It would not be men seeking me to find the way, perhaps not even men seeking God to find the way; but God in His infinite love, in the humility of a manger and the simpleness of a Baby, forever seeking men. "God, in Christ, reconciling the world unto Himself."

"You've found a text," said my husband. "Shall I get you a soapbox?"

Two
The Ancient Poem

Before my couch is the light of the effulgent moon.
Perhaps it is hoar frost on the ground.
Raising my head, I gaze at its brightness;
Lowering my head, I think of home.
　　　　　　　　—Li Po (A.D. 701-762)
　　　　　　　　(Poem on the ginger jars,
　　　　　　translated by L. Carrington Goodrich)

In my complacent ignorance I had always pictured China
as a warm, sunny country. In spite of the specific instructions
from the Board to take plenty of winter clothing to Peking,
China was the Orient; and to me, the Orient meant hot
weather. Our first Chinese winter furnished another of the
enlightening experiences that China was constantly giving
me. It was cold, bitter cold. The wind that blew down on
Peking from the Gobi Desert felt as if it had been swept
across Arctic ice. And seeing red lacquer temples and green
pagodas through a whirling snowstorm was like living in a
mixed-up dream. Fred finally bought a ponyskin coat for me
from a Mongolian peddler. The Chinese teachers had their
long garments lined with fur, but most of the populace kept
warm by donning layer after layer of padded trousers and
coats. Their clothing was so bulky that if a child fell over, he
couldn't get to his feet and someone had to come and pick

him up. I understood now why the pastor of the church had told me that the seating capacity of the pews was ten in summer and eight in winter.

The winter passed swiftly, though, for we were very busy. We worked many hours a day at language school and at home. Until we could communicate with the Chinese in their own tongue, we could not begin the work which we had come so far to do. Our mission considered language study of primary importance. No matter how much Fred fretted and complained that his medicine was getting rusty and he must see some patients, there stood the inexorable rule that two years of language had to be passed before he could take on the responsibilities of the hospital. He was to be thankful for that rule in the years to come. I was given a little more leeway as to time, but we both had to pass five years of language study before we could be voted back after our first furlough.

So we kept at it, that first winter in Peking, and at last our diligence began to bear results. We practiced on anyone who would talk to us. We were still far from *thinking* in Chinese, but we could understand a little and we could, by repeated efforts on our part and an uncanny perception on the part of the Chinese, make ourselves understood.

Emboldened, I set out to learn another skill without which I had been told one could not get along in China: bargaining. One day in November as Fred and I were walking about the temple fair, I had spotted an incense burner, a tall pagodalike brass piece about ten inches high—a hideous thing, I was to learn later; but being new to the beauty of simple bronze, I thought it was typically Chinese and I wanted it badly.

The shopkeeper was immediately aware of my interest. After the usual exchange of greetings, I ventured to ask in my classroom Chinese, "To hsiao ch'ien?" "How much, how little money?"

"The price is fifty dollars," said the shopkeeper, rubbing the brass with the sleeve of his faded coat. "But you have just arrived in our country and I want you to have this, so I will give it to you for forty dollars."

Um, not bad, I thought. Exchange is almost five to one. Less than nine dollars our money. But I mustn't forget this bargaining business. I'll begin ridiculously low.

"That is very kind of you," I said, "but I really cannot spend more than ten of your dollars for an incense burner."

"I am very sorry, T'ai T'ai," he replied. ("T'ai T'ai" meant "Honorable Mrs.")

He put the incense burner back on his improvised shelf, a board on two packing boxes, and smiled sadly. Round One was finished and we retired to our corners.

Many times that winter I was tempted to meet the price of my smiling, innocent-faced shopkeeper as he went from forty to thirty-five, to thirty, to twenty-five. I could hardly resist as his smile disappeared and his eyes grew sad. I would look from the lengthening face of the shopkeeper to the stern face of my husband and come away each week without my incense burner.

Then suddenly it was blazing spring. The Orient with its heat quickly redeemed itself. Within a week we were to leave Peking and continue language study at the cool seaside village of Peitaiho, northwest of Peking. We were eager to get to our first mission station, Tsining, but the missionaries there had written that on no account were we to bring First-Born into the heat of the Shantung Plain before September. In the midst of the packing, I remembered the incense burner and dropped everything for one last round with my shop-

keeper. Fred came along to pick up some old coins he had
seen at another shop.

"We are leaving Peking, as you know," I began. "Do let
me have the brass piece for ten dollars."

"Yes, you are leaving," he replied, "and though I cannot
afford it, I will give you the incense burner for ten dollars.
It will mean that my old mother and the children will have
to go without food today, but I want you to have it. Though
I lose money, I want you to have it." He actually brushed
away a tear with the back of his hand. For the fraction of an
instant I wavered, but I did not lose the fight. Fred, who'd
been off buying the coins, came up in time to rejoice with me
that, for once, I had stood my ground when left on my own.

As we were leaving the temple grounds, on an impulse I
ran back to the shopkeeper. "You and I have had an interesting winter of bargaining," I said. "I am new to your country,
as you have said, but I am going to be here a long time. I
want to learn how to bargain properly. Tell me, how much
did you really pay for this incense burner in the first place?"

The shopkeeper laughed and said indulgently, "Just three
dollars. Good-by, T'ai T'ai. I lu ping an—all the way, peace."

We had a glorious summer at Peitaiho, aside from Fred's
swimming miles and scaring me to death by staying out of
sight for hours. There were sharks off the coast. Sometimes
I would be so furious that I'd wish they'd bite him; then I'd
be so frightened at the thought that I would walk out into
the sea as far as I could just to be that much nearer to him.
I dared not swim out for fear of the sharks. He could never
understand why I worried. He could swim, couldn't he?
Cramps? Nobody ever had a cramp who used his head. And
he loved the ocean and the gulls and the feeling of being
alone in creation.

First-Born added a few words to his vocabulary and learned to walk by digging his fat toes into the wet sand of the beach. He was so fat that his little mouth was lost in a hole in his face. The Chinese thought that anyone who was fat was beautiful. I took it rather badly the first time a friend tried to compliment me by saying, "Teacher-mother, how fat you are!" The only thing that troubled our Chinese friends was that the baby had blue eyes. Once when some country women were watching me bathe him, one of them said to the other, "She'll kill that child, washing him so much. How beautiful he is! So fat, so pretty, so white. If only he didn't have those goat's eyes."

At last the day came when the train puffed into the Tsining railway station. What a welcome we had from our fellow missionaries, the Eameses and the D'Olives and the Walters, Miss Stewart and Miss Christman; and from the Baptist friends who lived across the city—the Connelys, Miss Smith, Miss Frank and Miss Lawton. They were all at the station to meet us. Their first words were prophetic of what our life in China was to be.

"The city was taken over by bandits last night," Frank Connely said casually, picking up a suitcase and maneuvering me through the crowd.

"Bandits!" I gasped.

Our senior missionary, the Rev. Charles Eames, who was hurrying along behind us, stepped up to the rescue.

"There is nothing to worry about," he said quietly. "Shops will be looted; there may even be some shooting, but life for us will go on as usual. Really, there is nothing to worry about."

Maybe we should get right back on that train, I thought. Fred looked as if he were enjoying the excitement. Just the kind of an adventure he'd looked forward to, I could read behind his twinkle.

But the streets were quiet as we drove through them in our cavalcade of rickshaws. In Peking I had been surprised to find that all Chinese houses were behind walls. Here, too, the streets were lined with mud or brick walls; closed doorways with scrolls of letters across their tops and down each side marked the entrance to a private courtyard. For that matter, our compound was walled and the spacious grounds of each of our homes were surrounded by another set of walls. We did have access to one another through a path that ran along the back of the compound—an arrangement that was to stand us in good stead in the years to come when it was too dangerous for us to be on the street.

We stopped first at the Eames house where we were served tea. I was impatient to see our home. And what a surprise I got when I saw it! The thatched-roofed hut of my imagination turned out to be an imposing structure of gray brick that looked like a small factory with a front porch. Our house had been the one most recently built. The other houses on the compound were more in keeping with their Chinese background, with lattices of Chinese design and pillars on the porches. There had been an outcry when the first two-story building went up, many years ago; it would be possible for *foreigners* to look down from a point of vantage into the courtyards below. But by the time we arrived, a few of the more progressive Chinese inside the city wall were building two- and three-story houses themselves.

Fred picked me up in his arms, carried me across the threshold of our new home, dumped me in the front hall among the luggage and was off to see the hospital.

The house looked huge after our two small rooms at the language school. We had a living room, a dining room, a kitchen *and* a study on the first floor, and three large bedrooms and a small one on the second. There was a third floor that could be finished off if we ever needed it.

"We'll never get this much furnished," I told Fred that evening as we sat in borrowed chairs before our own fireplace. "Mrs. D'Olive said something about furniture made at a model prison. Somewhere in these trunks I have a furniture catalogue. We can show them pictures of what we want. I'll fish it out and we can have a couch and a chair made to begin with."

"I'm glad we brought our own beds, even though the freight was so terrific. And we're lucky to pick up the dining-room furniture that belonged to that couple who've gone home. What were their names?"

"I didn't get it."

"Well, honey, there's one room you won't have to worry about furniture for—our goldfish bowl of a bathroom; doors in three of the walls and a window off a porch on the fourth! Did you find out what time of day the man comes to empty the can?"

(The can arrangement didn't last long. While walking along the Grand Canal one day we discovered a house deserted by the Standard Oil Company when the last foreign resident left. Fred climbed to an upstairs veranda and saw through the window that there was a good bathroom in the house. He wrote at once to the office in Shanghai for permission to buy the outfit complete with pipes. He installed it himself and designed the septic tank from one of his medical books on sanitation.)

"Now tell me all about the hospital," I said as we drank our bedtime coffee.

"There's too much to tell and you're tired. I'll take you over and show it all to you the first thing in the morning."

That night when I got up to cover the baby—and for months afterward—I looked down the stair well to see if one of those bandits had broken into the house and was even now on his way upstairs.

Right after breakfast next morning we walked the half block and crossed the road to the hospital. Could it be called a hospital? The wards were rows of mud huts; the beds were boards on trestles. There was, however, a good little operating room in a small brick building which also housed the out-patient department. I fell in love with the little room that was the pharmacy. The shelves were filled with beautifully painted porcelain jars. I found it difficult to believe that they held such modern and prosaic things as zinc ointment and unguentine. I felt that if I lifted lids I would find tiger claws, lizard skins, and scorpion tails.

The operating room was across an open courtyard from the wards.

"What do you do with postoperative cases in the dead of winter?" Fred asked the immaculate operating-room supervisor.

"We just wheel them across to the ward on a stretcher and pray that they won't get pneumonia," he replied. (There were no antibiotics.) This was only one of the reasons why, some time later, we converted a well-built school building into a very usable sixty-bed hospital.

We got a language teacher at once, for Fred was determined to complete his second year by January so that he could take over full responsibility for the hospital. He was allowed to take a clinic for only an hour a day and the rest of the time had to be devoted to language study. Adopted Uncle Eames, being a minister, would be delighted if Fred could relieve him in time for the spring itineration trips to the country Christians. Young Mr. Wong, our teacher, had a silvery laugh and a pleasant disposition. He was one of twenty-seven children, only three of whom lived to grow up. Old Mother Wong was a tiny woman who looked like a gnarled crabapple tree. She always ended the story of her children by saying with a sigh, "I would have had more, but my husband died." Fred operated on her for an inflamed appendix when she was well over seventy, and she walked after a fractured hip and recovered from pneumonia several years after that.

After he had passed his examinations, Fred went out every morning and came back late at night. He took time out only for a brief lunch and a more leisurely dinner. I would beg him not to go back to the hospital at night when he was so tired, but he would insist that sleep was half of getting well, and he wanted to make sure that everyone was going to settle down for the night. He did everything—surgery, medicine, obstetrics. We had a good Chinese surgeon off and on (whenever we could persuade one to leave the port cities and come into the interior for much less pay). Chinese doctors seemed to prefer surgery and they were very adept with their hands. Getting an internist was another story and was probably the reason Fred eventually became a specialist in internal medicine. And we had an excellent obstetrician. Dr. Kung was a dear, tiny woman who had stopped counting after her thousandth delivery. It was only when she was on vacation or when her strength gave out that she had to call on Fred to take over.

Almost all the patients were very ill. Few came to the hospital in those days unless every other means had failed to cure them. Typhoid, dysentery, malaria, an occasional case of smallpox were apt to be found in the course of a day's rounds.

I helped out wherever I was needed—sorting linen, making inventories, making rounds with the superintendent of nurses whenever she needed me; and I taught classes in nursing ethics, English, and bedside care to the students in the training school.

The missionary wives had had servants for us waiting to be interviewed. They assured me I was to make my own choices, however. Servants who worked well for one family did not necessarily do so for another, and servants who had been failures with one family sometimes turned out very well for other families. We finally settled down with Hu Shih Fu, the cook, an old man who made noises as if he were cooling broth all the time he was cooking, and who did not like to have me in the kitchen trying out my own recipes; Li Ta Ke, the gateman and gardener; Chen Wu, the houseboy and washerman; and Ning Ta Sao, the amah. I rebelled at having so many. Why did I have to have all these servants around? I soon found out. It took all morning for the cook to do the shopping; he had to bargain over the price of every egg. Our food bills would have been astronomical if I had attempted the bargaining. Li Ta Ke raised the vegetables for our table, did the errands in a different part of the city from the food market, bought light bulbs, carried mail, took notes to people in the city, was gateman, telephone and messenger between the hospital and the house. Chen Wu did the washing and ironing, and there was a lot of it during the hot season with Fred's daily uniforms; he did the cleaning and dusting and there was a lot of it during the dust storms. Ning Ta Sao looked after the children.

Ning Ta Sao was an arrogant, uninhibited little woman who was a constant challenge to me because I simply could not stand her. As time went on, neither her disposition nor mine improved.

"I feel terrible about this," I told Fred. "Here I am a missionary and my attitude toward that woman is anything but Christian. I ought to love her—she needs love; and I cannot bear to have her near me. What am I going to do?"

"Let's face it," he replied. "You two are not temperamentally suited to each other. We'll get her another job. You will find that you can love her easily if she is a bit farther away from you."

But I was not willing to fire her when I knew so well that the failure was not hers but mine. In a short time the problem solved itself. She ran off with a married man, and was soon happily settled as the proprietress of her "husband's" grain shop.

I struggled on without an amah, running home between classes at the hospital to see if everything was all right. Then one morning heaven opened. When I came into the garden on one trip from the hospital, a happy little woman with a pock-marked face was hanging diapers on the line. They were snow-white.

"I hope you will not mind, T'ai T'ai," she said when she had taken a clothespin out of her mouth. "My name is Chang. I came to apply for work and while sitting idle waiting for you, I did this washing. I hope T'ai T'ai will not mind."

T'ai T'ai did not mind at all! From that day on, Chang Ta Sao was a member of the family.

A short while later, special services were being held in the church next door and Chang Ta Sao attended Christian worship for the first time in her life. She came home with tears in her eyes.

"I can't believe it, I can't believe it," she kept saying, "I'm only the Fourth Girl Child; I never even had a name. I'm a poor, poor woman that nobody knows, and yet Christ who is God died for me!"

Then it was true. Those words could pierce the heart, could open a whole new world. It was a first experience for Chang Ta Sao, and for me; we were both overwhelmed by it.

I envied Chang Ta Sao. Though it took her two years to memorize the few simple sentences in the catechism, she never tired of it. She would say the same thing over and over again as she leaned against the swing where First-Born was playing, pushing it back and forth with her swaying body, droning away the same words day after day.

"I should think that you'd be so bored by now that you'd want to throw the book away," I said to her one day.

"Every time I read it, it seems more wonderful," she replied. "Doesn't it seem wonderful to you, too?"

I wished fervently that it could mean that much to me.

For I was having trouble with my soul again and at a time when I wanted to be thinking only the happiest of thoughts. Fred, First-Born and I, with Chang Ta Sao, traveled to Cheeloo University Hospital in Tsinan where Dr. and Mrs. Randolph Shields took us into their home to await the arrival of our Second-Born. After nine tranquil, radiant months, I was more depressed than I had ever been.

"Even my faith is gone," I told Fred. "If religion means anything, it should be a stand-by when you need it. My religion is no good to me at all. I am depressed when I ought to be happy, and I have not one ounce of courage left to face the labor ahead."

"You're not in any position to judge your religion or anything else when you're not up to par physically," he said. "When this is all over and you are completely well, you can make your pronouncements. When you come right down to it, is there anything of importance in your past life that you would want changed?"

I thought about it for a few minutes, wanting the answer to be a truthful one.

"No, not one," I said slowly.

"Of course not," he went on. "You admit that 'all things have worked together for good' in the past; there isn't any reason to suppose that they won't in the future. It's a good verse to hang on to."

The onset of a difficult labor followed shortly after. With all my strength I clung to the verse he had given me. Then the blessed relief of the anesthetic, and my vision—if vision is what one calls a more-than-dream.

I was moving back in Time—down a long, long road by the side of which the women of the ages were standing, presenting me with gifts held in their outstretched hands. The gifts were their suffering and pain. Because through the ages women had suffered, it was now possible for me to have my baby without pain. As I went back in Time, I knew beyond all doubt that God *is*. I felt sorry for people on earth who had to make an effort of faith in order to believe. Here in Reality there was no striving for belief; one simply knew. It was the greatest peace I have ever known.

Then words began to swim into my consciousness—stubby, blunt words through the haze of the anesthetic, and the doctor's voice: "She'll never get these shoulders through. . . ." And later, "Nurse, kao su Hsien Sheng shih i ke nan hai tze" —"Tell the father it's a boy."

We named him Carl Robert for Fred's father and for mine.

"Two sons. You are blessed," said our Chinese friends when we got back to Tsining.

"Honey, I want you to meet Mr. Yang Ping Nan, the Magistrate from the county seat, Hsiang Wen," said my husband, coming in for his tea one afternoon. He ushered in a dynamic-looking gentleman wearing a loose-fitting foreign-style jacket.

"I am honored to meet you," I said.

"It's no honor, believe me," he replied in excellent English.

"Wait until you see Hsiang Wen."

The two men took out their pipes, exchanged brands of tobacco with the usual ritual, and settled down to talk. Chen Wu brought in the tea.

"I'll pour your tea and leave you to your discussion," I said.

"No, no, no. We want you to hear this," said the Magistrate, and launched into a vigorous recital of his plans for Hsiang Wen, punctuated by rapid puffs on his pipe.

Mr. Yang had given up the chair of sociology in one of Peking's leading universities because he wanted to see if what he had been teaching in the classroom was applicable to the poorest county in the province.

"Eventually our plan will take in fourteen counties," he said. "You know the setup—agrarian reform, mass education, flood control. . . . My immediate problem is to stamp out opium smoking. And here's where I need your help. Doctor, haven't you got something that will stop the horrible craving? I've arrested everybody caught smoking the stuff, men and women (that's why we want you to come too, Mrs. Scovel), and they are all going mad in the prison up there. You can't do this to people. Isn't there *something* you can give them?"

"Yes, there are several methods being used," Fred replied. "I'd like a chance to try out the one I read about just the other day in the *Journal of the Chinese Medical Association.*"

"Whatever it is, it will have to be cheap. I haven't much money for this program, and this item doesn't come under any category," said the Magistrate, reaching for a homemade cooky.

"It'll be cheap," said Fred.

Cantharides, the drug called for, could be purchased inexpensively in local medicine shops. This was ground to powder on a stone mill, mixed with vaseline fifty per cent by weight, and bandaged to a spot the size of a silver dollar on the patient's upper arm, the bandage to be left on overnight. By morning a large blister would have formed. With a hypodermic needle and syringe, the fluid from the blister would be withdrawn and injected into the patient's pectoral muscle. I could hardly believe that it would work, but Fred was eager to try it out.

"How soon can you come?" asked the Magistrate. "We'll need you at least three weeks."

"I'll have to arrange for the children," I said. "The women on the compound will run in every day and Chang Ta Sao is wonderful with them. But it won't be easy to leave them for that long a time."

"Fortunately the hospital isn't too full right now. Dr. Liu can carry on with the men and Dr. Kung with the women," Fred added. "How about Monday?"

Mr. Yang Ping Nan certainly carried us along on the wave of his enthusiasm.

"First I will take you to the museum," said the Magistrate soon after our arrival at his headquarters. "Be careful as you step over the doorsill. I've collected all the stuff of historical interest and put it into this little room. Don't expect too much, but we do have a few good things. Confucius himself was once the Magistrate of Hsiang Wen. Here is one of his shoes."

"Such a long shoe," I said. "Was Confucius such a big man?"

"Stop asking embarrassing questions," he replied. "How do you expect a cloth shoe to last two thousand years? Someone has to make a new one occasionally and every pattern must be taken from the last shoe made. Eventually Confucius will have been a giant. Just out here to the right is the mound where he stood when he preached to the people. I gave them a good talk from that spot myself the other day."

I wanted to linger in the museum, to touch the bronzes

that Confucius had touched, but we were swept along by this
new day for Hsiang Wen and were powerless to stop long
enough to discover what place the old might have in the thinking of this present moment. Mr. Yang hurried us on toward
the jail where the opium smokers were imprisoned, the
women in one building, the men in another.

"Here we are," said the Magistrate. "I hope that treatment
of yours works. These folks are pretty miserable."

At first the patients took the treatment to be slow torture.
It meant a sleepless night from the discomfort of the burn. But
on the whole they were good sports about it and when they
saw how the craving began to leave them after one injection,
they accepted the plaster gratefully. After three or four injections they were well enough to be discharged, and the
craving had left them never to return unless they deliberately
went back to their opium smoking. Fred was delighted and
so was the Magistrate.

One morning after a delicious breakfast of crisp, fried cab-
bage leaves dipped in beaten egg, hot cereal gruel and long,
unsweetened crullers, Fred and the Magistrate went off on a
trip to examine the widening of the dikes. I was left alone to
change the dressings. Fred had applied the ointment to the
men's arms the previous day while I was doing the women's
section; this morning I was to take a look at the blisters to
see how they were rising. Those in the women's ward were
coming along nicely.

By this time I knew the men pretty well, and when I entered their ward, I noticed that there were several newcomers
in the group. I began the usual banter. "If you will get me a
stepladder, Mr. Tall One, I will change your bandage." I
was met with a sullen silence. Strange, I thought. They
usually enjoy a laugh. Perhaps the dressings were more painful than usual. It didn't take long to discover that the men

had removed the dressings and had wound a layer of gauze around their arms with no medicine underneath.

"What is the meaning of this?" I demanded sternly. "Are you babies that you are not willing to stand a little pain for your own salvation? You know that you will be executed if you are caught smoking again. The doctor has left a hospital full of sick patients to come out here to help you, and I have left my babies at home to give you my time so that your children will not have to suffer from this terrible habit of yours. And you—big, strong men that you are—will not even accept one night's pain to help yourselves. Stand up here, every one of you, and I will again apply the ointment."

At night I went back to see the results. But I had had time to think, and by this time I was frightened. I remembered all I'd been told about loss of moral integrity among opium addicts; how, when thwarted, they would not stop at anything, even murder. Why hadn't I just backed out of the place that morning saying, "All right, all right," and left it for the men to take care of when they returned? No, I had to wax eloquent. Where were Fred and the Magistrate anyway? They should have been back before dark.

The prisoners slowly surrounded me as I came into the room. One small kerosene lamp hung from the ceiling, making a circle of light on the clean straw covering the floor. There was not a smile on anyone's face as the men drew within that circle of light.

They know the doctor and the Magistrate are away, I thought. They could finish me off in a minute and then say I never came into the prison. I looked at the guard at the door; he could have been my little boy, and . . . Oh, no! His gun was plugged with cotton, I remembered. No help from that direction.

A huge man who seemed to be the leader stepped forward.

"T'ai T'ai," he began, "I have something to say to you."

This is it, I thought.

"T'ai T'ai, the men have asked me to speak to you. They want me to say that they are very sorry for what happened last night. After all that you and the doctor have done for us, we want to assure you that what happened last night will never happen again."

What a relief! The tension had snapped and we were all laughing. I thanked them for their cooperation, changed the dressings and got out as quickly as I could lest anyone change his mind. But not without giving them the farewell that never failed to amuse them—"Pu sung, pu sung."

It is a delightful custom of the Chinese to accompany a guest out of the door to the main gate and then to walk with him some distance down the road, the guest all the while protesting, "Pu sung, pu sung—don't bother to accompany me. I am not worthy of such honor." These prisoners, not being allowed to even approach their own door, took a wry pleasure in the parting words, "Don't bother to accompany me along the road."

By the time two weeks were up the Magistrate was complaining that the treatment was too successful. "These fellows are eating me out of house and home," he said, running his finger along the inside of the collar of his black uniform. "Their appetite had been so deadened by opium that they ate nothing at all when they first came in. Now they're hungry again and enjoying it. Look at old Wong. He's gained pounds."

"Yes, the men are fine," Fred said. "I only wish that I could have had as much success with the women. They are so much harder to cure. That one old lady in the east wing is beating the wall with her hands and begging me to give her opium or kill her. I'll try her on glucose injections today but it will cost you money, brother.

"When you women go in for anything, you never do it halfway, do you, Honey?" he added, turning to me.

In no time at all the three weeks were up. It would be so good to get back to the children, but we hated to leave the village of Hsiang Wen. We took a last walk around the top of the wall and watched the sun set over the rows of thatched houses.

"I'm so glad you could be with me on this trip," Fred said to me. "It's been interesting, hasn't it?"

"Yes," I said, remembering the episode of the prisoners, "and I'm mighty glad to be going home with you, too. Do you think the children are all right?"

"Sure to be with Chang Ta Sao looking after them," he assured me.

Only one more night and I would be seeing them again. It must be bedtime for them now. Chang Ta Sao would be standing between their beds with her hands folded in prayer.

"Cheemee, Kalo [her pet names for Jimmy and Carl], pi shang yen—close your eyes. Wa men ts'ai t'ien shang ti Fu—Our Father who art in heaven." Then sentence by sentence she would repeat the Lord's Prayer in her own language. They would tease her as usual by not saying amen until she had called each one of them by name.

"Amen, Cheemee."

"Amen."

"Amen, Kalo."

"Amen."

During the summer of 1932, Evy Shields and I took the children to Peitaiho to escape the heat. So Fred was alone in the house when the cable came—Father Scovel had died suddenly from a heart attack. Fred shut himself in his room until Li Ta Ke, the gateman, knocked softly at the door and said,

"Don't cry any more, Doctor. It's too hot." The logic of it made sense and Fred could face the world again.

We urged Mother Scovel to come to China, and bravely she packed and sold and stored and came out to us; but she was determined not to be a burden. We were able to get a small house for her at the other end of the compound, since that was what she wanted, and she soon became Beloved Grandmother to the whole community. She taught English to hospital staff members and in the schools; her home was a haven to which we all turned; and she could read Browning and Thackeray to children and make the reading fascinating.

One of her ministrations was to give up her little house, in December of 1933, and to move into ours to look after the family while I was at Cheeloo University Hospital for the birth of our first little girl, Anne Elizabeth, the Golden-Haired One. The big house was filling up.

Beloved Grandmother often said that her mission in coming to China was to amuse the missionaries with her brand of Chinese. She learned to speak the language in her own fashion, to the amazement of our Chinese friends who wondered that such an ancient lady should even attempt study. She did remarkably well except for occasionally misplacing a word, as she did that evening after dinner when she said to her maid servant, "Big Sister Wu, go into the bedroom, open the top drawer, look into the left-hand corner and bring me the kindling wood."

With never a smile Wu Ta Sao did exactly as she had been told and returned with a small box of toothpicks!

There were times when Beloved Grandmother and I had our difficulties, when our quiet disagreement left Fred puzzled and helpless. But if we did not always see eye to eye, we did see heart to heart. I wonder what we would have done without her. In addition to hospital work, there was that five years of language study to complete before furlough. For my classical examination I was translating a long poem of Po Chu Yi. How I mutilated that beautiful poem! After the examination had been passed, I found Arthur Waley's translation of it and tore mine into bits.

And there was the daily teaching of the children to be done. For their first year they attended the Chinese kindergarten and had as their teacher a very pretty curly-haired Chinese girl who became my close friend. She was the only curly-haired Chinese I ever knew. Since there were no Chinese schools in Tsining that would prepare our children for school and life in America, I had to teach them myself. We had a classroom and went into it every morning at eight-thirty. We used the Calvert Course, a correspondence course sent out by the Calvert School in Baltimore. I knew nothing about teaching, but the instructions were so clear that "wayfaring men, though fools, need not err therein," to use Beloved Grandmother's quotation from Isaiah. I stuck to my guns and saw each day's lesson completed before play could begin. Fred was amused by our being so conscientious and came in to snap a picture of Second-Born and me sitting up in bed with high fevers, Calvert books spread out before us.

But the children had fun, too. The boys had a feud with the Li boys, the sons of a schoolteacher next door; the cook's children were "on our side." The feud necessitated much stalking through grass and running through gardens at top speed. The Golden-Haired One helped to roll out the dough, cook (and eat quantities of) the long, round noodles for the cook's table.

One afternoon following an unusually tiring morning at the hospital, Fred and I went for a short walk in the nearby wheat fields. We came back refreshed, as we always did after a few moments out there in the quiet. As we entered the house we heard great thumping noises coming from the nursery overhead. In alarm we dashed for the stairs and reached the nursery door breathless. Nothing seemed amiss; there were our two innocent sons peering under the bed. What had caused all the noise?

A huge, roly-poly figure in a cassock crawled slowly from under the bed with a toy truck in his hand and an embarrassed grin on his face. He looks just like Santa Claus, I thought—the same apple cheeks, the same benevolent rotundity, the same beatific, jolly smile.

Our guest delivered the retrieved truck to First-Born before turning to us with a courteous explanation of his presence under our son's bed. He was Brother Linoldhus, a German lay brother from the Catholic monastery six miles north of Tsining; one of the priests was ill, and he had cycled over to ask Fred to visit him. Li Ta Ke had informed him that the doctor was absent but would soon return, so he had taken the opportunity to become better acquainted with the young men of the family. From the affectionate smiles with which the boys regarded him, it was obvious that he was already accepted.

Brother Li, as he was always called by Chinese and foreigners alike, spoke to us in Chinese. We did not know any German and he did not know any English. Chang Ta Sao was highly amused that two foreigners had to speak Chinese in order to be understood by each other. Didn't they even know their own language?

A continual flow of Chinese was coming from Brother Li now.

"As I was coming through the village today, a smart young fellow called me a foreigner. I got off my cycle and called him over. The usual crowd gathered. 'Young man,' I said, 'how old are you?' 'I'm eighteen,' he replied. 'So, you've been in this country only eighteen years and you call me a foreigner. I've lived in this country for over twenty years.' How the villagers laughed!"

We liked this cheerful, friendly man as much as the boys did. That afternoon began a friendship that still endures. And although we had no intimation then of the dreadful years ahead, Brother Li was to be the instrument to bring us help when we needed it most. But that is a story that belongs to a later time.

One never knew what a day would bring forth in that city so far from the stream of the world. A Chinese boy knocked at our front gate one morning with the message that Fred was needed at once; a foreigner was dying in the fur-buying place across the canal.

"A foreigner?" the doctor asked. "Are you sure? There are no foreigners in Tsining except at our missions. Never mind. I'll be ready as soon as I pick up my bag."

The boy had been right. The man, a White Russian, was dangerously ill with pneumonia. In those days before anti-biotics, nursing care was essential if he were to live; so Fred brought him home, and the whole family, including the children, nursed him back to health. From then on, the Russian fur-buyers would have turned the world upside down for us and even juggled it a while with Venus and Mars for our amusement. Fortunately they could speak English. They were a gay lot, those Russian boys, and the children loved them. Their laughter and rollicking music always made us feel as if a blast of clean, fresh wind had blown through the house.

Oh, the wonderful dinners at the fur-buying warehouse, with all the food brought in from the port city—liver paste, egg-plant fixed in a special way, caviar, salads, the table bearing up proudly under the weight of the elaborate hors d'oeuvres

called "zakuska"! There would be hot borsch soup with a
dollop of heavy cream floating upon its crimson surface, Kiev
cutlets of pounded chicken breasts waiting to be pricked
open with a fork to release the flow of hot melted butter,
piroshkis (triangles of pastry filled with chopped savory meat
and hard-boiled eggs), desserts, coffee and chocolate bonbons!
Then the ride home under the brilliant stars, the sound of the
rickshaw-puller's feet echoing hollowly against the boarded-up
shops in the deserted streets. Our little dog, Ber-ber, barking
with staccato insistence, would wake the gateman as we pulled
up in front of the house.

"Who is there?" the gateman would call sleepily.

"Bandits!" my husband would reply in a gruff voice. The
door would immediately be opened for us.

I wonder how many children in the world have camphorwood
boats sixty feet long to use as a playhouse. We certainly didn't
know what we were getting into that day when Adopted
Uncle Eames asked us casually, "Wouldn't you like a nice
wooden boat for your children to play with? You can have it
for about fifty dollars."

The boat in question had been used by the evangelistic committee for reaching the floating population on the Grand
Canal. It had never been an unequivocal success, tending to
tip over in a high wind. There were two good-sized rooms in
it, one of them with a small kitchen attached. The evangelistic
committee, being short of funds and finding that the canal
people could be reached as easily by wheelbarrow along the
bank, had tried in vain to sell the boat. Its unseaworthiness
was well known along the canal. Adopted Uncle Eames
thought he had found a way out.

It was not until after the purchase was a fait accompli that we realized that the boat was fully half a mile away and in the canal.

"We'll take care of that," said Adopted Uncle, who always took care of everything; who was our rock, our fortress, our bulwark of love.

One night it rained, and the next morning the roads were covered with soft mud an inch deep. Sixty coolies hauled the boat out of the water, up the short incline and into the muddy road. Soon the "ayaho, ayaho" of their chant could be heard as they slid the huge bulk along the main thoroughfare. The children left the breakfast table to see what was happening.

"Daddy, Mother, come quick! A boat on land! Why, look, it's stopping right in front of our house!"

And then everyone looked at everyone else with a "Now, what?" expression on his face. The boat was far too wide to get through the front gate. Nothing to do but call Lao San and his workmen. While all the astonished traffic was held up in both directions, the front wall, twelve feet high and a foot thick, was torn down, and the boat slid across the wet grass to its final resting place under the trees.

Not until some time later did we learn that the Christians of the community thought the doctor had had advance warning of a flood, as Noah had had. The doctor and his family would, of course, be spared because of this preparation.

Not long after this, we actually had a flood, and though its waters never reached the city, its tragedy did. The Yellow Dragon was always bursting its bonds. Through the centuries the water had come down from the hills, depositing layer after layer of silt, so that now the floor of the river was many feet higher than the surrounding land. It could be kept in its channel only by high dikes. A few holes in one of these had passed unnoticed, and now the whole countryside was flooded.

We took a trip down the canal by boat to see the extent of the devastation. It could have been the ocean, except for the trees sticking their tops out of the water like growing celery. Villages, constructed entirely of mud brick, had been washed away.

We took with us Mosely Eames, the teen-age son of Adopted Uncle. As the corpse of a man floated toward us, I did my best to divert the boy by pointing out a submerged tree on the other side of the boat. I thought I had succeeded. On the way back the same corpse, or another, came in sight.

"You again, pal?" said Mosely quietly.

Our city was the terminus of a branch line leading to the main railway. This was the outlet to safety for all the flooded area, and thousands of people collected at the railway station. Illness broke out, babies were born under freight cars, and our hospital was filled far beyond capacity. Fred and the hospital staff became a team that worked as one man. The challenge of the emergency called out the best in each member of the staff. For days nobody thought of sleeping. Fred had to insist that they take time out to eat.

Nobody could guess how many months it would be before the waters would recede. The Yellow Dragon was in no hurry to decide where it would cut its new channel. Governor Han Fu Ch'u did an excellent job of moving each village as a unit to a place where it could make a fresh start. Each person's name was carefully written in a register as was the place where he had formerly lived and the place to which he was going. In this way friends and relatives did not become separated. The Governor provided food and transportation for the journey and even vacated a large section of his palace so that the refugees would have a stopping place en route to their destination.

After the waters had subsided, we heard the exciting—and to me somewhat alarming—news that Governor Han would make an official visit to the hospital to thank the doctor and his staff for all they had done. I did not have a notion of the protocol attendant upon a Governor's visit. I asked myself, "What would I do in America if a Governor came to call?" That didn't help a bit, and there was no one to ask. I would just have to pretend that the Governor was a stranger coming to town for an informal cup of coffee. Coffee it would be, with brownies and ice cream. I sent to the fish market for a cake of ice and we borrowed the biggest freezer on the compound. We had no idea how many there would be in the Governor's party.

I had a few bad moments when I saw two truckloads of soldiers milling over the front lawn setting up machine guns. Did they all expect to be fed? Why were they setting up machine guns, anyway? "To protect the Governor, of course," the cook enlightened me. For a brief second I wondered what would happen if the Governor never came out of our house—if he had a heart attack and died there. Suppose he should get acute food poisoning and collapse? Had the cook been careful not to get any of that dirty ice into the ice cream?

The two boys were having a wonderful time with the soldiers, who were showing them how to fire a machine gun! I had no time to make a tactful rescue; the Governor and six giant bodyguards in long silk Chinese garments were walking up the path and into the house with Fred. They were chatting away as if they had known one another for years. There would only be these seven to be fed. When they were seated, I gave a nod to the cook to come forward with the coffee tray. Standing in the doorway with his mouth wide open and his hands hanging limply at his sides, completely overawed at having such an august personage in the house, he could not move a step.

I got up and did the serving myself. Apparently the Governor did not know I was in the room, so engrossed were he and Fred in their discussion of the flood. "More brownies, Governor Han?" I asked, passing him the plate. He took three.

"And let me fill your cup."

He passed it to me sideways without turning his head from my husband. He liked his ice cream, I could see that. I'd been a bit worried about it because most Chinese dislike anything made with milk or flavored with vanilla. I'd given this a heavy dose of maple and caramel.

"Doctor, are you a Christian?" the Governor asked as he finished his coffee. "But of course you are. I do not need to ask that question. You wouldn't be doing what you are for my people if you weren't a Christian."

As they rose to leave, the Governor said, "Doctor, I don't understand this at all. Most of the American men I know have to wait on their wives, but you seem to have this one pretty well in hand. Thank you both for everything. Good-by."

"And I never gave you away at all," said Fred when we were back in the house. "I let the Governor go away without ever telling him the truth."

Three
The Gourd

"The passengers think you two are on your honeymoon," said the stewardess. I cannot remember on which of the Dollar Line ships we were traveling from Shanghai to San Francisco for our furlough year at home after five years in China.

"Our honeymoon! With three children?" I asked.

"They think the doctor has been married before—the children are all blonds and you have such black hair," she said. "And they think it is very generous of you to take your mother-in-law on your wedding trip!"

It was June of 1936. We had had a spectacular send-off at the railway station in Tsining, with flags and banners and even a band which tootled its songs as we said good-by to our friends. It stopped playing long enough for the school children to sing their farewell song. The Chamber of Commerce was there to a man to express their appreciation for what the hospital had meant to the community. (We had been surprised to find a full-fledged Chamber of Commerce in Tsining.) It was hard to say good-by. These had been such rewarding, happy years that we hated to leave.

But America is a wonderful country too! We hadn't realized how wonderful it was until we came into it after six years away. There was hot running water, crisp celery, smooth roads, and comfortable cars in which to ride over them. There were

rolling hills, clean villages with tall white spires catching the
sun. We could sit together as a family in church instead of
separating at the door for the men's side and the women's side.
There were friends who had known us all our lives. There
were family and home. My beloved father and mother were
suddenly converted into my children's grandparents, who
scolded us for not being strict enough with them and then
spoiled them outrageously themselves.

The year passed quickly. Fred attended clinics at Cornell
University, taking a course in X-ray diagnosis to help him in
one of our major medical problems, tuberculosis; and he was
buying equipment for the hospital. I was buying shoes for
the seven years ahead; patronizing every counter of the five-
and-ten; buying bolts of cloth for pajamas, underwear and
curtains, and yards of dress material for the Golden-Haired
One and me. The winter clothes could wait. I always knitted
dresses and suits for the children each winter, and yarn for
these could be picked up in Japan on our way back.

There were days when the newspapers made us wonder if
we would ever get back to China. Remembering my qualms
of five years ago, it seemed ironical that now I had to pray that
I might be willing to remain in America if that turned out to
be God's will for us. I did not even try to defend myself when
friends said, "You are crazy to take those children out there
at a time like this." There was no explaining the deep compulsion in any way that would make sense.

But we got off, and Beloved Grandmother was with us,
willing to face whatever might come.

While we were still on shipboard, it was announced that
the Japanese army had landed at Shanghai. We could take
our choice of getting off the ship at Japan or going on to
Hong Kong. There seemed a slight chance that we could

obtain passage from Japan directly to our province, Shantung, so we disembarked at Kobe.

But we did not get away from Japan as easily as we had hoped. We spent futile weeks trying to obtain passage and permission to travel. The Presbyterian missionaries took us into their homes, though it cast suspicion upon them for harboring such close friends of their enemy, China. The David Martins loaned us their dear little house at the foot of Mount Fujiyama for several weeks.

What a gem of a country Japan is! It was here that Fred first began to work with pastels. One of our neighbors, a China missionary refugee too, would go off into the woods each morning with her box of chalks and a pad of paper, and come home at night with her achievement for the day.

"Look at this one," she would say, laughing. "Did you ever see such a tree?" We hadn't. "But you have no idea what it has done for my morale," she would add.

As the days wore on and Fred became more and more frustrated at not being able to get back to his work, I suggested that he, too, might take up drawing.

"Me, draw?" he protested. "Never. When I was in school I got my poorest grades in drawing." But I sent to Tokyo for the materials.

One rainy day I said to him, "Go upstairs and take a look at Fujiyama. It's just peeking its head above the clouds. And here, take these with you. Not one bite of dinner do you get until you have put something on paper."

We were both surprised at the results. To some discriminating individuals his painting might have appeared a very amateur attempt, but to me it was as if he himself had created the beautiful, snowcapped mountain.

Back at Kobe we made every attempt to get on to China.

Reluctantly we decided that Fred would have to go on alone and leave the rest of us in Japan. He talked it over with a friend in the United States consulate, and though nothing official was said, there was a sympathetic understanding of Fred's desire to get back to his hospital. The first step was to secure a passport for himself alone—all five of us were now included in his. Great care had to be exercised because the true reason for obtaining separate passports could not be told. No official sanction could be given to a civilian for taking himself into the middle of a war.

We two walked into the office of an under-secretary that gray, drizzling afternoon, feeling the burden of the separation before us. I sat down on one side of the room and Fred on the other. We could not trust ourselves even to look at each other.

"Name? Age? Which one of you will have the children? Have you ever been divorced before?"

Divorced? The ludicrousness of the situation dawned on us. The secretary thought we were seeking a divorce! Well, she would just have to go on thinking it.

Not many days later, when the clouds were so thick that I couldn't even see the ship in the bay, Fred stepped into a little gray cutter and was taken out to sea, the long V of ripples widening the distance between us. I watched the small boat disappear into the wall of mist and wondered if the children and I would ever see him again.

Barbara Hayes, another China missionary refugee, and I kept trying to find passage for our families. It did not look as if the war would end in the near future and we decided that, come what may, we were going back to our homes in China. Together we walked the streets, going from one office to another. At last we persuaded one company to take us on board the *Havel*, a little German freighter. The captain did not like missionaries and was perturbed when he found that some twelve of us were booked to travel with him.

It had not been easy to manage alone the passage, visas, finances, children and Beloved Grandmother. I hadn't realized how much I had come to depend upon Fred for everything, especially for thinking out loud to. We hadn't heard from him in weeks. The newspapers in Japan had repeatedly told of the bombing and complete demolition of our city, Tsining. It was the repetition in the papers of the term "complete demolition" that gave us hope. Too many "complete demolitions" couldn't mean accurate reporting. But the question remained, where was he? Would he get our message? Would he be on the dock to meet us?

It took seventeen days to make what was ordinarily a three-day journey. In spite of Germany's being an ally of Japan, the ship was held up by the Japanese authorities at every port. Sometimes we were held in quarantine several days before being allowed to proceed into the harbor. The passengers became one family, and the distraught captain an anxious father to us all.

But at last we *did* put into port at Tsingtao, and Fred *was* on the dock to meet us; and he had brought Chang Ta Sao with him. By some miracle our cable had reached him. Though he could stay with us only a few days, we took comfort in being in the same country together. We decided reluctantly that, for the present, it was best for the family to remain in Tsingtao rather than to risk the dangers of the road while armies were on the move. We were able to rent a house and we unpacked our Lares and Penates and set up a new home. Then Fred went back to Tsining to continue his hospital work. He did not open our big house, but made himself as comfortable as he could in Beloved Grandmother's smaller one. Letters were frequent and we settled down to the long winter ahead.

It was late November when I received his telegram:

HOSPITAL FULL OF WOUNDED SOLDIERS
NEEDING OPERATION. NO ETHER

"He must want me to buy ether and bring it in to him," I said to Beloved Grandmother. "There is no other way to get it into the interior; but I just don't see how I can do it. How can I leave the children and you at a time like this?"

"If it is right for you to go, the way will open," Beloved Grandmother replied. "Chang Ta Sao and I will look after the children with no trouble at all. Only—do come back for Christmas, both of you. That will give you more than three weeks there."

"Don't worry; we'll be here for Christmas!" I said.

I went from shop to shop, buying a can of ether here and another there. I also bought Christmas presents for the children and wrapped them in gay kite paper at odd moments. I was determined to be back with them for Christmas, but so many things could happen. At least they'd have their presents.

Supplies were not coming in and ether was hard to find. I finally collected a suitcase full of it. The next step was to get on a train. All of China was on the move. Crowds of refugees clung to the sides and covered the roof of each train. People were traveling in both directions—in toward the line of battle and out to the coast again. They seemed to feel they were safe as long as they were moving.

We were only a few miles outside of Tsingtao when the train screeched to a jerking stop. At once the myriad passengers started to shove and claw their way out of the windows; all exits were jammed. I didn't understand what was going on but I had to protect that ether from damage. Whether or no, I was swept along with the refugees who swarmed down the sides of the train and scattered over the fields to cast themselves flat in any available ditch. As I threw myself down alongside the suitcase of ether, fear and understanding reached me at the same moment: Japanese bombers were flying low overhead.

Finally the engine tooted, and there was an equally mad scramble to get on again before the train started. A few miles farther on the same thing occurred: the jarring halt, the frantic rush. This time I sat still. I thought it safer for the ether—and for me—to avoid the jam. Again and again the train came to a stop and each time I had the luxury of a few moments of space around me, tinged with the thought, however, that I was a sure target.

After an all-day ride, the train pulled into Tsinan, where I had to make connections for Tsining. I battled my way out of the station and selected a rickshaw from the crowd of them that hemmed me in. It took me across town to the other railway station. Here people were packed in a radius a half mile deep around the building—all of them waiting and hoping for transportation. I could not move forward one inch through the mass.

In desperation I told the man ahead of me that wounded Chinese soldiers would die if I did not get through to them with the medicine I carried, and asked him to pass the word through the crowd to the station master. I don't know what the message sounded like by the time it got to him, but eventually he came out with a squad of policemen. People were unwilling to give up their places so the policemen had to take small rope cords and strike at the people on either side to make a pathway to the train.

The policemen lifted me into the baggage car; it was crammed with soldiers but again they beat a path through

to a seat for me. I sat bolt upright on the hard bench with
the suitcase of ether in my lap, completely immobilized by
the soldiers jammed close on either side, and went sound
asleep. When I wakened the train was under way. A soldier
was asleep against my right shoulder, another on my left
shoulder, one across each knee, and two across my feet.

"At last," I said to myself, "I've solved the problem of how
to keep warm on a train."

From time to time someone would wake up and start a
conversation with me. The soldiers could not understand why
I was traveling alone under such circumstances in order to
help them. Why should anyone care whether they lived,
suffered or died?

"Brother, please do not smoke in here," I would say to them.
"Please do not smoke near this suitcase. It is filled with ether
and may explode."

"What difference does it make, T'ai T'ai, to be blown up
here or a few days later on the battlefield?"

"One very big difference, brother. I shall not be with you on
the battlefield!"

Wonderful, wonderful people! They could always laugh.
They had learned, over the long centuries, never to take
themselves, or life, too seriously.

I had wired Fred when I began the journey, and he met
me the next morning at Yenchow, the nearest railway station
on the main line. With unutterable relief I handed over the
ether. Our city had not yet fallen, Japanese newspaper reports
to the contrary notwithstanding. As we rode across the flat
plain with its fields sprouting winter wheat, Fred outlined
his plans.

"You know the rumors we are hearing about the on-coming
army. They may be true and they may not, but the young
girls in the nursing school are afraid and want to go inland to

safety. I can hardly keep them here against their wishes. But the Boys' School at Tenghsien has closed and the boys have come home. Do you suppose you could take some of the most promising of those boys and give them a short nurses' aid course? Then we'll put them on the wards and teach them as they go. A few of the older nurses have family responsibilities and can't leave. We'll put them on the women's wards, and the boys can work with the men. With all these wounded, most of the patients are men anyway. What do you think?"

"It sounds like a very good idea," I said. "But what about the children and Grandmother? I promised we'd both be there for Christmas."

"Yes, I know. . . . Well, we'll see what we can do in the next three weeks, and if there is any possibility at all, we'll try to get out for Christmas. If not, you'll have to go back alone and . . . but I can't let you do that."

Somehow or other the work was accomplished. The boys were given the fundamentals and an older nurse instructed on how to carry on. We even managed to work in a birthday party for Fred, inviting a few friends from the city. It was an evening to be remembered. We sat around the fire singing Christmas carols, each in his own language; the old German woman and her son singing "Silent Night, Holy Night," the Chinese singing it softly in Chinese, the Americans humming softly too—all of us with our eyes on the German woman's beautiful face, as her still lovely voice rose above the rest.

And then it was time to take the journey back to the children. What a trip the two of us had! We climbed in and out of train windows, were carried along by the surge of crowds, ate whatever scant food we could find along the way. But we made it! We arrived in Tsingtao on the evening of the twenty-first of December.

Since the Christmas gifts were already bought and wrapped,

we planned to use these last few days making popcorn balls with the children, melting old candles into wax stars with wicks (for the Adopted Aunts and Uncles), and decorating the house. We sank exhausted into bed, expecting a long night's sleep.

But I could not sleep. At first I thought it was because I was overtired; but gradually I realized a firm, insistent urging, as if God were trying to speak to me.

"Get up. Leave the city at once, all of you. You are to go back to Tsining to your home. Now."

This is just plain silly, I said to myself. Who would dream of taking the children and Beloved Grandmother directly into the line of battle? Why, I couldn't face the trip myself after these last days on those awful trains!

But long before morning, I knew that I would have to wake Fred and tell him. No, I wouldn't have to wake him.

"You know," he said, "I have the strangest feeling, a strong compulsion that we must all get out of this city and go back to Tsining—children, Mother, all of us. It seems crazy. You know I'm not like you, seeing visions and dreaming dreams; but this is it and there is no doubt about it."

"I know," I replied. "It's like Lot at Sodom, only this time the wife is not going to be turned into a pillar of salt. I'm sure that we must go."

Beloved Grandmother did not seem at all surprised when we told her. Had she, too, had a vision? Once again she was ready to disrupt a peaceful life and to go with us into danger. We found that she could go by a special train that had just been put on, for which we would be able to buy reservations. We telephoned the two "ladies" from our station, Miss Christman and Miss Stewart. They, too, had been waiting at Tsingtao for an opportunity to go back to their work, and hadn't heard about the special train. (The unmarried women of the station were always called "ladies" by the children to distinguish them from "mothers" who were not "ladies"!)

We worked all day packing. We put the children's Christmas gifts in a separate suitcase, for it looked as if we would spend Christmas on the road. We went to the landlord, who was convinced that we were insane; we got Beloved Grandmother and the ladies off on the train; we wired young Adopted Uncle, Deane Walter, who was already in our mission station, to meet them with his car at the railway junction. We learned later that that train was the last one to leave Tsingtao for many months.

Fred and I, the children, and Chang Ta Sao were going to attempt a cross-country trip of something under seven hundred miles in order to take with us the Ford truck a friend in America had given us for use as an ambulance. Before daylight on the twenty-third we started out, the children excited with the new adventure. Chang Ta Sao was sure that she was going to be seasick all the way. She was.

Looking back on it, I can remember only snatches of the journey, as one recalls a bad dream. We went through a winding river eight times, never knowing how deep the water in the middle of the stream might be. The truck had double wheels in back; we crossed one bridge that was only as wide as the inner wheels so that we bump-bump-bumped over the stumps of piles that held the bridge. We spent the night at Ichowfu, another of our mission stations, with Katherine Hand. Katherine could hardly have been more surprised when we drove up to her gate. She hadn't seen one of her own countrymen for months.

In spite of Katherine's entreaties and the temptation to spend Christmas with her, we hurried off early next morning for another grueling day across the level plain. (The plain was level enough but the road was anything else but.) At dusk snow began to fall, and by dark we found ourselves behind a column of marching soldiers whom we took to be Japanese. We were afraid to ask. Apparently the soldiers thought that the truck was part of their own unit, for they paid no attention to us. The marching file eventually turned off. Some time later the road petered out and became a small village. As a last straw the truck slid into a deep hole previously used by the village animals as a wallow.

I often wonder what the villagers thought when that snorting monster of a truck came to such an abrupt halt at the edge of their village that cold winter's night, and such queer-looking people piled out into their street. Exactly as we would feel if a spaceship from Mars landed on Main Street in River Bend, I suppose. No white person had ever been in the village before.

"Hsiao h'ar che ma pang, lien che ma pei," the villagers said as they crowded around us. ("So fat the children, so white their faces!")

"Where have you come from and what do you want here?" a thin-mustached old gentleman asked Fred.

"Ni kan. T'a ti t'ou fa ch'uan pei la!" "Just look," said a young girl carrying a baby, "the little girl's hair has all turned white."

"It isn't white, it's like gold thread," said a woman who might have been the girl's mother, "and it's all in little circles. See?"

She pulled out a ringlet from the Golden-Haired One's head, and was delighted when it snapped back into a tight curl. At once everyone, young and old, wanted to try it. I had all I could do to keep my daughter from being frightened as I held her in my arms. Fortunately she was a very outgoing, friendly child and rather enjoyed being the center of attention; but the crowd almost smothered us.

Fred asked for oxen to pull the truck out of the wallow, but all their animals had been commandeered by the army. He and a few of the men went off to the surrounding villages to see if they could find some oxen. The other villagers pressed closer, feeling our clothing and pinching the children's cheeks. The questions they asked were endless; and we were so tired.

At last a motherly looking woman came out of her house, took in the situation at a glance, and having elbowed the people out of her way, swept the three children into her capacious arms.

"Come into my miserable hovel," she said to us. "Here, T'ai T'ai, sit down on the bed. Boy, get some straw for the fire. I'll have some soup ready in no time. You are so cold and hungry."

She called it a miserable hovel; but she said the words as a queen would say them, asking you into her palace. A palace could not have seemed more inviting.

Fred didn't come back and we grew even more tired and hungry.

The night wore on. I sat on the board bed with the weary children and could not keep from crying. First-born, puzzled at this phenomenon, crawled over beside me and whispered, "Don't cry, Mother. Everything will be all right. God will take care of us."

Finally Fred returned with the news that no oxen were available anywhere. What were we to do? The village men were not easily thwarted. They put their backs to the huge, awkward vehicle and by sheer manpower lifted it out of the muddy pit and wheeled it into the road.

"Shall we stay here the rest of the night?" Fred asked. "The villagers want us to spend the night here and go on in the morning. We are about five hours from home, if nothing else stops us. One of the men has offered to go with us to show us the way." (When our guide returned to his village he had a

Bible and other reading material for the village schoolteacher to read to them all.)

"Well, what do you say? We'll do whatever you want," said my husband.

It was not difficult to see that he was longing to get out on the road again, to finish this ghastly journey and see us all safe at home.

"Let's go on," I said.

"But not until you have had some of this hot soup," said our hostess, dipping a gourd ladle into the simmering kettle. The light from the fire caught the satiny sides of the gourd as the soup, with its hot chunks of sweet potato, slipped into the heavy porcelain bowls. Never was hospitality more gratefully received.

At last we said our good-bys, after expressing our gratitude as best we could, and started out with our guide on the final lap of our journey. Aside from having to get the magistrate out of bed to give us permission to go through one walled city, nothing untoward happened; and not long before dawn, the car turned in at the mission compound. It was Christmas morning.

Christmas morning and home, with Beloved Grandmother and Stella Walter there to welcome us! Stella had opened the house, had it thoroughly cleaned, taken all the furniture out of the storeroom and arranged it exactly as it had been the year before. The beds were made and, joy of all joys, she had put up a Christmas tree and decorated it! We opened the suitcase full of Christmas gifts and laid them under the shining tree to be unwrapped later that morning.

Tired and thankful, thankful, thankful, we all fell into bed.

A few days later, Fred came back from the hospital with a strange look on his face—joy? bewilderment? wonder?

"What is it?" I asked.

"I've just learned," he told me quietly, "that the Chinese have begun to plow up the roads we came over; they're planting them with winter wheat so that the enemy won't find any road at all. If we hadn't come the day we did, we could never have made it."

Four
The Grape

Three weeks later our city fell to the Japanese. I had been doing the rounds of the hospital one afternoon, chatting with the patients and giving each one a flower. Even the men liked to hold a blossom in their hands.

Now I noticed that the planes were zooming lower and lower, and that the sound of the guns was getting louder and louder. One deafening detonation must surely have awakened the children from their naps. I hurried out of the hospital and saw that planes were strafing the courtyard and the roads nearby. Keeping close to the high compound walls, I reached the street and ran as fast as I had ever run. From the sound I thought thousands must be running behind me, and I turned to see that I was leading the retreat of what seemed to be the whole Chinese army. Well, they would have to continue without my leadership. I slipped in at the gate of our compound, negotiated the open space between the street wall and the house, and arrived, breathless, in the front hall just as the children were coming sleepily down the stairs.

Try to keep life normal for them, I thought.

"Let's have some fun this afternoon. Let's take a plate of cookies and some books and go down into that little cellar room that Daddy has built for us to play in." It was a bombproof shelter—we hoped.

I am not sure the children had ever been fooled by my

efforts over the last weeks to keep things normal—to continue
with school every day, to move casually to some other place
in the house when the bullets started to come through the
windows. I have a suspicion that they, too, played the game,
because they didn't want me to be frightened. Now they ami-
ably agreed that playing in the little room would be fun.

The cook's wife and children were already in the cellar.
We sat on the floor and told stories, first in Chinese and then
in English, lifting our voices in what First-Born called a
"quiet roar" in order to be heard above the noise of the guns
outside. We ate cookies and waited. We had no way of telling
which way the battle was going. Once I came upstairs and
found the cook standing in an open doorway watching the
progress of the fray.

"Hu Shih Fu, come down into the cellar with us. It's dangerous here," I said to him.

"Never mind, T'ai T'ai, pu yao chin. I'm all right here. . . .
Ai yah! What was that?"

"That was a bullet through your hat, Hu Shih Fu. Now
will you come down with us?"

The battle lasted only three hours. It seemed like three
years. The din grew so terrible that all I could think was, "If
only the noise would stop! Let them come in. Let them take
the city—anything to have it quiet again."

But when the battle closed we were stunned by the ominous
silence that fell upon the city. The next morning there was
a Japanese flag flying from every shop front.

It was a strange feeling to be "the enemy"—completely at
the mercy of an army that had been promised the freedom
of the city and who took unspeakable advantage of that freedom. But the American flag was still respected by the Japanese,
and at least for the time being, our compound and the people
in it remained unmolested. Thousands of men, women, and

children flocked into the compound for refuge, and it was heartbreaking to have to turn away the thousands more for whom there was no room.

We did our best to provide shelter for the refugees. Most of them had been able to bring food with them. Sanitation was the major problem; Fred realized that an epidemic in the crowded compound would threaten the refugees with perhaps even more danger than there was from the enemy outside. Deane Walter was in charge of the committee who collected able-bodied men to erect hasty shelters and make bore-hole latrines, and try to control the myriad flies. We lacked sprays in anything approaching the amount needed, so an offer was made to the children: three pennies for a hundred flies. Dead flies. The response was so overwhelming and the weather so hot that Deane found it impossible to count the corpses of the disintegrating insects, and quickly changed the offer to three pennies an ounce.

Military victory can be a terrible thing—an evil, corrupting, fear-generating horror. As we walked the streets from our compound to the Baptist mission to see how our friends there had fared during the battle, evil was so palpable in the air that you could almost reach out and touch it. Half the shops were closed and the best wares buried lest they be confiscated, but saki must have been available by the barrel. Drunken soldiers roamed the streets. Women, no matter how old, hid out in the fields at night, so a shopkeeper told us. I could not believe it and thought he was exaggerating the danger, but the day came when I, a Christian missionary, was glad to see that the army had shipped in a trainload of prostitutes. Poor, hard, unhappy little girls!

There were those among the Japanese, officers and soldiers, who hated the whole situation as much as we did—more, perhaps, because it was closer to them. Our compound, our home, was a comparative lake of peace in this morass of mud. Many times a day the doorbell would ring and our few words of Japanese would make a soldier welcome. But I never heard the clomp of army boots upon the stone walk without a moment of fear.

At the beginning this feeling of fearful uncertainty was almost overwhelming. What was happening? What was going to happen? What was the rest of the world doing? Did our families at home know what had happened to us? We could learn little of real fact, although there were constant rumors. One recurring rumor was that the Chinese army was about to recapture the city. Certainly we could hear continual firing in the outskirts of the city and there were times when the guns sounded much closer. But the weeks passed and nothing happened. We gradually grew accustomed to having the soldiers drop in, and began to take the firing for granted.

In an effort to keep up morale and to break the monotony of our restricted life, we celebrated every celebratable occasion and some that are not ordinarily considered so. We had always been a station that made the most of any opportunity to have a party—the anniversary of someone's coming to China, engagement anniversaries as well as wedding anniversaries, everyone's birthday—including George Washington's, which was celebrated by an Early-American fancy dress dinner—and St. Patrick's Day. The same scanty food would be served, but it was a challenge to cook it or serve it just a bit differently; and it gave us a chance to be together, to hear Adopted Uncle Eames tell his jokes, and to exchange the latest rumors.

One day, six months after the city had fallen, I was dressing for a luncheon party the Walters were giving to celebrate Stella's birthday. Bertha Smith, the children's Adopted-Aunt-from-across-the-city, had come in from the Baptist mission and was sitting in the bedroom with me. I remember I was tying the bow at the neck of my yellow cotton maternity dress when the sound of a shot zinged through the air.

"That must be near here," I commented. But gunfire was so commonplace that we went on talking without a second thought. Another shot crumpled the quiet.

"Fred will probably be late to lunch," I said. "He's so busy at the hospital now. But there is still plenty of time, isn't there?"

It was then that we heard the gateman's wife lumbering up the stairs in a great effort of speed. She threw open the door and stood there quivering.

"They've shot the doctor and we can't find his body!" she blurted out. (She told me later that she had insisted she be the one to tell me because she would break it to me gently. "After all, one needed to be careful," she said, ". . . in your condition.")

In her crude way she did break it to me gently because I didn't believe her. I did not believe her at all. "Now, Li Ta Sao, just because you have heard shots near the hospital, it doesn't mean that the doctor has been hurt. You are always worrying."

The gateman appeared in the doorway. "Please, Teacher-Mother," he said gently, "will you go and see?"

As soon as we reached the street, I knew that it was true. Not a word was spoken, but people were looking at me with such compassion in their faces. At the hospital gate I faltered; could I go on? Bertha caught my arm fiercely. "Come," she said. "God can take care of this, too."

Stella Walter met us at the door. She had come over as soon as she had heard the second shot. I looked at her mutely, and she answered my unspoken question. "He is alive. He was shot in the back and the bullet went all the way through his body. Dr. Kung is with him. She cannot tell yet how badly he is hurt."

As we hurried up the stairs she told me briefly what had happened. A drunken Japanese soldier had come into the hospital courtyard waving a gun and looking for nurses. (The gun wasn't loaded, but nobody knew that then.) Fred and a few of his staff had gone out to stop him. Two of the boys in the nursing course took the gun away from the man; another went out into the street to find a soldier on duty who would taken the drunken one away. But the soldier from the street, either misunderstanding the situation or interpreting it as a slur on the Japanese army, drew his own gun and forced the boys to return the weapon to the drunken soldier. Then he immediately left the compound.

By this time the drunken soldier was furious. He put a clip of five bullets into the gun. He singled out Fred, perhaps because he looked different from the rest—taller and wearing his white uniform—and motioned with the gun for him to lead the way to the women's quarters. Fred stepped into the path, thinking to guide him to the back gate and out into the street. The rest of the group scattered.

Fred was about fifteen feet ahead when the soldier shot him. A second bullet went wide of its mark because Fred had fallen into a flower bed. ("Not *fallen*," he protested to me later. "I knew I'd been shot, and people usually lie down when they're shot. The flower bed looked like a nice, soft place.")

As he lay there, the berserk soldier came and stood over him, with three bullets left in his gun. (Even now I am weak with the miracle of it. "God sent an angel to touch that gun," said Brother Li later.) The soldier aimed at Fred's head and pulled the trigger. Drunk as the man was, he could not miss, but the gun did not go off. People who know those Japanese guns tell us that they never jam—not even when they are hot

from having been fired all day. Again the soldier tried, and
again; finally he wandered off into the street. After a few
moments Fred was able to lift himself and walk into the hospital—that was why his body could not be found.

It was typical of him that, with two first-class rooms empty,
he had put himself to bed in the third-class ward with the rest
of his patients. I went over to him, afraid of myself and of
making a scene in front of that roomful of sick. "How are
you?" I said. "Will you be . . . all right?"

His face was flushed and his eyes showed the strain, but
he answered quietly, "We won't know for a few hours yet.
But don't worry. Please, honey, don't worry."

The external bleeding had almost stopped, but there was no
way to tell whether the liver had been damaged. We might
need surgical help and need it badly—and Fred was the only
surgeon. I did what I could to make him comfortable, as
cheerfully as possible, but underneath I was desperate. I had
to be alone for a minute to get hold of myself and to say a
fervent prayer in private.

As I opened the door, I saw a beautiful sight: Lay Brother
Li was bounding up the hospital stairs. "Is it true?" he gasped,
out of breath. "Will he. . . ?"

"Yes, it is true," I said. "As to the rest, it is in God's hands.
We won't know for at least twenty-four hours whether he is
safe from internal hemorrhages."

"What can I do for you? I was on my way to the city."

"You can take the message out. Get it to the nearest American consul if you possibly can."

I seized some blank temperature charts and wrote a report
of the incident, ending with the plea, "Please send help as
soon as you can. There is no other surgeon within this area
of five million people." (Our Chinese surgeon had fled to
West China a month earlier because he did not feel that he

could work under the Japanese.)

I quickly folded the papers and gave them to Brother Li. "Do get this out as soon as you can."

"Depend upon me. God give you courage," he said, and hurried down the stairs, tucking his cassock around his portly waist as he went out to pick up the bicycle he had dropped at the door. There was something very comforting in the sight.

Someone had gone for Beloved Grandmother, whose little house was at the opposite end of the compound. Later our wonderful friend, Dr. Kung, who stood staunchly by us through it all, remarked, "I never realized before what the long heritage of being a Christian through many generations meant. Mother did not come in screaming or wailing, as we would have done. She went to him smiling, and took his hand. None of us could have done that."

As I sat beside the bed, looking across at Beloved Grandmother, we were overwhelmed with wave after wave of gratitude that he was still alive. And, too, it was so like God to have sent Lay Brother when He did. Now there was hope that another doctor would arrive.

I watched Fred's respiration: the pulse held strong. No sign of internal bleeding yet. (God, O God, don't let anything happen to him!) Suddenly I remembered the children. I must tell them before anyone else had a chance to. I told Fred where I was going and that I would hurry back.

I was too late. Precious old Chang Ta Sao, overcome with grief and anxiety, had somehow got hold of Fred's bloodstained shirt and was sitting in the middle of the nursery floor, rocking back and forth and wailing, "Your father was shot. Your father was shot!" while the stunned children huddled in a circle around her. They looked up at me as I came into the room and did not say a word.

"Yes, Daddy has been shot," I told them, "but he is all right.

Chang Ta Sao, please get up. The doctor is all right and is going to be all right. Come, children, we are going over to the hospital now. You can see for yourselves that he is only hurt a little. Chang Ta Sao, you come too, and then you can bring the children back home and give them their tea."

When the Golden-Haired One saw Fred, she went over to the bed and very quietly felt him all over from head to foot to see if any part of him was missing. Reassured, the children went off with Chang Ta Sao and Beloved Grandmother went with them to be sure they were no longer frightened.

Fred slept at intervals during that long day, while I stayed with him, checking pulse, temperature, respiration. Occasionally I would look up to find him watching me with a semblance of the old grin on his face. By nightfall we knew that the immediate crisis was over, and the prayers of intercession became prayers of gratitude. As soon as we felt sure that he could be moved without hemorrhaging, we put him on a stretcher and brought him home to the quiet of his own bed. Every person who had ever known him, it seemed, had come to the hospital and demanded to see for himself that the doctor was alive. At one point during that interminable day I had counted seventy-five people jammed into the room and out into the hall. Their loving solicitude was touching, but Fred was still in danger and that had to be our first consideration.

Among the refugees living on the compound were several Chinese businessmen. A few of them were firm friends of Fred, although they had never been moved to become Christians; but most were shopkeepers whom he hardly knew. These men went to the pastor of the church next door and asked, "Sir, may we go into the church? We would like to kneel down and thank the God who saved our doctor's life."

The Chinese church next door had come to mean a lot to us. It had no beauty of architecture, being of the same gray-brick "factory construction" as our house, but helped a little by tall, slim, glass windows. Too, the service was not the hushed, dignified one we were used to. Though our splendid Chinese pastor tried his best, nothing could prevent an occasional outburst from someone breaking into the service to announce that "Uncle Wong has just come in from the village and you'd better hurry home." During prayer a dog might brush past you to pick up the steamed bread the child next to you had dropped. Beloved Grandmother's first Sunday in church had been quite a shock. I did not help her any when, in reply to her question, "Myra, what are those Bible verses written on the black lacquer pillar?" I replied, "It says, 'Don't spit on the floor.'"

But these were the "outward appearances" we completely forgot as, Sunday after Sunday, we worshiped with our Chinese friends. There was a holiness about the church that was good for the soul. We all sang together lustily, "Chi-i-i-i lai! Ch'uan shih chieh ti tsui jen" ("Arise, all ye of the world who have sinned") and such old favorites as "What a Friend We Have in Jesus." Miss Christman pumped faithfully at the little organ, Fred played the violin, and I directed the choir. The preaching was done not by the missionaries but by the Chinese pastor; for the church had fulfilled the aims of the Board of Foreign Missions in becoming self-governing, self-propagating, and self-supporting. When the pastors and elders had called upon us that first autumn of 1931, we mentioned a tithe of our salary as our regular contribution to the church, and met a situation which we have never experienced in any other church in the world.

"That will be too much," said the pastor. "Save part of your money for starting new work. You see, we are self-supporting and we do not want too large an amount to come from foreign sources."

I could not always understand our pastor's sermons, which were delivered at the speed of Morse code and with no more inflection. But I loved to sit in the choir facing the congregation of earnest, seeking faces—old Feng Ta Sao with her patient, tranquil smile; the robust local carpenter; the intelligent young professor with his head cocked to one side; the mother with her crying baby, rocking her body back and forth and patting the baby without taking her eyes from the pastor's face; the ancient anesthetist, dozing as if he had succumbed to his own ether. He would awaken presently, and fix the pastor with that rapt attention one uses to cover a doze. And the slim bamboos, swaying against the front window beyond the crowded pews, were a benediction in themselves.

The church was opened the morning after Fred was shot, though it was a weekday, and more than a thousand people knelt to give thanks to God for saving their doctor's life. I could not leave him to attend the service, but Adopted Uncle wrote us an account of it, telling how the pastor had taken this opportunity to tell again the story of Christ's coming to earth and giving His life for us all.

"So God uses even the wrath of man to praise Him," the letter ended.

We talked about it as Fred lay there—how you work so hard on the mission field, year after year, with no apparent results. Then suddenly one day, doing just the next thing to be done in a long routine of things to be done, something is accomplished, some wall broken down—not by your planning at all, but by the very circumstance of the hour. But Fred was embarrassed beyond words when people said to him, "You are just like Jesus. You shed your blood for us."

Brother Li was one of the first visitors to call after we had moved Fred home. He had got his message through and had taken the first train back to tell us about it. Dr. Theodore Green would be arriving from Tsinan almost any time now.

"But how in the world did you manage to be here at the very moment when we needed you most?" I asked.

"Ah, that was God's doing," he replied. "I was cycling in from the monastery to the railway station, and I thought to myself, I'll just stop by and see the doctor and his family for a moment. I can take the road past their house as easily as any other. But no, Father Superior doesn't want me to spend so much time visiting unless I have business. I cannot honestly say that I have business there today."

At this point, he had come upon an overturned ox-cart which blocked the road completely. Estimating that it would be a good three hours before the road could be cleared, Lay Brother took it that the Lord Himself had barred his path. There was nothing to do but take the other road, past the doctor's house.

As he pedaled into the south suburb, he felt a tenseness in the atmosphere. Something had happened. He called to a passing Chinese, "Peace to you, brother. How are you today?"

"Aya! Sir, have you not heard the terrible news? The doctor has been shot. It is rumored that he—"

"Oh, no-no-no! It cannot be!" Brother Li had raced to the hospital and had met me just coming out of Fred's room. I pondered again upon God's perfect timing.

Brother Li was a machine-gun conversationalist. "Did I tell you the fun we had at the monastery last week? One of the new priests is—what did you call it the other day? An eager-r-r beaver-r-r? The Old Brother who rings the bell for prayer at four A.M. has been doing it for years. How Old Brother loves to ring that bell! But this new young man decided to relieve him of the job. Nothing the old man said made any difference. So some of us fixed the bell so it wouldn't ring. We left the rope intact, but wired the clapper so it wouldn't swing when the rope was pulled. Poor young man! But he took it well. He is so young, and he will learn, he will learn. We all have had to. It is not good to take oneself too seriously, is it?"

What a man Lay Brother is, I thought. I wonder what the rest of his family is like? How could his mother stand to be separated from such a son for over twenty years? I thought of the story he had told me of his mother's death. One morning at about two o'clock he had been awakened by a bright light shining all around him. At first he thought that he had fallen asleep while reading his book and had not turned off the light. But this light was far brighter than any other he had ever seen. While he was puzzling, his mother came into the room. "Son, I have come to say good-by," she said. He knew then that she had died, and that God in His infinite mercy had granted him this blessing that he see his mother once more. It was six weeks later that the letter got through telling him that she had died, and the date and hour of her death. He was not at all surprised to find that it coincided perfectly with the time of his vision.

Now he was off on another story.

"Last week I went down to the railway station with a truck to pick up some boxes of clothing. On the way back the Chinese guards stopped me and wanted to know what I had in the boxes. 'It would be better for you not to know,' I said to them. That did it. They demanded that I open every box. 'O.K.' I said (I say O.K. just like an American, don't I?) 'O.K., you've asked for it. You want those boxes opened? Then you take the responsibility for what happens. Do you still want them opened?' They started talking among themselves, not knowing what to make of this crazy man. Well, I'd teased them long enough, so I leaned over and whispered, 'Brothers, I've got Japanese devils in these boxes. If I open them you'll have devils all over the countryside.' They had a good laugh at that and said, 'We might have known that Lay Brother would have something up his sleeve.' I asked them, 'Why else would I wear such broad sleeves?' They love a joke, don't they?"

Fred was amused, but he was looking very tired.

"One would think that you never had a serious moment," I said, laughing. "Let's go downstairs and have a cup of coffee. It's time for Fred to have a nap."

"Brother Li, you've made me feel like a new man," said Fred. "Happiness is good medicine."

"Happiness is my mission in life," Brother Li replied as he rose to go.

"Happiness is my mission in life." I thought of the words as he pedaled out of the front gate and I remembered the day Brother Li showed me the pair of shoes he was making for an old priest who was having trouble with his feet. He had explained his contrivings to make the shoes comfortable.

"You are wasting your time making shoes," I said to him. "You would have made a wonderful priest. Why didn't you go on and study to become one?"

He had looked at me as if I were a child. "You do not understand," he said. "I make shoes for God."

Dr. Green arrived next day and immediately gave Fred a thorough examination. It was unutterable relief to learn that the liver had not been damaged and that no surgery would be necessary; the deep wound was beginning to heal and, given time, would take care of itself. It only remained to see that the dressings were changed daily.

Work at the hospital went surprisingly well in Fred's enforced absence, with the staff taking care of patients, and the supervisor of the operating room doing what minor surgery he could handle. Members of the staff came to Fred's bedside for consultation, and carried out the treatments he directed.

Dr. Green did what he could in the few days he was with

us, but he soon had to return to his own work at Cheeloo University. His biggest service was during the repeated investigations by the Japanese army. The first—and from my point of view, the worst—of these had occurred before his arrival; within an hour of Fred's being shot, a military doctor had come to the hospital to examine the wound. Powerless, I watched him fish dingy-looking forceps from one pocket, a metal box of alcohol swabs from another, and with these doubtful objects probe deep into the wound. From then on I stood guard over Fred and would let no one but Dr. Green, or later our own staff, touch the wound.

Another military doctor, whom we called "The Terrible," arrived every morning at six o'clock, ordered the gateman to lead the way, and then kicked him all the way upstairs! I made sure that the dressing was always finished before his arrival so that there would be "no need to do more than look at it." If the surly examiner moved to touch the wound, I would step between him and Fred. When I think how powerless I was to save the gateman his daily kicks, I marvel that I got away with it.

A few days after the shooting, the General in charge of the town came to apologize. He was a soft-spoken, white-haired gentleman whom I liked at once. He seemed genuinely grieved at what had happened.

"But, Honored Lady," he said at the conclusion of a long interview with Dr. Green and me, "how did you succeed in getting the message out? This doctor-from-the-distant-city says he is here because you sent for him through your consul. But how did your consul know? I assure you that within half an hour of this dreadful occurrence every road was closed and every means of communication no longer available to you. I have checked back on everything very carefully. We know, too, that you have no radio transmitting apparatus." (This all had

to go through an interpreter, the tallest Japanese I have ever
seen.)

"My dear General, there is one more thing you know, isn't
there?" I replied. "You must know that I cannot tell you how
I got the word out." Brother Li had taken the road to Yen-
chowfu not ten minutes before every traveler on it was examined.

"We accept your apology," Dr. Green went on, "but, General, we are citizens responsible to our government and we
would be wrong not to let our consul know what happened."

"I understand," said the General, running his hand over his
short-cropped hair. "But this may mean my dismissal. You
see, I did not report it."

"Oh, General, I hope it will not mean that," I said, and
meant it.

(A year later he paid us his final visit, coming to say good-by
on his round of official calls before being transferred to another
city.)

"But now, may I see the doctor?" he was saying.

We went upstairs and we all began to talk of our happy
days in Japan. Then the interpreter said, "The General wants
to know if you want the man who wounded you shot."

"No, by all means, no," said Fred vehemently. "What good
would that do? He was drunk and didn't know what he was
doing. He had nothing against me personally. I feel sorry for
the poor fellow. I hear he has been sick and was left behind
by his regiment, and has nothing to do all day except to get
drunk and make trouble."

"Then, sir, what do you want?"

"I'd like to see better discipline in the city when the soldiers
are off duty. Do you know that no woman is safe in the streets?
And this isn't the first time that a civilian has been shot,"
said Fred.

"It shall be as you wish, Doctor," said the General. "You speak of having climbed Mount Fujiyama. I came here expecting to find an enemy and I find a man whose heart is as kind as Fujiyama is high. Good-by, sir."

From that day on, order was restored. The reason for it was so obvious that when we took our first walk through the city after Fred's recovery, merchants came out of their shops to shake his hand and to say, "Thank you, Tai Fu. You have saved us."

But the poor sick soldier was shot at last. I had asked about him over and over again and had received only evasive answers. Finally an officer said to me, "Madam, do not ask about him, please. We know how your husband feels, but this was a very bad man. Your husband was the seventh person he had shot."

One day the tall interpreter came to call, bringing a box of candy bars for the children. It was the first candy we had seen for a long time.

"My mother sent these from Japan," he said. "I want the children to have them. May I see the doctor? My former visit was an official one and today I want to say personally how sorry I am. I have many American friends and this grieves me very much."

Coming into the bedroom a few minutes later with a trayful of tea things, I stopped aghast at the threshold. The interpreter was lying face down across a chair drawn up beside the bed. His long samurai sword was dangling on the floor, and such contortions as he was going through! Fred did not look at all concerned.

"What on earth——" I began.

"I'm showing the doctor how to do the flutter stroke," said the interpreter. "I am a swimmer. I have just been telling him how I swam in the Olympics against Johnny Weismuller."

"I don't mind so much getting shot," Fred said to me one day, "but I surely do dislike being apologized to!"

This time the Major, the highest ranking officer in the whole area, had sent notice that he would arrive with his retinue. (I could never figure out why the Major seemed to have a higher position than the General.) Our Chinese friends were worried about the visit. "Remember, he is a very great man," they said to me. "If anything goes wrong, there may be retaliations upon us."

"Nothing will go wrong. Why should it? There is nothing to worry about," I told them with more assurance than I felt.

Just now, within a few minutes of the arrival of the great man, I was anything but confident. I had asked the children if they would like to wear the kimonos made for them in Japan by the mother of their little Japanese friend. They would help me serve tea to the Major in Beloved Grandmother's Japanese wedding cups. The two boys allowed themselves to be persuaded, but with no enthusiasm. Little Golden-Haired One could hardly wait.

There was a bang on the door and I took the Golden-Haired One by the hand and went downstairs; the boys followed reluctantly. The Major had arrived. He stood there scowling. A round-faced man he was, with a huge sunburst of a beard surrounding his face like the rays of the sun itself. I had never seen anything like it before. Neither had the children. I began to talk feverishly lest they make some remark about it.

The Major stalked upstairs and into the bedroom, brushing aside the doctor's greeting with a wave of his hand. He stood at attention and delivered his oration. It was translated by his interpreter. His official duty done, the Major sat down in a rocking chair and relaxed. Like a flash, the Golden-Haired One streaked across the room and jumped into his lap. She leaned back against his shoulder happily and began to pull the hairs of his exquisite silky beard, one by one.

What do I do now? I wondered. How can I get her to stop? How will the Major take it? He may be very sensitive about that beard. I motioned the child to get down.

"My dear lady," said the Major in perfect English, "please do not disturb your little girl. It has been a long time since I have had the privilege of holding my grandchildren on my lap. Do you mind if she stays here?"

The next day the Major's orderly called to present a package to the Golden-Haired One. It contained a beautiful Japanese doll.

On January 10, 1939, little Fourth-Child was born—a beautiful yellow-haired baby with stars in his eyes.

We named him Thomas Scott Scovel.

Fred was now back at work in the hospital and I was busy at home, adding the care of a new baby to the teaching of the other three children. The Golden-Haired One was really too young for school but she loved to sit at a desk and color a picture—anything to feel that she was part of the classroom.

It was best to keep busy in the house, or at least near the compound. If we went for a walk of any length, we had to bow to the Japanese guards at the gate. This meant a really low bow from the waist. It is not easy for Americans to bow low; and this situation was not made any easier for us by our having to cross a wooden bridge just before we got to the guards. Across the bridge were nailed steel rails which clearly read, "Bethlehem, Penn."; so we were furious before we even got to the guard at the gate.

But we truly had much for which to be thankful. We had enough food—of a sort; we had a good home and enough clothing and bedding to keep us warm, and we had friends.

God was good to give us such friends as the adopted aunts and uncles in the compound. They were really more than friends, they became our family. Then there were the Baptist mission aunts and uncles, the Russian fur-buyers, the Catholic priests and nuns, Brother Li, the Swiss nurse from the north suburb, the German friends who sang, and the Chinese with whom we lived and worked daily. We spoke Chinese far more hours of the day than we did English. Such good hosts were our Chinese friends that we forgot we were guests in their country and thought that China was our home.

It is difficult to choose out individuals above others—the teacher with the brilliant mind with whom Fred delighted to converse, the manager of the Standard Oil Company in our inland city who was lonely for life in Shanghai, the owner of the ancient pickle factory who came out of seclusion to help us with the refugee camp (and who wore an arm band that read REFUGEESCAMP!). (How we loved to take visiting friends through that pickle factory with its acres of huge porcelain vats containing every variety of local vegetable aging in its own particular brine! Inside there were special cheeses made of bean curd and kept at just the right temperature to grow an inch or so of feathery, yellow mold.)

There were others of our friends, but there is still enough fear left in our hearts to keep from naming any except those who, by now, have gone far beyond fear. It has been a long, long time since the tranquility of China was broken. Even as long ago as the summer of 1940, fear struck the heart of a little family who were among our dearest friends.

Five

The Chrysanthemum

"Han Fu Liang is in jail!" The cook brought the news with our breakfast pomelos. "You know that Little Teacher's husband has been a leader of guerrilla troops out in the country. I can't understand why he, an educated man, the principal of a school, should want to be a soldier. You know our saying, 'One does not use good iron to make nails nor good men to make soldiers.'"

"But how did he get caught?" we asked.

"He came in last night to see his family, and some Judas told the Japanese. They arrested him at the railway station this morning." Hu Shih Fu snuffed and snorted his contempt.

"And do you know what Wang Lao San heard him say to the men who arrested him?" he asked as he brought in the eggs. "'Yes, I am your enemy. I have worked against you and I will work against you.' That's what Principal said."

The Japanese were shrewd enough to recognize the potential value to them of such a loyal man. It would be worth while to win him to their side; they used every means to do it. When they found that their arguments, their promises, did not sway him, they put full responsibility for her husband's life or death in Little Teacher's small hands. "If you can persuade him to come over to our side, he will be released," they told her. "If not, he will be executed. It is entirely up to you."

"Little Teacher, how can you bear it?" I asked her.

"God gives me strength," she said, "but do pray for me. I am so afraid I will weaken."

Finding that she could not be moved, they tried to use the two children.

"You don't want your daddy to die, do you?" they said. "Go in and tell him that if he will work for us, he will live. He may go home with you and your mother now."

But those little children had the courage to say, "Daddy, the soldiers have told us to say this to you, but you do what God wants you to do."

Han Fu Liang asked for his Bible and read it through three times during the following months of imprisonment. All of that time he was questioned again and again, especially concerning the American missionaries.

"It is true, isn't it, that they are spies in the employ of their government?"

"No, it is not true."

"Then how do they get their money?"

"Well, you see, it is with them as it is with us in the support of our temples. Several old women [sic!] in America give of their money, a few cents here and a few cents there, and thus the missionaries are supported."

"That is very hard to believe."

One day the Japanese officers came to him with a letter. It was one of those being sent routinely by the consulate to all Americans in China urging them to leave on a ship sailing from Shanghai.

"Now you will know for certain that these foreigners are spies for their government," they said to our friend. "Here are their orders to leave at once."

"You will see," he replied. "They will not leave. Some of them have already left, but that was because of bad health or because their furloughs were due. This letter will not make any difference. The ones who are here will stay. You will see."

It was the evening of Thanksgiving Day, 1940. We had all been across the city to the Baptist mission to have dinner with Adopted Aunt and Uncle Connely. We had eaten all of the traditional Thanksgiving dishes, some of them planned for months in advance, the ingredients purchased on furlough and carefully hoarded. We had sat around the living-room fire with the traditional stuffed Thanksgiving feeling. We had sung, "For the Beauty of the Earth" and "Come, Ye Thankful People, Come" and each of us had had his separate memories. Now we were back at home. The children had been put to bed and Fred and I had settled down in the little up-stairs room over the kitchen which I used as a study, a sewing room, and a place to bathe the baby. On this cold night it was the warmest room in the house. And now we had one more thing for which to be thankful—the mail had come.

In the midst of reading those wonderful letters from home, Fred handed me an official-looking letter. It was the one from the American consulate. "May we advise you that . . . the ship will leave Shanghai on . . . Women and children are especially urged to . . ."

"I just can't walk out and leave a hospital full of sick patients," Fred said flatly.

"Does this mean that I will have to go alone with the children?" I faltered. "We've talked this over so many times. It's the same old circle—is it right to keep the children here? Is it right to leave you here alone? In the end will separation from you be harder on the children? I'm never myself when I am away from you, and the children feel it. I've prayed and prayed about this and the only thing that comes to me—and it always comes—is the verse, 'For ye shall go out with joy, and be led forth with peace: the mountains and the hills shall break forth before you into singing and all the trees of the field shall clap their hands.' If I am led forth now, it will not be with joy, it will be with agony."

"We've had such a wonderful day," he said, "so very much to be thankful for! Let's not say any more about this tonight. Let's go to bed thinking about our happy Thanksgiving and trust Him to guide us to His decision for us. In the morning we will tell each other what He has made clear to us."

By morning I was still disturbed. I had a decided assurance that the right thing to do was to stay, but I couldn't be one hundred per cent sure that it was not my own strong desire to stay that made me think it was divine guidance. We had both been so critical of missionaries who had failed to heed consular warnings in the past. We had vowed that we would never fail to take the advice of our government, and here we were doing that very thing. Again the old treadmill of thoughts —suppose we were lined up and shot? Suppose the children should have to *see* us being shot?

"Thou wilt keep him in perfect peace, whose mind is stayed on Thee—whose *imaginations* are stayed on Thee."

If this thing is right, it is right all the way through, no matter what may come, I thought. I have to take only one step at a time.

"Another cup of coffee, dear? More milk for your cereal, First-Born?" I went on with the usual routine of breakfast.

"No, thank you, Mother," said our ten-year-old First-Born. He looked across the table at his father; then he turned to me, and said steadily, "I heard you two last night when you were reading that letter. I don't know what *you're* going to do, but I've prayed to God about it; I'm going to stay."

"That just about makes it unanimous." His father smiled.

What a wave of relief swept over me! And through all the

troubles that followed, we never doubted that this decision was truly God's decision for us.

Little Teacher's husband was kept in jail for many months. One night a Korean interpreter came to him and said, "The whole garrison is changing. I am the only one left who knows you are here. It might be a good time for you to walk out."

Sitting in our garden one moonlit night, our friend told us his story. When we heard how he had answered his questioners, we were glad that we had not caused his prophecy regarding our staying on at our work, to fail.

Early in the spring of 1941 Beloved Grandmother returned to America to keep a promise made years before that she would be with her sister on her Golden Wedding anniversary. We hated to have her go, and she hated to leave us; but with the future so uncertain it seemed the only wise thing to do.

One day after she had gone, I was shocked to hear First-Born telling Second-Born and the Golden-Haired One that he thought I was going to die.

"She gets whiter and thinner and she is in bed all the time and Dr. Kung comes every day," he was saying.

I called each of them to me separately as I lay on a cot in the garden and told them the wonderful secret. It was such a happy day. The sun sparkled on every leaf. After I had been carried into the house, the Golden-Haired One flew across the room, knelt at the side of the cot, buried her head in my lap and whispered ecstatically, "Baby, I'm your sister."

But aside from a few oases of happiness, it was a grim summer. I managed to get permission from the Japanese to travel to the coast with the children, hoping to find some relief from the fever. "Huo T'ai," the Chinese called it, "the fire pregnancy." With no pun intended, it was the "freezing" that finally cured me. I was too frightened and there was too much to be done to indulge myself any longer. Japan was freezing all American assets in China in retaliation for a similar move made in the United States on all Japanese assets. I was caught with almost no money. Luckily we had friends in Tsingtao who loaned me enough to buy the railway tickets for our return to Tsining.

When I tried to buy the tickets, I found that money was almost the least of my troubles. The Japanese no longer permitted any Americans to go into the interior. I kept pleading, "I must get back to my doctor husband before it is too late."

("One look should have been enough to convince them," Fred said later.)

They examined every inch of my luggage. The new baby clothes helped to reassure them that I wasn't trying to smuggle something in that way. The guards almost balked when they found my brother's army address on a loose slip of paper in my address book. They puzzled over it for a few moments; I offered no explanations and they went on with the examination. Miss Christman, one of the "Ladies," was traveling with us; we had another very bad moment when the soldiers were leafing through her photo album. She grew more and more nervous as they turned the pages. I could see that she was at top tension when they stopped to look at a full-page photo of her brother in the uniform of World War I, broad-brimmed hat and all.

"So-o-o . . . American cowboy," the examiner remarked, and turned another page.

Just as the train was about to pull out, two more guards came aboard and took away my travel permits and passport. Those hard-fought-for permits . . . the weary miles I had trudged from government office to government office, always in the heat of the day, to obtain them. And my passport! Without it I was helpless. Would I never see any of them again?

By now it was late at night. I undressed the tired children and put them into their berths, wondering as I did so if I would have to get them up, dress them and get them off the train. No, I won't, I resolved. If they get us off this train, they will have to drag us off.

The whistle was blowing when an officer rushed into the car and put the precious documents into my hands. He looked at the sleeping children, then at me. "It is difficult these days," he said with a sad smile. "Good luck to you." That officer never knew how close he came to finding himself in the happy embrace of a foreign woman.

"And he got his wish; you did have good luck," Fred said when I told him the story. "You got here. I was afraid you'd never make it. And here we are with only eleven people in the house to see that we do no wrong."

I had arrived home to find nine Chinese soldiers, in the employ of the Japanese, on duty in the house guarding Fred, and two Japanese soldiers quartered in the study. Their total mission seemed to be to watch his every move. It was disturbing, of course, but we had lived on the edge of danger and difficulty for so long that the thing that bothered me most in the whole absurd business was the bayonet scratches on the piano where the Chinese guards had rested their guns against it.

I consider it positive proof of my husband's genius that he was able the next day to have the nine Chinese guards removed by the simple expedient of telling the authorities he did not think it suitable to have me alone in the house with that many men all day while he was at the hospital! Headquarters, however, refused to withdraw the two Japanese soldiers; evidently they felt I would be perfectly safe with them. As I was.

We have so often wondered what became of those two fine young Japanese soldiers. They themselves closed the door to

the study when they first took up residence there, and it was
never opened except when we knocked at it each evening to
give them a plate of cookies or a bowl of fruit. They had all
their meals sent in, and even took their baths in the middle
of the night so as not to disturb us. We never heard them talking to each other. During the day they spent their time looking
after the cook's baby or playing with our children in the yard.
I longed to know more Japanese. Once when an interpreter
came in on hospital business, we learned that the sister of one
of the boys had begged him to become a Christian before he
had left home. After some effort we were able to get a New
Testament in Japanese. The young man seemed very grateful.

It was certainly no trouble to have them in the house. We
even felt a little sad, after their many weeks with us, when
they came to tell us they were being sent to Singapore to fight.
Night after night I prayed for them, never trying to fathom
what their living might mean—to my own brothers, for instance, who might one day be in that very place fighting. I
knew God was able to sort out my prayers and use them.

Before leaving for Singapore the guards returned with an
interpreter to thank the family for all that had been done for
them and to say "Sayonara," that loveliest of all farewells,
"Since it must be." After calling on us the Japanese guards
called at the home of each of the servants to thank them. When
we got back into the study, we found that the desk and papers
on it had remained untouched. There was not a single cigarette
burn on any of the furniture. We wondered how many of our
American boys would have done as well in a Japanese home.

It was autumn again—the autumn of 1941. There were chry-
santhemums in every conceivable corner; pots of them in the
dark musty teashops, large gardens full of them ready for the
annual chrysanthemum shows, great golden sprays of them

spilling over the backs of the junks on the canal. There were crisp, white, snowball ones, and tawny sparse-petaled ones like dragons stretching their claws in the sun. And in our own garden little Fourth Child ran about trying to catch the butterflies as they lit on the beautiful blossoms. It was time for me to open Beloved Grandmother's house, which had been closed since her return to America.

And at last it was over. I lay in Beloved Grandmother's big mahogany bed thinking that to have produced five such wonderful, healthy children was a good job well done. Five children. A perfect family. Chang Ta Sao came in with Judith Louise in her arms.

"Oh, Teacher-Mother," she exclaimed, "at last the brown-eyed ones have started to come!"

The miracle of it was that this baby, who was so beautiful that she might have been carried off from a Reuben's canvas, had not been born in a concentration camp, or in the corner of a prison yard, though she might easily have been in those troubled days. She had been born in Beloved Grandmother's bed, cared for by our own doctor. I couldn't help thinking of the words of one of our oldest friends: "I have had many troubles in China. Most of them never happened."

But some of them did happen.

"Today is another week," Fred said as he got out of bed that Monday morning of December the eighth—still Sunday, the seventh, back home in Mechanicville. I was never to hear him say it again without shuddering; but then it seemed like such a usual Monday morning. We were on our way downstairs for breakfast when Second-Born came running up the stairs to meet us.

"There are Japanese soldiers guarding our gate," he said.

Fred went out to ask the reason why, but the answers he got

were noncommittal. Not long after breakfast an officer, followed by a group of soldiers, came up the front walk with the characteristic cl-lump, drag, cl-lump of heavy army boots—the sound that never failed to produce a sinking heart. The door opened and the officer said, "You are under arrest."

We stood in the front hall, stunned. Fred spoke to the officer. "May I ask why we are under arrest? Have we done something we should not have done?"

"You know very well why you are under arrest," the officer replied. "These are your orders."

The Brown-Eyed One, just ten weeks old, began to cry. The officer said, "Here, let me hold her." As he rocked her in his arms, he read to us the document from Tokyo.

"You are not to leave the house. Everything you formerly owned is now the property of the Imperial Japanese Government. . . . There, there, don't cry, little one, everything will be all right. . . . You are to make lists in triplicate of everything in the house. Your money is to be counted, the house searched in the presence of this officer. . . . There, there, don't cry, don't worry, little one."

This day was a blur of soldiers milling all over the house, upstairs and down; of lists being made, corrected, remade; of the scramble to find food enough to feed all the soldiers who were tearing our house apart. I remember looking around the table and thinking, "Thou preparest a table before me in the presence of mine enemies."

Night came. The soldiers were getting ready to leave when a message came from headquarters; they were to bring Dr. Scovel with them. Fred walked down the path through the garden, chatting to the soldiers as he went. How many more times would I have to watch him go, not knowing whether or not he would return? Or would this be the last? "Don't worry about me, please," he had said. That is easy to say, I thought.

He was back within an hour. The chief officer at headquarters had been most kind and communicative.

"I suppose you know that Japan has declared war on America. Several American cities have been bombed. We have not come away unscathed either," he told Fred. In the light of what happened that day at Pearl Harbor, we have always wondered why he added that last sentence.

For the next ten days we were not allowed to admit patients to the hospital. Then the Chinese Chamber of Commerce requested the Japanese to permit the doctor to carry on as usual, and the request was granted.

It was quite an experience to be interned in one's own home for a year. We were guarded by Chinese soldiers, one of whom used to sit on a soapbox at the front gate and embroider beautifully on pieces of grass linen, his gun propped up on his shoulder. Fred was the only one allowed out of the compound, and he was permitted to go only as far as the hospital, a few doors down the street from our own gate. We read our books over and over again, going through sets of Shakespeare and Thackeray that before had only been dusted. We bicycled around the tennis court for exercise. We had picnics on the roof and in every corner of the yard, and did all the things we had always thought we would do if only we had the time.

Once we had orders to prepare for repatriation. Trunks were packed, examined by the Japanese, repacked, kicked open and the contents strewn; repacked, re-examined and finally sealed shut. But nothing more happened. Every time an officer came to call, we would ask him, "When do we go to America?"

"Wait one week. If you do not go then, wait one month. If you do not go then, wait one year," was one not-too-helpful reply.

One day, after many weeks of waiting, we asked an officer the same old question, "When do we go to America?"

His English was not too fluent and he had to think a long time. Then he said, "Long, long ago."

"That's just what I thought," I told Fred. "That settles it. We unpack the trunks and go back to living normally again."

There was a new arrangement at the hospital. A Japanese who called himself a pastor-doctor had been appointed superintendent; he came down from the capital city once a week to make his inspections. He was a member of the newly formed Church of Christ in China. (The already existent Church of Christ in China, consisting of many denominations working harmoniously as one church, had been functioning successfully for many years.) The pastor-doctor seemed also to be a member of what was called Special Services, whose duty it was to investigate subversive activities. It was difficult to figure out just what the pastor-doctor was doing. We had a good time together one evening as he taught us to sing a hymn in Japanese, "Where He Leads Me, I Will Follow." His prayer before retiring that night was in English, heavily sprinkled with the Japanese word "No" which he seemed to use merely for emphasis. Or was it the English word "No?"

"Doctor very good man. No. Doing very good work. No. Bless him and his family. No."

Fourth Child fell to the floor while he was jumping on his bed one morning and broke his thigh bone. (What a day that was!) Pastor-doctor was most gentle and skillful in applying the cast after Fred had set the leg; we were so grateful to him for his ministrations that day. Once I asked him why he didn't wear the uniform of the Secret Service—or rather, Special Services—Department. He seemed very shocked at my question and said, "I am not worthy of it." Altogether he was a very puzzling person.

One day during the six weeks that Fourth Child's leg was strung up on pulleys, a soldier from the ranks, whom we had never seen before, knocked at the door. He made us know that he wanted to see the boy with the broken leg. He stood at the foot of the bed for a long time, watching Fourth Child play happily with his white rabbit, which ran all over the bed and nibbled at his cast. Sobbing great sobs, the soldier turned and plunged down the stairs and out the door. We have been forever in the dark as to what prompted his visit or why he was so moved.

The next problem that presented itself was that we ran out of money. "Hu Shih Fu," I said to the cook at last, "as you know, this is all the money we have left. Two dollars in this currency won't buy much, but it ought to be enough for food for your family and ours for today. I suppose people can't understand why I still have a cook when we haven't one cent of money. They don't know that you haven't been paid, and that you have brought grain in from your land to share with us, and that we share the little we have with you. I feel very bad that we haven't been able to do more for you. Perhaps you can find another job."

"No, no, Teacher-Mother. I will stay here. We have talked about all this before. You are doing your best and we are doing our best. But what shall we do now that the money is gone?"

"I don't know, Hu Shih Fu. We have learned the meaning of the prayer, 'Give us this day our daily bread.' God has answered it so far. Just think what a miracle it was that we were given a sack of rice last week. God has not forgotten where we live."

That very afternoon a member of the Japanese consulate called to give us five hundred Chinese dollars from the International Red Cross. We had had no idea that the world knew we were still in Tsining. "Comfort money," they called it. I hope the International Red Cross knew what comfort it brought. First of all, I paid Hu Shih Fu; then we laid in a supply of fresh vegetables to supplement the diet of lentils and blood sausages our German friends had given us.

And now it was Christmas again. There was no money to buy gifts for the children; every cent of the five hundred dollars had to be used for food. But there was a precious evergreen in the front yard; we would cut it down and decorate it. There must be *some* evidence of Christmas in the house.

This was not the first time we had been faced with a presentless Christmas. Once the gifts we had ordered from a mail-order house failed to arrive, and the Russian fur-buyers came down from Tientsin in the nick of time, their arms full of bundles. One package contained a toy gun that worried me. The rule of our house had been no guns to play with. Guns were used to do harm. We were people who healed. But the boys wanted guns so badly. I finally rationalized myself into agreeing that, since the children knew how I felt about it and that I would never buy them a gun, it might be all right for them to accept this gift of the kind Russian uncles.

But this time there were no Russian uncles. I looked through the trunks and found a few books I had meant to save until the children were older—*Huckleberry Finn, Pinocchio, The Stars for Sam.* There were some scraps of cloth with which I could make and dress rag dolls for the girls. Fred carved out a horse's head, painted it, and put it on a broom handle for the boys. A strip of fur from the bottom of my coat made a glorious black mane. Christmas cookies would have to be omitted. There was no sugar.

There was no sugar at all. I had hoarded half a cup of it, but a Japanese officer called one cold afternoon, bringing with him a little prostitute waif who looked so thin and so sad that I took out the sugar for their coffee. I put a meager teaspoonful into each cup, but after the coffee had been handed around, the poor little girl crossed the room, took the sugar bowl in her hands and emptied its entire contents into her coffee. If I tended to regret the loss of the sugar, I had only to think of those burning eyes as the girl gulped down her coffee. My children could do without cookies.

"Teacher-Mother." It was the gateman with a message. "The Catholic Sisters are here making their Christmas calls." (Each year they came to thank the doctor for what he had done for them.)

The Sisters had brought a package which they now gave to the children. "You must open it carefully," they cautioned.

"Oh, Mother, look! Little angels and stars, and oh . . . they are made out of sugar cookies!"

"Sugar cookies! Sisters, how on earth did you——" I stopped myself. "Really, you shouldn't have done it," I finished feebly.

They ventured a smile at each other and began at once to help the children hang the little angels on the Christmas tree, insisting that a few cookies must be eaten while working.

"And you must come over to the church and see the crèche," they urged. "The children of the school are giving a play."

"Perhaps we may be able to get permission from the Japanese this once," I replied. "It is such a special occasion."

The crèche with its exquisite figures, made by a brother of one of the nuns and brought out carefully from Germany, the old carols sung in stilted English by the Chinese children of the school—this was Christmas.

And Mother Superior confessing to me, "I vowed that these poor Sisters, who have gone without so much all year, would have sugar for Christmas, even if it cost every cent we had in our meager treasury. So I bought a few pounds though the price was unbelievable. The Sisters insisted on dividing the sugar in half and making cookies for your children. We all love them very much, you know. I remember so well when little Golden-Haired One was a baby. It was the first time I had ever called on you. Do you remember? I hadn't seen a white baby in fifteen years. She looked like a little cherub. And now look at her, chatting away in Chinese to our girls. The children are pleased with the cookies, then?"

This—*this* was truly Christmas.

Six
The Peach

There was nothing we could put a finger on, but something was in the air. We found ourselves becoming squirrels; we hid things. We took all of Beloved Grandmother's old family mahogany and stowed it behind a chimney in the attic. Then we built a false wall across the room and plastered it over to look as if there were nothing behind it. We took our precious music records and slid them down on ropes between two walls. We scrambled up to hidden recesses under the eaves and concealed our best-loved pictures. Fred filled an old camphor box with our wedding silver, sealed it shut, painted it with a heavy coat of white lead, and buried it in a deep hole under the porch, along with his stamp collection, Father Scovel's pulpit Bible, and the children's baby books. We had no money to hide.

We tried to spread the remaining furniture around to look as if nothing were missing. Beloved Grandmother's things were no problem; they had been brought up from her little house, and the Japanese did not seem to know that that house existed. Once started, we couldn't stop. One room in the attic had an outside window and a door leading into the attic guest room. The room was as apparent as the front street gate, but we put away dishes, some cherished curios, a few more pieces of furniture, and plastered the doorway shut.

The plaster was still wet, the door clearly outlined, when a

Japanese officer and five soldiers arrived to search the house. Had they been tipped off? The officer was either extremely stupid or extremely kind; I incline toward the latter view, for he found nothing. He stood with his back to the plastered doorway while his men made a cursory search of the guest room, looking behind chairs, under the bed and in the drawers of a washstand. They went through the house in the same manner and then left.

Why were we hiding things? We said little to each other, and nothing in front of the children, of the fear that hung over us. Yet I couldn't believe it when the Japanese officer began his polite conversation that afternoon in early March of 1943.

"We fear for your health, here in the interior. Everything is so dirty." It looked like a routine call, but he shifted uneasily in the rocker. Now he leaned forward. "So we are putting all foreigners together in one place where we can look after you properly under hygienic conditions."

"Oh, you mustn't worry about us. We're making out very well and we'd be much more comfortable in our own home." I was slow to catch the implication of his words.

But Fred looked very serious. "When do we leave for the concentration camp?" he asked. "And, by the way, where is the camp to be?"

"You will leave the day after tomorrow for Weihsien, halfway between Tsinan and Tsingtao, Doctor. Here is the paper with your instructions." He edged to the front of the rocker. "Well, I must be going now. I'll be here at five in the morning to take you to the station."

"Why are you doing this to us?" I asked as the officer rose to his feet.

"Madame, it is in retaliation for what your government is

doing to Japanese civilians; your country is putting them into concentration camps."

"But that can't be true!" I protested. "I *know* my government would not do such a thing. I was in America during the first World War and a German even taught in our school. They were not put into concentration camps."

The officer only smiled. "What's the use of trying to explain it to her?" the smile said.

I was furious but I tried to hide it. After all, the poor fellow had been duped and deluded into believing tall tales about the United States.

"I'll see you at five, the day after tomorrow," he said as he left.

Well, at least we knew now what was going to happen to us. In a way it was a relief. We wouldn't have to worry now every time the boots came up the walk. We were not going to be shot; we were going to an internment camp. We could take our beds with us, the instructions said. They were to be shipped ahead. Ahead? We were leaving the day after tomorrow. There was a lot to be done. Another glance at the instructions informed us that we were to take all the food possible. We had no money to lay in a supply, but we did have enough to buy a large sack of whole-wheat kernels. I would send the cook to the market at once and have the kernels broken on the large stone mill. But first we had to tell the children. To this day they hold it against me that I told them we were going on a camping trip.

Early next morning John and Agnes Weineke of the Weimar Mission across the city came with a large pillowcase full of the little fruit cookies called "pfeffernuesse." They had stayed up half the night baking them. (One cooky apiece was to be our dessert for weeks.)

"How did you find out so soon?" I asked them.

"Trust the grapevine," Agnes replied. "The whole city knows it. Pfeffernuesse keeps forever so you won't have to worry about these drying up before they are used."

Chang Ta Sao was sure that she was "going to prison" with us. The Japanese officer had to tear her away from us that cold gray morning. The last time I looked back, she was still sitting in the middle of the dusty road; her hands covered her face and she was rocking back and forth as she wailed her grief. For the first time since I had told them, the children were shaken. They never saw her again.

The mission compound at Weihsien we knew very well, but it looked sadly different to us when we arrived there next evening. Japanese officers were living in the homes where we had been entertained so hospitably in the past. School buildings were barracks—the girls' school for the women and the boys' school for the men. But, unbelievably, we were not separated. We were to be together as a family in two tiny rooms in a small courtyard shared with five other families. Our beds, sent ahead, hadn't come nor did they for several weeks. We lay down with the children on the cold, damp bricks and tried to sleep. I was sick, sick, sick; but I would have to pull myself together. I would have to learn to take it and to keep cheerful. Before morning I knew that it was not fear that was disturbing me; it was pregnancy. Wave after wave of nausea was all too familiar a symptom to be passed off as anything else. I had ample time to consider the chances for a child born in prison camp. Those long hours before daybreak were an all-time low.

Hygienic conditions indeed! The first thing the men did the next morning was to wall off a corner of our small courtyard as a latrine. (It was in constant use as everyone had "camp tummy.") The next project was the building of a stove out of old bricks. Having scrounged (a good camp word) coal dust from the coal the Japanese officers burned, the men would sit down on the ground, mix the coal dust with mud, form it into balls and set it out to dry in the sun. This was the fuel we used in our fireplace type of stove.

But for the first few weeks Fred had all the work to do alone. I tried again and again to get up and finally got it through my head that it was harder for him to have to clean up after me *and* dress the children than it was to just dress the children. Poor, dear man! I will never forget his efforts to get the Brown-Eyed One's dress over her wiggling, fat body, nor my agonizing to get my hands on it. "Worse than delivering a head through a contracted pelvis," he would mutter.

It was wonderful to be sleeping in a bed again and not on the cold floor. And I was more than grateful for all the kindness being shown me. Every day someone would come in with a tray of some precious hoarded delicacy. A bowl of mushroom soup became water from David's well, though I never had David's courage to pour it out upon the ground. Every drop was consumed and enjoyed, in spite of the sacrifice of it—perhaps *because* of the sacrifice of it.

Two of the nuns offered to go on teaching the two older boys. The new teachers were careful to send home each book for us to look over before they gave it to the children lest it contain some Catholic doctrine that we might be unwilling to have the children learn.

And there was the cold, bitter March day when everyone was away from the house. The bare branch of the stripped tree was tapping at the window with such a melancholy sound that I burst into tears. The tapping of the branch became a knock at the door.

"Come in," I said, when I had dried my eyes. Into the room

stalked a tall nun wearing a blue habit with a stiff white headdress sweeping up in wings from her scrubbed, shining face. She began to talk volubly in what I took to be Dutch. When she saw that she was not being understood, she made a quick tour of the room, searching everywhere, and finally found what she wanted underneath one of the beds— a basket suitcase overflowing in all directions with dirty clothes. The thought of that ever-filling basket and my inability to do anything about it had been one of the reasons for my tears. She took the clothes away and brought them back a few days later transformed into sparkling clean and neatly ironed garments. The children called her "the Dutch Cleanser," and until the day when the bare branch against the window became a bough of pink, and I knew that I could face the world once more, the Dutch Cleanser, bless her beautiful soul, performed these devotional ablutions once a week.

It was indeed good to be up again, to be taking some of the burden from Fred so that he could be free to work in the hospital. A small building had been set aside and the sick of the camp were taken care of there. The doctors and nurses had gone from door to door, asking for each family's supply of drugs, huck towels to be used for operating towels, and bandages. It was a little frightening to give over everything for the common good when you did not know when your own family was going to need a drug that might already have been used up on someone else. But people were generous. The doctors had been allowed to bring in their instruments, and soon a reasonably well-equipped hospital was set up. We feared epidemics, but aside from "camp tummy," none broke out. When people complained to Fred that there seemed to be a lot of sickness, he would say, "It's only because you know everybody and you know when a person is sick. There are really fewer than the average number who are ill."

We never ceased to marvel at the way the fifteen hundred people in the camp met the emergency—people from all walks of life, businessmen (two of them millionaires), Belgian and Dutch priests, nuns from several different countries and from different orders, beachcombers, Protestant missionaries, and prostitutes. These last came into camp with lovely auburn, gold, or platinum hair. As time went on, inch by inch of black, gray, or mouse appeared at the hairline, the children wonderingly reporting the progress of it on each individual.

We hadn't been in camp overnight before one of the millionaires planted gladiolus bulbs. When they bloomed, their flaming flags made us lift our heads a little higher as we walked by. We thought it was a little disconcerting to the Japanese to see the way this conglomeration of humanity formed itself into a community, elected its officers for self-government and appointed various camp duties. Three big kitchens were set up and the food doled out to us so that one could either eat it on the spot or carry it home. The children took turns standing in line with the bucket, for we preferred to eat together at home perched on beds and trunks with a small table between us.

We were more than grateful for being allowed to live together as a family. One of our two small rooms was so filled with beds that the only way to get across the room was to kneel from bed to bed. This took care of the children, and our double bed all but filled the remaining room. To Fred, the greatest horror of internment was sweeping underneath those beds. But the two little rooms became home to us. There were curtains at the windows and a clean cloth on the little table. Our Chinese embroidered piece hung on one

wall. We called it our culture corner. This, and a drop of
perfume on my handkerchief, kept me from forgetting there
was another world.

There came a time when the curtains at the window had
to be cut up and made into clothing. These were the curtains
that had hung in the schoolroom at home in Tsining. They
were of dark blue coolie cloth with appliquéd suns and
moons on them, and though these had been carefully ripped
off, Fred's pair of shorts showed very clearly the outlines
of sun and moon over each rump, much to the delight of the
whole camp, especially when he bent over to do his stint of
a thousand strokes at the communal pump each evening.

Our own courtyard was a cross section of the entire camp
—a Greek restaurant owner and his wife; a Belgian with his
wife and two boys; an American missionary couple, a British
businessman and his wife, their twin boys and an adorable
little girl whom everyone called "Queenie"; and another
British businessman who had a Russian wife and two teen-
aged children. In spite of the rumored "affair" of the Belgian
wife, the continual Mah Jong playing of the Russian wife,
and the continual pot-scouring of the Greek restaurant owner's
wife (putting all the other housewives to shame), we all got
along well together. We learned to walk softly on those days
when one of us had had all that he or she could take, and to
shut our ears tactfully when the angry shouts from one room
became too loud.

Fred was studying calculus. "I can think of only one thing
worse than being interned," I told him. "Being interned and
studying calculus." Certain of our number volunteered to
teach the eighty classes in adult education, and one could study
anything from flower arrangement to—well, calculus; and
there was a full-fledged school for the children.

Sometimes I worked in the kitchen with a group of women,

helping to prepare the stew, paring endless mounds of vegetables that seemed to vanish without a trace in the huge
cauldrons of water. One of my jobs was to help make breakfast "porridge." Orange peelings were collected from those
who had been lucky enough to bring fruit in with them.
These were dried and then cut into tiny pieces, an infinitesimal
amount of sugar added and boiled with hunks of stale bread
that had been allowed to soak overnight. This made a hot
gruel that had better staying qualities for the working men
than tea and dry bread—all we were allotted for breakfast.
Our family was able to avoid the hideous porridge for several
weeks, until the cracked wheat gave out. Breakfast of whole-
wheat porridge with no milk would have been a delight to
us if we had not had to endure the smell of frying bacon as
the Russian wife prepared quantities of it. She sometimes
gave us a little bacon fat, and this we would use to fry
potatoes fished out of the weak stew and covered with one
or two beaten eggs for the seven of us. It was a feast for us,
and to this day it is a favorite family dish, prepared now with
lots of bacon and lots of eggs.

The eggs were purchased from the black market and it went
against my conscience to use them.

"I know we don't actually buy the eggs ourselves," I told
the family, "but I don't like the idea of asking anyone else
to sin for us."

For the black market was run almost entirely by the Catholic
Fathers who did not consider it a sin, and who did it as an act
of service for the entire camp.

"If we are caught and executed for this," they would say,
"well, there will be one less priest in camp, but if one of the
fathers of a family is caught, there is the added suffering of
his wife and children."

The priest at the head of the whole project was a mild-mannered, saintly gentleman who belonged to an order whose priests take the vow of silence. He had done almost no talking in his fifteen years in the monastery, and now he was thrown into this vocal vortex of humanity where all such vows had to be laid aside temporarily. The priests used a clever system to inform each other of the arrival of a Japanese guard while the actual buying was in progress. Priests were stationed at intervals in all directions from the scene of the buying—a corner of the back wall where the Chinese could bring their eggs, peanut oil, fruit and vegetables. As a guard approached, one watcher would scratch his head, the next man getting the signal would flip out his handkerchief, the next would bend over to pick up something, and in no time at all the news had spread, and the buyers and sellers would retreat to a place of safety.

One day the Silent Father was almost caught. He disappeared into a latrine, took off his cowled cloak, and came out smoking the cigarette of a man who had gone in before him. But though the Silent Father was threatened many times by the Japanese officers in charge, he still continued his benevolent, nefarious practices. At last he was caught with a chicken in his hand and was given his sentence—solitary confinement in the small shed near the homes of the officers.

His reply must have been somewhat disconcerting. "Thank you so much," he said to them. "I am used to solitary confinement and I like it. In my cell at the monastery I was always alone and I could pray. Here in camp I have little opportunity."

Overnight he became the camp hero. Children wrote him notes and slipped them under the door of his shack; women saved the choicest food and prepared it especially for him. The officers in the nearby houses frowned upon this but had little to say. They would play Mah Jong until two or three o'clock in the morning, and what really troubled them was that this prisoner had the horrible habit of awaking at four to begin his devotion with loud hymns of praise. It was thought best to release him, and he was soon back at his old post by the outside wall.

Thoughts of food filled all my waking hours. Nutritionists, interned with us, assured us that we would not starve to death on the diet we were getting. "Do our stomachs know that?" my husband wanted to know. Mine felt as if it were in the last stages of starvation. Within reason, one could have all the bread one wanted, as the Japanese had confiscated large quantities of white flour, and the Belgian priests had constructed ovens and were the self-appointed bakers. The children were continually filling up on their nicely baked bread, but the adults found it more and more difficult to face the endless slices with nothing to spread on them to make them palatable.

These same nutritionists, realizing the lack of calcium in the diet, prepared ground eggshells for the pregnant and nursing mothers. We met everyday for "tea" of ground eggshells in bonebroth.

Eggshells in bonebroth! When all I wanted from life was a plate of fried oysters and a mound of salted peanuts, and to have hot water enough to be clean just once. To look at my beautiful baby all grimy was bad enough, but to have to do it on an empty stomach was even worse. I vowed that I would never again accuse poor people of being shiftless and lacking initiative. I could not get my mind one peg above that plate of fried oysters. And I could do with a chair to sit on.

"People are imagining all sorts of things about what we are suffering," I said to the missionary next door as we were doing our washing together, "and all I long for is food and a chair with a nice, comfortable back. Anyone with a baby in front needs a chair in back."

"I wish you had the nice little rocker I brought out from America with me," she said. "It belonged to my grandmother. I tried to bring it into camp with me but the Japanese wouldn't let me. Only beds, they said, could be brought. This little chair was so comfortable—it just fit the small of your back."

"Don't talk about it," I said.

"You know, for the first time I realized how much God expected of Lot's wife, telling her to leave her beautiful home in the city, with all those little treasures she'd been accumulating for years, and not even look back once. I tell you I looked back a good many times when I left my house."

Lot's wife again. So much had happened since that night we had decided to leave Tsingtao. If I had it to do over again, would I do what I had done that next day or would I stay on in Tsingtao? I had to admit that I would have gone on into Tsining even knowing what I knew now.

"You're very quiet," said the husband of the missionary next door as he came out of the house with a few more clothes for his wife to wash. "Come on into the house a minute. We have something for you."

"I wanted to give it to you, but he wouldn't let me. He wants to have the fun himself," said his wife.

We wiped the suds from our hands and went into the house.

"Shut your eyes. Now open," said our friend.

In his hand was a luscious Shantung peach. At the very sight of it I felt a lump rise in my throat. I knew that he had risked the danger of dealing with the men outside the wall, and oh, the peach was so beautiful that I had all I could do to keep from bursting into tears.

"This is for you," he said, "but I will give it to you on one

condition—that you do not share it with anybody. You are to
eat the whole thing yourself."

After the long days of gristle floating in water with a few
anemic vegetables added, the peach was from heaven. In the
end I broke my promise, as he knew I would, and gave each
member of the family a bite of it.

Time lay upon us like a weight, but life fell into a pattern.
There was the one daily pail of hot water, and a small one
at that, for all the washing that needed to be done for the
seven of us, including faces, hands, baths, and clothes.
Little Brown-Eyed One, obsessed with getting her hands into
any water available, would start calling "wata, wata," as soon
as she was dressed. She would sit in the dust of the courtyard
happily washing handkerchiefs in her little basin as long
as I was there to work beside her.

But life in camp was not all drudgery. The Negro band
from the Peking Hotel was interned with us and they put on
a dance every Saturday night. We were fortunate to have
an excellent musician who led eighty voices in a glorious
Holy Week production of Stainer's "Crucifixion." Hearing
that music in such a place at such a time was an experience
to remember. The solemn occasion was not without its moment of humor when the Japanese commandant walked down
the aisle, having arriving late, to the chorus singing at its peak,
"Fling wide the gates, fling wide the gates, fling wide the
gates!"

The boys, now aged thirteen and eleven, were busy with
scouting, organized games, and watching the baseball league
with another Catholic Father hero as pitcher. The scout badges
were squares of green felt with the scout emblem embroidered
in gold by the nuns.

The Golden-Haired One was happy as long as there were

people around and she went from courtyard to courtyard, calling on her little friends and talking with their mothers and fathers. She came home with such bits of information as, "The little Russian woman in the next-courtyard-from-the-corner fought all night with her husband. She has a black eye. She told me she was going to leave him as soon as she can get out of here."

Or, "You know the family that lives next to Susie's? [The other millionaire family.] Well, the children say they've never had such a good time before in all their lives. The mother used to leave them to the Nanny, that's a kind of amah, and go to a lot of parties and things all the time. Now they're having so much fun together that they don't want to leave even when the war is over!"

Then one day little Fourth Child disappeared. We thought he was with his favorite, the kindergarten teacher. When he didn't come home, we sent the other children to his usual haunts to find him. One by one they came back without him. No one had seen him. Fred got the men of the courtyard to help him and they scoured the camp. The child just hadn't been seen by anyone. I was so weak from anxiety that I could only lie on the bed and pray. By late afternoon Fourth Child still had not returned and the Japanese guards joined the search. They even let the men go outside the camp to the garbage pile to see if he had wandered out when the men had gone out to empty the refuse. (That ghastly place, the garbage pile, where poor, hungry Chinese beggars waited to snatch the awful refuse that we, hungry as we were, could not eat!)

By this time the whole camp was alerted. We prayed as we had never prayed before. Then, just before dusk, he was dis-covered leaving the Japanese Commandant's headquarters with an apple in his hand. He had had a wonderful day. The officers had taken him home with them and had shown him a cow and the new puppies and had given him candy and this apple and— "Mummy, you're crying. What's the matter?"

The Japanese loved all growing things, children and plants. One afternoon when I was at home alone, a Japanese guard knocked at the door. He said something in Japanese that I didn't understand, but he finally made me know by a gesture of his hand that he wanted a pair of scissors. He was very gruff about all this and I couldn't imagine what he wanted with scissors until he pointed to the straggling tomato plants growing at our door. We had decided, after much discussion, to plant tomatoes instead of flowers in our two-by-four garden, since the children would need vitamin C. They were in for a good bout of deficiency if they were to depend on our tomato plants! When summer came and the pitiless Shantung sun beat down on our one-story house, we scrounged a piece of matting and made a slanting roof over the windows to keep the worst of its rays from penetrating. This shaded the tomato plants, which shot straight upward in pale shoots that bore no sign of fruit on their stalks. The soldier spent the afternoon skillfully trimming them, and in time the plants were prolific. He did not smile once, in spite of my repeated efforts to be friendly, and I never found out whether he felt sorry for us or for the tomato plants.

I was ironing a little dress one morning when a friend of ours from the British American tobacco company dropped in.

"Where's Fred?" he asked.

"Over at the hospital, I suppose. Sit down there on the bed. And excuse my back. It's a major operation to turn around in this room. How's everything with you?" I asked.

"Oh, fine. I hear Fred has a new recipe for tobacco," he

went on. "I'd like to try some. Would he mind?"

"Of course not." I passed him the tin and went on ironing. He filled his pipe, lit it and took a few puffs.

"Say, this is good—really good," he said. "How did he make it?"

The men swapped recipes for tobacco just as the women swapped recipes for making pancakes out of soppy bread porridge.

"I'm not quite sure," I began. "I know he got the leaves from some of the priests who seem to be able to get them in. It must be grown near by."

"It is. At one time we had this whole area planted in good seed. I never thought the day would come when I'd be smoking the stuff almost straight from the fields. But go on with the recipe."

"You know the usual routine, I suppose, choosing out the good leaf and stripping away the stems and veins. Then he spread them out on that flat stone outside the door and smeared them all over thickly with some kind of goo."

"Yes, yes, I know. But what was in the goo?" he asked.

"I really don't know. You'll have to ask him. I know there was tea in it and that the pharmacist made him an extract of licorice. And then, of course, there was honey.

"Ah, licorice. That's the flavor I was wondering about. Then what?"

"He spread the goo over the leaves, added another layer and smoothed it on again until he had quite a pile. Then he rolled the whole thing up in one of my precious pieces of old sheeting; using my even more precious clothesline, he tied one end of it around a tree for purchase and wound the rope around the roll of tobacco, squeezing it with all his strength until he had a long 'sausage' completely covered by rope. This had to be dried and he put it up on the tin roof and had to run home from all meetings whenever rain threatened. After all this tender care, he used my best carving knife to shave the tobacco into shreds. Greater love hath no woman than this—that she allow her husband to use her best carving knife for shaving tobacco. Fred will be flattered that you like it. Do you want some to put in your pouch?" I asked as I circled the starched ruffle with my iron.

There was no answer. There was not a sound in the room. I twisted my head around and saw that I was alone. "How long have I been talking to myself?" I puzzled, and went on with my work.

In a few moments he returned, his face a morbid shade of gray-green. "Whew! That stuff is powerful. I couldn't take it. I doubt if anyone outside of a longshoreman or a missionary could," said our friend from the tobacco company.

I loved doing the ironing, but the sweeping was another thing; I tried to get it done before Mr. Davies arrived. He was a man well along in years, a member of our own mission, and a tower of strength to me as the days went by. He would come into the room at about the time I would be sweeping the floor and, knowing that I would never let him do the work if he asked, he would take the broom from my hands and begin to scold me.

"Haven't I told you before that this is not the way to sweep properly? First sprinkle the floor with water. Where is that basin I used last time I was here? I wonder if you will ever learn. [I liked mud even less than dust.] Now, sweep toward the door with long, firm strokes—like this."

He didn't stop scolding until the floor had been swept. Then he would put the broom back in its place, smile with satisfaction and sit down for a while to philosophize. He was suffering from diabetes and I worried about him. I knew there were times when there was nothing at all that he could eat.

"What have you learned so far from this concentration-camp experience?" he might ask.

"I'm not at all sure that I have learned anything," I would reply, "except perhaps that one must walk to the edge of the gangplank and jump off before one can know that the limitless sea is actually there."

"Fairly good, but I don't like your metaphor. Say, rather, that you have learned that you are a child standing on a table, and that if you jump, you will surely find yourself in the arms of your Father."

"But you have to jump," I would say.

"Of course," said our friend, stroking his neat white beard.

Every month on a certain day the whole camp was turned out on the athletic field to be counted. The daily roll call was rather casually taken, courtyard by courtyard. On this scorching August day, the fifteen hundred of us were lined up in rows of one hundred according to our assigned camp numbers. It should have taken a matter of minutes to count us; it took hours. Someone was at the hospital; another had lost his number, two were watching the ovens and shouldn't leave, and so forth. Children cried, babies vomited, adults fainted, and still one person was missing. It turned out to be the man they were sending to round up the others! After what seemed an eternity spent in a furnace, we were dismissed. I took the children back to the house while Fred went to the hospital to take care of the new influx of patients. Our old friend should have gone to bed at once. Instead, he came to see if we were all right.

"Lie down there quietly with the children and I will tell you a story," he said. "Once upon a time there were three ducks, a mother duck, a father duck, and a baby duck. While they were out walking one day, they came to the bank of a swollen stream. Father Duck said to Mother Duck, 'You swim across first; Baby Duck will follow you and I will come last to see that there is no danger from the rear.' So Mother Duck struggled bravely across and reached the bank safely. Baby Duck had a more difficult time but he made it, and at last Father Duck succeeded in getting across. They stood on the bank, shook their feathers, and, said Baby Duck with a sigh of relief, 'Isn't it wonderful that all five of us got across safely.' Now why did Baby Duck say 'all five of us'?"

"I suppose Mother Duck was pregnant," I offered.

"Silly! Mother Ducks don't become pregnant; they lay eggs, remember? You have a one-track mind these days. No, you see Baby Duck was a Japanese army duck and he couldn't count!"

I knew now what Jesus meant when he warned the people to beware of wars and rumors of wars. There were times when the rumors were almost worse than the wars. One could hear anything in camp. One group made it their business to start rumors just to see how credulous people could be. The rumors kept getting more and more far-fetched until the bubble finally broke with the report that Churchill and Roosevelt had been on their way to call at the camp in person to do something about getting us out, when Churchill's camel got stuck in the sand at the edge of the Yellow River. When the rumormongers found that some people would actually believe this, they gave up in disgust and tried to find another method of relieving their boredom.

I was better off than most of my co-sufferers because, for them, time stretched endlessly ahead, while I had something lovely to look forward to at the end of a fixed period of time— the birth of my baby. It gave me something to count toward, something very much worth living for.

Then, like a flowering cactus, the bulletin board blossomed

a white notice. There was to be an exchange of internees! Japanese from the internment camps in America (then the Japanese officer in Tsining had been right after all!) were to meet Americans from the internment camps of Asia at the neutral port of Goa in Portuguese India. There the exchange would be made. We only half believed it, but again the old question had to be faced—would we have to be separated? For there were only five categories under which we could apply for repatriation; women and children came under one heading, but there was no category under which Fred could apply. We went to ask the advice of the obstetrician who was to take care of me. She did not say it in so many words, but she made it clear that anything might happen to me at the delivery—even death—and that I was in no condition to travel alone. Since we knew that the baby probably would be born en route, her question, in a low voice, "What would the children do then?" was more than enough to swing the decision. We filled out the papers waiving my right to repatriation and settled down for the "duration" (another good camp word).

A few weeks later we were sitting on the stone in the courtyard after the day's work was done. The children were in bed. Fred and I were having a few moments before going in when Ralph Lewis, another of the doctors, stopped by and dropped down on the ground beside Fred.

"I suppose you've heard that the list is up," he said.

"What list?" Fred asked.

"The list for repatriation," he replied.

"How can you be so calm about it?" I asked. "Isn't your name on it? Oh, I do hope so. You and Roberta have had to be separated so long."

"Yes, my name is there. So is yours, you know?"

"There must be some mistake," said Fred. "We made out

papers some time ago waiving Myra's right to go. No telling what might happen en route; we didn't dare let her go without me."

"Well, your name is on the list too, Fred, and so are all the children's."

We couldn't believe it, not even after we had lit matches and read the names on the bulletin board.

Such a fever of excitement as we were in! One moment we would be filled with hope and the next minute plunged into despair, dreading the disappointment if our plans should once again fall through. And suppose that at the last minute they took Fred's name off and made me go alone with the children?

But we went ahead sorting and packing our few belongings. Everything possible was to be left behind for those who were to remain; for of the fifteen hundred people in camp, only three hundred of us were chosen for repatriation. I exchanged my dresses for a few maternity clothes offered to me by a woman who had already had her baby.

At last the day came when the three hundred chosen ones were to leave the camp. Another three hundred internees from the Cheefoo camp had been brought in the night before to take our places.

We were led through the streets of the camp, crowded with people calling out "Good-by, and good luck!" then out of the gate, down a steep little hill, across a small stream and into a grove of trees. We sat on the ground to await the coming of the lorries that would carry us to the railway. The Brown-Eyed One crawled into my lap, and Fred took her little hand in his. The other children were exploring the grove, happy in a new adventure.

Fred and I were very quiet, filled with conflicting emotions. Fear—were we really being taken out to safety or was this a trick, a way to rid the camp of three hundred extra people? Sorrow at the thought of those who were left behind, and joy—surely joy that we were at least outside the gate with the real possibility of freedom before us. A light breeze brushed the trees and the leaves stirred.

"Fred, they are clapping their hands!" I said. "The leaves are clapping their hands! The verse is coming true!"

Just then the whole hillside before us burst forth into singing as the fifteen hundred clambered for places along the wall and raised their voices in "There'll Always Be an England," "God Bless America," and "God Be With You Till We Meet Again."

We went out with joy, and were led forth with peace: the mountains and the hills broke forth before us into singing, and all the trees of the field clapped their hands.

Seven

Lao Shou Hsing,
the Birthday Fairy

Ralph Lewis made his way down the car toward us, lurching back and forth with the movement of the train, picking his way between the sleeping bodies on the floor. He reached the place where we were sitting and leaned over to ask confidentially, "Have you noticed the ankles?"

"Yes, I have," said Fred. "Is there anything we can do about it?"

The two doctors went on talking. I remembered something about swollen ankles and poor nutrition and could see that the men were worried about us. The trip from the internment camp to the seaport of Shanghai should not have taken more than thirty-six hours. None of us knew why it was taking three days. We would go a few miles and then stop for long periods of time. The food had long since been eaten—all that had not spoiled the first night—and we were so crowded that it was almost impossible to sleep. First-Born and Second-Born and the other boys of their age had kept on their feet so that the older folk might have a place to sit. They would stand up as long as they could and then lie down in the aisle, curling themselves up as small as possible to avoid being stepped on. I looked down at our boys' ankles; swollen, yes, but not as terribly swollen as some of those sitting near us.

Would we ever get to Shanghai? There we would at least have food and water. The hours inched by and at last we neared the city limits. The train stopped, we thought to get the all-clear signal; but when it started again it was going in the opposite direction and this it continued to do for an hour or more. At once the rumors began to fly.

"Back to Nanking! They're taking us back to Nanking! We'll be put in a camp there! The repatriation is off. . . ."

Late in the afternoon the train stopped again, and when it started this time, it was headed in the right direction.

At long last we arrived in Shanghai and piled out of the train. The railway station had just been bombed—in fact was being bombed as our train had been about to pull in. But the unloading was allowed to proceed, our men grumbling at the weight of the heavy trunks some of the women had insisted on bringing out of camp. Lifting a heavy trunk, even with plenty of help, was almost more than most of the men could manage.

We were crowded into buses and taken out to the campus of one of the universities; I think it was St. John's. Oh, the smooth, green lawns! We stumbled out of the buses and stretched full length on the sweet-smelling grass.

Here we were to await the arrival of our repatriation ship. The time was filled with endless inspections of what luggage we had. It meant constant repacking and we were so tired. But there was just a little less to pack after each inspection.

American money was one of the objects of search. Hems of dresses were felt carefully, shoulder pads ripped open, shoe soles torn off, and long hair thoroughly combed out. The girl in line in front of me turned and whispered, "What shall I do? I have an American check that my father sent me for Christmas two years ago. It is tucked into the roll of my hair." It was too late to do anything about it. When the Japanese police woman reached us, all she said was, "Never mind taking your hair down." We never knew why this particular girl was thus exempted.

It was with mixed feelings that we boarded the Japanese ship, the *Teia Maru*. We were not at all sure where we were going to be taken. The *Teia* had come over from Japan carrying American repatriates from that country. Later a missionary already on board told me that as we walked up the gangplank she had turned to a Japanese officer and said, "I take it that the people with the blue rosettes in their lapels are the diplomats. Who are these now coming up [indicating our large family] wearing red rosettes?"

"Those," he replied, "are the hardened criminals."

When we were given our accommodations, I was surprised to find that the three youngest children and I had been assigned to a very good cabin with three berths. Fred and the boys were down in the lowest hold where the wooden bunks had been hastily erected to hold several hundred passengers. The boys, now thirteen and eleven, were suddenly thrust from their sheltered living into a maelstrom of life in the raw; for in this hold, under these terribly crowded conditions, were men who were constantly drunk. Some of them smuggled women into various off-corners (some of the corners not so off!). There were constant fights with knives or fists. All of this became a daily occurrence to the boys. They said little but they looked very thoughtful.

Our ship had formerly been one of the French Line's "Three Musketeers." It had been called the *Aramis*, and had been a beautiful ship in its day, but after its capture it had been allowed to deteriorate. There must have been a quantity of excellent wines and liqueurs on board, for these were now being sold to the long-deprived men at exorbitant prices. Since the Japanese yen was the only currency we were allowed to use, and since it all had to be spent while on board, it was no trial at all for the drinkers to pay the amounts demanded. Even the missionaries were willing to spend ten of these Japanese dollars for an extra cup of coffee now and then.

I found it more and more difficult to eat the food set before me. The diet of rice filled with worms was almost more than I could take.

"Eat it," Fred would say to me, "eat every bit of it."

"But the worms!" I would protest.

"You're just lucky to be getting that much extra protein," he would reply.

Fred was getting weaker too. It struck me with a blow when I discovered that all of the passengers had to reach out for the handrail in order to pull themselves up the short flights of stairs. One day when Fred was carrying the Brown-Eyed One up a ladder, his knees buckled under him and he fell. Fortunately neither of them was hurt.

"It's the vitamin B deficiency," Fred told me. "We'll make it up when we get on board the other ship at Goa."

There came a day when I was too weak to get out of bed. I just lay there wondering what I was going to do. Fred tried to help me up, but I could not stand on my feet. I had been saving one can of evaporated milk so that if there were no milk at all when the baby was born, we could at least have something to start on. There was a great feeling of security in owning that can of milk, and it was with difficulty that Fred persuaded me there just wouldn't be any baby unless I drank it then. He borrowed some cocoa from a woman down the hall, heated some water and gave me drinks of the chocolate throughout the morning. By night I was able to get up again.

"Darling," I said to Fred one morning, "stop reading for a minute and look around the deck."

He looked up from his Bible and saw at once what I meant; people sat propped up against smokestacks or lay full length, chins cupped in hands; every person in sight was reading a Bible! This, by the way, was the first time I had ever seen a woman smoking a cigarette as she read her Bible. The only other books allowed us were Japanese propaganda leaflets, which the children used for making paper airplanes and flying darts. With the exception of the Bible, nothing written or printed could go with us out of camp, and if the Bible were marked or underlined in any way, that too had to stay behind. The Golden-Haired One had prayed that the Japanese would not take away her Bible, and as the examiner had flipped through its pages, not one of the many marked verses did he find.

The ship continued on its course, down the coast of China to Hong Kong, on to a port not far from Manila, then to Saigon (a wonderful day it was, sailing up the Mekong River with lush green on either side), then Singapore, through the Straits of Sunda, past Karaktau, the volcanic island which upset half the world by its eruption; steadily nearing Goa, our neutral port of destination on the west coast of India. At no port en route were we allowed to disembark; in fact, the ship always anchored well out to sea.

At the Philippines we had taken on more internees, among them the wives of some of the men already on board. It was a glorious day of rejoicing; some of the couples had not seen each other for two years.

Soon after this new influx of passengers, I was standing on deck near a group of them one morning when they began to pass around a box of salted Spanish peanuts. For all those months at camp I had been dreaming of salted peanuts. I wanted some of those peanuts so badly that the craving for them could hardly be suppressed. I was standing a little apart from the group and only with difficulty could I keep from thrusting myself forward. I waited greedily as the box passed from person to person. Surely they had seen me there. But no, they went on talking and laughing and the box of salted peanuts went the rounds and was put away.

Fred found me later lying on the berth crying uncontrollably. Taking me in his arms, he tried to quiet me. He was greatly relieved when Dr. Harold Loucks came in for his daily call. (We hoped Harold would deliver the baby if it were born en route.) In our embarrassment at being caught thus, the story was blurted out. Harold asked his usual daily questions about my condition and went out. He came back in a few minutes with a medicine glass filled with the precious salted peanuts. "Just what the doctor ordered," he said. It did not lessen my embarrassment, but I ate the nuts one by one, chewing each nut carefully, lingering over each one. To this day, when any lack of security threatens, I find myself having to go out to buy peanuts.

The days went by. There were games with the children and there were long hours of interesting conversation on deck with many colorful people: the General, a Canadian who had spent years with the Chinese army and who told tales stranger than fiction; the maiden authoress who had had a child for the experience of child-bearing and who smoked long black cigars in the evening; the beachcomber who, since coming on board, had beaten up so many people that he had been confined to the brig on deck. The two boys held conversations with him. They had to be careful because at times he was really violent.

Conversation, Bible reading, and an occasional card game helped to count off the calendar. It was during a rather boring game of bridge that we came to realize the danger we were in. Our foursome was sitting on deck under a lifeboat, using it as a shield from the tropical sun. One of the men began to speak in a low voice. "Don't tell this to the others. I wouldn't tell you except that I've got to tell somebody or bust. The other night I came up here completely frustrated by this awful inactivity. I rammed my fist against one of these lifeboats in desperation. My fist went straight through the wood! So I made a tour of the deck. Not one of these boats is seaworthy. That accounts for the fact that we haven't had a boat drill since we've been on board. Fifteen hundred of us, and no way to save us if a submarine happens to mistake us for an enemy! It's a great life . . . if you live."

Goa at last, her lovely green hill topped by the old-world church of St. Francis Xavier; the comforting smell of wind blowing across earth! I am sure I am a direct descendant of that first little fish that crawled up out of the ocean to dry land. Now, after all the miserable days at sea, we were allowed to walk along the quay and a few steps farther down into the green fields near by. Fred couldn't understand why I hadn't learned to love the sea during our many voyages. Whenever we sailed past a visible stretch of land, he would ask, "Do I have to lash you to the mast as they did Ulysses to keep you from striking out and swimming to shore?"

We had expected that the Swedish ship, the *Gripsholm*, would be there to meet us. We scanned the horizon each day but no ship came in sight. Again we were set upon by rumors, this time in the form of a pun. "Goa is as far as we are Goan." It wasn't very funny, and when you'd heard it even a few times with fear at the pit of your stomach, you were ready to throw the next punster overboard.

But one day the dream came true. A tiny speck appeared on

the horizon and the news sped through the ship like a grass fire.

"The *Gripsholm* is coming! The *Gripsholm* is coming!" Fifteen hundred of us crowded the forward decks. We sang, we waved handkerchiefs, we shouted. Then, first one of us and then another remembered the Japanese on board the incoming vessel who would have to take our places here. Why had these Japanese, so well off in America, chosen repatriation? No doubt we would find out when they arrived.

I was humiliated to have the first-hand evidence that what the Japanese officer had told me in Tsining was true. The Japanese, so soon to board this ship carrying with them American cameras, sewing machines, good shoes and clothing, had chosen to return to Japan in many instances because it was their only hope of being reunited as a family, the father having been interned in one camp and the mother and children in another. No doubt there were zealous patriots among their number too, but it was clear they had no idea of what lay before them; nor, if the tales of the American repatriates from Japan could be trusted, of the weight of suspicion that would fall upon them as soon as they reached their ancestral shores.

One youngster had a photograph album which she showed to a missionary from Japan. It contained several photos of her brother in the uniform of the United States Army.

"Do destroy these, or give them to me to keep for you," the missionary pleaded. "This can be a source of great difficulty for you."

But the girl remained firm.

"Surely the authorities of Japan will excuse those who, like my brother, have remained loyal to the United States, for they were brought up from childhood there."

It was evening and the exchange was to be made the next day. We were to board the *Gripsholm* in the morning. Officially none of us had even seen one of the Japanese from America, but there had been many instances of "fraternizing," since both parties could hardly wait for news of what was happening in their respective countries. Now Fred and I were standing on the deck of the Japanese ship watching the clean, fine-looking officers from the *Gripsholm* as they walked back and forth along the wharf.

"I wonder if one of them has an orange in his pocket," I said. Dear Heavenly Father, would I ever again be able to think of anything except food?

Yet when it came, the abundance of it hurt us. We had lined up that morning single file and had presented our papers. We were asked not to go below until our cabins had been thoroughly cleaned. The whole ship looked spotless to us— gleaming white smokestacks with the blue and gold crest, shining brass, freshly uniformed staff. While we were still waiting, the Red Cross personnel lined us up again. Each of us was to receive a gift of the hugest chocolate bar I have ever seen. Those in the approaching line were beside themselves with impatience, so those of us in the line with bars already in our hands would break off a piece to give to someone who had not as yet passed the table, admonishing him to return the piece when he had received his own bar.

And now a smörgåsbord was being prepared on deck. The waiters found it difficult to get through as the people crowded for a sight of the food. Whole roasted turkeys, whole cheeses, whole hams, heaped-up salads, gallons of fruit juices, real butter and snowy Swedish breads were being brought up from the galley, and with the arrival of each tray, cheers would ring out.

Fred and I stood a little apart to avoid being crushed in the surge forward to see each tray. "I can't bear it," I said, "when I think of those who are left behind. The whole camp could be fed for a week on this one meal. This is a strange experience, isn't it? Now we are free and have everything; the day we dreamed of has come, and it is the very dream-come-true, the abundance, that hurts."

"I know," he said. "I suppose we are in a position to appreciate the riches of life more fully than almost anyone we know, and yet we will never be able to accept them again complacently."

What a feast that was! But how very little we could eat. It was frustrating to see all this good food and to have a stomach shrunk to a size that could hold only a small helping. The fruit juice ran like a river in flood and I could get down only one glass of it. We found that it was days before some of us could digest anything as rich as whole milk. The Brown-Eyed One was the wise one of the family; she didn't try to eat some of everything, but contented herself with applesauce and bread and butter.

On the second day out at sea I met the captain. With my characteristic inattention to stripes and bars, I thought he was a steward.

"When will we reach New York?" I asked him.

"That I am not allowed to tell you," he replied with a kindly smile. "This much I will say—you will not arrive before I do."

"Somebody else may arrive before either of us gets to New York."

"Now, my dear, you are not to worry about that arrival. I will get you to New York in time, and if I do not, we have three doctors and six nurses and all of the needed equipment to welcome the coming one."

And we will use it, I thought. This passenger was due to arrive three weeks before we could possibly reach New York.

Gradually it began to sink into our consciousness that we were free, that we were approaching friendly waters, that we could give way to the luxurious relaxation of free people. Strangely, it was only then that I began to have nightmares. Up to that time, even when there had been much to fear, I slept well each night and was kept in peace—the peace of God that passes understanding. "If I could only accept Him fully with my subconscious mind as well, I wouldn't have these terrible dreams," I told Fred.

I would hear again and again the scuff-clump-scuff of the heavy-booted soldiers coming up the walk. The soldiers would take Fred off and I would hear a shot; or we would all be lined up against a wall and I would be trying to give the children that one last reassuring word that would take them into heaven without fear. I would wake up shaking as if I had malaria and it would be a few minutes before I could realize that we were all safe and on our way home.

Home was a wonderful word to think about; home and family, after all these years of separation! We had had an unexpected thrill in finding a large packet of letters waiting for us at Goa. It had been two full years since we had received a letter from anybody, and it hadn't occurred to us that there would be mail en route. To my intense relief I learned that my father, a semi-invalid, would be waiting to welcome us home. During the two years of no letters I had dared to hope that he would live to see us again, and God had answered my prayer. I found, too, that I had my first sister-in-law. Letters were wonderful.

Some farsighted person had seen to it that copies of current and back issues of magazines were placed on board our ship. We were amazed to find that in the comparatively short span of two years the language had changed so that it was often unintelligible. What was a "WAC" or a "WAVE"? What was "ack-ack"? Above all, what was a "jeep"? Every other paragraph contained a word that made the meaning of what we read obscure. We finally guessed that a "jeep" was some kind of vehicle and at last someone found a picture of one and it was passed around the ship, so that that mystery, at least, was solved.

Port Elizabeth on the tip of South Africa, and what a warmth of welcome! The whole city turned out to meet us. We were surprised to see so many people in uniform. One could hardly find a man or a woman on the streets in civilian clothes. It was good to feel pavement under my feet and to look up to tall buildings again. We stood still for a moment, looking up at the American flag flying from one of the buildings. It was the first time we had seen it flying for years, and I, who had always scoffed at sentimental patriots, who called myself a citizen of the world, wept at the sight of it.

The children's one memory of Port Elizabeth is that each of us was given a whole pint of ice cream and that the Brown-Eyed One ate hers at one sitting, a feat which none of the rest of us could accomplish.

Leaving Africa, we sailed toward the coast of South America and on up to Rio, that fabulous city with its emerald harbor. The ship's doctor advised against going ashore. "The baby is a week overdue," he warned.

"I can't miss the one opportunity of a lifetime to see Rio," I said. "The baby has taken so many chances so far, can't we risk one more?"

We were soon walking up the quay toward a sparkling white building where members of the Evangelical Church were waiting to take us out to see the city. A dear little picture-book lady stepped forward to greet us. She was Mrs. Oliveira. She told us afterward that when she saw the five children, she said to the man in charge, "Oh, do let me have that family."

"You are certainly a brave woman to have taken this family," my husband told her. "It would be difficult to find a larger one or one in a more bedraggled state. At least we are now shod, thanks to the American Red Cross who rescued Second-Born from his barefoot bliss just before we got off the ship."

We had such a memorable day. We were driven by Mrs. Oliveira's chauffeur to the top of Sugar Loaf to see the beautiful panorama below. The boys were intrigued by the charcoal-burning attachment at the rear of the car. There were many such in Rio since gasoline was scarce due to the war. Mrs. Oliveira then took us to her sunny home at the seashore to spend the rest of the day. The next morning, before the ship sailed, our new-found friend was at the wharf to see us off. She had brought a gift for everyone of us, including the baby for whom we were restlessly waiting.

Rio de Janeiro was still two weeks from New York. In some ways they were the longest two weeks in the seventy-two day voyage. We learned later that there had been a large number of bets laid as to whether or not I would reach New York before the baby's arrival. Fellow passengers also amused themselves by choosing names for the child. "Gripsholm Maru," for both ships, was one of the gruesome suggestions.

But at last the journey neared its close. The boys' only regret was that we hadn't been hit by a torpedo so that they could put to sea in one of the Gripsholm's well-equipped lifeboats. The F.B.I., having come aboard at Rio, combed the entire ship. We did not seem to be suspicious characters, much to Fred's disappointment. He wanted a chance to chat with those men.

We were gathering on deck for our usual evening prayers. The nuns would soon be singing their beautiful "Stella Maris" and the whole ship would be joining reverently in the singing of "God Bless America" as we had every evening since leaving

Goa. One of the ship's officers came up to a Red Cross nurse and, motioning across the deck to where we were standing, said, "Can't you do something about that woman?"

"Why should I?" the nurse asked.

"She's three weeks overdue."

"I guess you can stand it if she can."

"But you don't know what I'm up against. The ship's manifest has to be complete before tomorrow. We don't know whether we are landing with fifteen hundred passengers or fifteen hundred and one. And besides, that one is going to be an alien, don't forget. This ship is flying the Swedish flag, and if the kid is born outside the three-mile limit, it'll be a Swede. Do you know how many complications that will cause? Brother! Well, see to it that she either has it tonight or not until every last man is ashore."

"Aye, aye, sir. Just anything you say, of course."

The next night the ship moved slowly into the harbor. There before us were the shores of our own country. We could see the headlights of cars slipping through the blackness. What would it feel like to ride in a car again?

Daylight of December 1, 1943, and the whole ship going completely mad! Before us stood the Statue of Liberty. We were all shouting, singing, dancing. Fred took me in his arms and together we danced around the deck.

"We're home," he said to me. "We're home!"

A Catholic priest standing near us took off his hat and addressed the Lady in the Harbor. "Old girl, take it from me, I'll never go so far away from you again that I can't be repatriated by streetcar."

"How much longer will it be before we get off the ship?" the children asked.

"Several hours yet," said a passing steward. "You ought to get off about lunchtime."

Lunchtime. Then I would have to see the ship's doctor. There was no use putting it off any longer.

"No!" groaned the doctor. "You can't do this to me. We've had everything ready for you for the last three weeks. How many times have we had to resterilize that maternity packet? Now everything is locked up; the quarantine officers are on board. Listen, you can't have the baby now. Do you hear me? You can't have it now. Go down to your cabin, get into bed and don't move. I'll call for an ambulance right away and it will be on the dock when we get there."

I felt like repeating the nurse's words to the ship's officer, "Aye, aye, sir. Just anything you say, of course."

I lay in my bunk as quietly as I could. Fred sat beside me holding my hand. It was then that I named her, knowing for a certainty that it would be a girl—Victoria—"Thanks be unto God who giveth us the victory."

Lunchtime came and went. Mrs. Ruth Shipley herself, the head of the United States Passport Division, newly arrived from Washington, cleared our passports for entrance. At last the gangplank was down and our family were the first passengers to disembark.

"You would fix it so that we go off before the diplomats," said Fred.

The ambulance was waiting for me, but what would we do with the children? We piled them all into the ambulance with us. There they sat in a row watching me with agonized expressions on their faces as I winced with pain.

"Drive to the hotel," I said to Fred. "You and the children get off there and I'll go on to the hospital. You know how it is with me. Some day I may learn how to have a baby quickly, but you'll have plenty of time to give the children their supper and put them to bed. Then you can come up to the hospital and we'll have the baby in peace."

The ambulance sped on through the city. I was determined that the baby should be born before Fred could get there. He had had to bear enough of my suffering already. The radio had been giving hourly bulletins, "*Gripsholm* races with stork!" But of this I knew nothing.

Met by Dr. Theodore Reed, the kindest of doctors, I was cared for lovingly and skillfully and, of necessity, with celerity! Victoria Fairchild Scovel was born before I reached the delivery table. An intern came in when it was all over.

"You came thirty thousand miles," he said, "and you couldn't make the last three feet."

Eight
The Mei Hua
(Flowering Plum)

I don't expect heaven to look any more wonderful than Presbyterian Hospital did that next morning when I woke up. It was all over—the danger, the dirt, the hunger; the baby was perfect, if weak and tiny. And the nurses and doctors and dietitians were so good to me. I was among people who really cared.

We had apparently made the headlines in our "*Gripsholm-races-with-stork*" episode, and everyone was being very careful not to let the press in to see me. There was a hospital rule to the effect that newspapermen were not allowed in the maternity ward for publicity purposes. This meant no visitors except the carefully screened few, and I enjoyed the quiet with only the family and a few friends.

We had hoped that Beloved Grandmother would be in New York to meet us, but she was suffering from a virus infection, and her doctor advised against her leaving Cortland where she had gone to visit her old friends. Instead, Beloved Grandmother asked our cousin, Harriet Day Allen, who was more like a sister than a cousin, to meet us in New York. Harriet took over the care of the children at the Prince George Hotel.

The morning after our arrival, Harriet took the children down to breakfast in the coffee room. Fred had left early to get our baggage through customs. As the children sat eating piles of pancakes, a gentleman came into the room, and finding no vacant table, sat down with Fourth Child and the Brown-Eyed One. When his order of bacon and eggs arrived, he pushed the plate away from him and called the waitress to complain about the cooking of the eggs. The Brown-Eyed One pushed the plate back in front of him, saying, "Eat it. It's food."

We literally sneaked out of the hospital and down a freight elevator the day I was discharged, Dr. Reed coming with me to put me into a taxi that would take me to the railway station. I rather doubt that the press was that interested in me, but at any rate, either we avoided the reporters or they weren't there in the first place. Fred and the children met me at the station. We were to spend Christmas in my home in Mechanicville, and Beloved Grandmother would join us there.

Christmas in the bosom of my own family was all that I had dreamed it would be. But now we had to hurry on to Rochester, New York. Fred was to work in the medical department of Eastman Kodak. No one could guess when, or if, missionaries would get back to China, and the Board had asked us to find other work if possible. Fred wanted to do something for the war effort but was not well enough or strong enough to enlist. He had lost forty pounds from his already thin frame. At Eastman he would be working for the navy.

"You'll never find a house," my father warned. "Do you two have any idea what housing is in this day and age?"

But again I had a Bible verse to cling to. In the first batch of mail to reach us at Goa, a friend had sent a verse that had become a prayer: "Behold I send an angel before thee to keep thee in the way, and to bring thee to the place which I have prepared." Fred went up to Rochester for one day and found the first furnished house in the whole city that had been on the real estate list of available houses that year. It was on the list for one hour on the only day that Fred was able to be in Rochester for house hunting.

Life in Rochester was perfect. And to make it even more perfect, we had a visit from the Magistrate of Hsiang Wen. He was now a famous man, serving on international committees for which purpose he was in America at the time.

After dinner that night I said to him, "Come now, you are no longer a magistrate; you're taking orders from me. Let's all do the dishes together because in the first place, I want them out of the way, and in the second place, I don't want to miss a word of your conversation."

"I'd love to help with the dishes," he replied. "Nobody but you would ever ask me to wipe dishes."

When the last pan had been washed and the sink cleaned, I reached for the bottle of hand lotion on the shelf and poured a generous dollop into my palm.

"Just like American women," said the Magistrate. "The hardest-worked women in the world, but they never forget to be beautiful."

In the living room, puffing his English pipe, he was thoughtful. We had asked him to give the Littlest One her Chinese name.

"I've got it," he said. "Mei Hua is just the name for her. 'Mei' for America and 'Hua' for China. All of your children have this 'Hua' character in their Chinese names in accordance with true Chinese custom, so this is entirely appropriate."

"Mei Hua. I like it very much," I said. "It's the name of a flower, isn't it?"

"Now you are getting your Chinese characters confused," he said. "The two characters for Mei Hua, the flowering plum, are different ones and are spoken in a different tone. Here, give me that envelope. I'll write them for you. See? These are the ones for the flowering plum. She is as sweet as a flower. Call her that, if you like."

"Oh, I remember the La Mei Hua!" I said. "It is like no other flower on earth. We had a bush of it in our garden in Tsining. The colder the winds blow, the more profusely it blooms and the more fragrant it becomes."

"That's something else again," said the Magistrate. "But do you know that some famous gardeners tie ice along the boughs of the La Mei in order to improve its flowers?"

"If our daughter could be like the La Mei!" I said. "Fragrant in the midst of adversity . . ."

"Before my 'Woman-from-the-inside-of-the-house' becomes even more confused, let's get back to the original idea," said my husband. "I agree with you. 'America and China' is just the name for her."

"We shall call her Mei Hua, certainly," I said. "You two can think of her as 'America and China' if you like, but I shall think of her as the La Mei."

America and China! The boys used to say there was only one thing wrong with our kind of life—when you were in America, you wished you were in China, and when you were in China, you wished you were in America. America certainly looked wonderful to us this time. I never turned on a hot-water faucet without being thankful for that continuing warm stream flowing from it. The children would fill a glass with cold water, drink what they wanted from it and put the remainder on the shelf above the sink to be drunk later. And coffee! To be able to have coffee again! We drank nine cups a day the first month we were home.

We were appalled by the amount of food people wasted— whole slices of bread, leftover meat, fruit with a small spot on it, all dumped into the garbage can. I remembered every day what a peach had meant to me, or that handful of peanuts.

When we were in camp, we used to joke about eating in a restaurant when we got out: we feared we would forget ourselves and say to some well-dressed man at the next table, "Pardon me, sir, but are you going to eat that piece of steak you've left on your plate? If not, I'd be glad to eat it for you."

The day the war ended we had invited friends for a picnic supper at a nearby park. The food was spread out on the table and we were just ready to eat it when every whistle and bell and automobile horn in the city suddenly went wild.

"The war must be over!" we said to one another. First-Born ran home to get the news over the radio and hurried back to tell us it was true.

"Isn't it glorious? Isn't it wonderful? Now those back in camp will be free! I almost wish I were there today, don't you darling?" I asked.

Fred was looking up across the treetops, a sandwich halfway to his mouth. "I must write the Board tonight," he said.

He went back to China alone. No passports were being issued to women and children nor was there any passage available for us. Fred went out on a troop ship. He wrote long, daily letters of his trip to our old mission stations through north and north central China, trying to find a location for his future medical work. He enjoyed the survey, traveling by train, by river boat, by cycle, walking miles and miles over the Shantung roads, sleeping at night with the farmers who gave him their best accommodations—the barn with the animals because the heat from their bodies made it the warmest room in the house. He had a wonderful reunion with the friends in Tsining and was almost caught by Communist troops when he all but presented the wrong pass. It had been a temptation to remain in Tsining, but the Communists were so active there that he feared that no work would remain open long. The hospital was being run by one of the nurses, so he left it at that and went on down to Anhwei province.

He finally chose Huai Yuan, a village at the fork of two rivers. Our mission hospital there had been doing excellent work before the war. Now there was nothing left but the shell of a building. Floors, window frames and doors had been torn out, and every movable piece of furniture had been removed. Soldiers who had been left behind because they were ill were lying on the dirt floors.

Fred's first task was to get these patients moved to a better location and then to clean up one small building so that he could open an outpatient department. He found a man in the village who had once been a nurse in the hospital, and another who had been a laboratory technician. A former hospital coolie was added to the staff, and the work began. So great had been the former reputation of the hospital that as soon as the doors were opened, Fred was deluged with patients.

Then, almost at once, a cholera epidemic confronted the meager staff. A village doctor offered his services and the tiny crew worked day and night. There were no beds at all, and the cholera sufferers were stretched out on the floor of the clinic building so that it was hard to avoid stepping on them. The treatment was normal saline solution intravenously, and the small still was kept going constantly to prepare it; one of the valuable men had to run it day and night. When they could go on no longer, Fred and the village doctor took turns lying down for a few hours at a time. Of the more than two hundred patients they treated in their small clinic, not one was lost from cholera, though two died later from kidney complications.

No sooner had the cholera epidemic subsided, and fortunately it was a mild one, than the two rivers flooded. The hospital, located on a rise of ground, became the scene of all the activity of the village; families moved up by the hundreds, as did the merchants with their wares. Even the post office set up shop on the compound. As the waters receded and life began to fall back into a normal pattern, a plague of locusts descended upon them.

"I had seen enough movies to know what that cloud of locusts descending upon the land and destroying the crops would mean," Fred wrote, "but I was not prepared for the personal annoyance of having them up my pants-legs. Shake them off and they come back with their sisters and their cousins and their aunts. How they get into the room, I don't know, but they are into everything."

The locusts were a small variety, and after they had eaten their fill of green stuffs, they were unable to rise from the ground. They died by the thousands, and the ensuing stench was hard to endure.

Fred had many difficulties and we missed each other unbearably. It is better not to recall my year in America without him; each day was a heavy link in an endless chain that grew heavier and heavier as I dragged the weight of it around.

But one evening when a Fuller brush salesman was sitting in the living room ready to show us his wares, the telegram arrived granting us a passport and announcing a sailing for us all, including Beloved Grandmother! At once there was a cyclone of joy in that room. We screamed, we danced, we hugged each other. First-Born finally made himself heard. "Let's get it down to a quiet roar," he said with his characteristic chuckle, which is really a vocal smile. (First-Born is the only quiet Scovel.) It was then that we discovered the Fuller brush man standing in the middle of the floor with a dazed expression on his face.

Beloved Grandmother had not been at all well. Her right arm was showing the effects of Parkinson's disease. But with her usual high courage she insisted that we must all be together in order for Fred to do his work efficiently and happily.

"Then he will not have the anxiety of separation," she said, "nor will he need to waste energy worrying about us."

She even managed to persuade her doctor that it was the right thing for her to do. So her passage was booked with ours, much to the delight of the children.

That trip has still a nightmare quality for me; the one compensation is that no other journey since has seemed difficult. During the final packing, and en route across country by train, the three boys had bouts of virus pneumonia; they were still weak when we reached San Francisco. The day before the ship was supposed to sail, Fourth Child was rushed to the hospital for an emergency appendectomy. Fortunately the ship was delayed and Fourth Child was carried aboard on a stretcher. I could not have managed alone; but John Rosengrant of our Board was on hand to put us all on the *Marine Lynx* that December day in 1946.

We passengers soon rechristened the ship the *Marine Stinks*, which was probably quite unfair of us. It was a troop transport that had been hastily converted for use in sending out missionaries. We slept in the hold of the ship, some two hundred of us—in canvas bunks hung three deep—and kept telling one another how lucky we were to have any transport at all so soon after the close of the war.

On Christmas Day I was stricken with lobar pneumonia. I dimly remember crawling out of my bunk early that morning, before the children were awake, to arrange the crèche on top of a suitcase with the gifts beside it. It was an endless task; nothing would stay in place because the ship was rolling and pitching—and so was I. At last the task was finished and I collapsed on my canvas bunk. For me the rest of the day was, mercifully, blackness.

Many, many times during our life across the world we

have had occasion to be grateful for friends. This was one of them. Dorothy Wagner, the beautiful new recruit for our station, Huai Yuan, took complete care of the two little girls. Stella Walter, who was to join Deane in Shanghai en route for Shantung, was also on board. She looked after the older children. A young bride who was a nurse gave Beloved Grandmother constant care.

One always awakens from a nightmare, and this was a happy awakening. As we approached the harbor, the ship's doctor wired for Fred to come out with the pilot boat to help me to land.

"Trust you to do something different to get to see your husband an hour ahead of time," he said as he extricated himself from the children and made his way through the pile of suitcases to where I was lying.

We left the two older boys in Shanghai to attend the Shanghai American School, and the rest of us were soon on our way to our new station in Huai Yuan.

For the past year Fred had been living in one room. "I couldn't bear the big empty house without you," he had written. But now we had arrived and the children were surprised to see their father lift me over the doorsill like a new bride. He set me down in what would soon be the reception room but which was now the room in which he had been living. I was shocked when I saw it—and I had expected the worst, knowing what he could do to a house in a week's time if I were away. I looked around at the camp cot, the desk, the chairs— every surface covered with a conglomeration of tins of food, books, medicines, papers, a clock to be fixed, a couple of stones picked up on the mountain, a clean shirt half unfolded. . . .

"Now I am disappointed," he said when he saw the look on my face. "I worked so hard to clean it all up for you."

It was fun to be making a home for him again. The house

was huge. It had been built by the father of one of the former missionaries as a gift to him and his bride. Nothing had been spared to make the house beautiful and useful. Many were the tales told of the dinners and parties held in that house "in the good old days"; for the people of the community loved Duboise Morris and his wife and enjoyed recalling the days of their sojourn among them. The house was surrounded by a garden and we never tired of hearing of the exquisite roses, of the chrysanthemum shows held here to which the gentry from miles around would come to enter their choicest blooms. The garden had been allowed to run wild during the war years; when we moved great yucca plants, we would find beneath them such rare shrubs as the delicate tree peony. The smaller "Poet's Garden" was across the little bridge in a quiet spot. A stream of water flowed lazily through it and one could picture the poets of those bygone days writing their verses in the little covered "t'ingtze" or summer house with its lacquered pillars and pointed roof.

It embarrassed me to live in such a "mansion" when there was so much poverty around us. I would seek an opportunity during conversations with our new friends to apologize for it, saying that ours was the largest family and that none of the other missionaries needed such a large place; that we didn't really need such a large place either, but that the house had been assigned to us, and so forth. One day a Chinese doctor from the hospital was sitting in Fred's study looking up something or other in a medical journal; he heard me telling all this to a guest who had dropped in. When the visitor left, Dr. Li said, "Why are you always apologizing for this house? Do you feel that you cannot be a good missionary because of it? The house doesn't matter at all. It is what you are, not what you have, that counts with us Chinese. The man who lived here before you did a great deal for this community. For one thing, he used to persuade the gentry to show their best paintings in exhibitions for the poorest school children with the result that you will find an appreciation of art and calligraphy in this little village that you do not find in many of the cities. I'm from the city myself and I know."

"I've noticed that too," I said.

"But it was what Dr. Morris *was* that attracted men to him and made them willing to take out those valuable paintings and show them. He talked to them about Christ, but more than that, he showed them what it meant to live a Christlike life, to care whether or not those poor children saw the beautiful in life. You mustn't be concerned because of the house. We don't hold it against you. People feel free to come here; weren't there fifty of us singing on the terrace Sunday night? Why don't you relax and enjoy your home?"

Work at the hospital mushroomed. The doctors saw some hundred and fifty patients a day in the outpatient department; the hospital itself had been opened. It was astonishing to see how ingeniously the staff had improvised equipment. Test-tube racks had been carved out of wood; bedside tables had been constructed and the tops covered with tin; thermometer trays were of wood with handles for easy carrying; charts were printed on the street by the local printer; a stretcher was made of old piping. The wheels didn't work very well but it was usable.

To equip a hospital beginning with nothing, at a time when no equipment was available, had taxed everyone's ingenuity. But such organizations as the British Red Cross and UNRRA (through the China organization, CNRRA) came to the rescue. The British Red Cross gave beds—the first requisite. Later our Board bought a shipload of army surplus and that helped all our hospitals as they reopened. However, one does not pick and choose gifts, and there were great gaps in what was needed to carry on the work. At one time Fred had written, "I have two hundred beautiful red corduroy bathrobes and not one aspirin tablet." Narcotics were almost impossible to get and presented a real problem in postoperative care. Alcohol was distilled from local wine and the ward smelled more like a tavern than a hospital.

Added to the routine hospital work were a biweekly clinic for the many sufferers from kala azar; a school of nursing and a school of midwifery, both schools meeting government requirements—and all of this accomplished in less than two years.

In spite of his busy schedule Fred managed to spend a little time each day with his family. This he was determined to do, having been alone for thirteen months. In the midst of a teeming clinic he would let the patient out of his consulting room, and before calling in the next, he would climb through a window and come home through the back garden. After a fifteen-minute lunch during which I read a little from some book that would interest the whole family (a ruse to keep him a few minutes longer), he would climb back through the window, open the door and admit the next patient.

"Those farmers would get discouraged if the nurse told them I'd gone to lunch," he would say. "That would mean a couple of hours to a Chinese. Most of these folks have come miles to get here and they have to wait too long to see us as it is."

Sometimes in the late afternoon the whole family would climb the hill behind the compound, walking out past the deep well a quarter of a mile from the house where the ascent began. We would meet the hospital water carriers with their dripping kerosene tins, now converted into water buckets, slung from a pole on their shoulders. They would be singing in spite of the fact that they were tired, having had to carry all the water that was used in the hospital.

One evening just at sunset we started out on a picnic. It was a lovely evening; the quaint old village with its stone houses was painted a soft rose by the setting sun. Two little Chinese waifs ahead of us were leaning against the carved stone pillars of a memorial arch, their baskets of fuel grass lying at their feet. Bright blue jackets and the red trousers of the smallest one gave just the right touch of color.

"What a picture!" I said as we approached. The youngest child called out a greeting. The older one tried to but couldn't speak. She was in the act of blowing a great wad of bubble gum into its bubble! It broke against her dirt-stained face as we passed.

"And what wouldn't *Life* magazine give for that picture!" said Fred as he helped the Brown-Eyed One over a bump in the road.

Beloved Grandmother was now confined to her bed except for a short time each day when Fred and the gardener lifted her into a chair by the window. Again she had a small house of her own near us. It was difficult for her to hold a book in her hand, but her son read to her and Dot Wagner wrote letters for her and the Golden-Haired One sang her favorite hymns by the hour. So fertile was her mind and so well stored that she told me once that she had never exhausted the possibilities of what she could recall of the poetry and the literature she had memorized. Each day, too, she would choose one of her old friends and in her mind go down the street to that friend's house and try to remember everything she had done with that friend and the places they'd been together. I am sure that part of each day was lived in the memory of the husband who adored her.

Two women servants looked after her as if she had been their own mother, and the hospital staff enjoyed dropping in to see her. In her quiet little house at the end of the garden, the hospital pastor would often be found consulting her about his work.

"Are you giving enough time to your sermon preparation?" she asked him one afternoon.

"But, Venerable Lady, God has promised to put the words into our mouths."

"Into your mouth, yes, but not into your head," was her reply.

"I'll remember that," he said, laughing. "I must thank you again for your generous gift to the new hospital chapel. The little organ was all that we needed to make it complete. Some day we must arrange to wheel you over so that you may see it."

"Describe it to me," she said to him. She could see the chapel in her mind's eye but she never tired of hearing about it. "My daughter tells me that it was just a storeroom before you made it into a chapel."

"Originally it was a guest reception hall, a room for small tea parties, art exhibitions, and so forth. The hall had been built in perfect Chinese architecture with lacquered pillars supporting a curved roof of tiles. When we moved the packing boxes from one end of the room, we found a round window with the crosspieces carved in a bamboo design forming the lattice. A touch of gold on the leaves here and there accentuated the cross and gave us our worship center. The carpenter became so interested that he carved an altar table to match; the student nurses brought brass candlesticks. Each of us has had a part in it."

"You have done very well. The hospital should be proud to have such a pastor," said Beloved Grandmother.

"Actually I have done very little. There was one thing I wanted and the carving is even now being done. On the back of the pulpit, facing the preacher, are to be the words from the twelfth chapter of John, 'Sir, we would see Jesus.' You see, Venerable Lady, I am even now heeding your advice."

In the spring of 1947 the two boys came home from the Shanghai American School and saw their new home for the first time. They brought with them two of their classmates whose homes were too far-distant for them to return for the short vacation. The Golden-Haired One, now in her early teens, was ecstatic.

"At last there will be some excitement around here," she said.

But she was disappointed. The boys, with the lethargy of adolescence, spent the entire vacation moving from one horizontal surface to the other—out of bed, to the dining table, to the living-room floor, sprawled out with books, back to the table, back to the floor with the record player beside them.

"Mother, they are horrid!" she said. "I had planned so many hikes up East Mountain, picnics to the Milk White Spring, games on the lawn, and they won't move!"

We hadn't been back to Tsining to visit our friends. Beloved Grandmother had spoken often of her furniture and her familiar belongings which had been left behind. Travel was dangerous but we decided to risk it and see what we could do about bringing our things to Huai Yuan. My diary records the trip:

May 9, 1947. Taught school in the morning. Dot came over to look after the family while we are gone. Started for Hsüchow at noon. A perfect day. Stayed with the Hopkinses at night.
May 10. Drove to Chin Hsiang riding on top of a truckload of matches covered with a very slippery straw matting. Held on for dear life. We'd been warned that if we fell off, the truck would not stop. Too dangerous going through Com-

munist territory. Road perfectly awful and had to watch boughs of trees above us. Truck broke down; had to change radiators en route. At Chin Hsiang, ran into Kung Yu Chen [one of the nurses from Tsining] who brought us to the offices of an official where we slept. Met Elder Han and some of the Christians. They are so discouraged.

May 11. Waited for trucks to come through from Tsining to be sure road was safe. Two trucks had been taken and six people killed the day before. Tore through another patch of Communist territory and got to Tsining and the Baptist mission a little after noon. Mary and Frank were thrilled to see us as we were to see them. [There were no missionaries at our compound then and we had planned to surprise our Chinese friends.]

May 12. What emotions flooded over us as we went into our old home—lived in by Communists, Japanese, and Central Government troops, yet in good condition. Chang Ta Sao came in to help us. How I hugged her! She looks a lot older. She has a grandson and is as proud of him as she can be. Chen Wu died of tuberculosis. Hu Shih Fu has gone, too. Gateman and family back in country.

May 13. Opened secret room and found all in good condition. Hole under porch broken into—silver and stamps gone! But nobody touched things like the horrible Peking incense burner in the attic! Started packing. Out for all meals with friends. Oh, it is good to see them! Church has raised funds to repair and redecorate.

May 14. Tea party in afternoon given by street Elders. Packed the trunk so full we couldn't get in one toothpick more, but never mind, we're off tomorrow.

May 15. Started out from Tsining at seven A.M. driven by dear Brother Sophronius from the Catholic mission (who offered to do it). Schools lined up, even at that early hour, to wave good-by. Drove to Hsüchow and then on to Sui Ning where we stayed all night at the Catholic mission with Father Brice, a young American from San Francisco. He opened all his stores and feasted us royally. Learned the next morning that I was the only woman who had ever stayed at the monastery. He could hardly have turned me out at midnight.

May 16. Rode all A.M. through wheat fields looking for a bridge to cross. Had a narrow escape as bridge cracked. Another time, truck almost turned over. Arrived at Ku Chen, couldn't go by truck to Pengpu. Freight train coming. Got coolies and threw everything on, including piano. Stayed at chapel in kindergarten for the night.

May 17. Oh what a thrill to get home! Dot met us at the door with "Mr. and Mrs. Livingstone, I presume." Fred had a three-day growth of beard. Children were wonderful. Grandmother had had a bad spell but is better.

We had a year of peace in our lovely home in Huai Yuan, then . . .

"Must I always be planting heavenly blue morning-glories and having to leave them before they bloom?" I asked as I handed the letter back to Fred. He had stopped in the garden with the mail on his way to lunch. I dusted off my knees and went into the house with him.

"We won't have to face moving again for a while yet. I'm getting to hate it as much as you do," he said. "The letter only asks us to consider the need for a doctor to teach in Ling Nan Medical College in Canton. As I see it, I can't possibly leave this place now. There's still too much to be done. We couldn't move Mother anyway. Let's forget it. I'll write them a note this afternoon."

I knew he would not forget it. When the mission asked him

to do a thing, he usually did it. I knew, too, that the mission would not have asked him to consider it without having weighed the relative needs in both places. Teaching was the work he loved. He taught all the time he was in the hospital, nurses, doctors, technicians. Our friend the Magistrate had been urging him to go into medical education for years.

"Don't stay on in a small mission hospital," he would say. "When you die, the work will die with you. Get out and do something big for China; teach and train men to carry on after you've gone. Remember our proverb: 'If I can help one hundred men, why should I help ten? If I can help a thousand, why should I help a hundred?'"

We had to consider also the rumors that the Communists had an army five miles away and could come in and take the strategic village at the fork of the rivers at any moment. Wouldn't it be better to get Beloved Grandmother out now while it was still possible? *Was* it possible to move her at all? No, it certainly was not. An elderly woman, partially paralyzed, how could we think of moving her all those hundreds of miles, on and off trains, across crowded station platforms, through cities and into crowded coastal steamers? It was out of the question. Come what may, we would have to remain where we were.

But I must not close the door in God's face, I thought. I picked up the prayer notebook from the table beside me and wrote out a list of all the reasons why we could not possibly go to South China. At the top of the list I wrote, "Moving Beloved Grandmother," and I added, "the new and difficult language . . . the necessity of finding another doctor to take over Fred's present work . . . uprooting the children again. . . ." It was a formidable list, even for God.

I had not written "another packing up," though I had been

tempted to. Little things like that I should be able to take care of myself. It had been so much fun unpacking the things we had brought from America to make this house a home. When I had had the trunks removed to the attic, I had hoped they would remain there for a long time. I looked up at the oil painting I had carried all the way by hand. Would I have to start all over again? The dishes, the glassware . . .

"What are you laughing about, Mother?" asked the Brown-Eyed One, coming into the room.

"I was thinking of the time when we unpacked the glass-ware. Do you remember?"

We had just unpacked the navy-surplus drinking glasses, which were unbreakable. The boys had been tossing them back and forth, dropping one on the rug occasionally to prove their indestructibility. Our new servant came into the room.

"Wong Ta Ke, did you ever see glass that would not break? Look," I said to him as I threw the tumbler on the floor. It crashed into a thousand pieces. Wong Ta Ke looked at the doctor with a shall-we-put-her-in-a-straight-jacket expression on his face. No amount of explaining ever convinced him that I had not been temporarily deranged that winter morning—throwing glasses on the floor and saying they wouldn't break!

There was no doubt but that the war was moving closer to us. After a terrible battle to the north, the wounded were being sent into our quiet little village by the hundreds. The mission primary school was temporarily converted into a field hospital. The army doctors worked day and night. Most of the operating was done by our doctors at our hospital. Second-Born and I went over to the school that first morning to see what we could do to help. The patients were lying on the floor in an unbelievable condition; their dressings had not been changed since they had received first-aid treatment on the battlefield; their faces were still caked with mud and, worst of all, they had had nothing to drink. Second-Born and I went from soldier to soldier passing out cups of hot water. (Cold water is believed to be harmful to anyone. No one in Shantung would think of ever drinking anything cold.) The men who had tetanus couldn't open their mouths and they looked at us in anguish. We took wet cotton and squeezed water between their clenched teeth. Then we set to work to wash faces and hands. The flies swarmed over their wounds, crawling over the eyes of the men, who were too weak to brush them off. Second-Born went back to the house for a DDT spray and to get some of the other women on the compound to help. (They had not heard of the wounded in our midst and came at once.) So diligent was Second-Born in his spraying that after three days it was almost impossible to find a fly. The whole missionary community helped daily until the soldiers were moved to a base hospital in a larger city.

One morning not long after this I was suddenly called from the schoolroom to see two policemen who were waiting in the living room.

"We have come to tell you to leave the village before noon today," said one of them.

"Why?" I asked.

"Because we have word that the Communists will be in the village by noon. You should leave at once."

"Thank you for coming to tell us," I said, "but I am afraid the Communists will have to take us along with the village. The doctor has gone to the hospital at Showchow for an emergency. He cannot return for two or three days at least. His venerable mother lies paralyzed upon her bed. So, gentlemen, you see we cannot leave."

"Oh. We are very sorry," the policeman replied, "but . . .

well, perhaps the need to leave may not be urgent. Who knows?"

I went back to the schoolroom wondering what would happen to us before night. Nothing did. Nor did the Communists enter the village. Some time later we heard it might possibly be that the chief of police had been wanting our house for his headquarters and that he had been using this method to have it evacuated, but this story was never verified.

The village remained peaceful, and June of 1948 found us in Shanghai attending First-Born's graduation from high school. We came back together to Huai Yuan until it was time for him to leave for America for college. I had known all his life that this would come, but I was not prepared for the tearing of my heart as the river launch took him away. We did not know, though we might have guessed, that our days in that lovely village were numbered.

"But Teacher-Mother," the hospital pastor said, "the doctor cannot leave us. You must not let him. This hospital is like a baby—less than two years old. It cannot walk alone. A mother does not leave her baby with others until it is able to walk."

"Pastor Chang," I said, "the doctor loves this hospital as much as if it were his own child, but it is not his child; it is God's child. Doctor Scovel is only the amah, and God is able to find another amah for it. He will not leave unless another doctor comes. And surely we cannot move Beloved Grandmother, so do not worry."

In the end it was Beloved Grandmother who settled everything. She called Fred to her one afternoon and said, "What's this I hear about your being asked to go to South China to teach?"

"Oh, it's just an idea the mission had," he told her. "Don't worry your head about it. I can't possibly go; too much to do here and no one to take over if I did want to leave. Did you think we would go off and leave you here alone?"

"I don't see why you couldn't take me with you," she said. "Do you think because I am almost eighty years old I have no interest in seeing new places? Besides, you have always wanted to teach; you are a teacher to your finger tips—from a long line of teachers. It seems to me that the mission is entirely right in sending you to a medical college.

"But, Mother, the mechanics of such a move alone would—"

"If it is right for you to go, God is perfectly capable of taking care of the mechanics of it," she said.

Beloved Grandmother learned that the Lutheran mission had a plane which had been flying in behind the lines of battle to rescue missionary personnel, and she made it financially possible for us to use this means of travel.

We were to meet the "St. Paul" at Pengpu, the nearest landing field eight miles down the Huai River. (The Lutherans had two planes, the "St. Peter" and the "St. Paul." The pilot used to say he was always robbing Peter to pay Paul until at last the "St. Peter" was grounded!)

Just at this time, too, Dr. Marshall Welles from one of our mission hospitals in a port city offered to come into the interior to take over the Huai Yuan hospital. This was a brave move on his part because it meant leaving his family.

Sitting in church that last Sunday morning, I went down the list of insurmountables in my prayer book; the new doctor, moving Beloved Grandmother, the difficult language. . . . Well, we would just have to learn the language. I looked up at the carving above me, the tiny gold-leaf petals of the La Mei Hua, the flower that flourishes in adversity. What a symbol for the Chinese church! And a good symbol for me to take as my own. But there were times when I would so much rather have put down roots and become a carrot.

The coolies had come before daylight to carry out the baggage. I had gone through every room in the house for the last time. We closed and locked the doors, walked through the garden, past the morning-glory plants, to Beloved Grandmother's cottage. She had already been moved to the smaller bed upon which she was to be carried. As we reached the big gate at the entrance to the hospital, the sun was just beginning to spread its gold upon the river below us. The moment we stepped out into the big thoroughfare, a loving crowd surrounded us. A huge pole of firecrackers was raised and the first one in the string set off. The ever-enlarging procession moved toward the river bank where the launch was waiting. Such a spluttering of firecrackers! Such farewells from every doorway! The firecrackers never stopped until the whole family was safely on board the launch.

As it drifted slowly from the shore, and the faces of our friends became smaller and smaller, I thought of Paul leaving the people of Tyre as they had come to the river bank to see him off.

Our friends upon the shore were singing, "God Be With You Till We Meet Again." We floated farther and farther away from the singing until the last thread of song spun itself out.

We will never meet again, I thought, never this side of eternity. O God, be with them; be with them.

Nine

The Bamboo

The "St. Paul" dropped down upon the airstrip at Canton and taxied to a stop. We had been all day in that bucket-seat plane, part of the time flying over mountains at eleven thousand feet. Beloved Grandmother and the children had been as blue as a Chinese rug from lack of oxygen. Now the doors were thrown open and the sweet, fresh air rushed in. The sun was setting and beautiful White Cloud Mountain had its head in a heaven of rose. Paul Snyder, a new Adopted Uncle, drove up with the hospital chauffeur in a shining ambulance, and Beloved Grandmother was taken at once to the well-equipped, modern Hackett Medical Center where Fred was to work.

As Beloved Grandmother was wheeled down the green parquet corridors and into her sunny room, Fred and I looked at each other, marveling at what we saw.

"Am I walking in my sleep?" he asked. "This place is like a dream come true. A few hours ago we were seeing the small beginnings of medical missionary work, and this afternoon the efforts have become reality."

It was thrilling to see the Chinese chiefs of staff in their long white coats, followed by the inevitable brood of residents, interns, and medical students. Except for the faces above the coats, this might be any hospital in America. Nurses rustled starchily as they carried out their ministrations. One of them was explaining the earphones at the head of Beloved Grandmother's bed.

"It's almost time for evening devotions," she was saying. "We broadcast them over a public address system morning and evening. We like the idea of earphones instead of a loudspeaker; then people are free to listen or not as they choose. Here is your bell. If there is anything I can do for you, push the button."

"You'll only be here for a few days," I told Beloved Grandmother. "As soon as we are settled, we'll be taking you home." She was never to leave that bed. Her Parkinson's disease, with complications, was advancing more rapidly than we had thought.

We were soon settled in a double house in one corner of the hospital compound. Dr. Cheung and his lovely family of teen-agers lived in the other half of the house. I was a long time getting to feel that that house was home. I felt as if I were in a new country. The language was so very different, the scenes were different, though at least they looked like the geography book. Gradually we made friends and entertained and did enough living in the house to have it begin to envelop us with warmth.

Of all the rooms in the little house, I liked the schoolroom best. Here I could look out over the fields to the distant horizon. In the foreground was the canal that ran past the back wall of the compound; here women were at work, washing their vegetables or their clothing or their babies. A flame-of-the-forest tree made a beautiful silhouette against the bright blue sky. It was difficult to keep my mind on the teaching before me.

Calvert was fun to teach. One never knew what was coming next. It might be "the tremendous and appalling boom" when the world broke off from the sun, or it might be an answer to a routine question such as Fourth Child gave me one morning.

"If a man found buried in the ground a coin which was dated one hundred B.C., would the coin be authentic or not?" I asked him.

Quick as a squirrel he replied, "Of course not."

"How did you figure that out so quickly?" I asked.

"Simple," he replied. "B.C. Bad coin."

Into the schoolroom one morning was wafted the syncopated "thoom—ta-ta-tum" of distant drums. Three pencils were dropped, three chairs were pushed back and three pairs of eyes looked questioningly at me. It was no use going on; if the dragon boats were coming, the children would have to run out on the porch to see them. I wouldn't miss that sight myself.

The slim, graceful shell, ninety feet long and one man wide, was just coming into sight. The rowers cut the water with the precision of Radio City Rockettes. The "dragon" in the center writhed and tossed his head to the beat of the drums beside him.

"Is it a really, truly dragon, Mother?" asked the Littlest One.

"No, it's just a man with a big dragon's head made of cloth. He is shaking it around with his arms. See, there are his legs in his blue pants."

In a matter of seconds the boat whisked out of sight. But another would be coming in a moment; the rowers were practicing for the races on the great day of the Festival of the River God.

"Let's get on with today's lesson," I said. "If we keep our minds on it, we can finish by one o'clock. Perhaps we can persuade Daddy to take one of the little picnic boats and go down the river to watch the practice while we eat our lunch."

Teaching the children, three of them in three different

grades, now took all morning, but here I was not needed in the
hospital. The nursing department was well organized under
the leadership of Rena Westra and Martha Wylie; Dorothy
Snyder, Paul's wife, taught English and had Bible classes for
the student nurses. So I spent my free time helping in the
School for the Blind.

It occurred to Alice Schaefer, the principal, that a little
knowledge of the hospital beforehand might soften the blow
later if any of the blind were to become patients; so we invited
the blind from the school, according to age groups, to spend an
afternoon at the hospital and in our home.

It was always fun to entertain them; everything seemed to
give them pleasure. The older women liked the rocking chair
best. Each one of them would take a turn having a good, long
rock. The older boys liked the refrigerator. What a joy it
was to have that refrigerator! After the hot summers in Tsining
and in Huai Yuan, with no refrigeration, where we had to
drink tepid water and throw out any leftover food each day,
Beloved Grandmother had insisted that we have a refrigerator
if we were going down to the heat of South China. Actually,
South China was much cooler, being near the ocean, than
either Tsining or Huai Yuan, but the refrigerator still saved
us money on our food bills. Beloved Grandmother little
guessed, when she gave us that refrigerator, that it would be
used as a toy for blind children. The boys liked opening the
door and feeling the rush of cold air on their faces. Each one
would be given an ice cube to hold and they would have such
fun with the slippery, cold, square things in their hands.

Today the youngest children were to be "shown" the hospital. The cook and I were setting the table for tea.

"The table will be crowded with fourteen children sitting
here," said Ah Yang with a twitch of her long black braid.
"And all of them blind," she sighed. "They will surely break

things. Why do you use these beautiful thin cups, your very best ones? They can't see them anyway."

"But they can feel them," I said, "and these cups will feel different from the ones they use every day. They will be careful, I know."

We took the children to the hospital first. We gave them rides on the elevators, whizzed them down corridors in wheel chairs and on stretchers, gave each one a turn at lying on the X-ray table to reach up and touch the cone which would take a picture of their insides and show us what was wrong if they were ill. The children's ward was the most fun of all. Here the chairs and tables were just the right size, and here was the huge doll house with its tiny furniture. We decided that they must have one of their own.

Then the children took hands and in pairs they walked back to our house for tea and cakes. And Ah Yang was convinced at last that not a thing on the table was unsafe in those deft, sure little hands.

By late November of that same year, 1948, we were watching at the bedside of Beloved Grandmother daily. She would look up at us and say, "Oh, children, why can't I die?"

On December second, her prayers were answered and she left her tired body lying there on the hospital bed. We were thankful that she could go; we had even been praying that she might be taken from her suffering, but we were in no way prepared for the sudden emptiness of the world without her. In that first hour we learned the meaning of the word bereft.

The next morning, after making plans for the service to be held in the hospital chapel, Fred went out with one of the men to make final arrangements for the interment. I picked up Beloved Grandmother's Bible. There on the flyleaf was a quotation from a poem by Whittier. I had often read from this

Bible to Beloved Grandmother, but I had never seen the poem before. When had she copied it in? It had been over a year since she had been strong enough to hold a pen in her hand. It was her message to us for this very day.

"Yet love will dream, and Faith will trust,
(Since He who knows our need is just,)
That somehow, somewhere, meet we must.
Alas for him who never sees
The stars shine through his cypress trees!
Who, hopeless, lays his dead away,
Nor looks to see the breaking day
Across the mournful marbles play!
Who hath not learned, in hours of faith,
The truth to flesh and sense unknown,
That life is ever lord of death,
And love can never lose its own!"

The Littlest One was sure that Beloved Grandmother had gone straight to heaven that very day, taking her body with her. The child had stayed with friends during the simple ceremony in the chapel. That evening after the body of Beloved Grandmother had been laid to rest in the beautiful English cemetery by the river, the Brown-Eyed One, the Littlest One, and I were taking a stroll out past the hospital buildings.

"Oh," said the Littlest One, stopping in the middle of the walk, "Beloved Grandmother forgot her clothes!"

"She won't need her old clothes in heaven," I said. "God will have lovely new ones waiting for her."

"What will they be like, I wonder?" said the Brown-Eyed One. "Nicer than our clothes; like that light, Mother, don't you think so?" And she pointed to the laboratory on the top floor where all the fluorescent lights were lit, spreading a radiant glow across the treetops.

The Communist army was moving South and the Nationalists were preparing to defend Shanghai. A telegram from the children's school announced that Second-Born and the Golden-Haired One were being evacuated on gunboats. Their destination was not made known, but America, Japan, Okinawa, or Hong Kong were the rumored possibilities. We prayed that it might be Hong Kong so that they could come home to us. For several days we heard nothing further and then the looked-for telegram came with the thrilling message: "ARRIVED HONG KONG, COMING HOME."

It was a wonderful reunion. Second-Born had completed his high-school work. The Golden-Haired One was desolate at having to leave her singing teacher, but somewhat cheered that she would be going to school in nearby Hong Kong. No, they didn't know anything about the fighting except what they had read in the Hong Kong papers—that Shanghai had been "liberated."

The army is moving rapidly, I thought. It is only a question of time now.

We were grateful for the few extra months with Second-Born, but it seemed no time at all before we had to take him to Hong Kong to see him off for America and college. The plane was an eagle carrying off our son in its talons. And we had to leave the Golden-Haired One in Hong Kong to begin her new school year.

Back in Canton the air was taut. Every day brought news of the approach of the Communist army. I was so tired of excitement. This time my reaction to imminent danger was no longer exhilaration and challenge; my only feeling was one of numbness and my only urgency was to finish the sweater I was knitting for the Golden-Haired One so that I could get it to Hong Kong before we were cut off.

The "liberation" itself, on October 14, 1949, turned out to be peaceful enough—one army marching in as the other army marched out. It might have passed as any other day had not the retreating army decided at the last moment to blow up the Lingnan bridge on its way out. A crash like the rending of the earth at Judgment Day threw garish colors across the sunset sky and all was quiet again.

Soon there were Communist soldiers all over the streets, many of them from our former province of Shantung, as I discovered one day when some of them were billeted in the school building next door.

"I go housie," I heard the Brown-Eyed One saying; then the slam of the screen door and the creak of it opening again. "I come out housie."

Why is that child talking baby talk? I wondered, and left my letter writing to see what was going on. Straddling the ridgepole of the building next door was a row of Communist soldiers. Below in the garden the children were teaching them English!

"You mustn't listen to this little one's English; she is teaching you baby talk," I said to them in the northern dialect into which I always lapsed in an emergency.

"Where did you learn to speak Chinese?" one of them asked.

"Oh, I'm an old Shantung countrywoman," I replied, and went on to tell them about the place where we had formerly lived, far to the north on the Shantung Plain.

"I know, I know!" the soldier said. "My home is in Yenchow, twenty-six miles from Tsining. Now I remember where you lived. You come up the main road from the railway station, cross the little bridge, and just before you get to the Memorial Arch, on the right-hand side of the road, is the hospital. Your house is on the left farther down the road."

"Don't," I said. "You are making me homesick."

"*You* are homesick, T'ai T'ai, what about me? It has been years since I have seen my home."

Such a happy fraternizing was frowned upon, and the soldiers never appeared upon the rooftop again.

We loved these Shantung soldiers who reminded us so much of the friends we had left behind. It always surprised the soldiers to find people who could speak their own dialect; and after our struggles with Cantonese, it was a relief to us to be able to express ourselves freely once again. In some ways we seemed less foreign to the Shantung boys than the Cantonese whom they could not understand. And, as in almost any country in the world, there is a lasting feud between the north and the south.

"T'ai T'ai, from what country do you come?" one of the soldiers asked one day when we were crowded together on a river boat.

"Sir, I dare not tell you," I replied.

"Ah, yes, America. We thought so. America is a good country. We Chinese have always been friendly with America. There are many Communists in America."

When Fred made rounds in the wards where many of these wounded Shantung soldiers were lying, it was like walking through a country teahouse—everyone talking, telling stories, asking questions, and the ambulatory patients preparing special bowls of meat dumplings which they made on their little charcoal stove. It was a favorite northern dish and one they knew would please the doctor. They loved to talk to him about their old homes and their families. Later, when one of the accusations against Fred was that he had neglected the Communist soldiers who were his patients, I was indignant.

"How can they say such things about you?" I remonstrated.

"I could have done more for them than I did," he replied. "After they were up walking around, I only went in to see them every other day."

"But they didn't need medical attention then," I said. "They were really ready for discharge; and look at all the work you had to do with the hospital full of really sick patients."

But all this was much later. Now he was a hero, and how he hated it! One awful day, the Central Government planes had flown over and the bombing that had come upon us filled the the whole city with terror. The fearful staccato of the anti-aircraft guns, so close to our house, was almost worse than the deep boom of the bombs. Ah Yang, our beloved little cook, with no thought for her own safety, first ran to see if we were out of danger. She herded us into a hallway where double walls would keep the flying shrapnel from hitting us, then tried to comfort the Littlest One, who was crying against my skirt.

When it was all over, we found that a bomb had struck just in front of the house and another just behind us. Over a hundred of the wounded were brought into the hospital, and we were all kept busy binding up the wounds. It was heartbreaking to see the people going from bed to bed hoping to find their loved ones, their lost children, or the mothers of their children. Tears could not be held back when one man fell to his knees beside his heavily bandaged wife, sobbing, "You are all I have left. The children are gone, the house is gone, but you are here, you are here!"

A few days later Fred went over to the hospital earlier than usual. It was Sunday and not many people would be around. A poor coolie woman had had her leg blown off and needed a transfusion. She had no relatives left, and since Fred was a universal donor, it would be simple enough to give her a pint of blood. (It always seemed "simple enough" to give someone a pint of blood. I used to wish, for his own good, that he was not a universal donor. "It doesn't mean that you have to donate blood to the universe," I would tell him.) This time he swore the nurses to secrecy, had the blood removed in one room and carried into the patient's room to be administered.

"In these days of anti-American propaganda it might upset her if she knew she had American blood in her veins," he explained.

But the story leaked out and Fred was one of fourteen heroes chosen to receive the special Communist award of a "golden" fountain pen. It was with difficulty that he was persuaded to attend the ceremony.

"I don't like this idea of singling people out," he told them. "We are *all* working to help those who come to us for medical attention; this was nothing special or different. Some of the patients need drugs, some of them need operations, and what they need, each one of us here tries to supply. This woman just happened to need blood."

But the crest of the wave spilled over and there was a gradual ebb in the popularity of the foreigner. As one friend put it, "We were allowed to attend the Christmas pageant, yes; but for the first time in all my years in China, not a bathrobe of mine appeared as a Wise Man's robe!"

Ginger, the cat, was lost. It was impossible to accomplish anything in the schoolroom until something was done about finding him. I didn't dare to take the children with me on the search. I had looked out of the schoolroom window a few minutes earlier in time to see a woman in the shack across the canal skinning an animal for the family pot. The tawny fur falling away from it was suspiciously like Ginger's.

I gave each child a written assignment and started out on my unpleasant errand. I hadn't gone ten steps before I met the gardener coming in with the precious pet in his arms. A tragedy narrowly averted—if only I could spare the children other blows as easily!

There was the afternoon when the two little girls ran to me crying.

"Mother, we don't want to be killed. We don't want to be killed," they wailed.

"What is all this silly talk?" I asked. "Nobody is going to kill you."

"Yes, Mother. That girl in the gray uniform told us to come in and tell you to go to America, and that if you don't go, we will all be killed," the Brown-Eyed One insisted.

Why, oh, why couldn't they pick on somebody their own size? I wondered.

"She's just saying that to be funny," I said. "You know how Brother likes to tell you frightening stories to scare you just for fun? Well, that is all this amounts to. Run and get your faces washed, and dress your dolls in their party dresses. Aunt Rena has invited you to a doll's tea party, and she has the material all cut out for new pajamas for them. She's going to help you make them this afternoon."

Bless Adopted Aunt Rena who entertained them through the long afternoons when it did not seem safe for them to play outside in our own compound, when they might have had to hear something that would fill them with terror, as they had this time.

Always the question kept pounding into my mind: Had we been right in staying on in China? As medical workers, interested only in the welfare of the people, we had been so confident that we would be able to work under the Communists. We all had the interest of the common man at heart, didn't we? We had talked about it and prayed about it. We had written First-Born saying, "This is your decision as well as ours. It may mean being cut off from you for years. It may

mean that we will not even be allowed to send or receive letters. If you would feel better if Mother and the children were
in America, please say so, won't you? We can trust you to
tell us the truth about how you really feel."

"I've thought about it a lot," he had replied, "and it seems
to me that I would rather know that somewhere in the world
my father and mother were living happily together than to
have you two separated. My only unhappy times as a child
were the times when you were away, Dad. And as I see life
here in America, I realize that we as a family are closer together across the miles than many here who live in the same
apartment."

Second-Born, with his realistic idealism, had added, "I
don't see that you two will have a leg to stand on if you go.
Why should you leave? You still have work to do, haven't
you?"

And now the Golden-Haired One was leaving for America.
Though the separation, with all its uncertainties, cut through
to our hearts, it was a relief to have one more child out to
safety.

The three children who were left with us seemed to be
having to bear the brunt of it all. The accusations made against
Americans—that they were living in imperialist mansions,
controlling all the finances, receiving higher salaries, and so
on, did not apply in our case even in one particular instance.
We were living in a duplex with a Chinese doctor (his side
only was screened). Deep-voiced, gray-haired Dr. Cheung
had been in complete charge of the hospital for the past twenty
years, carrying the burden on his stocky little frame without
a tremble from the weight of it, and what an excellent job
he did! Fred was more than delighted to be in a place where
he did not have to worry about administration; he did not even
know about many of the finances of the hospital, nor was he

the highest paid doctor on the staff. The Chinese children in the school next door must have been puzzled by the contrast between what they heard in class about Americans and what they could see before their eyes. Why had the doctor come to China then? Their teachers had an answer.

One day, when our three were playing in the yard, a group of children from the school joined them.

"Do you see that woman sitting on the porch?" one of them asked.

"Yes, she's our mother," was the reply.

"No, she isn't your mother. She stole your father away from your real mother in America and made life so unhappy for him there that he had to leave his practice and come to China."

The good joke was shuttled around the compound, and there were many references to me as the "concubine." It was all very, very funny until we realized that the Littlest One was not eating. At first we thought she might be coming down with measles or chicken pox, but soon her loss of security revealed itself.

"Mother, are you a witch? Can you turn yourself into something that you aren't?" were some of her questions.

It was only after a long time and after many reassurances with stories of "when you were a little baby inside me," that she began to feel secure again.

To all outward appearances, life went on fairly normally. We were allowed to go and come as we chose as long as we kept well within the city limits. For that matter, no Chinese could leave the city without permission either. It was a bit disconcerting at times to be called a Russian devil as we passed. People seemed to think that any foreigner now appearing in their city streets must surely be a Russian; and that was not far from the truth since there were few foreigners of any other nationality in the country. But the screws were gradually being turned. Visitors calling at our home were compelled to register in a book stating their name, age, nationality, profession, and the purpose of their visit to us. They were required to leave any package which they might happen to bring with them at the gatehouse with the guard until their return from us when they signed out, giving the time. We feared to have our Chinese friends get their names in what we felt sure was a black book, but it did not deter them from coming.

Once when we were all out for a short ride in a rickshaw we passed a group of primary school children marching to a meeting. One of them called out, "Look, Russians!" and the rest of the children took up the cry. Knowing how our three might react to *that*, I looked back quickly to their rickshaw to see how they were taking it. The situation was ripe for an international incident. I needn't have worried. They were accepting the ovation with bows to the right and to the left like visiting royalty.

Strange, incongruous things were happening which would have been highly amusing were it not for the rising tension. One Sunday all of the employees in the hospital were called upon to march in an anti-American parade. (It was in vain that the hospital administration pleaded that such an exodus would deplete the staff to a point where it would be impossible to care for the patients, let alone take care of an emergency. The reply came back, "What are you putting first, the lives of a few individuals or the State?") There was some question in Fred's mind as to the wisdom of our walking through the streets on such a day, but the bishop was counting on me to play the hymns for the union service, and since we would probably be taken for Russians anyway, we decided to risk it.

The Anglican church, where the service was held, was across the street from the Russian Trade Embassy, and as we ap-

proached we saw that part of the street was fenced off so that
no common person could interfere with the arrival of important
guests at a cocktail party now in progress. The guests were
arriving, one to a car, an American car. It would not do to
crowd two or three in one car together. So, as our Chinese co-
workers from the hospital were marching in an anti-American
parade, and as we were trying to listen to a sermon by an
English bishop, his voice was being drowned out by the
Russians entertaining their Chinese guests with such American records as "Rose Marie, I Love You," played over a
raucous loud-speaker.

Parades were the order of the day. One of our dearest
Chinese friends, a devout Christian woman who was obliged
to march in many of them, said to me one day, "I welcome
every opportunity to walk through the streets of this city.
There is nothing these people need more than love. I look at
them as I pass and love them. I pray for them too and, do you
know, they go home never knowing what hit them!"

It didn't seem like China any more. Nobody smiled or
laughed out loud. The wonderfully apropos quips were
dropped from all conversation. Suspicion and fear were tangible enough to touch, and there were accusation meetings held
against Fred and our closest friends. That Fred neglected
Communist soldiers who were his patients, that he con-
trolled the finances of the hospital, that he was a spy of
American imperialism were some of the trumped-up charges.
This I rebelled against with all my being.

"What can you do, which way can you turn, when you have
no recourse to justice?" I would ask Fred. For no explanation
of an action, no answer to an accusation was accepted by those
accusing.

Fred took it far more philosophically than I ever could. But
one morning we found the vicious placards posted on the

walls of the hospital. When he saw that some of the signatures were those of his own students whom he had worked with and loved, it seemed as if his heart would break.

"What they say is not true," he said sadly, "but I suppose that if they had asked me, I could have told enough that *was* true for them to make a case against me. I am human, I make mistakes. Perhaps this amounts to the same thing."

"You may make mistakes," I protested, "but you have never wilfully done anything against anyone. You wouldn't hurt a snake. And every single soul around here *knows* that the accusations against you are not true!"

That was the diabolical part of it. It was as if the Communists were saying, "You all know these accusations are not true; we, too, know that they are not true. But we have absolute power to make them as if they were true. This too can happen to you."

As the loud-speakers blared out speeches of frenzy against us all day long and night after night until midnight, I wondered how long my sanity would hold out. "God has not given us the spirit of fear; but of power and of love and of a sane mind." Power, love, sanity! I tried to hold the words in my mind.

There were some evenings when the Chinese gentleman on the nearby balcony would play his accordion. We could not see him clearly through the heavy bamboo sprays, but he appeared to be in uniform. When the accusation meetings were at their loudest pitch, he would play American folk songs. We never found out who he was and he may never know how grateful we were for his friendly hand of song across our darkness.

On December 3, 1950, we registered our application with the police for permission to return to America. Fred had hoped to complete the medical lectures he was giving before applying, but the day came when one of his Chinese colleagues at the Medical College telephoned to say, "Don't come in for your lecture today under any circumstances." The walls of the college had been plastered with accusations against Fred, the sight of which his friends were trying to spare him.

"But I have only two more lectures to give before the course is completed," Fred replied.

"Just forget about those two lectures and don't come down here at all," his friend warned.

A day or two later, following an official injunction that no patient was to allow himself to be treated by a foreign doctor, Fred's work at the hospital too was finished. We sat in the cold, damp house huddled around the fireplace, popping the last of the popcorn sent out from home, playing games with the children, and waiting for the permit to come.

Christmas came and still no permit had been issued. The gardener, intimidated, refused to bring in the Christmas tree or to allow anyone else to dig it up and put it in its pot. But the Chinese engineer in charge of repairs for the hospital went out and cut down an evergreen from his family burial plot. "These children are going to have a Christmas tree," he said.

It was a strange Christmas morning. We had decided against taking the children with us through the streets to church. It was well we had. Just as we were passing a primary school, we heard jeers and looked up to see forty or more children on the roof spitting down at us. Fortunately there was a good wind and the barrage missed fire.

"I'd feel differently about it," I said as we walked along, "if it weren't that I never get up that high without having the desire to spit down on someone myself. Wasn't it Richard Halliburton's poet friend who, on top of the Matterhorn, looked at the beauty below him and came out with the unpoetic remark, 'I could spit a mile'?"

One morning there were chalk marks on the walk in front of the house: "Imperialist dog, do you not yet know enough to leave China?"

Well as we knew who had put them there, and how little it had to do with our friends and colleagues, the chalk marks on the cement hurt. And part of the hurt came from the stricken looks of our co-workers as they too read the words.

"Darling," I said, "do go to the police again and ask them if we may leave. I can't bear this any longer."

"I know, Honey, but it was only day before yesterday that we went, and the officer said no permission had been given," Fred replied.

By now we both knew the route to the police station blindfolded. We had made thirty-two trips (and presented twelve photos) in order to get permission for the Golden-Haired One to come in for ten days on her last visit before leaving for America. But she *had* been allowed to come in, which was an unusual concession.

And there were the constant questionings. We were at a distinct advantage during these hours of examination because we did not need an interpreter and could speak directly to our questioners in Mandarin, the official language. The missionaries who had never lived in the north and the businessmen who did not speak the language were at the mercy of their interpreters.

One Sunday morning we had been called in for another of the questionings. For some reason we were alone with the examiner; usually the room was full.

"Why did you come to China in the first place?" the examiner asked.

Fred was trying to avoid the pitfall that China was a needy country and he had come to help; he hesitated a moment to phrase his answer.

I turned to him and said quietly and quickly in English, "Don't you think the real reason we came is because Jesus said to go into all the world and teach and preach and heal?"

Fred turned back to the police official to give that answer in Chinese and found him smiling and nodding in complete accord with what I had whispered to Fred. But the serious, dead-pan expression returned to his face at once as he barked out another question.

The day the chalk marks appeared on the walk, Fred went to the police station alone. When he came into the house some two hours later, I knew at once that the permit had not been granted.

"Do you remember that crazy Western movie we saw?" he asked as he helped me remove the chalk marks, "the one about the fellow with the two guns shoving the little guy into the corner and saying, 'You can't go and you can't stay. What are you going to do?' I've been thinking about it all the way home.

"Here is something for you," he added as we went into the house. "I thought you deserved a little surprise." And he gave me a tiny package containing the beautiful opal stone that we had looked at so often in the jade market.

Two days later the permit came through. Though it had seemed like an age of time, we were actually far more fortunate than most people in obtaining the permit in less than two months.

On January 24, 1951, we left Canton. Our staying on under the Communists had justified every person who left early because he felt he could not work under this regime. We had been so sure that we could. By far the most difficult thing we had to face was not the suspicion, not even the accusation meetings, but seeing our Chinese friends placed in an impossible position because of our being there. Any move toward us on their part put them in the bad graces of the Communists. We urged them not to come to see us, not to speak to us when they passed us on the street. We dreaded the consequences of their having anything to do with us. In spite of our entreaties they had continued to come to see us at our home, and now two of them braved censure and came to the railway station for a last farewell.

"At least we did not have the heartache of listening to 'God Be With You Till We Meet Again,' " said Fred as the train pulled out of the Canton station.

At last the border, the gates flung open and the neat, black-uniformed Hong Kong police saying, "Welcome to Hong Kong!" My knees felt weak. I threw my arms around our faithful Ah Yang, who had elected to live in Hong Kong and had left China with us. With my head on her shoulder, I cried and cried and cried.

How great a deliverance! How great a deliverance! was all I could say or think. Why had we been allowed to come out, and why were some of our dearest friends still back there in solitary confinement in prison? We did not deserve it; we did not deserve it at all. How sweet it was to breathe the air of freedom; how beautiful would be the low white house, the soft green meadows, the flowering dogwood of River Bend!

I looked up at Fred. His gaze was down the long silver tracks, but he was not seeing them.

"I wonder where we'll be two years from today," he was saying.

The Epilogue

It is but a few months more than two years from that day. We are in India, crumpling the newspaper wrappings from a pair of Chinese ginger jars. We found them, quite by chance, this afternoon in the junk shop kept so carelessly by the old Sikh gentleman with the long white beard. There on his shelf were the lovely green jars, sitting squat and proud among the empty bottles and broken tins. We have brought them home to our summer cottage in the foothills of the Himalayas.

"Look at it," Fred is saying as he places one of the jars in my hands.

He is now Professor of Medicine at the Christian Medical College at Ludhiana in the Punjab, and we have come to this hill station to study the language. It is strange to be starting a new life in a new country—a country as big, as colorful, as confusing as India. And yet there is a familiarity that is frightening. What course will India take? Are we beginning a new life, or are we facing the same old round of uncertainty and difficulty, the same old troubles?

The same old troubles—those which we would never have chosen, but which we wouldn't have missed for anything in the world!

Whatever comes, we will not be facing it alone. I hold the cold stone jar against my face and thank God.